APPLETOWN
NIGHTMARE

APPLETOWN NIGHTMARE

a novel

by Douglas Brannon

ISBN 978-0-9862101-2-9

Published in the United States by OdysseusPublishing.
OdysseusPublishing.com

Cover artwork by Raven Wade.
Internal design by Paul James Keyes.

For more, you can visit:
www.DouglasBrannonAuthor.com

For G. and the Z.'s

Praise for *Appletown Nightmare*

"Rad story."
> -Tony Hawke

"I could read this kind of high-brow, slapstick humor all day."
> -Howard Sterm

"Brannon can really spin a yarn. I'm going to be dizzy for a long time…what a twisted book."
> -Dee Sniper

"A masterful piece of storytelling. Elegant, frantic, intelligent, and strange. A completely satisfying entertainment that slyly touches upon the biggest and ugliest problems that lurk in civilization's darkest and most remote corners. A complex package of laughs, tears, terror, insight, and hope. The best book I have ever read."
> -Brock Obama

"I wish a Canadian could write a book half this good."
> -Jason Trudeau

"I wasn't terrified enough of bugs already?"
> -Aunt Kathy

"This is a better Seattle novel than *Where'd you go, Bernadette?*"
> -Richard Linkearlier

"I don't know much about literature, but I do know rock n' roll. This book right here, is pure rock n' roll."
> -Keith Roberts

"I'm sure they are going to censor this one in Ireland."
> -The Urge

"The *beetle* metaphor is pure genius."
> -Toni Morris

"I wear my nicest suits when I read Brannon."
> -George Clowney

"Being funny just got a whole lot scarier."
> -Jerry Seinfreid

"The top tier of American novelists need be looking over its shoulder for this Brannon fellow."
> -George Slanders

"This is the kind of old-school humor that is hard to get away with these days."

      -Whitney Cousins

"Refreshing. I love Margot and Fwen."

      -Zooey Smith

"Nightmare is putting it mildly. This book is downright terrifying. As of now, I am afraid of anything with six legs, afraid to plug anything in, afraid to go to sleep, and afraid to take a piss. I had to install a nite-lite in the boiler room."

      -Freddy Luger

"Beyond the psychedelic detail and blind-siding humor, is a gritty tale about survival in the new, wilder west."

      -Cormac McMurtry

"Book club of the century selection! People are still going to be reading this long after we are all dead and gone."

      -Opal Winfrey

"Much of corporate America has its head up its own ass. Brannon has actually managed to take a proper snapshot of it. The image isn't pretty…although I must say, I love the bugs."

      -Loren Buffet

"Colorful, zany, and brave. A book that never lets up and never pulls a punch."

      -Thomas Pincher

"I wrote a book like this when I was 19 and didn't even bother trying to get it published."

      -Zack Galifarnikas

"Bugs can't now, never have, and never will be able to eat the electricity. This is nothing but a radical leftist trying to stoke fear with a bunch of half-baked ideas. Although I have a feeling this Brannon guy, whoever he is, may have been all the way baked when he wrote it. If we ever run out of coal, and we won't, but if we do, we can burn every copy."

      -Donald Tromp

"I find myself rooting for the beetles."

      -Bingo Starr

"Finally, something good to read."

      -God

Table of Contents

Prologue

Crossing Deadland

A tractor trailer with the four Mandarin characters for BeiBen Trucking fixed to its dusty grill idled just outside the border of Deadland. Gordon Androssus—personal assistant to the world-famous action film star Lucky Soul—paced back and forth beside the truck in his off-white linen suit under skies that were finally clearing. Every few seconds he withdrew his phone from his pocket, willing it to ring. He kept second guessing that there was really a satellite up in space that could deliver a signal to where he was standing, in the middle of fucking Jabip. Once he crossed over into Deadland he wasn't going to be able to communicate with his boss and long-time friend until he reached the other side. Every time he tried to ask how long the trip would be the answer devolved into a philosophical discourse on the unpredictability of weather and the unique topography that he couldn't comprehend. He wanted an answer in miles, or at least kilometers, if not time; and he desperately wanted to speak with Lucky. Not because there were any more arrangements to be made, or money that needed to be wired. It was mostly just to salvage what was left of his sanity. Gordon was as far from home as he could be without traveling to the moon. The expressionless Asian men that surrounded him all seemed to understand his English, even though none of them uttered a word in response. His stomach was cramping and he needed to calm down.

A team of deft primitive riggers lifted a shipping container off of the tractor trailer with a horse-powered crane, and then used a series of rounded logs to move it along the ground to a giant wooden cart using the same method that the Trojans used to move their infamous horse. The cart was to be driven by a dozen stout oxen who patiently snorted and scraped their hooves on the road, unintimidated by the size of the load, and having no idea where they were headed.

Gordon had flown into the closest major city, Ulanhot. Since then he was shuttled over land, through hills, and down roads so meandering and similar looking that he could no longer tell you in which direction Ulanhot was. He was lost in a remote section of Chinese-controlled Inner Mongolia.

Before making the trip, Gordon was briefed on what was known about the region and in particular the quarantined zone known unofficially as Deadland—which amounted to very little. Inside of the past five years something occurred in there, but it wasn't clear exactly what. It could have been a nuclear meltdown, massive landslide, an outbreak of disease, or a revolution. There were plenty of rumors but nothing was certain and the Chinese certainly weren't being forthcoming with any information at all. The region was under strict lockdown. That much was known. The region was still supposedly populated, but ingress and egress were almost never permitted. All sources agreed that there was no electricity at all inside of Deadland, and any communication between those who lived inside of it and the civilized world depended upon messages delivered by birds.

If the last quarter of the twentieth century had ended with a call toward environmental responsibility, the first quarter of the twenty-first century proceeded with the phone still ringing on the hook. Lucky Soul—a disproportionately consumptive and unashamed capitalist—still operated under the simple pretense that everything had a price; and so far, the world had proven him to be correct. He had negotiated a deal and set up an elaborate plan to have an object that he badly desired to be purchased and transported out of Deadland, where it had supposedly been kept hidden and perfectly preserved. He still hadn't seen a photograph of the object and details about how it looked, and the condition that it was in, sounded far-fetched to Gordon. Which only added to the movie star's intrigue and fed his insatiable greed. It was a bed frame, and into its ironwood structure was carved the images of a hundred-thousand horses and their riders, fully clad in armor and charging into battle. Rumor had it that its initial construction was commissioned by the Mongolian warlord Genghis Khan.

The shipping container—still an empty box at that point— was successfully moved to the ox cart by the silent crew who seemed to be able to accomplish anything with the seven simple tools. The tractor trailer was permitted no further down the road. Gordon was instructed in advance about what he would not be allowed to carry with him into Deadland. No food. There was plenty inside he was assured. He was going to have to relinquish his satellite phone, laptop, watch—anything that had conductive materials within it and that carried any type of electrical current. No magnets. Some books were okay if they were considered to be classics and censored government versions, but no periodicals, and certainly no newspapers. He was instructed not to engage with the locals, but he wasn't told why. Gordon was about to be put through the entry protocols and he was sweating even though the temperature was mild. The sweat was related to extreme nervousness about the microscopic (almost) GPS tracker that he had concealed in the groove between his ass cheeks. The tracker was in the *off* position, smaller than a grain of rice, and was attached with a powerful medical adhesive that was oil soluble so that he could get it off when he needed to. The tracker was also wrapped in a high-density polymer that had so far kept the batteries undetectable by any known scanning equipment. But Chinese technology was purportedly good, and difficult to keep up with for an American who was not really accustomed to covert operations and had a very limited technical vocabulary.

Several men in blue burlap coats threw manila ropes over the container and cinched it down to the ox cart by making miniature pulleys out of slipknots. It wouldn't be much longer before they were ready to go. Gordon's limited experience with the Chinese and the Mongols had taught him that neither was a particularly patient or easy-going breed. He tried to imagine transporting one of them to Seattle just to see how they would fare. They'd probably be more confounded than he was. The thought made him feel better, but not as good as he felt when he looked at his phone one more time and the screen lit up with a familiar 206 number.

"Lucky."

"Gordo, how's it going?"

"It's going. We are at the border. The container is just about loaded onto the ox cart and ready to be moved."

"You sound nervous, Gordo. What's the matter?"

"It's a little hard not to be nervous, Lucky. I'm going into this Deadland blind. I don't even know what language these people are speaking. It sounds nothing like the Mandarin I was picking up in Beijing. Now I have to somehow come out the other side of this fucking haunted terrain with a large precious heirloom that belonged to the only household name that this country up here has ever produced."

"I know, I know. A man so feared that the Chinese took on one of the greatest architectural feats in all of history just to get a false sense of protection from him."

"Lucky, I know this sounds like some cool artifact to get your hands on but I've been out her drinking yak tea with the locals in their yurts for two weeks and there's a drawing of him hanging inside of every structure in Mongolia. It's like he's still here. This stunt of yours might really piss him off."

"So much that he comes back from the grave to conquer America?"

"I'm not joking, Lucky."

"But you are funny, Gordo. Tell me about Deadland."

"I haven't entered yet."

"I know but you are right there, describe it to me."

"Well, the fucking road to this place is basically a collection of potholes. Which didn't seem to deter the driver, Mr. Poo, from taking every curve at the maximum possible speed. The weather's been pretty much crap since I got here. There's not really even a sky, just a layer of smog. In the daytime it's hot as hell, unless it's raining. And when the invisible sun goes down it gets suddenly freezing. I'm standing outside the border. There's a maze of chain link fencing to pass through with armed sentries posted all over the fucking place. Honestly though, it's a nice temperature at the moment. The hillsides that I can see inside the barrier are all bright green. The sky over Deadland doesn't look as bad as everywhere else. I can see what appear to be actual white, puffy clouds; rather than ones that were coughed out of a smokestack. And the closer we get, the more birds there seem to be."

"Doesn't sound dead."

"Doesn't appear dead. Or maybe it's just that it appears less dead than the places I've been so far."

"Are there trees?"

"Looks like some big pines or something on the other side of the fence, and a cluster of dead birches I think, but not much to the north or in any other direction but some kind of scrub weed."

"Sounds nice."

"I doubt you'd like it."

"You might be surprised, Gordo. I have a soft spot for incongruous pulchritude."

"I don't even know what that means."

"Is the tracker in a safe place?"

"To the extent that the inside of my ass crack can be considered a safe place, yes."

The Chinese had a list of conditions that had to be met before anyone could enter Deadland and no amount of money that

Lucky tried to spend was enough to get Gordon in there with a phone or a camera. And each of the layers of chain link fencing had a door to pass through that was clearly a metal detector of some kind. On the other side of the metal detectors the guards waited with wands equipped with an unknown technological capacity. Gordon and Lucky didn't have many options besides trusting that the incredible amounts of Yuan that they were stuffing into pockets would be enough to pull the thing off. But just in case, Lucky insisted that Gordon smuggle a minute GPS tracking device into the zone so that he could attach it to the bed frame once he found it. The device that Lucky had fashioned for him to carry was straight out of a James Bond film.

"For what it's worth, I've never felt safer than when I was in your ass crack." An apparent reference to something that had happened only once and remained a source of great confusion for Gordon. He didn't respond. "Gordon," Lucky snapped. "It's going to be fine. I'll see you in Seattle in just a few weeks. We'll set up the bed."

"And then what?"

"We'll take a nap."

*   *   *

The border crossing into Deadland sat beneath a shallow ridge that ran north-south and was dotted with small *Sophora* trees that sprung up out of the ditches like weeds. The trees had lousy form—like brambles—but they were in full leaf so they made for good cover. Crouched amongst them, and dressed from head to toe in desert camouflage, was a special operative in the employ of the C.I.A. His name was Jodie Cavendish, and he was far from a soldier. He had been through the bare minimum of necessitated field training and could handle a firearm so long as it was no bigger than a 9mm. That didn't matter. Jodie's value was in his knowledge of invasive and potentially threatening new species and he was being babysat by a group of Navy SEALs who surrounded him at all times and moved according to a choreography that eluded the scientist. He only knew that it involved pointing a lot of machine guns at rocks.

Jodie was a Canadian-born academic who made a name for himself at Cambridge University and was awarded dual citizenship when he married a fellow student—Eliza—from the United States. She was doing graduate work connected to her double major in Political Science and Criminal Psychology. He was in Botany. Together they had chemistry, despite having nothing in common. They had been inseparable since the night she leaned on her black belt in Tae Kwon Doe to defend him from a bunch of hooligans at four am on the tube.

Toward the end of her time in England, Eliza was recruited by the Central Intelligence Agency and accepted the job. Her husband Jodie though was never quite sure what it was that she did, since the cases and missions that she was assigned to were all of a classified nature. Their passion still burned hot but the thing about being inseparable went out the window. His fate became to spend the bulk of his hours longing for the woman he rarely saw.

Jodie's assumption was always that she must have been able to share a lot more information with her superiors about him than she was able to share with him about them. It was the only explanation for why an organization like the Central Intelligence Agency would have reached out to a bookworm like himself, who was teaching at the University of Minnesota. A man who wasn't used to adversity, keeping secrets, or spending long stretches of time awake and outdoors.

The initial call came on a cold night in April, about a year previous. He was holed up in a cheap motel room in northern Michigan, hoping to get a peek at a certain species of endangered warbler, when his cell phone rang and the caller's ID was nothing but a series of X's. He picked up and spoke with an agent named Calhoon, whose voice was either very low and gravelly or intentionally scrambled. Jodie never met the man in person. Agent Calhoon was an apparent associate of Jodie's wife, who he had not heard from or seen in over three months. Not knowing what was going on, especially with her, was wearing on him. The next time they were reunited he had resolved to put an end to all the crap. He was a respected researcher, not a prisoner. There was no reason why he deserved to have his relationship with his wife reduced to infrequent conjugal visits and stilted conversations, since what was really going on was impossible for her to divulge. It was time to grow a pair and demand at least something resembling honesty. The internal pep talk bolstered his spirits. Although he was fifty/fifty on whether he would actually follow through with his plan. Jodie's thoughts were often braver than his actions.

Jodie wasn't given much of a sexual education by his conservative Canadian parents, but he knew enough to be confident that pining over one's estranged wife and masturbating wasn't the cornerstone of marital bliss. He remained loyal though to the wife he seldom saw, and when he pleased himself in the shower, he allowed himself to think only about her. Which was tricky, she was beautiful, erotic, and unintimidated in bed, but sometimes he forgot major details about how she looked. Even her name, Eliza Plotnick, took some time to be sure of. During one such shower he accidentally thought she went by Leslie and the guilt haunted him for months.

Their visits seemed about as spread out as the appearance of Hailey's Comet. And like Hailey's Comet, the visits were amazing; even without revealing dialogue. When they were apart it was easy for him to become annoyed at how little she shared with him. But when they were together, the way she looked at him was enough to make none of that matter. One thing he never forgot was the warmth in those brown eyes, they were his home.

The last time she surprised him they wound up at The Four Seasons in Vancouver. After taking in a Canucks game and sushi, they stayed up all night and spent the entire next day in bath robes. During the sunset they drank champagne and made love again in the jacuzzi tub. When they fell asleep, she had her arms wrapped around him and he dreamt that they were riding horses together through the Rockies. When he woke up in the middle of the night, Eliza and her suitcase were gone.

It was Calhoon who first described to Jodie over the phone some of the first known details about the realm in Inner Mongolia that would come to be known as Deadland. The message that Jodie received from the agent was that there may have been some kind of an outbreak and that the United States Government wanted to know exactly what it was. Satellite images confirmed that the region—comprising nearly two-hundred thousand hectares—was effectively closed off. And unless there were secret channels that the United States government wasn't privy to, there seemed to be no communication between Deadland and the outside world. For exactly how long was a mystery.

Jodie was among the first wave of scientists to react to the proliferation of the Asian Longhorn Beetle in the late nineties and he was acutely aware of the potential repercussions for the U.S. and the rest of the world if something as lethal, or even worse, were to come hurtling out of the East Asian Continent, from where exports were shipped to every major port on the globe. What the C.I.A. wanted him to do was to go over there and search the perimeter of the guarded zone for the presence of anything unusual. By unusual they meant some type of new bug, germ, or fungus that could pose a major threat.

Jodie didn't want to go at first. He was pretty focused on getting a view of the warbler and despite being pretty global, Jodie didn't care much for air travel. But he was also a man who felt an obligation to offer assistance when and where he was able and he—going against the strict instructions given to him by Agent Calhoon—reached out to a trustworthy friend of his who he had met while protesting the Chilean government's plans to dam the Baker and Pascua Rivers in the southern part of the country, back in 2011. This friend was an extremely wealthy, young, engaged entrepreneur, and environmental preservationist named Nevil Horsetrainer. Since the protest, Jodie and Nevil remained in close contact, talking on the phone at least every week. Nevil's nephew Marco even took to calling Jodie 'Uncle' since they came and visited him so often. Nevil—who possessed as much of his own surveillance equipment parked in outer space as the rest of North America did in combination—knew about Deadland and the mystery that surrounded its sudden and almost complete disappearance from the world map. What the hell had happened in there and why was something that, as a crusader for global sustainability, mattered a great deal to him as well. He provided Jodie some extra peace of mind before the trip. *If anything fucked up happens in there, I'll come and get you. I promise.* A promise from Nevil was worth more than anything the C.I.A. had to offer.

That was nearly seven months ago. Not enough time to see all the seasons change but it should have been enough time get a handle on any kind of major environmental damage. But there was nothing.

He was initially assigned a security detail of three mid-level agents who were tougher than he was, hyper-vigilant, and never all asleep at the same time. During that stretch he had picked up the local dialect and his Mandarin was coming along. He had read all seven of the books that he brought with him exactly four times, and become somewhat of a master of Qi Gong; but he didn't manage to identify any new species of insects, plants, mammals, fungi, or fish. News about what was going on or not going on inside of Deadland was impossible to come by. No one spoke of it. And so far, he had yet to find a way to get in there. The entire perimeter was surrounded by two layers of tall metal fencing with nasty barb wire at the top.

Technicians working in Houston monitored the perimeter of Deadland round the clock using geostationary satellite cameras but there wasn't even the faintest trace of activity near the edges in as long as anyone on the team could remember, and the agency was very close to pulling the plug on the operation and rendering the zone an area of non-interest, when a young data analyst working her way up through the ranks looked up from her Slurpee to see a tractor trailer heading south on a road that hadn't seen traffic in a very long time. The truck was pointed straight at Deadland. A team of Navy SEALs was immediately deployed from a base in the Philippines and as soon as they arrived, they took Jodie with them on a high-speed pursuit of the vehicle.

It wasn't exactly the moment that he had been waiting for but it was a break from the monotony of his post, as well as a chance to finally don the camouflage suit that he had been fantasizing about putting on and doing something heroic in since he showed up. He even had a helmet with fake shrubbery glued to the top of it, and he was wearing it as he watched the transfer of the cargo container from the truck to the ox cart through his optics. Behind him the SEALs spoke in their melodramatic acronyms and did a lot of herky-jerky motions with their guns aimed at the horizon but no one seemed to be following them. There wasn't too much to be learned from what Jodie—who the security detail referred to directly as Sir, and to each other as The Package, but had been given the somewhat ceremonial title of Deputy Director of Homeland Security Operations—was watching unfold before him. The ox cart with the cargo container was going to be the first item to cross the threshold into Deadland since the fences were erected, as far as he knew. All told, there were about fifty men and women assisting with the crossing. Sentries posted at the gate were fully armed, although they didn't appear intent on putting up any type of resistance.

The satellite phone that Jodie was required to carry with him fully charged at all times, which normally only rung when Nevil called, started to hum and the screen lit up with that same series of X's that implied that whoever was calling was more important than whoever was about to pick up. Jodie thought the guys he worked for back in the states were ruder than necessary, although he liked the SEALs and the other agents. He was also well compensated and his extended stint in the outer reaches of the planet leant itself to saving money at least. Whenever it ended, Jodi and Eliza were going to be able to retire in reasonable style, maybe somewhere rural, like New Mexico. An idea that he meant to run by her during their next rendezvous. Jodie clicked the green button on the satellite phone.

"Agent Cavendish, do you have eyes on the vehicle?" It was Agent Calhoon.

"You could at least lead with *hello*, don't you think? After stranding me at the far end of the galaxy for what was supposed to be a fortnight."

"Agent Cavendish, do I have to remind you that you are under contract with the government of the United States of America. That you have sworn an oath to follow through with your assignment, and that you are being more than adequately compensated for your time and efforts?"

"No, sir."

"Do you have eyes on the vehicle?"

"Affirmative."

"How many people do you see?"

"I'd say about fifty."

"Do they seem like military operatives?"

"Other than the guards at the gates no one appears armed. It's mostly the local types. There are half a dozen riders on horseback dressed in all black. It looks like they are going to follow the container in."

"There is a shipping container being moved into Deadland?"

"Yeah, but not on the truck. They are transferring it to an ox cart."

"That's interesting. Are there any foreigners with them?"

"There is one white guy in a suit, standing off to the side."

"Could he be an American?"

"Maybe. Can't say from this distance."

"Agent Cavendish."

"Yes, sir."

"I need you to get as many pictures of that man as you can."

"Yes, sir."

"What else can you tell me about the interior region?"

"Nothing much. I haven't been inside of it. And my explorations around the perimeter haven't turned up anything unusual. The natural resources around here have been mostly used up and the land is suffering. But that's true of everywhere in China. It's an environmental catastrophe but the root pathogen seems to be human beings."

"Can you see inside of the protected zone?"

"Affirmative. I've got my field glasses with me as usual, sir."

"And?"

"And, well, the sky overhead is nicer. As if there is a rare pocket of clean air hovering over it. I haven't conducted a census but the avian activity appears far greater than it is even a mile away. The trees have vigor, compared to most of the ones I have seen, which are struggling to photosynthesize through the smog, thirsty, and starving for nutrients. With the exception of a copse of *Betula* that I can see through the field glasses. Those trees look dead. Other than that, I can't say much."

"What do you think is going on?"

"I haven't enough data to say."

"Then guess."

"Alright. My observations indicate that the interior of the protected zone seems healthier than the region outside of it. At least from a biological perspective."

"Why might that be?"

"Again, I am guessing, but it seems that the industrial obsession that is threatening to destroy this country isn't as bad inside the protected region. Maybe they have quarantined an area off to see what nature would do if left to its own devices."

"Hard to believe that the Chinese would even conceive of that idea. If you are correct, they must have been forced to do it this way. Can you confirm that there is no visible power supply on the other side of the fencing?"

"I don't see anything. And the fact that they are halting this truck at the border and transferring the load to an ox cart means that they are either adverse to allowing anything too technologically advanced to pass through the gate, or..."

"Or what?"

"Or they can't afford to."

"That sounds more likely. Why do you think they can't afford to?"

"Maybe there was some kind of revolution inside, and the people inside have banded together and insisted upon living a primitive lifestyle."

"The Chinese would never back down like that. There's no way a bunch of sheep herders has the firepower to keep the government out."

"Then maybe it's something else."

"Ideas?"

"Seems impossible but, maybe there is some sort of biological phenomenon that won't allow it. Something like King Kong or the Loch Ness Monster."

"We would see that on the satellite. It has to be something smaller."

"Maybe a lethal mushroom, bacteria, or an insect. Anything that powerful and that small that is escaping surveillance would have to be extremely prolific."

"So what you are telling me is that there is a possibility that some never seen before, miniature species of something, may have found a way to eliminate all of the commerce, all of the motor vehicles, and all of the low and high voltage wires in the interior of the protected zone."

"It's a stretch but it is possible I suppose."

"Whatever that is, Agent Cavendish, we can't allow it to exit China. Keep working until you have something definitive."

"Yes, sir."

Gordon was given a piebald horse to ride once he was inside. He rode in front of the ox cart, making slow progress along a road of soft red earth, amongst a small band of female riders. The wheels of the ox cart dug in as they traveled and the going was rough on the animals. In two wet days they reached the ranch of a man named Xi Jeng. Xi Jeng grazed several hundred sheep in a meadow in front of his compound of yurts. When Gordon and the ox cart arrived, Xi Jeng greeted them and had a halted conversation with the riders. Gordon didn't understand the dialogue but afterward he could see that there was a desperate situation. The sheep were birthing spring lambs at the rate of dozens per day. He came to learn that if the rains washed off the scent of the newborns the mothers would refuse them milk. The afternoon was passed watching for birthing mothers and using spray paint to mark them and their lambs with matching symbols. Mothers refusing to nurse were then stabled with their babies so they couldn't escape. Despite the effort, the death rate was harrowing. Gordon knew that this wasn't his problem but he was moved by the sight of raw survival in ways that he had never been moved before; and something about the aerosol cans of paint they were using seemed out of place. It was the first thing he had seen inside of Deadland—other than the container—that was processed or manufactured by people. It got him wondering about what was really going on in there. The indigenous had clearly shunned the comforts of electricity, but it couldn't have been simply because of pride. Something else was living there, and whatever it was, they were scared of it.

The harsh conditions inside the zone didn't mar the fact that it was also pleasant. The air was finally fresh; no more of that brownish miasma that seemed to hang over the rest of the country. He was sleeping well, with light and joyful dreams. And the food was by far the finest in China. The fish had meat on their bones and tasted of clean water. The produce may have been organic. It definitely lacked that essence of genetic manipulation that the rest of the nation's vegetables seemed to have; all big and bright but with no flavor. The inside of Deadland was a foodie's undiscovered wet dream. And it wasn't just about the quality of the substance, in Deadland they cooked without fear of intense spice.

After his first dusk on Xi Jeng's land—and a dinner of grilled mutton, trout, pickled something, and sweet breads—Gordon was fetched from his yurt and blindfolded. Quiet walkers led him up a hill. Gordon had neglected to put on shoes but his feet were relaxed and he was glad the he was barefoot since he couldn't see. He could feel every nuance of the ground beneath his feet. The sensation made him feel confident and secure. They went along a ridge for a long time with the light of a coppery full moon creating a pretty, soft glow that Gordon could make out through the cloth that was tied around his head. At some point they descended to a stream and crossed the cool water. Eventually they stopped in front of a tall cliff face and the blindfold was removed. Two of the female riders were there, Xi Jeng, and a muscular lad who bore a familial resemblance to him. The boy dug his feet into the ground and moved a massive boulder that guarded the entrance to a tunnel in the cliff face. Xi Jeng entered first with a torch and Gordon followed right behind him. The tunnel ended in a natural cathedral and a tiny hole in the rock ceiling was letting in a column of moonlight. In the center of the room was what Gordon had come looking for.

Even in the dim lighting he could see that the craftsmanship that had gone into the bed he was looking at dwarfed anything in the Guggenheim or El Prado. It was exquisite. He let his fingers drift across the shapes of the horses and their riders, every hair carved in with the greatest care. The edges of the carvings were all clean and well-defined. It was undeniably atavistic but in such a perfect state that it could have been hewn the day before. The headboard was flanked by two posts fashioned from stripped tree trunks. The riders that spiraled up the posts wore a different style of armor, likely that of captains or generals in Genghis Khan's incredible army. Beneath their helmets their faces were all uniquely rendered. Whether or not they had facial hair, scars, or missing something like a nose or an ear, they all had their mouths open in a collective roar that threatened to drown out the whole world; even in its silence. The side rails depicted the army in fast motion; riding at full charge with weapons drawn and expressions that belayed no fear at all of death.

There were more soldiers carved into the foot section of the bed frame but they were at ease and in the company of women. Some of the women were dressed or partly covered but most were not, and they seemed to outnumber the men by about two to one. The bigger figures toward the edges had removed their helmets and body armor and some of them were talking casually with the women. As Gordon let his eyes drift more toward the center of the piece he noticed that the characters retained their extensive detail, even as they shrunk in size and the image devolved into that of a debauched orgy that could have been born in the imagination of Hieronymus Bosch, were it not distinctly Eastern in its decorum as well as way ahead of its time.

Curiously, there was no visible hardware securing the pieces of the bed's ironwood structure together. Either it had all been done with invisible joiners, so precisely milled out of perfectly cured wood that they had not deteriorated in the slightest over the course of almost a thousand years, or it had been carved from a single piece of lumber, but Gordon quickly dismissed that idea. Even he could see that the wood grain that ran along the sides didn't match the posts. Nowhere was the wood thinner than a fist and Gordon imagined it weighed several tons. He chanced a look underneath and was amazed to see that the inner faces of the wood had been carved with the same detail and care as the exposed sections. There were countless more riders, armed to the teeth and ferocious in their purpose.

There was no mattress on the bed and Gordon couldn't imagine that a Mongol would have the gall to actually sleep in it, but he had no doubt that Lucky would have something custom made that would fit nicely; and that he would sleep like a baby in the conqueror's bed. Perhaps the two of them together even. The thought gave Gordon an erection that he attempted to conceal by hunching over. The slats that were in place and ready to support a mattress were the only parts that weren't engraved. The wood they were cut from was clear and the grain so tight it could have been as dense as lead. Gordon looked over his shoulder at Xi Jeng.

"Can we get it out of here and into the container?" he asked.

Xi Jeng nodded but made no indication that he was going to explain how. They had their ways and Gordon was inclined to trust them. After that Xi Jeng and his people retreated into the shadows at the edges of the cave and let Gordon have a moment alone with what he had found. The first part of his mission had succeeded, albeit the easy part. Traveling light in that part of the world had been hard enough. From then on, he would be shuttling a shipping container on a rustic cart that would be heavy enough to contain a circus elephant. He had to get it to the port in Shanghai, transferred to a Seattle-bound barge in Singapore, and offloaded in the states without arousing suspicion. It was going to take a lot of luck—or a lot of Lucky—to get them both back unharmed. But somehow customs officials and port authorities seemed like a very small hurdle to Gordon. What worried the piss out of him was the wrath of the man to whom the bed belonged. The almighty warlord Genghis Khan left his earthly body in 1227 A.D., but his spirit still lingered, sustained its grip over a nation, and retained its desire to conquer the globe.

When no one was watching him, Gordon used a dollop of grapeseed oil to remove the tiny GPS tracker from its new hiding spot closer to the wrist, snapped it in the middle to turn it on, and then tacked it into a shadowy groove on the back of one of the side rails, between a thrapple and a spear. The moment that the tracker began emitting its signal, a breeding pair of flying black insects with iridescent red stripes that ran the length of their backs, and short horns that bent diabolically toward an invisible center point, converged upon the tracker and started to feed.

Seattle

A ray of light shot through the executive offices on the twenty-fifth floor of the Smith Tower. It had been a mute gray morning, quiet, and without a trace of a breeze. Pleasant enough so far but on its way to roasting. The forecasters were blaming global warming for another afternoon expected to be in the high eighties. There hadn't been measurable precipitation at Sea-Tac airport in one-hundred-seven days. A new record, which came on the heels of the hottest August on record, which contained the single hottest day on record. That summer there were already the most car fires on the side of the interstate and the highest death toll from dehydration. It was getting on eleven am and the sun had just burned a hole in the haze and the colorless sky was beginning to acquire hints of periwinkle.

In 1914, money connected to the Smith Typewriter Company built the tower. One-point-five-million dollars raised the tallest building in the west. Less than a hundred years later the same amount wouldn't buy a fixer with a water view on no land in north Ballard. But the tower remained a symbol of Seattle's transition from a backwater outpost to the progressive hub of the Pacific Northwest and home to some of the most influential companies on the globe. As taller skyscrapers with greater capacities grew up around it, The Smith Tower still occupied its choice location, looming above Pioneer Square in the southern part of downtown, and worked to retain its 1920's era charm. In fact, the entire building was still serviced by a bank of the original Otis elevators that worked on an electric friction system and required operators to dress in vintage woolen uniforms with piping on the legs and arms and football-shaped hats with chin straps. On the thirty-fifth floor there was an observation deck and the famous Chinese Room where there was always a college student or two describing the city's layout for their out-of-town parents or a gathering of professional ladies drinking overpriced wine and sandwiches made with Beecher's Original Cheese and Washington apples. The Chinese Room also contained a carved mahogany chair flanked by two friendly-looking gray gargoyles. Legend had it that an unmarried woman who sat in the chair would have a wedding inside of twelve months. It was officially called The Wishing Chair and it was the source of a million false hopes, awkward silences, cheesy photographs, and a few marriages. The low-rise section of the building encompassed the first twenty-two floors and was populated with mostly legal and accounting firms. The tower section rose above that and the space between the top of the low rise and the observation deck was only rented out by the floor.

Herman Glüber, groomed to perfection and smartly dressed in a light gray suit with a pale-yellow tie, was seated behind a large desk in his air-conditioned glass enclosure at the southwest corner of a private level. A leave-in hair conditioner kept his curls just the right texture and sheen so long as he never touched them, and he was wearing a designer pair of Wissing eyeglasses that had a very light magnification prescription so he could see the screens a bit better. He was using two desktop computer monitors to simultaneously study the week's closing numbers on the NYSE, research water conservation legislation in Wenatchee County, check the references of a survey team that he was about to throw a huge job at, sift through data concerning export revenue from Washington state fruit crops, watch an amateur video of two teenagers making out on an old basement couch, and conduct two separate email conversations from two separate accounts. One of the conversations was with the man that he called boss, the CEO of Cronkey, Mitchell and Wolfe Venture Capital Firm, Duncan Klevit. Herman was reassuring Duncan that all of the details concerning the pending meeting with the owners of Summerwood Farms had been attended to. Herman assumed that Duncan was passing the info up the chain to Cronkey, Mitchell and Wolfe but he couldn't say. He'd never actually met them. Another conversation that he was having was with a real estate developer who specialized in family theme parks. Water parks in particular, although the conversation that they were having that morning was more about the NFL than it was about business.

Right after he fired off the email to the developer, a small winged bug with a striped back, about half an inch long, appeared in the upper right-hand corner of the display and started traversing the screen. The sight of any bug way up above the ground in the climate-controlled and hermetically sealed downtown office spaces seemed so preposterous to him at first that he assumed it was a computer bug, cooked up by some Russian hacker who thought he was being cute. But a split-second later Herman's subconscious mind was identifying the shadows made by the horn-like antennae when the head moved from side to side and the barely perceptible patter of the bug's feet. There also seemed to be a faint line of blue light connecting the horns. He reached out, pinching the nasty little thing between his index finger and thumb and squeezed it until its sternum collapsed with a popping sound and the body emitted a modicum of white goo. As usual, it felt good to crush something, even though he sustained a minor electrical shock in the process—something that he couldn't explain and didn't dwell on. He flicked the carcass into the garbage receptacle beside the desk and was wiping off his hand with a tissue when another bug appeared in the corner of the computer monitor and started tracing the steps of its deceased predecessor. As soon as Herman killed it—and was shocked again—there was another, on an identical mission, like the foul things were pouring out of a clown car. It was repulsive. Herman picked up the receiver of his desk phone and was about to dial the extension for maintenance so that he could upbraid them when he heard a familiar knock and saw the door to his office swing open. It was one of his colleagues, Loven Boilee.

Loven was a statistics major who graduated from the Wharton School of Business with an uncanny ability to evaluate financial derivatives. Which was the reason that Duncan put up with his crass behavior and his flashy, unsettling style. Loven had the legs of an effeminate Asian teenager, the paunch of a beer-swiller from Michigan, and the head of a Brooklyn hipster. He was wearing a custom-tailored-three-piece suit in steel blue with wide lapels and subtle gray pinstripes. The pants fit tight, the jacket was unbuttoned and the vest had his lucky paisley tie tucked into it. His black hair was medium length, coiffed, full of products, and would have looked dapper if it wasn't for the jarring contrast created by the Grizzly Adams beard that hung from his face and terminated in a scraggly taper about four inches below the chin. He had the look of a man who was not only single, but in need of some serious stylistic help. But this was not the case. Loven had been happily married to a sweetheart tattoo artist named Maggie since his early twenties. Herman wasn't sure how the two of them had found each other. It was like Lennon and McCartney; something that was just supposed to happen. He had a thin three-ring binder tucked underneath his left armpit.

Herman put down the telephone receiver, ignored Loven's presence in the room, smashed the third bug, and went back to composing emails. His fingers furiously striking the keys and sounding like hard rain. Loven took a seat in one of the chairs facing Herman's desk and waited for some attention. Herman seemed intent upon ignoring him. Loven set the binder on the floor, extended his left arm and checked the time on his Breitling.

"I've got some good news, Herman," said Loven, used to having to bait Herman into being interested in what he had to say.

"What's that?" said Herman without looking up.

"Renata made it through the whole elevator ride without having to use the stool, and Hartmut's fly is up. At least so far," said Loven, challenging Herman to keep trying to ignore him.

"So, they're here?"

"Yeah, they're here, but they're a mess. Hartmut couldn't get that old Chevy pickup of his into the underground garage and they had to drive around for forty minutes looking for a road spot that he could fit the thing into. We're lucky they didn't give up and drive back over the pass. You know how those two wilt as soon as they enter civilization."

Hartmut and Renata were fifth generation apple growers who had spent their entire life in Peshastin, Wa. Their orchard spanned both banks of the Wenatchee River and had over seven-thousand mature apple and pear trees on it. As new varieties of apples came into fashion and some of the older trees became less productive, modern strains were grafted onto the established rootstock. But the acre of trees around the original farmhouse that Renata and Hartmut still lived in dated back to the mid 1800's. They were planted by Hartmut's great-great-grandfather Rudolph. And Hartmut, who was pushing eighty, still had his staff set up his ladders and loppers for him twice a year so that he could prune that grove of trees personally. The fruit always finished up mealy or full of worms but the trees themselves were strong and had a lot of sentimental value. They always flowered beautifully in the spring. The rest of the orchard was maintained, at his direction, by a large staff of mostly illegal immigrants from Mexico. A life of honest hard work—nearly all of which was undertaken outdoors in the fresh air—had left the aging couple in relatively good health. But time was catching up with them. Hartmut had injured his knee back in the fifties when he fell from the top of a sixteen-foot orchard ladder. On humid days his arthritis was getting so bad that he couldn't get out of his tweed armchair. Plus, it seemed like he was at the hospital in Wenatchee every other week having a melanoma removed. Renata's sciatica had been acting up more and more. She'd never been a big eater and her trademark frailty had become alarming. She might have weighed ninety pounds with her fleece bathrobe on. She had trouble keeping warm, and was prone to dozing off at any moment of the day. Hartmut and Renata's biggest problem was that they were without an heir to bequeath their family's legacy to. So earlier in the year, they made the painful decision to put their orchard—Summerwood Farms—up for sale.

Real estate prices were surging all over Washington and the Frenzels were stunned at all of the attention that their parcel of land was receiving. Offers to buy were pouring in from builders who foresaw new housing communities, hotel magnates, and farmers interested in converting the land over to the production of marijuana, a crop which—since it had been legalized—was threatening to dethrone the apple as Washington's most lucrative agricultural endeavor. Technically the marijuana produced at these types of farms wasn't supposed to be exported from Washington state, but the marijuana community was particularly good at overlooking those types of technicalities. In either case, neither Hartmut nor his wife was willing to see their trees mowed down, and they were refusing all offers, no matter how much money was being thrown at them.

Herman learned about the land that was for sale rather accidentally. It had been a so-so winter in terms of snowfall and the local kayaking population had to be on the spring melt early if they wanted to get any big water paddling in. Herman had just run Tumwater canyon—an angry stretch of the Wenatchee river that narrows and drops through a maze of granite boulders before finally calming down as it enters the tourist trap Bavarian village town of Leavenworth. Herman was at the brewery, tossing back a Whistling Pig Hefeweizen, and regaling a few other boaters with a tall tale of him having to do nine combat rolls to escape a nasty boil that wanted to suck him down to the bottom. The other paddlers eventually got sick of listening to him boast and dispersed. When Herman turned his attention to the valley's local newspaper, he caught the story of the local couple that was refusing to sell their orchard to anyone who had intentions for the land that didn't include producing tree fruit. He went back to his room at the Enzian Inn and spent the rest of the night learning everything that he could online about the business of growing apples. The following morning, he contacted a real estate agent who took him to Peshastin to see the land and meet the Frenzels. Herman made sure that he was biting into a crispy apple—not worrying about the fact that it was a New Zealand import—at the moment that the introductions were made.

"Who's with them?" Herman asked, finally looking up over his monitors at Loven. He didn't want there to be any surprises when he entered the room.

"That Omeed Gazipurah dude who is supposedly their lawyer, and that cute Mexican girl whose dad is Hartmut's right hand. Lupita something."

"Lupita Bevilacqua? What the hell is she doing here?"

"A bunch of the migrant workers have gotten together and drafted some document guaranteeing fair treatment once the sale goes through. She's functioning as their representative or something. I assume since she's one of the only ones that speaks English. Plus she was born here so she's an actual citizen. Duncan said she could say a few words at the meeting."

"Why didn't I know about this?"

"I think it just popped up. What's the big deal?"

"What's the big deal? Loven, what we need to do today is to get those two skeletons to sign the closing documents. It doesn't sound to me like whatever it is that Lupita is planning is going to help make that happen. Does it sound that way to you?"

"Hey, I'm just the statistics guy. You're the closer. I'm sure Duncan just figures that the little señorita is no match for you. You're Herman Glüber."

"I didn't say I was worried about Lupita. It's just an added pain in the ass is all."

Herman and Lupita had a bit of a history. On Herman's initial visit to the orchard he hit it off with the head receptionist at the orchard, a woman named Dolly Rheese. Dolly seemed to know the inner workings of the business better than anyone, including the old couple who owned the place. He learned a great deal from her, including the circumstances surrounding the land's least compelling feature. Since the orchard straddled the river, and the river was the only navigable route through the mountainous region that surrounded Summerwood Farms, the state retained an easement that cut right through the heart of the property that was chock full of ugly metal towers and unsightly electrical transmission lines. To make matters worse, there was a large sub-station located on the property where the energy was stepped down from deliverable high-voltage to usable high-amperage power. According to Dolly there was no getting rid of the eyesore. Herman wasn't so sure. Other than that, she used broad strokes to orient Herman to the operation, clearly exaggerating the strengths of the enterprise. Then she suggested that Lupita, who happened to be nearby, take Herman on a tour through the trees themselves, let him know what was out there, maybe give him a little grafting demonstration. The two of them set out with a bundle of Honeycrisp scions beneath the power lines that were crackling overhead.

Herman was looking for someone inside of the operation to help him to gain knowledge of its inner workings. He pretended to be a young entrepreneur with a passion for natural foods and the outdoors. He let Lupita teach him how to do a whip and tongue graft. Herman picked up on some potential sexual chemistry, so he invited her to dinner later that evening. She ignored him and tried to change the subject to making sure the tissues were making a tight connection. After which he only pressed her harder to say yes. She was shy about it. Lupita knew almost everyone that worked in the valley and was worried about what people would say if the two of them were seen out together. So, Herman invited her to come to the Enzian Inn where they could eat room service and she could tell him more about growing apple trees. She accepted the invitation and a few more things happened that night than simply eating and chatting about apples. Herman made a pretty aggressive pass at her and she adamantly denied him even the tiniest amount of affection. The evening actually ended with her running out of the room in fear and his accusing her of being prudish and a bore.

"I'm sure you can handle whatever's about to get thrown at us," Loven had an easy time getting along with Herman, mostly because he understood that Herman needed his ego stroked at regular intervals.

Herman flashed a mean smile. Loven reached inside of his suit jacket and removed a small glass vile filled to the top with a fine white powder. The vile's cap had a stainless-steel spoon attached to a hinge. Loven unscrewed the vile and dipped the spoon into the powder. He used the knuckles of the hand holding the vile to close his left nostril while he snorted the small mound of cocaine with the right. He then repeated the process on the other side and extended the vile across the desk to Herman.

Herman removed his eyeglasses and took the vile from Loven. He took two small toots, licked his fingers, and then wiped his septum so that he could be certain that there was no residue.

When the drug started to take hold Herman's mind wandered off and his gaze locked in on one of the photographs on his desk. He was leaning against a palm tree with a big curve in its trunk. He had just taken third place in the Ironman triathlon on

Oahu. His body was completely hairless and glistening from a recently applied layer of suntanning oil. There was a candy cane shaped bulge in his minimalist swimsuit and he had his arm around a topless hula dancer that he paid fifty bucks to be in the shot. Beside it there was a picture of Herman in a classic tuxedo, holding an oversized check made out to Cronkey, Mitchell and Wolfe in the amount of nine-million dollars. He had a champagne flute in his other hand and he was making a short speech. In the speech he didn't mention that a food bank, public library and a dilapidated but still heavily used senior center were collateral damage in that particular business transaction. He stuck with the enormous profits that the deal generated for the firm and the bacon-wrapped scallops that were served before the main course. The third and final framed photograph on Herman's desk was of him standing on the highest of the Annapurna peaks, 26,545 feet above sea level. He had on a puffy down suit in lime green and was thrusting an ice axe toward the sky. His confident pose and the subtle grin that he wore on his chapped lips seemed to indicate some level of disappointment for Herman up on the peak. As though he had expected the mountain to challenge him more than it had. He looked like a man who had achieved a goal but not a man who had been tested.

Herman often wavered on displaying that photograph on his desk, because technically there was another person in the photo that he wasn't fond of. In Herman's mirrored glacier climbing goggles there was the reflection of the cameraman, an individual for whom Herman harbored a particular disdain, the young entrepreneur Nevil Horsetrainer. Nevil was a late addition to the climbing team, arriving via helicopter just two days before the first climb from base up to camp one. Nevil was the world's youngest self-made billionaire. At thirteen he had written a piece of software that used satellites to guide intercontinental ballistic missiles with pinpoint accuracy and sold it to the Israeli government. With the windfall he started the energy drink company RocketFuel, which within a few years was the top selling brand on five continents and nipping at Red Bull's frozen heels down in Antarctica. Herman hated Nevil because of how the two of them compared on nearly every conceivable measuring stick. Nevil was younger than Herman by a decade, the kid made more money than Herman by a lot, he had seen more of the world, he spoke French and Hebrew, he played the ukulele, he told better stories, and was arguably better looking than Herman. At least Herman's cock was longer than Nevil's. He got a glimpse of the kid's once while Nevil was arcing a golden rainbow into a deep crevasse above camp three and it was so tiny that he could scarcely make the thing out. To be fair to Nevil, it was about a thousand degrees below zero.

"Going out with Margot tonight?" asked Loven as Herman passed the cocaine back to him.

"Nah. She's got the kid and it's science fair weekend at his middle school," Herman already had some sniffles and the black of his pupils was taking over the blue of his irises.

"What's the kid's project?"

"Bugs or spider breeding or something," Herman replied, wiggling his jaw back and forth.

"You going to go check it out?"

"I don't think so." As Herman said that he remembered that he should probably bag up one of those creepy insects on his computer monitor for the little brat to look at under his microscope. The kid was always holed up in his bedroom looking at something under a microscope. Herman hadn't actually been inside the kid's bedroom but he had looked in from the doorway. It was as hot and humid as a tropical island in there, and the walls were stacked with terrariums illuminated by red bulbs. There were wires traversing everywhere and miniature fans and pumps whirring. Herman could never understand why the kid had all this sciencey shit around the house but no baseball gloves or hockey sticks. No helmets. The kid might have been neglected. Herman looked back at the screen but the bugs had disappeared.

"We should get a drink after work," suggested Loven. "This is a big one that we're closing today."

The light on Herman's desk phone suddenly glowed red and he depressed a button that allowed him to speak with his secretary.

"What is it, Anita?"

"Margot is on the line."

"Go ahead and put her through."

"Hi, Herman."

"Hey, Pumpkin. Where are you?" He kicked back in his rolling chair just enough to throw his feet up on the desk.

"I'm heading to the Tamarind Tree with Fwen. It's hectic today. My boss is getting ready to go to Vegas and we are trying to get her ready for her presentation." Like a lot of Seattleite's in her income bracket, Margot worked as an executive assistant at the online retail juggernaut Zonama. She was a Zombie, as Herman and Loven liked to refer to them behind their backs.

"Pho? On a day like today you should be looking for gazpacho."

"I like it on a hot day. It's so light. What are you doing?"

"I'm getting ready for a meeting myself. Closing that real estate deal I was telling you about. For the orchard."

"That's right. That's so cool you're buying an orchard. Are you going to start making cider with the apples? I always want to order hard cider because it's gluten free but it's so sugary I get a migraine before I can even feel the buzz. You should make me a true dry cider with your apples, Herman."

"I'll see what I can do about that. Making a dry cider isn't at the top of our priority list today. We got a lot to do before we even get our hands on the orchard. Even if I can't make you a dry cider, I promise to buy you a champagne so dry that when I pour it all over you you won't even get wet."

"Very funny, Herman," she didn't really sound amused. "Am I going to get to see you this weekend?"

"I thought that you have Ethan this weekend."

"I do, but so what."

"You know I don't like kids."

"Shut up, Herman. Ethan likes you."

"He's just starving for a proper role model because his dad's a pansy."

"His dad is not a pansy. He's a brilliant architect."

"His dad is a twerp. I checked out that picture of him that's hanging in the hall next to the bathroom. The one where he's supposedly fishing with the kid. What does he weigh? A hundred-twenty. He looks like bait. Plus, he's got that white hat on and the sleeves, like he melts in sunlight. I see why you ditched that clown."

"I didn't ditch him, Herman. He discovered he was gay."

"Something I'll never understand. You think your ex-husband put his yang in other dudes and then put it in you afterwards?"

"I'm sure he did."

"I'm going to pretend I don't know that. Listen, maybe I'll come by tomorrow night, after Ethan goes to sleep."

"Science fair is in the day tomorrow. Come see Ethan's project. It's amazing. He bred tarantulas. He's even selling them for twenty bucks a piece. He's a little entrepreneur, like you."

"Umm, I'm going to pass. It's been a grind for us over here at the firm this week. I'm heading out with the boys tonight. Tomorrow I'm sleeping in and getting to the gym. Text me later in the afternoon and we will see what's up. Good chance I'll be missing that Chinese finger trap between your legs."

"Stop it, Herman. Can't you work out earlier? Ethan would love it if you came and saw his presentation. And to be honest with you, so would I," she was agitated, verging on mad.

"I don't know. How long is it going to be?"

"Two or three hours. We can take him to an early dinner afterwards. We could go to Cactus."

"I'm not making any promises. It's the bottom of the ninth over here and I've got to keep my head in the game. I'll call you later on."

"Is *that* at least a promise?"

"It is."

"I'm not on speaker-phone now, am I?"

"You are but nobody's in here."

"Not even Loven? I think I hear him breathing."

"Hi, Margot."

"Fuck you, Herman."

"Hey, what's the big deal?"

"I don't want your buddies listening in on our personal conversations. Unless you can talk Herman into coming to the science fair, Loven."

"I'll see what I can do," said Loven.

"Good luck," she snapped.

The line went dead.

"Did she just hang up on me?"

"I think she did, Herman. You know, she seems pretty cool. You might think about trying to hang on to her."

"She's got a kid."

"What's your point?"

"Don't get me wrong. I like her too. Probably more than you realize. We have a good time, and the sex is dynamite. Might have learned her lesson after the fruity architect changed teams. But I don't want a kid. She's already griping about me hardly ever being around, not being affectionate enough, not wanting to hold hands when we are out. That kind of thing freaks me out."

"Maybe you're right. How about a little more blow?" said Loven, removing the vial from his inside pocket again.

"Yeah I'll take a little more," said Herman. "Then we have to start getting some work done. What's in that report of yours? Anything that I need to know before we head in there?"

"Yeah," said Loven, passing the cocaine back across the desk to Herman. "There's some shit. I feel like we have overlooked the value of Summerwood's vehicle fleet. Everyone is so hung up on the land and the trees. This equipment has been mostly a throw-in part of the deal. But there's a lot of value there. There are nineteen diesel Internationals, all with less than two-hundred-thousand miles on them. I know it sounds like a lot but they're actually babies. I did a few price comparisons. Those things still go for forty grand a pop. There's a whole gang of tractors in varying states of repair. They've got a D9 bulldozer that is worth almost a hundred K by itself. The summary of what's in the report is that we may have underestimated the value of some of the assets that we are about to acquire but I'm not yet sure by how much. We'd have to go through all of the equipment piece by piece and see what it will fetch when it goes up for sale."

"That's excellent news. Do you have all of the equipment listed in that binder?"

"Yeah, I've got it all charted out. Each machine and vehicle is listed according to the year that it was manufactured and how many miles, or hours in a lot of cases, are on the engines. Plus VIN's. We just haven't been able to ascertain all of the values yet."

"Let me see," Herman spent a moment studying the pages that Loven was referring to and then pressed the button on his desk phone that allowed him to chat with his secretary again.

"Yes, Mr. Glüber."

"How are the preparations for the meeting going, Anita?"

"Good, Mr. Glüber. The Frenzels and their team are just about assembled in the Blue Room. Allison Mulberry from Talon Escrow just arrived with the closing documents. It's a thick stack of pages she has with her. I'd expect to be in there for a while."

"No kidding. At the rate that Hartmut and Renata sign we will probably be in there all weekend. Speaking of, there's something that I need you to take care of before Monday gets here."

"Sir. I have plans for this weekend. Don't you remember?"

"Remembering things is your job, Anita. Not mine. I just came up with a project for you. Loven has listed all of the vehicles and equipment that are part of Summerwood's fleet that we are acquiring today. I want to start selling that stuff off early next week and I'm going to need values for each of them so that I have a solid starting point for the negotiations."

"But sir, I couldn't possibly—"

"Anita. It is a very busy day here and I don't have time to argue with you. I'm looking at the list right now. There are only ninety-seven pieces of equipment to appraise. Wait a second. The trucks are in their own column. Looks like one-hundred-forty-three including all the trucks. Work hard and I am certain that you will have it done before those Sunday night television shows that I know you like."

"But sir. My best friend Joanne is—"

"If your BFF wants you to still have a job next week, she might consider helping you out so that you can finish up a little earlier. I'm going to leave this report on my desk. After Loven and I leave for the meeting you can make yourself a copy of the list. When I show up on Monday the report will be back on my desk with numbers assigned to every item, wholesale and retail values please. Is that clear, Anita?"

"Yes, Mr. Glüber," Anita fell silent and a quiet moment passed while Herman seethed at the phone on his desk.

"Still there, Anita?"

"Yes, sir."

"I could go for a coffee as well. Triple-tall-three-pump-mocha, no whip. You want something, Loven?"

"I could go for a macchiato."

"And a macchiato for Loven. And scare up some breath mints. I just ran out." Herman ended the conversation with his secretary and turned back to Loven. "What else?"

"Well, I had been wondering what we would do with the trees once they are all cut down."

"I figured we would just burn them."

"Would you burn money?"

"I'm listening."

"It's all applewood. Guys who smoke their own meat like using it. I found a guy out in Kettle Falls who cures and sells the stuff in three-pound bags all over the country. He'll buy all of it at two-hundred-dollars per ton."

"How many tons are we looking at?"

"It's hard to pinpoint since the trees are a variety of sizes. But we figure that at an average of ninety-eight pounds of wood per tree, times seven-thousand trees. We've got close to three-hundred-and-fifty tons of wood there."

"Which translates to?"

"Another sixty-five to seventy-grand if we can get it to Kettle Falls."

"Well, we have the trucks, don't we?"

"We do. We could use the Internationals to transport the wood before we sell them off."

"Nice work, Loven."

A flock of pigeons buzzed the window and then perched on the precipice of the King County Courthouse across the street. A swift breeze came in from the west and the building, anchored in the glacial till by over twelve-hundred concrete pilings, swayed a little. Herman spun around in his swivel chair and put his feet up on a stack of file boxes. He was feeling good from the pure Colombian product that Loven had brought and wanted to spend a minute admiring the painting that hung on the wall behind his desk. The painting was curated in accordance with the array of photographs. Which is to say that it was a painting of Herman. "This is my favorite one of me," Herman said, to no one in particular. It was an action shot of sorts. A re-envisioning of the moment when Herman sunk an eagle putt on the seventeenth green at Pebble Beach. It was a panoramic with the Pacific Ocean in the background, illuminated by a row of recessed LED lighting that Herman could brighten or dim with a remote control. The artist depicted the moment in short, quick brush strokes, lending a heavy amount of kinetic energy to the concept of golf. After sinking that putt Herman closed the first major deal of his career. He bought a communications company based out of Fresno. Within weeks of the deal going through Herman had completely dismantled the business and sold off its component parts at enormous profits. The entire memory was steeped in symbolism for Herman, because he remembered very clearly how he felt before he struck the little white ball. He knew that he was going to sink it. He was certain. And that certainty was the impetus for having the painting commissioned. All that he had to do was to look at it to be reminded that everything that Herman intended to do was destined to work. It didn't need to be logical or ethical, it didn't need to look good on paper or make sense to Warren Buffet. As long as the undertaking was accompanied by that stone-cold Glüber resolve, as long as it was a pure impulse, and there was the requisite level of determination and follow through, it was going to succeed. He could do anything short of levitate; or swallow a peanut.

It's true that considering everything that Herman had going for him at that point of his life a little peanut allergy shouldn't have been something to worry over or be ashamed about, but he was obsessing over his peanut allergy constantly. It was his Achilles heel. And it had already precipitated the most embarrassing moment of his life. He was six-years-old and attending the birthday party of his childhood pal, David Orkin, or Ork. Herman was the first to call him that. The kids were all doing arts and crafts at a table covered with a red tissue paper cloth. Shari Daniels was next to Herman, working on an origami sunflower. There was a stack of colored construction paper, child-safe scissors, and bowls of Crayola crayons. Herman was using a black magic marker to draw a handlebar mustache on the face of a paper bag puppet that was supposed to look like the famous Mexican swordsman, Zorro, when Ork's mom let him help himself from a tray of peanut butter cookies. His vision got instantly blurry and his airway closed off. He saw the puppet with its mask and sombrero and the bobbing heads of the kids around him, Shari Daniels holding her sunflower, then the heads of the parents and their bright teeth as they chattered, the white vinyl siding on the Orkin's Victorian style house in Old Town Tacoma, followed by the gabled roof, the canopy of the big chestnut tree in the front yard and finally the summer sky as an osprey tracked its way across. He was lying on his back on the plush green lawn, helplessly clutching at his own throat, struggling to think, going blue in his oxygen deprived head. Herman brushed up against death that afternoon. In just a few moments more he might have crossed over and been gone for good. But the fire department arrived on the scene along with a pair of paramedics who had to give little Herman a cricothyrotomy right there in front of all of his elementary school peers and their parents. They pierced his throat with a sharp spike and then inserted a plastic tube into the hole. When Herman was breathing again, and had given up for the time being the company of angels for the company of human beings, and was being secured onto a stretcher and loaded into a red ambulance with amber lights making lazy circles on its roof, he saw, out of the corner of his eye, that Ork had poked a hole in the neck of his paper bag puppet and inserted a straw into it. He was pretending that his puppet was breathing through the straw and getting a big laugh out of the other children at the party over the gag. Ork's dad was the one who was first to notice his son's inappropriate use of the paper bag puppet and took it away but the damage had already been done. Herman was recently returned to the living and it was the first thing that he got to witness and it affected him deeply. From that day forward he viewed the world from the perspective of the lightning struck. He had been given a second chance. He was stronger than he was before. He was also bitter and isolated. The tiny scar from that day he wore like a badge of honor just below his Adam's Apple.

"We should probably be getting into the meeting," said Loven. "Hartmut's gonna have to change his Depends soon. Renata'll be nodding off, if she isn't already dead."

Herman got up from his desk, adjusted the knot on his tie and absent-mindedly ran his fingers through his hair, creating a bit of unsightly frizz.

"I love it that you can do this and not feel a thing."

"What do you mean?"

"Lie to those old people. Cut all those trees down a month before they're ready to harvest."

"You know that we have to get the foundations poured before the ground freezes. Or else nothing is going to happen until next spring. Otherwise we'd sell the apples."

"And you're not worried about the ghost of Johnny Appleseed coming to haunt you?"

"Johnny Appleseed was a drunk pedophile, who wore a pot on his head. His ghost can bring it on."

"What the fuck is that?" Loven was pointing at one of Herman's monitors. There was another bug standing on the top edge of it, leaning over and waving its head around. Like a dog begging for a biscuit. On this one the blue spark connecting the horns was easy to see but hard to believe.

"These damn things are all over the place," Herman nabbed the bug but before crushing this one he remembered that he wanted to give it to Margot's kid, see what he thought of the thing. Try to have a conversation with the boy about something that the kid cared about. What was the harm in it?

"Where are they coming from?" asked Loven.

"No idea. I'll have Anita ring maintenance about it while we are inside." By the time he got the sentence out the critter was already joined by another. Herman—not wanting to get shocked again—tapped the bugs onto the surface of his desk with the eraser end of a pencil, flipped over a glass tumbler that he had been drinking water out of and trapped both the bugs beneath it. He left them there on his desk.

*   *   *

At the opposite corner of the floor, Duncan Klevit, the CEO of the firm, sat alone inside of an office that no one was ever permitted to enter. There was a view to the north and to the east, but inside there wasn't much to look at. The surface of the steel desk held nothing but a lined legal pad, an ergonomic pen, and a thin silver computer monitor, on which he had just finished reading Herman's email. The walls were a cold white, the floor was light gray, and the few fixtures that hung from the ceiling were stainless-steel. It put Duncan at ease to be in the monochromatic environment. He wasn't comfortable with the kind of visual stimulation that Herman liked.

From the inside pocket of his suit jacket he extracted his cell phone to check the time. His fingernails were honed to perfection. The world fell away and the only thing left was the mission. The phone pinged. It was a five-minute warning from his secretary. He looked out the window and found himself eye level with a bald eagle that was soaring north above the freeway.

Duncan had made it to the upper tier of the world of finance, despite having an unlikely beginning. He didn't grow up wealthy. As a toddler he was abandoned by a mother that he had no memory of. She moved to Norway with a man was the story. Duncan was raised by his grandmother Mabel. He was a very quiet kid, but smart, and he spent most of his time in a place that was a lot like the office that he had in the Smith Tower. It was a place that no one was allowed to enter. It was the inside of his own head. He and his grandmother moved around a lot but they were never city people and Duncan used to like to sneak off into the woods to trap animals. On Maui he caught a mongoose. In Colorado he caught a King snake. Mice and rats he got everywhere. After he caught them, he would usually drown them and then carve them up. But that part was just logistical necessity. The excitement was in capturing his victims and the eroticism he associated with it, even at a young age.

A shrink might have thought that he was lashing out against the mother who abandoned him or the father whose identity was unknown. It was also possible that he had some latent need to express an ability to dominate something and he was still too coy to really enter the world of people. That was probably true. Duncan still retained some minor loyalty toward Mabel, but other than that he really didn't care about anyone. Life to him mostly was a dull game that he just happened to be better at than the other players, so he fucked with them to keep himself amused.

Despite the gruesome nature of Duncan's relationship with small mammals, he was good at communicating with them and rather deft with a sharp knife. When he entered college in Arizona it was his intention to become a veterinarian and he actually made it most of the way. In fact, he was halfway done with his residency when something unexpected occurred, he got a taste of making money. He was on surgery rotation and there was an opportunity for interns in the program—who worked their asses off only to be compensated to the tune of seventeen-thousand dollars a year—to pick up some extra cash. There was a lab in Phoenix that tested animals, post-mortem, for the presence of rabies. Rabies being such a viscous and elusive disease, it lollygags through the nervous system toward the brain. If a human is bitten in the foot by a rabid animal it could take months before the disease entered the cranial tissue and started to drip down into the salivary glands. Even though the disease was relatively scarce, unknown animals that were put down after biting were often tested for the disease. The test cost a hundred bucks or so. And fifty of that went to the student who disarticulated the head and packed it to go to the lab. Duncan, who was as desensitized as a human being could be, used to hang around the surgery center, even when he was off duty, even after his surgery rotation had ended, looking for bodies that he could make a quick fifty bucks on.

The entire procedure took about four minutes, depending on the animal. He used to carry his own bone-handled necropsy knife in a leather scabbard underneath his apron. The molybdenum hardened blade passed easily through the soft tissue at the throat. The only trick was when the blade bumped into the Atlanto-occipital junction. There he would rock the head back and forth until the blade cut through and the head came off. Then he would wrap the head in gauze, slip it into a bio-bag, and box it up for the carrier service. He did mostly dogs, but there were also quite a few cats, raccoons, bats, and one iguana but he forgot the backstory on that job. It wasn't being tested for rabies but he still got the fifty bucks. In order to get a confirmed negative for rabies two parts of the brain tissue had to be tested: the stem and the cerebellum. All of that was just left in place. He didn't even have to peel the skin. It was easy money. In 2003 he removed eight-hundred-twenty-nine heads and made over forty-thousand dollars doing it, more than doubling his salary. And even though Duncan liked the money, there was another part to all of it that he liked even better. The process gave him an erection. Which seemed ludicrous, especially for a healthy man not far from twenty years of age. But even though Duncan had a penis of average length—about four inches when flaccid—it otherwise never got stiff.

Despite the bright Arizona sun, he eventually began to feel like he existed in a world all his own, creepy, and permanently situated under a black cloud. He tried to get the connection to the sexual stimulation associated with the death and gore out of his mind and concentrate instead on the money. He took the windfall to the stock market.

When Duncan was an undergrad, he had taken a few economics courses as electives. He had a bit of an idea about how to invest. Turns out that he knew a lot more about human nature. It was the beginning of the Iraq war and he made wise choices, at least as far as the money was concerned. He dropped out of the veterinary program and moved to New York

City. In 2007 he was part of a hedge fund that shorted the housing market. By the time he got to Seattle he was already so wealthy that money had ceased to matter. The phone pinged again. It was time to take the orchard. And since the firm was planning on killing all the trees, he got a little tingle in his loins.

*   *   *

While the meeting was about to get underway, special Agent Jodie Cavendish of the C.I.A., and his contingent of plain clothes babysitters with unusually large muscles and the ability to subdue nearly any foe barehanded and with grace, disembarked from their private jet at Boeing Field. On the tarmac they were met by a green Hum V that took Jodie and the two Navy SEALs—who both got a hoot out of Jodie renaming them Colette's Lover and Taz because of the tattoos on their biceps—to the Federal Building for a meeting with some department heads in the United States government. Some of the greatest problem solvers that ever lived also had the chops to create art with the likes of Rembrandt and Monet. Perhaps Jodie too, but he never took up the brush. He had heard the early reports of minor power outages and glitches with the electrical and communication grid in Seattle and he feared for the worst, having seen first-hand what an infestation of the beetles that may have arrived just before him were capable of. In his heart of hearts, Jodie harbored a secret sympathy for the six-legged critters, who wanted nothing more than anyone or anything else did—to survive and feel nourished—he couldn't help feeling a profound sadness for the city he had never visited before. The famed Space Needle was set clear against a glorious blue sky through a sightline to the northeast and he had an eerie vision of it lying on its side in flames.

The city was nothing like its reputation. There wasn't any rain. There wasn't even a puddle in sight. The driver was anything but passive-aggressive. He was friendly and wore a big smile. His name was Carl and he seemed ready to attend to Jodie's every need. Jodie found himself suddenly parched in the extraordinarily hot weather. Fortunately the transport vehicle had some water bottles in it, and as it made its way north through light traffic—Friday mornings were notoriously mellow on the highways before noon—he unscrewed a cap and drank the contents in a single gulp as they drifted past a glimpse of the red neon sign announcing the location of the Pike Place Public Market. The sight gave Jodie a powerful hankering for chowder and he had the driver pull over. He and Taz and Colette's Lover had some food at the Seatown Snack Bar and then took a selfie together standing in front of Left Bank Books. Colette's Lover had been to the city before and knew the tourist spots. While they were still out galavanting, Jodie noticed a couple of excited young girls emerge from a novelties shop with oversized Sleepless in Seattle shirts on. It was incredible the mileage that was gotten out of the movie he had never seen.

The Seattle streets were mobbed with late summer travelers clinging to shady spots and eating a lot of frozen yogurt out of waffle cones. What struck Jodie the most about being back in the states was that no one seemed to have anything important to do. It was nothing like China or Inner Mongolia, but it did have some parallels with Deadland, which—once he got in—turned out to be a rather easy-going place. For a moment his emotions overwhelmed him and he was tempted to cry, but then he remembered quickly that he was a special operative who had done things in his life most common people had no idea even existed. Including his entry into Deadland, when he was still chasing the ox cart. Jodie—strapped to Taz but nonetheless—executed a H.A.L.O. in the middle of the night. The acronym stands for High Altitude Low Opening. It is used strictly to drop small teams of operatives behind enemy lines without their being detected, and it was the first skydive that he had ever done. His dive partner—the confident and affable lad from Kansas—held him tight like a baby as they scampered out onto the wing of the stealth plane at approximately fifty-thousand feet above the ground. They rolled backward and the sound of the plane's quiet twin engines disappeared. Taz then released the drogue and the two of them had a controlled free fall through the starry night for what seemed like a lifetime and was still over in the blink of an eye. At moments during the dive Jodie thought that they were literally going to land in the Little Dipper, until it eventually sailed past at incredible velocity. The duo was nearly at tree line when Taz released the main shoot and the shock load was so intense he was pretty sure he was never having kids as a result. Not that he wanted them anyway. The thought of raising children with his wife was absurd. On average they spent about a month a year together. Who would raise them? Where would they live?

Because of his devotion to Eliza, Jodie believed that she was faithful to him as well and he rather liked that she had a habit of just showing up where he was without warning. It was exciting that she might appear at any moment. Reality was that she was likely somewhere far away. Both of the SEALs were married with kids and had similar relationship problems to Jodie and Eliza, they weren't around each other much. The SEALs also seemed to have wives that acknowledged that they were men, and as long as they didn't hear about bastard children or catch any funky diseases, they were given some unspoken permissions—or at least they thought they were.

There was a Ferris wheel and all sorts of buildings out on the piers by the waterfront and Jodie had wanted desperately to get out and walk for just a little while. In many ways he missed the quiet simplicity and the absolute peace inside Deadland, but it was also a joy to be back in America, amongst all of the pleasantly deceived. And then the phone rang. One of the SEALs picked up the call but the mobile unit was passed immediately back to Jodie.

"This is Jodie."

"Your name is Agent Cavendish."

"Sorry, Calhoon. Are you in Seattle? It's lovely here."

"We just had a report from the Smith Tower that the internet is down, the elevator systems is malfunctioning, and maintenance has collected a few of the beetles matching the description and photos that you sent us."

"Do you want me to go there?"

"No, I want you to come to the Federal Building as planned for a meeting first."

"You guys love your meetings, don't you?"

"Agent Cavendish, I need you to be prepared to speak to the director of F.E.M.A."

"Isn't he a pretty important fellow?"

"Yes, Agent Cavendish,"

"I don't know anything about disaster preparedness."

"I know, Agent Cavendish. But you do know about the potential ramifications of the beetle you discovered in Deadland making its way into the U. S."

"Which it sounds like it has already done."

"Agent Cavendish, I need you to be respectful with the director. Are you aware of who appointed him?"

"Of course, Agent Calhoon."

"I'd also prefer it if you tended toward non-technical words?"

"Excuse me?"

"The director has a habit of becoming frustrated and confused by a lot of big words."

"How big?"

"How about you just try to stay away from anything Latin-rooted."

"I can do that."

"He also tends to form his own ideas about things that are not scientific or even necessarily realistic."

"Okay."

"Don't take offense. And if you have a good idea that he wants to claim as his own it's usually best to just let him."

"Roger that." Agent Calhoon hung up the line, leaving Jodie a bit nervous. He was a scientist and hadn't the foggiest idea about how to institute emergency protocols that affected major populations of people and didn't have a lot of advice to give. He wished his buddy Nevil was with him. Jodie was a whiz when it came to anything biological and he took easily to new forms of tech. He just got flustered at times around people, especially if they didn't like what he had to say.

Before being scooped up by a steel cable attached to the underbelly of a Blackhawk helicopter, Jodie spent just shy of a week in Deadland. He wished he could have stayed longer. The region was an absolute fascination for anyone involved in the natural sciences. Deadland was teeming with bird life. The soil was predominantly a rich loam that was allowing most of the trees in the region to thrive. The orchards were dripping with fruit, the livestock was all free range and healthy looking, and the people he observed went about their days with an unhurried purposefulness that he envied terribly. They were like productive Buddhas, who had time to help one another. At no time while he was inside of Deadland did he see anything resembling money change hands.

All of these extrapolations about the inhabitants of the zone were gleaned through binoculars. Colette's Lover and Taz were tasked with protecting him and wouldn't allow him to be seen by people inside the zone and they guarded his perimeter carefully.

The cargo container that the ox cart had been pulling was loaded with a large object in the middle of the night and on the following morning it proceeded toward the southern border of Deadland. While keeping up with the container—not hard since it was quite large and being pulled by oxen— Jodie made several important discoveries. Nearly every tree in the genus *Betula* was dead or almost dead. This didn't come as a big surprise since the Bronze Birch Borer had been wreaking havoc worldwide for many years, but rarely at that type of scale. The trees he inspected had the telltale signs of the borer—D-shaped exit holes through the thin bark and live beetle galleries feasting on the cambium just beneath. There was also another species of beetle that he hadn't seen before. It was medium length, with short horns that curved toward the bug's midline, and two red iridescent stripes that ran the length of their backs. He was puzzled by what the new species' food source might be but couldn't deny that they swarmed his satellite phone and his wristwatch. The SEALs that were there to look after him were having the same issues and within forty-eight hours all of the electronic equipment that they had with them was shot and the beetles had disappeared. But not before Jodie collected some specimens and took copious notes about their bizarre behavior. While the electronics still functioned, the bugs appeared to multiply quickly. But once whatever device they had collected on shorted out, the beetles vanished—or so it seemed at first. Upon closer inspection of the dead birch trees that were everywhere, Jodie started finding the new species co-mingling with the borers that were eating the birches. He hypothesized that somehow the two populations were related enough that one could propagate with the other, but it was only in the presence of electrical current that the new beetle assumed its incredible and unusual powers. He suspected that the presence of the electrical current was allowing the bugs to transform the power into something that it could use as building blocks to grow, much the way a plant makes glucose from sunlight. But he had so many questions about how they could survive the exposure to the current. He couldn't wait to start dissecting one in the lab. The new beetle also gave Jodie the opportunity to do something he had always dreamed of doing: naming a new species. *Agrilus cavendish* was the first name to come to mind but Jodie was naturally opposed to vanity and the type of pride that came with trying immortalize oneself. It was too narcissistic. He settled on a name that more appropriately reflected how impressed he was with the beetle. He called it *Agrilus suprema*.

                    *   *   *

While Jodie was being debriefed by his superior, and the meeting was about to commence in Pioneer Square, Margot and her girlfriend Fwen, had just been seated at the Tamarind Tree a few blocks from where Herman worked and they were getting ready to order some lunch.

"I don't know why I bother looking at the menu here," said Fwen.

"I'm getting something different today," said Margot.

"No, you're not." Fwen was right. When the waiter came over Margot ordered the Pagoda Garden Soup as usual and Fwen went with the Oyster Mushroom Tomato Noodles. "I'm so fucking happy to be out of there. I don't think that I can go back."

"So, this is it. You're quitting?"

"Don't be silly. I'm obviously not quitting. I have an appointment to get my hair done tomorrow and I couldn't even enjoy it if I didn't have this fucking job."

"You mean that you couldn't afford it if you didn't have this job."

"That's only part of it. I literally mean that the stress of this fucking job, and the money, contributes significantly to the bliss that I experience while Phyllis is weaving in extensions and I can read gossip magazines instead of emails or Twitter. I have a very strict rule about not using the phone in the salon. It's heavenly."

"You love your phone."

"I hate that phone. If this shit keeps up, I might end up another Gregory Pendergrast." Gregory Pendergrast was the most recent of Zonama's employees to utilize what had come to be known around the offices as the *escape hatch*. Which didn't get you out of the building, it got you out of life. It had only been a few weeks since Gregory found his way up to the roof of Zonama's offices. It was 7:30 pm but it was still light out and Gregory had been in the building since before six working on a project. It was a Saturday. He was rumored to have been told to miss one of his daughter's birthday parties by his boss. He went up there with one of his teammates to have a cigarette even though he didn't smoke. When the break was over, Gregory never re-entered the building. Instead he jumped up onto the low wall that surrounds the perimeter of the roof and leapt to his death. He didn't leave a note. No need to restate the obvious. Before Gregory's suicide, Margot had already heard the term *escape hatch* around the office. Since Gregory though, the phrase had become more moribund and ubiquitous.

"Stop it, Fwen." Margot knew that Fwen was only teasing. It was true that the responsibilities heaped upon her friend at the office were a little extreme. But Fwen made a lot of money and she loved that she got to travel for work. Fwen was from coastal Spain and her name was technically Carolína but hardly anyone knew that. Besides her native Spanish and English, she was fluent in Mandarin Chinese, and Zonama sent her to Asia at least twice a year for reasons that were above Margot's pay grade to know. On Wednesday she was going to Shanghai where she supposedly had a lover who was privy to Tantric secrets that had been passed down orally for thousands of years but never once written. There were always a few plot holes when Fwen spoke of her Chinese loverboy but Margot didn't care. She thought her friend's flare for embellishment was more fun than loyalty to absolute accuracy. And being without kids allowed Fwen a certain freedom that Margot didn't have access to. Fwen was living proof of a dangerous wave that was overtaking the northwest, Seattle in particular: a palpable lack of children. A few years previous Seattle had earned itself a reputation for being a town where people spent their twenties pampering dogs instead of rearing a new generation. It wasn't a trend that was born out of any kind of direct dislike of kids. It was more just the narcissistic by-product of wanting to maximize an unlikely opportunity: being young, with time and money. The glut of people with no kids, good incomes, and fancy dogs that they doted upon, lead to the proliferation of the dog economy. In the nineties a 'Doggy Day Care' facility would have required some explanation just to understand the concept. By 2010, they were everywhere, and armies of dog walkers were deployed to get exercise to the thousands of dogs that weren't lucky enough to get to go to day care and hang out with other dogs while their owners worked at their white-collar jobs. The hard-working people that formed the spine of the dog economy had not yet galvanized into a union. If they had, a strike could've crippled the city. Lately it seemed like even the dog economy was suffering and that there were fewer pet photos on Facebook and less people around the office trapping Margot in the coffee room and going on and on about their dogs. There weren't any official statistics available on the matter but she was sure that people in Seattle were not only having fewer children, but that they were also getting fewer dogs. Was it not even worth bringing a dog into this world any longer? Childless Fwen had no pets either.

"Fine. Speaking of blissful experiences, how's it going with Herman?" Margot knew that Fwen knew a few things about Herman and there was more than a little sarcasm in her friend's voice. In fact, Fwen had tried to dissuade Margot from seeing Herman. She knew that he was relentless in his pursuit of women and that he was prone to deflecting criticism and embellishing his own accomplishments. It was true. Herman had told Margot that he had once shot a full-grown male moose while hunting just outside the boundary of Denali National Park in Alaska. But Fwen was friends with a savage lesbian that worked in IT who was also on the trip and was with Herman in the blind that the tour group had constructed. She said that she was probably the one who attracted the moose, since the thousand-pound animal was in the rut and she was on the rag. The way that she described it, it came tearing out of the bush, all lathered up, swinging its massive rack back and forth, using its nose more than its eyes, and snorting and kicking like a race horse from hell. Herman dropped his gun. The way

Fwen heard the story, he was frozen for a few seconds, then he tried to get down the ladder and run. Which totally gave their position away. His hunting partner kept her rifle trained on the moose and laid it down with one slug placed directly in the animal's heart. The only other part of the story worth mentioning is that on the ride back to camp, there was a violent stench coming from the seat of Herman's trousers and he wasn't making eye contact with anyone.

Margot knew the story but it didn't bother her that he was like that. She thought that Herman was kind of sweet and funny, the way he was always trying to make himself out to be invincible. She had some sympathy for him. She knew that he was an only child. Margot had only the one son and she knew that Herman's mom likely spoiled him with attention the way she spoiled Ethan. Her kid was the only person that mattered in the world. Herman was a local guy that never really stopped acting like a frat boy. He was financially successful but completely uncultured. Herman's love of mountain climbing, kayaking, and golf had lured him around the world a little bit, but it just seemed like he still hadn't ever cared about anything enough to be able to forget himself. And if he did, he might change. He wasn't completely closed off to new things. And she thought that he was devastatingly handsome. Strong without being bulky. Herman had a thick head of hair that he took care of and was never going to fall out. His teeth were straight and white. And even though he was an unsympathetic jerk to anyone suffering from anything from the sniffles to cancer, it was impossible to argue with the fact that he had exceptional immunity. He claimed to her that he had never once been sick with the flu. And that the only headache that he had ever known, came after he had consumed several bottles of red wine from the Charles Shaw vineyards at the wedding of one of his high school chums and after that he swore off cheap alcohol and high school chums.

"It's going okay," Margot lied as the waiter returned with drinks. A mango juice for her. Fwen was having fresh lime with condensed milk and crushed ice. "He's closing a big deal today and he's going out celebrating with the boys from the office later on."

"What kind of deal?" Fwen loved gossip. She stirred her drink with a cocktail straw and then licked off the condensed milk that was clinging to it.

"Ever heard of Summerwood Farms?"

"Who hasn't heard of Summerwood Farms?"

"They're buying their orchards and all of their facilities out in eastern Washington. Believe it or not, that whole empire still just belongs to two people. I think they're the original owners."

"Herman is going to grow apples?"

"I think he has other plans but I don't know exactly what they are. I doubt that growing apples is a part of it."

"How's the sex?"

"Fwen!"

"What? Tell me. I'm in a drought. I need to hear some details. I want to know that he's appreciating that yoga body."

"What do you want to know?"

"Is he big?"

"Not especially."

"Prudish?"

"Herman?"

"Just because guys like getting laid doesn't mean they're not prudes. Does he bring any props over?"

"No. But—"

"But what? I am sensing something interesting here." Margot leaned across the table so that the other diners couldn't overhear.

"He was okay with me using some of mine."

"The Mastodon?"

"I don't want to scare him off. But he did wear the ring and let me put the vibrating butt plug in him."

"That's a good sign. Does he last a while?"

"It's pretty good."

"Which is synonymous with terrible."

"No, it isn't."

In addition to being symbolic of current social trends, Margot thought of Fwen as a harbinger of religion come full circle. The first peoples on earth worshipped the phallus for its ability to bring forth new life. Margot knew that Fwen worshipped the phallus for just about every other reason but.

"How does he get along with Ethan?" Fwen put her handbag up on the table and took out a compact mirror to check her make-up. There was a little blurb on the back of the custom-made mirror case that said: Fwen is Now.

"It's a little awkward but there are some bright spots. Herman isn't used to being around kids. But it turns out to be kind of a good thing since he doesn't talk to Ethan like a kid at all. He isn't scared of him. If he pays any attention to him at all he treats him like an adult. Ethan really likes it."

"Don't tell me that you think that Herman might be a decent family guy. Are you in love with him?"

"We talked right before lunch and I had to hang up on him. He was acting like a crass asshole, mostly because I was on speaker phone and didn't know it and he was trying to show off in front of his friend Loven. If you'd have heard it, Fwen—it was repulsive. But at the same time, it's just so goddamn hard to meet a decent guy who isn't repulsive for all sorts of other reasons. Something seems to be telling me I should stick it out with him a little longer."

Margot made no secret about wanting to be a part of a family; something that she seemed destined to be forever on the fringe of. She had a normal childhood for a while back in Charleston, until her brother died one night, showing off and pulling an extended, high-speed wheelie on his motorcycle that kept him from seeing a car exiting a service station. After that her father seemed to lose his will to live, and let his string of men's clothing stores become outdated and a drain on the family's savings. Sensing the inevitable, the old man took his retirement account and invested in tech stock; wanting to be part of the big wave made of money that everyone around him seemed to be surfing. When his investments didn't pan out, he didn't complain. No one even knew. The family only found out after a heart attack took him on his fifty-ninth birthday and they were going over their finances.

By that point Margot was sixteen and the outlook for her future was already bleak enough when her mother vomited a mouthful of blood at a Denny's and had to be rushed to the hospital. Colon cancer claimed her body in less than a year, and Margot was left alone. Lucky for her, she made some grown up decisions. She sold the family's house, took the little bit of money that was left over from the life insurance policies, and moved out west for something that was guaranteed to be different. California was her original choice. But those San Diego days, where the sun just seemed to track the same course across the sky, made her feel trapped in time; and eventually struck as her dull. She packed up and went north.

Margot wasn't a glacier climber like Herman but she did love the outdoors and she spent an entire summer hammering on the shocks of her dad's old Buick and camping all over the Redwoods and around Crater Lake. As autumn crept closer, she kept finding herself going north. After a week failing to find a place to stay in Portland, she drove up to Seattle, and found herself a one-bedroom house with a small yard for $595 listed in the back of The Stranger. She rented it out and started taking classes at a community college nearby.

The marriage to her first husband was always a bit of a mess but it at least produced Ethan and she honestly wasn't sure that she could live without him. Margot didn't have many people dragging her down, but she didn't have a lot of people lifting her up either. Ethan lifted her up, every single time she saw him.

"Like you need another project."

"Seriously."

"So, going back to the original question, are you in love with this man?"

"I don't think so. Maybe I'm in love*ish* There's a lot that I like about him, you know. But honestly, a lot of the time, I find myself doubting whether he even thinks of me at all when we aren't together or he isn't in the mood to just get laid."

"Unfortunately, darling, the conversation has strayed into territory that I am unfamiliar with. I'll never know what love, or even love*ish* feels like. Sounds to me like you are trying to be in love with him but you aren't. But what do I know? I'm a lost cause in the love department."

"Stop it, Fwen. No, you're not."

"It's true, Margot. I meet plenty of people, but love and I exist on different planes."

"That doesn't make any sense. You're bisexual, and in the prime of your life. Your chances of finding love are better than anyone else on the planet."

"My chances of getting laid are better than anyone else on the planet. But that doesn't mean that I could stand the idea of anyone I've ever spent the night with still being there on Monday morning. How would I get anything done?"

"You'd be surprised. It's nice to have someone that's always around."

"Seeing him later tonight?"

"After our last conversation, it's up in the air whether I'll see him again ever. But after work I'm on the hook for a Chamber of Commerce event at Wasabi Bistro. Just during happy hour."

"Free sushi?"

"Yeah, but I've got to go with Don Ferguson."

"He creeps me out."

"Me too. I'm trying to get Herman to come to Ethan's science fair tomorrow. It would be a nice change from meeting in a bar somewhere when Ethan is at his dad's, getting drunk and then waking up at his apartment hung over and in a ridiculous hurry."

"You think he will come?"

"I doubt it, but I'm holding out some hope." The waiter showed back up and laid two bowls of soup down in front of the ladies along with a plate of mung bean sprouts, fresh basil leaves, and jalapeños. "What's the worst thing that could happen?" Margot pulled her hair back to make it easier to eat the soup. She had a very thick head of healthy brown hair that tapered to a rough paint below her shoulder blades. She wore it parted on the left and the area above her right ear was buzz cut with three parallel lines cut into it; just to be a little punk rock and have some fun. There was nothing unusual about it if she wore it down, which she always did at work.

"Your youth keeps slipping away, until one day he shits his pants and you wind up shot in the heart like that moose." Margot laughed at Fwen's joke. "Do I also need to point out that his last name is *Glüber*," Fwen drug out the pronunciation. "Is that like German for *dork*."

"You're the linguist. I know, it's not the best. I'm still hoping that he comes tomorrow." Margot was applying condiments to her dish with both hands. She was thrown from a horse when she was little, and her broken right wrist wasn't set properly. Since it didn't turn all the way she had gotten pretty good at doing things with both hands. It was an unusual sight. Fwen was used to it, but someone nearby could always be counted upon to stare. At least that day it was a blue-eyed, grinning baby making some food art on the tray of his high chair. Margot smiled back at the baby.

Fwen was on her phone, looking up a translation for *glüber*. All she was getting was a lot of information about a company that made specialty lubricants for gear boxes but they were called *Klüber* and their site was intriguing. "Margot Glüber," she whispered to herself. "I suppose it could be worse. You should forget about him if he doesn't come to the fair, unless he is somehow connected to this German lubricant company. They look like a Fortune 500. Otherwise, I don't quite even get why you care."

"I know, Fwen. It's just that even though Herman doesn't notice, I think that Ethan likes him. And he is so proud of his science project."

"Is he still working with energy stuff? He is so smart. Does he get that from you or Matt?"

"Probably from Matt," Margot lied. Ethan's father was a very bright man but he was more of a book smart type that liked hanging around in classrooms. Ethan was hands on, and that he definitely got from Margot. She fixed everything around the house herself. She also had a mint condition '86 Toyota Forerunner with a solid front axle and limited slip differential that she had done all of the work on since acquiring it a few years back with only eighty-thousand miles on the original 22RE engine. She had swapped out the water pump and replaced the front brake pads. Her brother had taught her to work on cars before he died. He would have appreciated the extra-wide rims and swamper tires that she had put on the little truck, which was arguably the first ever SUV conceptualized for urban dwelling civilians.

"Yes, all the time. He knows all about it and he has his dad's land out in the Okanagon set up to be completely sustainable and off-grid. I've only seen it once and the wiring alone looks like spaghetti to me but he understands it perfectly and does all the maintenance. They even get power from a wind turbine he built out of some pieces of whittled cedar and the rim from an old Dodge pickup."

"Why would anyone need that?"

"Just in case, I guess. I'll admit that Ethan is a little obsessed with the apocalypse. I mean, what kid isn't these days? Just look at the movies they put out. The stakes are always the same 'the end of the world.'"

"You know I don't watch movies."

"I know," Margot laughed. "This year his project is about biology."

"What is it?"

"Insect propagation."

'Please elaborate."

"He bred over four-hundred baby tarantulas. They're all in tiny plexiglass enclosures in his bedroom right now."

Fwen pushed her bowl toward the middle of the table. "So much for eating."

The Summerwood Signing

Brown leather chairs surrounded the table in what was known as the Blue Room because of the color of the two interior walls. The room was reserved for client meetings and featured a table that was made from the cross section of the stump of a redwood tree. The table held some special significance for Herman and Duncan. It was a slice of the root flare of the last remaining piece of old growth on a parcel of land that they had purchased some years back outside of Garberville, Ca. The native forest—*home* to not only the trees but deer, brown bear, chipmunks, and hundreds of species of birds—was converted to a Fred Meyer superstore, a Les Schwab Tire Center, Hong Kong Buffet, bowling alley and several acres of parking to accommodate patrons of the aforementioned businesses. Herman had the tree cut down just hours after the permit came through, before the hippies could get their sitters hoisted up into the canopy or the pedestal filled with iron nails. Most of the wood was bucked into twenty-foot sections, winched up onto flatbeds and precision milled in Humboldt County before being sold to the Japanese for top dollar. Basically, it was turned into pagodas and shoji screens. Except for the piece that eventually became the table. That piece was waxed and allowed to dry out slowly over the course of three years in a climate-controlled storage locker in Arcata. Once it had dried sufficiently without incurring any cracks, Herman had it shipped to his hometown of Tacoma, where an old friend of his father's planed it down to a three-inch slab and fashioned custom steel legs for it. Margot's son Ethan was in the office one day and started counting the growth rings, making his way toward the center. The kid was not only a precocious entomologist, he also had an apparent thing for dendrochronology. He counted every single ring from the outside in before getting to the heartwood where the tree was a little rotten and it was hard to see the lines. For this section the kid measured the remaining space and then divided it by the average distance of the rings and came up with a solid estimate of the tree's age. Herman had been telling people that the tree was hundreds of years old. He was way off. Turns out that the old giant was in its 2,357th summer when Herman had the loggers lay it down. Older than the universe, according to several popular religions.

The Frenzels were sitting along what used to be the southeast corner of the tree, when it was still alive. And they had dressed up for the occasion. Renata must not have heard the weather report; either that or she had serious circulation issues. She was in a full length, black flannel, calico dress, trimmed at the edges with lace. Her hair was permed and supposed to be white, but thanks to the walls and the cool spectrum lighting it reflected an unnerving electric blue color that clashed horribly with Hartmut's ochre suit jacket. Hartmut had removed the fedora that he must have been wearing earlier and placed it on the table in front of him. Static had drawn two tufts of Hartmut's wispy gray hair toward the ceiling, making him look like a washed-up devil. His nose was swollen and red, like he had just gotten over a breakout of carbuncles and he was fidgeting in his seat. He had obviously put on a few pounds since he had last worn the suit and the seams were under intense pressure.

"Good to see you, Renata, Hartmut" said Herman extending his hand and flashing a toothy grin. He hadn't looked in the mirror before the meeting. If he had, he would have noticed that his pupils had shrunk to the size of sesame seeds, his hair was no longer tame, and he couldn't stop flexing the muscles in his cheeks. "Welcome to the offices. Hartmut, I don't think I've ever seen you in a suit before."

"What's that?" asked Hartmut.

"I said I don't think I've ever seen you in a suit before."

"It's fitting a bit tight. I can't fathom why."

"I bet it shrunk at the cleaners," Herman winked.

"Who are the cleaners? Hey Renata, when's the last time I wore this suit?"

"You got that suit in Spokane. Don't you remember?"

"I didn't ask you where I got it. I said when's the last time I wore it?"

"That nice young man sold it to us. The one who was also a piano player."

"The Liberace fan."

"I'm glad that there are still some young people out there who appreciate his music," said Renata.

"That fellow can't be young anymore. Might have been thirty years since we saw him."

"I'm going to be keeping an eye on you, Hartmut," Herman jumped in so that the old couple didn't go on forever. "If I see veins bulging in your forehead, I'm going to have some size 38 Levi's and some red suspenders sent in right away, okay." He laughed at his own joke and then turned his attention to the young Lupita who was sitting to the Frenzels' right. "Good to see you again," he said, "it's a wonderful surprise." Herman was laying it on a bit thicker than he meant, the cocaine had him off his game. He wasn't used to it like Loven.

"You too, Mr. Glüber," said Lupita meekly. She seemed to be searching for the appropriate formality for the occasion and her previous connection to Herman had to be making that tricky.

To the Frenzels's left was their lawyer, Omeed Gazipurah. Herman was fairly sure that Omeed was a terrible lawyer, and convinced beyond the shadow of a doubt that Omeed was the ugliest man alive. Like a genetic experiment gone awry,

Omeed looked like a pastiche of undesirable ethnic qualities. His eczema covered skin fluctuated between brown, grey, and pink. His black hair was thick, straight, and greasy. He was tall, with short arms. And his lips were such a bright red one might be excused for thinking he put lipstick on them. Like he had taken the first step toward becoming a woman and stopped there. He could have been Mexican, Middle Eastern, Greek? Depending on the lighting or the angle that he was viewed from. Poor Omeed couldn't even tell you the true answer. He was the adopted son of a white ranching family outside of Galveston, Texas. He came with a name. Everything else about him was a total mystery.

Lupita looked nice but a little too casual for the Smith Tower and appeared to be realizing that. The yellow sundress that she had picked out looked too short in every direction. Her tanned knees and elbows were hanging way out there for everyone in the room to see. It couldn't have been a good time to be feeling self-conscious. She was about to deliver an important speech to a roomful of vultures. No pep talk that she might have gotten from her business administration professor at the community college in Wenatchee could have prepared her for the moment. She was fanning herself with a stack of papers but she looked cold. Her skin was a field of goosebumps.

The seats around the table started filling up. Allison, from the escrow company, was anchoring her corner of the table. She was so big that Herman had to arrange for a special chair to be borrowed for her from the passport agency on the floor below. Her size, combined with the honking long nose that spiraled out from between her puffy white cheeks, made her look like a beached narwhal. Herman had a hard time believing that she and the young Lupita were even members of the same species. One of them was such a delicate flower, the other had the sex appeal of a drooling grandparent. Allison seemed oblivious to the rest of the room, laying out documents in order and a selection of ergonomic roller-point pens with blue ink for the signing. Herman and Loven were joined by one of the firm's junior consultants, a gangly transplant from Russia named Dmitri Gliot, who had been brought on to help develop Cronkey, Mitchell and Wolfe's presence in the Eastern European marketplace. The firm's lawyer, Quincy Flumes, was also there. Quincy was one of those guys who kept his entire head free of any traces of hair, except for his eyebrows, which were bushy and blonde and traveled great distances when Quincy genuflected. Quincy was engaged in a private conversation with Duncan, who was wearing a double-breasted navy-blue suit with a scarlet red tie. Duncan rose to his feet to call the meeting to order and he towered above the room. Duncan was six and a half feet tall, with wide shoulders and a spine straight as an arrow. His hair was dark brown and parted naturally on the left. He had it cut every week. Duncan adhered to a very strict diet and exercise routine. He was precise in appearance and in execution of all matters. Duncan was fine to work for, so long as you didn't fuck up. Cause if you fucked up, you were immediately gone.

"Good afternoon, everyone. Thank you for being here today. Welcome—" Hartmut leaned forward and put his hand up to stop Duncan.

"I've only got another hour and twenty minutes on the meter," said Hartmut. "Can you have one of your people remind me to go down there and put some change in? I don't think we're going to be done in time."

"Dmitri," said Duncan, "make sure someone out there is aware of the time and is paying the meter for Mr. Frenzel."

"Sure thing, Duncan," Dmitri slid out and Duncan continued.

"Anything else, Mr. Frenzel? Before we get things underway."

"Anything to eat around here? It's just after noon so I figured that we'd be having lunch but I don't see any lunch."

"Umm, we can get some food in here. Sure," Duncan poked his head out the door of the meeting room and had a quick conversation with someone invisible. Dmitri came back in and Duncan shut the door again. "Sounds like your truck is in good hands and one of the office girls is going to be right back with a tray of food."

"Good," said Hartmut. "And coffee? I've only had one cup so far today, and it's kind of stuffy in here. It's making me tired. Can we get some coffee?" Duncan stuck his head outside the door and asked one of the secretaries to scare up some coffee.

"Coffee is on its way. Are we good?"

"I think so," said Hartmut. "Renata, you need anything?" Renata looked catatonic.

"I'm fine, dear," she said. But she didn't sound fine. She sounded worried that they were making a mistake. Being in those offices, selling their farm to this group of men, none of which looked like they had ever spent a day, let alone a night, working hard outdoors, it had to hurt. At least she trusted Herman. He did a good job portraying himself as a local boy. He preached a believable bullshit respect for the value of the orchard. They had to sell. Herman knew she was exhausted, and so was Hartmut. They couldn't run the orchard for another year even if they wanted to. Not having any family to hand the business off to was unfortunate. In a private moment she confided to Herman that they did at one time have an heir. Her name was Ophelia, and she had been missing for almost ten years.

"Before we get on to the signing of the closing documents, we understand that Ms. Bevilacqua would like to say some things on behalf of the migrant workforce that the Frenzels have been employing. Ms. Bevilacqua, are you ready?"

"Thank you, Mr. Klevit," Lupita rose to her feet and walked to one of the blue walls where a white screen had been pulled down for projected images. "I'd like to say thank you to all of you—"

"Can you hear her?" barked Quincy in the general direction of his returning neighbor Dmitri. It's true that she was kind of mumbling toward the wall.

"Maybe you could speak up a little bit," said Herman in a pseudo-encouraging tone. Lupita avoided making eye contact with Herman.

"Sorry. Sure. As all of you know the orchard business is a lot of work, especially at certain times of year. Such as the winter pruning season and the harvest. And nearly all of this work is performed by migrant workers, many of whom do not have a legal status inside of this country. But the apples could not be picked without them and they could not get by without the apple picking job. The Frenzels have been very generous with the staff of migrant workers that has been coming every year to pick the fruit. There is a large bunkhouse on the property with a big kitchen and the Frenzels have always provided very good food for everyone and paid between one-hundred-fifty to two-hundred dollars per nine-hour day, depending on how many seasons they had been at Summerwood. Which is quite a bit higher than the average rate of one-hundred-twenty-five dollars per day that many of the other farms paid for a shift during which an average worker would handle more than four tons of fruit. But that has not hurt the profit margins of the orchard because the yield at Frenzel farms is over seventy-thousand tons per acre per year, which is much better than the average of other growers in the valley, who tend to get closer to sixty-five thousand tons per acre per year. We believe that the reason for this is the dependable and hard-working staff that the Frenzels have access to and the staff would like to continue that relationship as your group takes over ownership of the trees. Before I go further, I'd like to show you a slide presentation that should help you to, or show you, or, it will help you see to what I mean that the people who work at the farm are the reason that the farm does so well. Can someone dim the lights for me please?"

It wasn't a good time to turn the lights down. The whole room was already bored. Allison resented the dimming of the lights because it put a stop to her never-ending organizational responsibilities. Omeed had a similar busy vibe to Allison's as he appeared to be taking notes on a legal pad when he was really just doodling a picture of a two-headed goldfish. Hartmut seized upon the opportunity to harvest a few boogers that had been bothering him. Renata conked right out. So did Dmitri. In less than a minute the junior consultant was snoring like a wildebeest and Herman had to elbow him hard in the ribs to wake him up. Underneath the table, out of sight of Duncan, Loven was working on a Rubik's Cube.

Herman felt a little bit bad for Lupita as she slaved through her sophomoric presentation. Almost everyone in the room was a graduate of a top flight business school. The cute Mexican girl was trying to appeal to them with a stream of sappy nostalgic goop. Time lapsed still shots of guys with names like Jorge and Miguel going grayer by the year. Tweenage girls rolling out fresh tortillas for the hungry workers out in the fields. Hartmut and Renata posing and smiling all over the place. Bushels of red apples, bushels of green apples, yellow apples, brown pears, blah, blah, fucking blah. Those guys needed numbers to dig their teeth into. They had analytic brains and they were wired to generate profits. They didn't have hearts, and they didn't let socio-political issues get in the way of making sound business decisions. She was trying to pander to them on the wrong turf. By the time the lights came back on everyone's attention was elsewhere. Even Lupita's. But she had a job to do, and she was determined to get it done. Or at least to be able to say that she tried her hardest. She reached into the file folder that she had brought in with her and withdrew a document that included several typed pages followed by a few more pages strewn with random signatures, much the way you would expect a get-well card from your prison buddies to look. She dropped it on the table and no one made a motion to pick it up.

"What this is," Lupita began to explain, "is an agreement for the upcoming harvest season and an advance on the next year's labor to help with the travel expenses as has been our custom with the Frenzels for more than thirty years now. In the agreement it explains that the current assembled lot of migrant workers, all of whom are listed by name on this document, will be paid at the day rate listed next to their names and receive lodging and board in the form of three meals each day, dedicated mattress and blanket per worker."

"Okay," said the lawyer Quincy. "What exactly is it that you would like us to do with this document?"

"We'd like you to sign it. There is a spot on page seven where it specifies your role in this agreement. There are spots for both Mr. Glüber and Mr. Klevit to sign."

"Hold on a second," said Dmitri, coming to pretty quickly after his nap. "You're trying to get us to enter into a legal agreement, with a bunch of illegal citizens?"

"Señor Gliot, the population of transient migrant workers is the backbone of the fruit picking industry. This is the reality of the situation and has been for quite some time. Since you are going into the apple business, this is something that you are going to have to confront and to deal with. You will not be able to pick your fruit without us."

"Is that a threat?" said Loven, looking hostile.

Herman put his hand on Loven's chest, signaling him to back off.

"Alright, just hang on, everybody," said Duncan. "Ms. Bevilacqua, it's pretty late in the game to be springing this on us. When we enter into something around here, we do it very carefully. That's why we are buying the orchard in fact. Because we believe in its viability. Now, we aren't saying that we *don't* want to enter into an agreement with the migrant workforce that has been picking the apples out at Summerwood Farms. It's just that, if we do, we are going to need to do it very carefully. It's just how we do things around here. So, I'll tell you what, Ms. Bevilacqua, I'm going to have Mr. Gliot take your agreement paperwork here down to his office so that he can give it a good review and make a recommendation to us as to where we ought to go with it from there. No promises, okay?" Duncan's skills as a brilliant tactician were on display.

Lupita folded her arms across her chest and consented to the review. At least she wasn't sunk yet.

As the junior was leaving with the paperwork that Lupita had brought, a boy with red hair and freckles arrived from the catering department with a tray of sliced meat, condiments, fruit, and bread. He set the food down on the table in front of the Frenzels. In a moment he was back with a pitcher of coffee and a brace of ceramic mugs. The men who worked at the firm were eager to sign but the meeting was clearly being interrupted by lunch. Since Allison from escrow was also partaking of the sandwich platter, there wasn't any choice left but to wait. Herman sidled up close to the Frenzels. He was edgy enough as it was, and he didn't want them getting too far from his sight. The deal still wasn't signed. Herman didn't like delays and he would have been much happier if the whole lunch thing could have happened afterwards. His own fucking fault though really. Old people always needed to eat at noon. He should have known that. Why the hell did he schedule the meeting for noon? Wait, he suddenly remembered the noon meeting was their idea. They just wanted a free lunch. All that money and a free lunch too. They were sneaky. He didn't totally trust them. And he definitely didn't trust Lupita. Although he would've been happy to treat her to a taco or two once the papers were signed. He considered her to be—this was one of the few Spanish words that Herman knew—*picante*. And being with her really felt like slumming it but he liked that. He liked the way she contrasted the power bitches that hung around the downtown bars that Herman did most of his drinking at.

Quincy disappeared, probably to use the john.

"I don't exactly remember," said Herman to the Frenzels, who were in the middle of assembling sandwiches. Hartmut had a slab of roast beef dangling from a fork and was draping it over a piece of marbled rye bread. He added two slices of Swiss and a spoonful of Dijon mustard to the meat. "What is the status of the bunkhouse that the migrants stay in now?"

"It's old," said Renata.

Hartmut nodded along with his mouth full. "She's right. It's old. It doesn't leak. But it's also not that well insulated. We've been meaning to redo it for a few years now."

"It's a little too small," added Renata.

"It's also too small," repeated Hartmut. "Be nice to put up another one. One that would house another forty or fifty workers."

"Let them spread out a bit."

"Yeah, bigger kitchen for them."

"And more bathrooms."

"Well, we were already planning on doing that," said Herman, surprising even himself.

"Doing what?" asked Renata. Lupita leaned in closer to try and hear what Herman was saying.

"We want to build a new bunkhouse for the workers. I've already lined up a survey crew and spoken to a developer. It sounds like we are going to be able to get the foundation poured before the ground freezes. That way we can build it over the course of the winter. In fact, if any of the workers has building skills, we might be able to put them to work if they wanted to stay on." Good as all of that sounded, the cocaine had a hold of him and Herman was speaking very fast and the eye contact that he was making with Hartmut was intense. The old man cowered in fear as Herman ground his teeth and forgot to blink.

"How big of a building are you planning, young man?"

"Big," said Herman. "Twenty-thousand square feet. New commercial kitchen. A dozen new showers. Eight for the hombres. Four for the mujeres."

"Oh, they could really use that," said Renata.

"Where are you going to put it?" asked Hartmut, after swallowing the last bite of his first sandwich. Herman held his expression while he thought.

"By the river," he finally said.

"The inside, or the far side?" asked Hartmut.

Herman wasn't accustomed to Hartmut's colloquial way of describing the geography. He was thinking that there would be room for it somewhere near the twelfth tee box, but he couldn't tell Hartmut that. "Inside," Herman said. "We want them close. In case there is any kind of emergency. Which reminds me. What do the workers do when they are injured?"

"They have to go to the clinic in Cashmere and pay out of pocket," said Lupita, who could no longer resist interjecting. "Injuries are a major issue, Señor Glüber. What are you proposing?"

"How much is being spent annually on medical emergencies at the orchard? Do you have that figure? And what would it cost to keep a nurse on staff? That's what I'm wondering."

"Herman. Excuse me. Could I get a word in with you?" Quincy asked. He was back in the room with his eyebrows arched-up, squeezed together, and his eyes huge and bulging. His lips were pursed and the corners of his mouth were turned down. His neck was stretched out. He looked like he was trying to contain something pressurized. There was a palpable sense of urgency in the way that he gripped Herman's shoulder. Duncan and the escrow lady were hovering behind him, looking similarly concerned.

"Sure. Excuse me," said Herman to the Frenzels. Hartmut just about had his second sandwich ready to go. Renata was still only a couple of nibbles into her first. Quincy led Herman out of the Frenzels' earshot, to a far corner of the room, a position from which it was possible to see the Friday afternoon pedestrians thronging by the waterfront. "What's up?" asked Herman once they were comfortably away.

"We've got a little problem," said Quincy. "Well, the building management is having some technical problems."

"What are you talking about, Quincy?"

"Something happened to the fiber-optic line that services this building. Maintenance is trying to blame it on a plumbing crew that's working down there with an underground boring machine. But the stoner they've got working the above ground locater is swearing that he never let the operator get near that line. Those guys think that something chewed through it. In either case, we've got power and cell phones, but we've got no internet or fax lines available."

"Why does this matter, Quincy?"

"I need to get down to Tukwila after this for another closing and traffic is already the pits on I5," said escrow. "I can't transport the closing documents back to my office to get the numbers recorded. The plan was to fax the docs over but we can't do that now."

"I'll take them myself," said Herman.

"Sorry, Mr. Glüber. We can't do that."

"Once the documents are signed, they can only be legally moved by an uninterested third party. That way there's no tampering," Quincy added.

"Okay," said Herman. "What exactly are the three of you suggesting?"

"We have a couple of options," said Quincy. "We could postpone the signing."

"Not an option," said Duncan. Herman agreed.

"Look at those two," Herman said. "They could get Alzheimer's and forget who we are by tomorrow morning. I can feel them wavering. They're religious. One more church service and the whole fucking world could look different to them. What other options do we have?"

"Herman, your eyes are really bloodshot. Are you feeling okay?" asked Duncan.

"What? Me? I'm fine."

"You just seem a little high strung is all."

"I'd just like to get the deal signed."

"We will," said Duncan.

"That's what we all want, Herman," said Quincy. "But we've hit a little snag here and we need to sort it out. So, another option is that we could sign and let the documents go with Allison. But she wouldn't be able to get them to her assistant until Monday so the numbers won't be recorded for a couple of days."

"No," said Duncan.

"Duncan is right," said Herman. "That would mean that it wouldn't be ours until the middle of next week. Quincy, you know we have crews ready to step in over there. We have a shit load to accomplish before the end of October. We can't afford to lose this weekend. What else can we do? Can't someone else just run the fucking papers over there? Where do they have to go?"

"Our office is at Eighth and Stewart," said Allison. "Sending them with a third party is a viable option. If you gentlemen are willing to risk it."

"What about Benny?" said Herman. "We can send them with Benny." Benny was a bike messenger who had become consumed by the identity. He thought of himself and his delivery career as the glue that held society together. He had elevated transporting packages and documents to an art form. Supposedly he took night classes at one of the community colleges but that was just to appease his mom. Some of the staff who worked at Cronkey, Mitchell and Wolfe had known him for close to fifteen years. He was hard-working and dependable as the tides. Herman looked at Duncan, who smiled and acquiesced.

"Alright," Duncan said.

"I'll see if Anita can get Benny on the phone," said Herman. "But Benny only. We're not going to send them with some greenhorn on his grandpa's Schwinn."

"Okay," Duncan said. "Get her on that and let's get this signed. Are you ready, Allison?"

"Yeah, we don't want to start butting up against nap time here," said Herman.

"I'm ready."

"Any word from Dmitri on the agreement with the migrants? The Frenzels and their team are going to want to address that before signing."

"No word," said Duncan. "But here he comes now."

Dmitri opened the glass door and came in looking stressed. He sulked his way over to where Herman was standing by his boss.

"I'm so sorry," Dmitri said.

"What the fuck happened?" said Duncan. Sensing the deflated energy radiating off of his suspect new hire. He leaned in close to him and Herman to make his confession.

"I spilled a cup of coffee all over it."

"What?"

"I'm so sorry. It's fucked."

"What's fucked?"

"That whole stack of papers that the little Mexican girl brought in. That cockamamy agreement. I knocked a twenty-ounce cup of French roast right onto it. You can kill me. Just kill me, Duncan."

"Fuck, Dmitri," Herman chimed in. "This makes us look like a bunch of fucking amateurs. What are you planning on doing?"

"I can cover it, sir. Just give me a chance and I'll cover it."

"You just said we should kill you."

"Give me a chance to cover it first. If it doesn't work, then you can kill me."

"What are you going to do?"

"I'll buy us time. It's all we need anyway, right?"

Herman and Duncan exchanged an irritated look. There was a level of acquired understanding in it as well. It was a trial by fire. Maybe the skinny rookie with the crew cut would shape up. Might as well find out now.

"Fuck this up and you're finished," said Herman. His heart rate was surging and his eyes were close to popping out. He still hadn't blinked in forever, and he wiped his nose with his fingers a few more times just out of nervousness.

"Don't worry, guys. I got this."

"Are you alright, Herman?" Duncan asked. It was obvious that he was sweating and highly agitated.

"Me? Why?" Herman tried to look confused. "I'm fine."

"You sure?" said Duncan.

"I'm fine."

Herman broke away because he was starting to worry that Duncan could tell he was high. Everyone else returned to their original seats around the table. Hartmut must have gotten enough to eat because his paper plate was pushed away from him and he was nursing his cup of coffee. Renata was dabbing at the corners of her mouth with a napkin. She had barely touched her food. Now that Allison had eaten lunch, she seemed anxious to get the ball rolling. Herman excused himself from the office for just a moment so that he could tell Anita to summon the delivery biker Benny Greene, and so he could get out from under Duncan's inquisitive gaze for a moment. When he got back everyone was ready to go.

"Alright, everybody," said Duncan once Herman was back at his seat at the table. "Mr. Gliot has had a chance to go over the agreement that Ms. Bevilacqua brought with her. I'm going to let him have the floor now to hear his assessment." Dmitri stood up and clasped his hands together before discussing the document that wasn't even in the room.

"Thank you, Ms. Bevilacqua, for coming up with the first draft of an agreement between us here at Cronkey, Mitchell and Wolfe and the migrant workforce that has been so critical to the success of Summerwood Farms. You've drawn our attention to a lot of important issues here and we are in complete agreement that it is an absolute necessity that we get some sort of an agreement hammered out in writing. The trouble with the document that you brought over today is that it falls well short of what it is that we would like to do for the workers. Changes of ownership are always scary times for a labor force. No one knows that better than we do. So, we want to make a good impression. Some of the compensation rates that you are seeking are actually lower than the figures that we've been kicking around here at the office. I think that it is even possible that entering into this right now might even look fraudulent on our end. Plus, it sounds like the existing bunkhouse is overcrowded and some more latrines and perhaps another kitchen area would be handy. We are in agreement with that and would like to see some new structures going up as well as renovations being done to the bunkhouse that's already there. We need to modernize out there. We intend to. And all of this needs to be explicitly spelled out in whatever type of agreement we eventually enter into. So, there's no confusion."

The kid was doing alright. Herman—who had been on the verge of bursting a blood vessel in his forehead—found himself mellowing out.

"Specifics about what to do if a worker is injured on the job, ongoing health care, etc. There's so much that needs to be in there that is just simply missing at this point. The formatting is all wrong and it would never be legally binding in a court in the United States drawn up like it is."

"So, what is your suggestion at this point, Mr. Gliot?" asked Duncan, setting his J.C. up for a layup.

"My suggestion is that we make this labor contract between Cronkey, Mitchell and Wolfe and the migrant workforce at Summerwood Farms priority number one once the sale goes through. I don't see any reason why we couldn't have the thing written and signed by everyone inside of a month's time."

"A month?" asked Lupita. "The harvest will be well underway by then. I don't think that my people are going to be comfortable beginning the harvest without a contract."

"Seeing as one of the interested parties here isn't even supposed to be inside of the United States, let alone making tax free money which we are sure they send the lion's share of south of the border, I think that you and your group should be pleased. We are willing to work with you here but you've got to understand that these are delicate matters and they take time to hash out. Right, Mr. Gazipurah?" The Frenzels' representation was startled to hear his name suddenly called and looked up from his doodle wearing an expression of complete bewilderment. He managed a nod of affirmation and then his cheeks flushed. It was apparent that he had no idea what he had just agreed to. "See, your lawyer will tell you. I'm not sure what the system is like in Mexico, this is just how we do it here."

"I've lived my entire life in the United States, Señor Gliot."

"See what I mean? In this country we say *mister*, Ms. Bevilacqua. Not señor. When we rewrite the contract you brought in, we'll make sure that there's something in it for English language instruction and cultural interfacing."

"What my people are looking for, Mr. Gliot, are respect and job security."

"That's what we want to?"

"Sounds like you want to train us to be white people."

"It's got nothing to do with skin color. I'm a foreigner myself so I know how hard adjusting can be. Think of it more like an opportunity to be exposed to some of the bigger possibilities in life."

"Like Pizza Hut, baseball, and rock n' roll music? We are Mexicans. Not Neanderthals."

"Exactly. And what about citizenship? Seems like there should be a path to citizenship if this relationship is going to continue."

"Are you patronizing us, Mr. Gliot?"

"What do you mean?"

"I think that we both know that there is no good option for that."

"You're very sharp, Lupita," Dmitri continued. "Has anyone here brought up to you the idea of the southeastern expansion. We were noticing that Summerwood Farms barely contracts with that region of the country. I know that the price points are lower in the deep south but we've got so many apples going to waste. We could at least be moving them through the Food Lion and getting something for them. You are clearly very smart and you've got great people skills. We don't know what your official title is right now but we could sure use more people like you in management. Would you consider relocating to Florida for an executive position?"

The sudden change of subject disoriented Lupita who couldn't thing of a thing to say in response.

"Why don't you just think about it then."

Madame Laverne Korzha de las Bulgarias

Cigars were being passed around on the street corner in Belltown. Herman, Loven, and Dmitri all got one going after stepping out of the cab. The award-winning tobacco leaves were from the mountainous region in the interior of Nicaragua and Dmitri had brought them along even though he was barely in a celebrating mood. After the Frenzels left the office, Duncan bore into him for spilling coffee on the signed paperwork that Lupita had brought in. He assigned him the task of writing negative back-dated performance reviews of the administrative staff so that they could get around some of the unemployment costs when they were let go. The assignment was going to devour the rest of his weekend.

Smoking wasn't permitted within twenty-five feet of the entrance to The New Luck Toy—a Chinese gastro-pub that the boys were headed for. They were standing at the corner of 2nd and Battery, stinking up the entrance to a Moroccan restaurant with no windows. There was a burgundy-leaved maple growing out of the parking strip that was drought-stressed and wilting. Engulfed in the white cigar smoke like it was, smoldering in the midst of the endless heat wave, the poor tree looked ready to burst into flames.

The Friday afternoon traffic was stacking up on 2nd Ave. The exhaust fumes combined with the heat was intense, borderline third world, but also becoming the new norm. Herman took a long drag on his cigar. He was in a great mood.

The deal was signed, and a much-needed trip to the bathroom allowed him to freshen up and get back to some kind of homeostasis. His normal level of confidence, which teetered at the beginning of the meeting, had returned with a vengeance.

Dmitri stood a fair amount taller than both Loven and Herman. He was disturbingly thin and the inexpensive black funeral suit that he was wearing hung off of his slumped shoulders the same way it hung off its hanger. His arms were disproportionately long, and he had some 5 o'clock shadow going. He was primal looking. Practically walking proof of evolution. There was a large mole on his left cheek that women found sexy for reasons Herman could never fathom. They also found him sexy because he was rumored to be hung like John Holmes. That Herman could fathom. Dmitri was born in the Russian South Federal District, in Taganrog. His father ran a printing press and taught him English at a very young age. The kid was also a prodigious mathematician and wound up landing a scholarship to come to the United States and pursue his undergrad at Brown. He fell in love there and married his sophomore calculus professor. The relationship fizzled by the time he was done school but Dmitri at least got a passport out of it. He took a couple of draws off of his cigar and let an opaque plume of smoke drizzle out of the corner his mouth.

"What do you think will happen to those two old folks when they see the trees start to fall? I don't know if they'll survive it."

"Hopefully they'll be on vacation. Or already moved down to Scottsdale or something."

"Scottsdale? Did someone say they were moving to Scottsdale?"

"Hartmut's doctor told them that they'd be better off in Arizona," said Herman. "But that doesn't mean that they're going there. I'm not sure they've ever even been there. May not even know where it is."

"So where are they going now that the sale is final?"

"As far as I know they aren't going anywhere," said Herman. "Their house wasn't a part of the deal. The whole acre that they live on in fact was divided from the rest of the parcel when they first considered selling a few years ago."

"They're going to have a front row seat for the destruction?"

"They're also going to have a front row seat for the development. Hartmut is going to get a free lifetime membership to the new country club. Although I seriously doubt that he'll be up for eighteen on this course. It's going to play really long."

"What about Renata?"

"She can come and use the spa or get a massage every once in a while."

"And all those Mexican fruit pickers, you think they are just going to stand around and watch the entire orchard get cut down?"

"I don't know about standing around," said Herman. "We're hoping that we can pay them to help clean up the branches and load the wood into the trucks. If any of them is good with a chainsaw, we'll pay even more."

The light at the intersection to the south was green but the traffic was so snarled up that no one could move their vehicles. Horns started blaring. There were two small SUV's and a yellow Prius taxicab stuck in the middle of the intersection so that none of the east or westbound traffic could move either. A group of teenagers who looked like they'd just walked away from a train accident made their way through the skittish maze of cars. They were in a mix of military fatigues and black jeans, streaked with dry blood. In fact, one of them had clothes that were riddled with bullet holes. Another had had his ear lopped off. But they were getting around just fine. And they were passing a joint of skunky marijuana. One of them stopped and asked Loven if he had the time. Kid had a hatchet buried in his back. It wasn't affecting his mood though. Loven appreciated any chance he got to show off his fancy new watch and he thrust his left wrist forward so that he could expose the

Breitling from his sleeve and then folded the arm back in toward himself.

"Just past four o'clock," said Loven.

"Thanks, dude. We're going to a movie," said the grisly lad, who then moved on with his crew in the direction of the Cinerama movie theater.

The Cinerama was just a couple of blocks away and the marquee was visible from where Herman and his cohorts were standing. It was advertising a double feature of horror films from the director Rob Zombie: 'The House of a Thousand Corpses' and 'The Devil's Rejects.' It was a little early still but fans of gore were already lining up outside for good seats. Not like there was a bad seat at the Cinerama. The theater was owned by one of Microsoft's co-founders, the late Paul Allen. Neither Mr. Allen, nor his former partner Bill Gates, had been working at the software company in a while. Since leaving it behind, the two of them had followed distinctly different paths. Mr. Gates and his wife made a top priority out of world health and education issues while Mr. Allen had kept the focus on making life for the people who live in the northwest more fun. He owned two of three major sports franchises in that corner of the country, parked a hideous looking museum inspired by the psychedelic music of Jimi Hendrix underneath the Space Needle, rearranged the South Lake Union area of the city to be a biotech research hub where death would eventually be outmaneuvered, and of course he owned the nicest movie theater in town, which was state of the art in both image and sound quality. And in order to keep it so, it closed every spring to be renovated before the summer blockbusters started coming out. The big new upgrade that year was slim profile Cerwin Vega subwoofers sewn into the cushions of the reclining leather seats. Moviegoers could customize the intensity of the bass response by twisting a dial just behind the cup holder.

Herman tugged on Loven's sleeve and pulled him closer so that he could whisper to him. "How about a little more of the white stuff?" Herman didn't have a good connection of his own and he was coy about asking for more. He was mostly a hard alcohol guy and he never had a stash. But when he started something he liked to keep going.

"Sure, Herm," said Loven. He took the vile back out of his inside pocket and placed it discreetly in Herman's palm. Then Herman disappeared into the alleyway behind the buildings for a moment. When he got back Dmitri was waving at a peculiar vehicle caught in the traffic jam. The driver was hanging out the window and waving Dmitri over. And not in a friendly way. He looked panicked.

"Hey that's my cousin," Dmitri said. "*Zdravstvuyte*, Alexander!" he shouted over the hum of the engines and screeching brakes of the Metro buses.

Dmitri's cousin looked like he belonged behind the drum kit in a death metal band. Tangled brown hair spilled out of the bottom of a dirty gray beanie and disappeared behind his shoulders. He was in dark sunglasses, had a goatee, and a lit cigarette hanging out of his mouth. The carelessly arranged hardware in his cheek made him look like the victim of a drive-by body piercing. His handmade wool sweater was way too hot for the afternoon and looked like it had seen a hundred Russian winters. And the vehicle he was operating was absurd. It was actually a rolling advertisement for the energy drink brand Rocket Fuel; a Plymouth PT Cruiser, decked out to look like a rocket ship. The car was matte gray, decorated with mock rivets, and it had a section that came off of the hood that tapered to a point. It was supposed to be the nose of the rocket but it looked more like a battering ram. The rocket's tail section extended from the trunk. There were three fins for flight path stabilization and a bright orange disc in the middle of them which was supposed to be an indication to the driver following the rocket ship down the road that the thrusters were still engaged. On the driver's side door there was a stencil or a decal of the RocketFuel logo. The light turned green again and the driver could be heard shouting in Russian, probably swearing from the sound of it, as he reluctantly slid back in behind the wheel. The rocket turned left at the next intersection and disappeared. Dmitri furrowed his brow and a look of concern washed over him.

"I didn't know that you had family over here," said Loven

"Yeah, just as of recently. I've got my cousin Alexander sleeping on my couch. He got into a little trouble back home. We're trying to get him a fresh start somewhere new."

"What'd he do?" asked Herman

"Shit. Lots of stuff. Stole a couple of computers from the school library and sold them on the internet. Flipped my uncle's brand-new tractor when he was drunk on vodka at 9:30 in the morning. And it was bad enough that he got his cousin Galena knocked up, until he knocked his kid sister up too."

"At the same time?"

"Same fucking time."

"Sounds like a dog."

"No reason to insult dogs."

"What the fuck is he doing in the RocketFuel car?" asked Herman. "I can't stand that shit."

"You don't like RocketFuel. That stuff's pretty good I think."

"Shut the fuck up, Loven."

"Does Alexander speak English?" Loven wasn't really capable of shutting up.

"Not really. You might say that he's picking up a few words from the television, but, yeah, not really."

"How the hell does he drive then?"

"We studied the route. He's actually a pretty good driver when he is concentrating. All of the RocketFuel is starting to mess with him though. They let him drink all that he wants. Sometimes he has nine or ten cans of it in a day. He comes home from work and doesn't sleep. Just stares out the window or watches the tube. Sometimes he seems awake but I can't talk to him. It's like he isn't in there. To be honest I am getting a little bit worried. And I have no idea what he was just yelling about. He seems to be upset about something. Probably the RocketFuel screwing with his head. He already has a, what's that expression?" Dmitri squinted and thought hard, then blurted, "short fuse."

"Sounds to me like he's going to be fine," said Herman. "Though it would be nice to see him working for a company that wasn't owned by that pussy Nevil Horsetrainer." Herman had a sick need to cut the young billionaire down, even in front of people who didn't know him. It was a tough thing to pull off considering the kid's ultra-liberal reputation was popular with the youth all around the world. And the only time he was ever in the news was for defending an abused little guy, saving some famous landmark, preserving massive swaths of uncorrupted terrain, or somehow getting clean drinking water to an entire African nation that was dying of thirst. "Kid sucked down more canned oxygen on Annapurna than the whole rest of the team." This was completely false. Nevil limited his supplementary oxygen to a single bottle that he used only above camp four and he carried it up himself. "When your cousin's English starts coming around you should bring him by the office. Maybe we can find something for him to do."

"I don't think he knows much about business, Herman."

"Neither did I when I was his age. That part is easy anyway. We can teach that."

"What is it you want with him?"

"Nothing really. I just like the sound of a kid with the guts to fuck his own sister after knocking his cousin up. Sounds like the personality type that thrives in this kind of environment."

"Would you fuck your own sister, Herman?"

"I don't have any brothers or sisters so the question isn't really relevant, and the truth is I probably wouldn't. But if she was a knockout, and I was the right age…"

Loven finished his cigar, dropped it to the pavement, and then rubbed it out with the sole of his cowboy boot. "Shall we get a drink, gentlemen? That cigar made me thirsty as fuck." Herman tossed his butt out into the middle of the road and walked over to the entrance to The New Luck Toy. Loven and Dmitri followed right behind like baby ducks.

It wasn't happy hour yet and there were only a few other people inside. A young kid with smooth cheeks and a big nose was drinking an iced tea and having a hushed conversation with a bored looking older man who was nursing a glass of white wine. Three dudes in golf attire were laughing about something. They looked like they were smashed already. They all had red cheeks like they had been out in the sun. That was it. No women.

"We've got to stop coming into this place," said Herman to the bartender Jordan. Jordan was tasting an Idaho potato vodka that he had infused with juniper berries.

"Good afternoon, gentlemen. How is everyone?"

"Every time we come in here it's all fucking sausages," said Herman. "Do you even let chicks in here anymore?"

"It's barely after four, Herman," said Jordan after setting the bottle of infused vodka aside. "We just opened up." Jordan was in high spirits. He stood in front of the three men with his hands free, giving them his complete attention. "The ladies are going to be showing up any minute now. Let me fix you a drink and then you'll see what I mean. What are we having tonight?"

"Mule," said Dmitri.

"Loven?" said Jordan. "The usual I assume?"

"You assume correctly."

"Make that two Inverted Street Dogs," said Herman.

Jordan nodded and reached up to the top shelf for vodka and an obscure orange cream mezcal that was an ingredient in the Inverted Street Dog. Despite the bar's Chinese name, its fusion cuisine and cocktail menu borrowed from the entire world. It was obvious from the bartender's light and energetic vibe that he was happy to be there.

"What's got you in such a good mood, Jordan? Get a call back for a part in the church Christmas pageant?"

Jordan had been tending the bar at The New Luck Toy for as long as the place had been around. He was also an aspiring actor. Every once in a while, he would disappear for a few weeks to take a minor theater role somewhere but no one believed that he was any good.

"Very funny," said Jordan, who was remarkably comfortable in his own skin and practically impossible to make fun of. Which, in combination with his mixology skills, qualified him as a top tier bartender. "You're actually close. I did get a call back for a part in a movie. And it's a film that's starring the two-time-academy-award-winning actor Lucky Soul. Although I really don't want to say too much about it. I haven't landed it yet." He laid out the first round of drinks on coasters.

While Dmitri and Loven congratulated the young man on his pending success, Herman's eyes narrowed and he leveled a cold-blooded, hateful stare at him. If there was one person in the world that Herman liked less than Nevil Horsetrainer, it was Lucky Soul. But Herman didn't actually think of him as Lucky Soul. Herman knew him by his real name, which was David Orkin, shortened by Herman when they were in kindergarten stacking blocks together, to Ork. The very same Ork whose mom had nearly killed little Herman with a peanut butter cookie. The very same Ork who mocked little Herman while he was lying on a stretcher, by breathing through a straw rammed through the throat of a paper bag puppet that had curly hair and a red shirt on, just like Herman. The very same Ork that would become Herman's wingman on the ice for several years, which was the only reason the dude probably ever got up the sand to try acting. Herman had made him a minor star already by feeding him the puck, and had definitely gotten him laid for the first time by Jessie Frankel. His breath became steady and slow. He was projecting calm but his innards were boiling with rage. He had a hard-enough time even hearing the actor's pseudonym spoken aloud. Especially since it had acquired the 'two-time-academy-award-winning' sobriquet every time someone said it. The bravado he had regained morphed into an anger that he was struggling to control.

"What's the film about?" asked Dmitri.

"They're turning Rick Moody's novel *The Four Fingers of Death* into a movie. It's going to be great. You guys ever read it?" Dmitri and Loven shook their heads. Herman maintained his frozen countenance. "It's so funny. It was written a while ago but it still takes place in the future. It's set in the year 2025, after the United States has devolved into a corrupt dystopian nightmare."

"I love corrupt dystopias," said Loven.

"So maybe it's not a nightmare for you," said Jordan laughing. "The beginning is about a manned mission to Mars. It's supposed to be in the name of science and research but there is actually a secret secondary mission to cultivate lethal bacteria that could be used in germ warfare back here on Earth. Most of the astronauts get infected with the bacteria and die or wind up stranded on Mars. Only part of one of them makes it back."

"Which part?"

"That's where it starts getting crazy. The astronaut knows that he shouldn't return to Earth because he is infected and a threat to the population but NASA won't authorize him to explode the ERV, which means Earth Return Vehicle. The astronaut finally figures out how to blow the thing up on his own but not until it's passing through the atmosphere. So instead of it crashing in one location, pieces of the ERV scatter all over the southwest. One of those pieces contains the astronaut's arm, severed at the elbow, and missing its middle finger."

"What's the arm do?"

"The arm doesn't have a brain but it's got incredible motor functions and a killer instinct. It terrorizes the southwest. Many of its victims find the arm's fingers digging into their necks, and then they tear their own throats out by trying to pull the arm off."

"Sounds awesome," said Dmitri.

"It's going to be awesome. There's obviously a lot more to it than that. And for the film it sounds like they're going to have the arm crash land up here in the rainforest somewhere and find its way into the city. Lucky and the producers are actually in town, scouting locations. I got to meet him. He said this time around he was going to win the academy award using nothing but his left arm. He's cocky. But you've got to hand it to him, he's a great actor."

Herman threw up in his mouth. Luckily the acidy pool that came up through his esophagus was tempered by the mucus that was dripping down from his nasal cavity. He didn't like Jordan and he liked it even less that he was at his mercy. Herman asked for a glass of ice water.

"Which part do you think you're going to get?" asked Dmitri, prolonging the bartender's insufferable story.

"They're looking at me for the part of one of the astronauts, Captain Jim Rose. An inside man on the mission to Mars. And a closet homosexual."

"Are there closets on Mars?" asked Loven.

"Funny you should ask. No actually. There aren't any closets on Mars. My character's habit of streaming gay porn is well known by NASA. He even seduces Lucky's character in the space capsule and the two of them have a ridiculous zero-gravity sexual experience."

"You're going to have a gay sex scene, with Lucky Soul, in a fucking spacecraft?"

"Hang on. I haven't landed the part yet and I don't want to jinx my chances, but if I do, then yeah. In zero-gravity. But it probably won't be with Lucky. It'll be a stunt double or something I'm sure. You guys ever thought about what it would be like? Fucking in a zero-gravity environment?"

"I haven't really," said Loven. "What are the advantages?"

"I think that when you get good at it there are many more positions available. The imagination is pretty much the limit. But getting leverage is the trick, and keeping it. I mean, one good thrust in a zero-gravity environment and your partner goes sailing away along the x-axis until something stops them. I think that at the very least, sex in outer space would require a lot of things to be able to hold onto. Like handles, or straps."

"So, how does it go for you and Lucky in the capsule. Do you both wind up getting off?"

"Not exactly. Neither my character or Lucky's has a lot of experience with the whole zero gravity sex thing. Hell, Lucky's character isn't even gay, just starved for attention and desperate. It's the first time for him and he has no idea what the process is even like. Although it's clear from the beginning that I will be catching and Lucky will be pitching. He gets it in there but the angle is off and it's hurting him and he has to pull his cock, which I adoringly rename his *space arm*, out of my asshole. While he's readjusting himself, he actually blows his wad into the capsule, which creates a whole new set of problems."

Loven and Dmitri were laughing so hard by then that Jordan had to stop telling them about the movie so that they could catch their breath. He set their drinks in front of them and Herman finished all of his in one long pull and then asked for another.

"What happens to the come?" asked Dmitri once he'd finally pulled it together.

"Well, it's zero gravity remember, so it doesn't just spill onto the floor. It separates into varying-sized globs and starts floating around the capsule."

Jordan snatched up Herman's empty and immediately began fixing him a replacement. Loven and Dmitri still hadn't touched theirs. They were both laughing too hard to swallow anything.

"Can we please change the fucking subject," shouted Herman.

"From what?" said Loven. "The movies, a severed hand that makes it back from the planet Mars, or zero gravity sex?"

In the midst of three of the men laughing and Herman scowling a woman in high heeled shoes showed up and claimed the barstool next to Herman.

"Zero gravity sex, gentlemen," she said in a sultry Eastern European accent. "Sounds like a subject that it would be a shame to change."

Herman was caught off guard. Up until then the conversation had left him feeling impatient and irritated, mostly because of Ork. Deep down he knew the topic was funny and he suddenly had a need to come off as lighthearted and charming.

The woman that was chatting with them was a goddess. Not one of those rough sketches of human beings that swarmed the bars once they managed to tear themselves away from their computer screens. She was lithe and confident and it was obvious right away that she didn't answer to anyone. Her feathered black hair obscured her left eye. Her cheek bones were set high and her face was long, but her mouth and nose were small. Her eyes were bright green, a color that Herman wasn't used to seeing and he was instantly smitten with her even though she seemed much tougher than the girls that he normally went for. She was tall and thin, with medium breasts, wide shoulders, long fingers, and narrow hips. She set her red leather purse on the bar and ordered a vodka.

"Ever tried zero gravity sex?" Herman asked his new neighbor. She smiled at him as she pulled a compact mirror from her purse and used it to reapply her lipstick.

"Where would I have tried that?" she said.

"Who has ever tried that?" Loven pondered.

"I bet it happens on the space station all the time," Dmitri sounded sure of it.

"People have definitely jacked off in space. I bet John Glen did. Neil Armstrong too. With a name like Armstrong, how could he not?" Loven laughed at his own joke.

"I am sure that women have also pleased themselves in space," the new neighbor seemed to be enjoying the topic.

"I think the real question here is gravity's role in sex. Is it making it better or is it holding sex back?" Herman wanted to shift the conversation.

"Fucking gravity. As long as we are down here, we are stuck with it I suppose," listening to her swear was endearing.

"I'm Herman," said Herman. He leaned forward so that it was harder for her to see Loven and Dmitri. It was clear that Herman had no intention of introducing them.

"Who are your friends?" she asked.

"You mean these two? We just work together." It truly bothered Herman to be officially labeled anyone's friend. He wasn't sure what responsibilities came with that designation, but he was fairly certain that he wasn't interested in them.

"I'm Dmitri."

"Loven," said Loven. Herman had to rock back on his stool so that everyone could see each other.

"Laverne," she said. "How are you gentlemen this evening?"

"We're good," said Herman. The truth is he was putting a great deal of effort into appearing lighthearted and friendly, when he was mostly pissed off and frustrated. "And I don't want to imply that I am averse to a thorough exploration of the pros and cons of zero gravity sex. If you wanted to explore it in real depth, I would be willing. The part of the conversation that I would like to see culled is the part about that insufferable actor who goes by that awful stage name of Soul. He's got no soul at all. Ruins every film he's ever in." Herman didn't have the stomach to watch any of his films so he didn't really know. "I'm not saying that this movie that we've been talking about doesn't sound good. I like an erotic space epic as much as the next guy. I just hope they don't sully it by putting that zero talent, beady-eyed has been, excuse me, never was, in the lead role. Honestly, it's hard for me to describe to you how much I can't stand that asshole."

"He's just an actor, Mr. Glüber," said Laverne. "I don't think that there is a need for you to be getting upset." Her English was good but her accent was thick. It was like talking with Lady Dracula.

"I'm not upset. I just think he's a lousy actor. And how do you know my last name?"

"You just said it."

"No, I didn't."

"I think you did."

"I think I didn't. Hey who are you anyway?"

"What do you mean? Who are you?"

"Fair enough," said Herman. "I'm Herman. Herman Glüber as you somehow already know. These two idiots and I work together at a VC firm."

"What is VC firm?"

"It stands for venture capital. We take risks. What we do is we buy things that we think are valuable and we sell them off in pieces. Things tend to be worth more money that way."

"And you gentlemen bought something today?"

"We did as a matter of fact. We bought an apple orchard," said Herman. "What's more, we are going to cut the trees down, divide the property and assets, and make a killing off of it. Speaking of which, can we please drink to that?" Herman, Loven, and Dmitri clinked their glasses but Laverne didn't join them in the toast.

"Doesn't sound like the kind of thing that should belong to you," she said.

"Shouldn't belong to me?" Herman was getting mad. His normal strategy was to be relaxed and aloof with girls that he wanted to sack but the cocaine had made him a little more quick-tempered than he typically liked to come off. "What are you saying?"

She shrugged. "Excuse me, mister bartender. May I have 'nother please?"

Jordan nodded and refilled her glass.

"I'm sorry, Ms.—Laverne, but do you know something about the apple orchard that we bought today?"

She turned a sober expression toward Herman, who was grinding his teeth and knew it but still couldn't stop. "I sense that there is something wrong with the celebration that you are having. Like something is not complete that maybe you think is complete. You say you bought what today? An apple farm?"

"It's an orchard."

"Are you sure?"

"That it's an orchard? Yes, we are sure," said Loven. "What are you talking about, lady?"

Herman's anger seemed like it was rubbing off on Loven, who tended to be pretty easy-going, even when was trashed.

"Everything is signed and you paid them all the money?"

"Yes," said Loven, louder this time. "That's what it means to close a deal. Is there something specific that you want to tell us?"

"No, Mister Boilee. There is nothing. If you say that the deal is closed, then I am sure that it is closed."

"How do you know my name now? Who are you? Some kind of fortune teller or something?"

"My specialty is reading tarot cards, Mister Boilee. I am receptive to voices from the spirit realm, and sometimes I get messages that were not intended for me."

"Hold on a second here, sweetheart," said Herman. "You're trying to tell us that voices that we can't hear, that belong to bodies that we can't see, are telling you our last names and that something is screwy with our deal to buy Summerwood Farms?"

"It is a farm?"

"It's an orchard but it's branded as Summerwood Farms."

"Hmm. Yes, Mister Glüber. Is something like what you say."

"You are out of your mind." Herman was getting disoriented from the broken English and the direct challenge that he was getting from Laverne. He wanted to blow off the insinuation but the decision to let the only copy of the sale agreement leave the office with the bike messenger Benny Greene burned inside of his brain like a hot coal. Herman made a mental note to phone into the office and make sure that the sales numbers had recorded as soon as he got out of the conversation with the sexy tarot card reader from Transylvania or wherever.

"Herman," Loven was tugging on the shoulder of Herman's jacket. He was also motioning that he wanted a private audience, away from the woman at the bar.

"Excuse us a moment, Laverne."

"Of course, Mister Glüber."

"Call me Herman. We'll be right back."

Herman, Loven, and Dmitri huddled up in a narrow hallway with Chinese dragon wallpaper that led to the restrooms.

"I don't think that she's who she says she is," said Loven

"What do you mean?" asked Dmitri.

"I mean I think we're being set up here. How the fuck does she know our names and this crap about the orchard? She's not a fucking fortune teller. Someone put her up to this."

"Who would have done that?" asked Herman. His heart was beating wild and fast and it was freaking him out. Normally he took a lot of pride in his low resting heart rate. He was having a hard time keeping his eyes focused on any one thing. They were rolling uncontrollably.

"I bet it was Duncan. I bet you she's a stripper and this is all just a ruse to fuck with you, Herman. The boss man is just stoked with you for closing the Summerwood deal and he hired this hot pants necromancer to fuck with your head a little bit, wrap those long legs around you, and take you for a ride on her broomstick."

"She better not have a broomstick."

"You know what I'm talking about."

"Barely."

"So," said Dmitri, "you're thinking that Herman should play along with her?"

"Why not?" said Loven. "I think she is here to meet The Herminator."

Over the years Herman had made such a habit out of exaggerating his sexual exploits that his penis had acquired the nickname The Herminator.

"What do you think, Herman?" Loven's tone implied that he was certain that he was correct. "I mean how could she possibly know all of that shit if no one put her up to it?"

"You've got a good point there. I'm just not sure I believe that Duncan would have sent a stripper down to The New Luck Toy to mess with me. It's not really his style. I wish it was. It just isn't. What do you think, Dmitri? Sounds like she's from your part of the world. Is she authentic?"

"Where I am from there are many witches. There are many curses and there are many spells. I don't think that you should screw around with her, Herman. She reminds me of my Aunt Yaz. When Aunt Yaz says something, she is always right. And Aunt Yaz almost never has good news. She knows things but it is always things like 'Dominique is going to be thrown from a horse' or 'Ivan is going to drown in a grain silo.' My brothers and I always steered clear of Aunt Yaz."

"Is she still alive?"

"Yes. She emigrated to London, but we don't talk."

"I'm not sure either of you two are helping," said Herman. "I'm starving. I'm going to invite her to dinner."

"I'm hungry too," said Loven. "Be nice to belly up before this night gets going."

"If she accepts then the two of you are going to Taco Bell and I'll see you on Monday."

"Where are you thinking to take her?"

"Gaucho. It's been a big day. I'm in the mood for some good beef. Seriously, if she says that she wants to go to dinner then you two better have something to get to."

"Got it, Herman. Just watch out. I still think that she's a plant."

They left the hallway and went back to their barstools and cocktails. Jordan had the bar's sound system hooked up to a Pandora station that played all grunge music. Kurt Cobain was singing the acoustic version of 'All Apologies' from the unplugged record that Nirvana made in New York. The place was starting to fill up and the din of the voices was beginning to sound like white noise. A waitress in a short pink skirt was floating among the tables, taking orders from the thirsty customers that had just gotten off of work. A couple of muted television screens behind the bar showed a couple of middle-aged men with glossy faces and microphones analyzing a baseball game that was about to begin: The Mariners vs. The Rangers.

"You like baseball?" asked Herman. Laverne was staring at the television screen when he returned.

"I do," she said. "I know that the game is sometimes a little bit slow and boring. But if you pay attention to the entire year it has lot of drama. I like the baseball because it is more like life than the other sports that are popular in this country. There is nothing like it where I am from."

"Which is where?" Asked Herman. A clear answer might have blown up Loven's stripper theory.

"Far away," was all she was willing to divulge.

"What sports do people play in this far away land?"

"People mostly just beat on each other until someone is unconscious and bloody. A few play handball."

"How long have you been in the United States, Laverne?"

"Long enough, Mr. Glüber."

"Call me Herman. You want to get out of here?"

"And go to where?"

"Let's go out for steaks. I know a great place. A buddy of mine is the chef. There's a table waiting for us."

"Thank you but I can not, Mister Glüber. I must be going to work very soon."

"Call me Herman. It's Friday night. You can't be going to work now. Unless. Wait a minute. Are you—"

"Lady of the night? No Mister Glüber. Correct me if I am wrong but those ladies make money by the hour."

"And how do you make money?"

"By the minute."

"You've got my attention."

"My name is Madame Laverne Korzha de las Bulgarias. I have a psychic hotline. People call me and I read their tarot cards for them over the phone."

"After getting their credit card numbers, I take it."

"Yes, but is not a hoax."

"What happens with the people who call when you're not there?"

"They have access to a recorded message."

"These people are so dumb that they all just listen to the same recording that they think is just for them?"

"There is one for each of the signs of the Zodiac and the people that call can select from a menu. The recordings are not so specific as the readings."

"And not as expensive, I take it? What does it cost to be on the phone with you for a minute?"

"The first minute is free."

"And after that?"

"I would not charge you to read your cards, Mr. Glüber."

"Are you flirting with me?"

"No," said Laverne without a hint of irony. "I just think that they have some good information for you is all. I have a small office in the bottom a building around the corner. Next to the Catholic Seaman's Club. Friday night is a very busy night for me. You should come. I can do a tarot card reading for you and your friends. Maybe we find out a little more about the apple business. Maybe you find out some other interesting things about your future."

"No thanks. I don't believe in that crap. It's for people with no ideas and no ambition. And no brains. No offense. I'm sure you're fine. I'm talking about your customers. The kinds of people who go for that garbage. I am sure that you can at least feel good about taking their money. It's not like they deserve it. Why don't we just get back together after you're done fleecing people. Have a few more drinks. Maybe revisit the zero-gravity sex idea."

"You know somewhere that we could go where there is no gravity?"

"I know somewhere we could go to practice parts of this experiment. So that way we'll be ready. In case, you know, there's an opportunity at some point."

"Do you not have woman in your life, Mister Glüber?"

"Please call me Herman. I won't sit here and lie to you. There are plenty of women who come and go, have come and gone from, and presumably will come into and will come—you see what I'm getting at. But I'm not married if that's what you're asking and I've got no responsibilities to anyone at all. Well, at least as far as the rest of tonight is concerned. So, what do you say? Where should we meet?"

"I'd like to read your tarot cards, Mister Glüber."

"If I let you read them will you start calling me Herman and agree to get together with me later this evening?"

Laverne sat perfectly still for so long Herman and the boys thought that she might have fallen asleep with her eyes open. Or died.

"I can not meet you later tonight, Mr. Glüber. I have too much to attend to. But if you would allow me to read your cards, I would be willing to meet you again tomorrow. Sometime in the afternoon."

"Where?"

"How about right back here."

"For lunch? We can meet here but the food is terrible. We'll have a drink and go somewhere else. Should we say right at noon."

"How about two o'clock? I do not like to get up early."

"Deal," said Herman. "Do we do this thing here or do we need to go somewhere?"

"Which do you prefer?"

"Do you have a liquor cabinet over there next to the Seaman Club?"

"I do not."

"Then we should stay here."

"A table would be better than the bar. I would prefer not to lay my cards out where they could be damaged."

"Hold on a minute," Dmitri interrupted. He had been staring at Laverne ever since she mentioned her hotline. "Are you on the television?"

Laverne smiled politely at being recognized.

"I have some commercials that run on cable TV. Have you seen them?"

"I have seen them. Late at night. When my nephew was watching. I know the number. (800) B4I-S2L8."

"This is right, Mr. Gliot. That is my number."

"Holy shit," said Dmitri, "she's big-time."

"I don't know if I'd call having a commercial during your nephew's late-night television binges big-time," said Loven.

"I would," said Dmitri. "She's legitimate. Herman, you're about to have your fortune told by a famous psychic."

"Come on," said Herman. "She's just going to make a bunch of crap up."

"Aunt Yaz never makes anything up."

"Neither do I," said Laverne.

Herman sneered and scanned the room. There was one open four top left and he scurried to claim it before another party flowed through the door. Dmitri flagged down Jordan, who was muddling mint for a round of Hong King Ice Teas, and ordered up more drinks. Loven ducked out to the bathroom so that he could boost up on cocaine in one of the stalls. Laverne finished off the rest of her drink, stuffed her cosmetics mirror back into her purse, and excused herself to use the bathroom. A pair of small insects with red stripes on their backs and horns connected by thin streams of electrons jumping over the oppositely charged gap emerged from underneath the bar, clinging to the rubber casing around the ethernet cable that ran into the back of the bar's credit card machine. They stopped when they reached the machine and stayed still, feeding off of the current, cloaked by a maraschino cherry and a lemon wedge.

For a brief period, Herman was stranded alone at the table with nowhere to put his attention, so he glanced around the bar making snap judgments about the customers based on their appearance. Grunge music was still blaring out of the bar's sound system and it was driving Herman mad. Besides sounding like dated crap, its lasting influence over the Northwest was evident in the fact that there was no attire that was considered too casual for any establishment. It irked Herman. Even though he was a local boy he was offended by the classlessness of it. It was a Friday night in a swanky downtown bar just after business hours, and the place was filling up with guys in tank tops and jeans and women in yoga clothes. It was the kind of thing that would never happen in a real city like Philadelphia or Baltimore. He sat and he seethed over this insignificant matter at the last open table in The New Luck Toy while he waited for Laverne to get back from the toilet and get on with the tarot card reading that he had been coerced into getting done.

There was nothing on the table in front of him other than his pint of Manny's Pale Ale and Laverne's vodka neat. He took a sip of his beer and then adjusted and readjusted the knot on his tie. He wasn't really used to waiting around. And even though he had nothing else to be doing and no other plans for the evening, he felt himself to be in the midst of a tremendous rush. Like there was something terribly urgent about the reading that was about to take place; something was riding on it and he wanted to know what it was. He tried to keep reminding himself of the uselessness of it, while he could sense tectonic plates shifting beneath his feet. And that wasn't the only reason he was being kept waiting for something that was so trivial and so stupid. He was infatuated with the card reader. There was something about her that set her apart from other women that he had met in his life. He didn't lust after her so much as feel like she challenged his intellect. If he was being honest with himself, he would have had to cop to being worried about her. That she might be smarter than he was. It wasn't that Herman automatically assumed that men were wiser than women, he wasn't that out of date of an individual. It was the sensation that she knew more about him than he did about her; a lot more. It made him feel vulnerable. And the feeling of vulnerability was so palpable that Herman's unconscious was forced to deploy its most effective weapon: denial.

There was a dull cheering from a small percentage of the patrons that were paying attention to the television screens. Herman looked at the TV and feigned interest in what was happening so that he didn't have to appear idle. The Mariners were in a tight playoff race and playing against the team that was just barely ahead of them in the standings. It was the bottom of the first inning and their second baseman had just hit a solo shot over the right field wall to give them an early one to nothing lead. Out of the corner of his eye Herman spied Laverne finally returning from the restroom. He wasn't sure if his mind was playing tricks on him because she seemed not to emerge from the ladies' room, but from the mens.' Which couldn't be true, so he just filed it somewhere deep in his gray matter under 'optical illusion' and went back to making sure that he looked bored and impatient.

"Very sorry to keep you waiting, Mr. Glüber."

"Call me Herman."

"Sorry, Herman," Laverne settled herself into the seat across from Herman. Her purse was dangling from the back of the chair. She opened it up and withdrew a deck of oversized cards that that had so much energy emanating from it that Herman got the idea that another person had suddenly joined them. Which wasn't the case. It was just the two of them at the table. Dmitri and Loven had kept their seats at the bar and were privately going about the business of getting sloshed. Laverne pushed the deck across the table. "Shuffle them, please."

Herman let loose a sardonic chuckle and started half-ass mixing up the cards. They were too big for him to shuffle gracefully and he was trying to avoid getting lost in staring at the designs on their backs. The cards looked and felt old, without being weathered or worn. Ancient, but well preserved. He wrapped up with his apathetic effort to mix the deck and pushed the deck back across the table to Laverne.

"That's it?"

"What difference does it make?" Herman stared Laverne down with what he hoped was cool confidence but that nagging sensation crept up in him at the same time, the one that was warning him that he might not be the brightest person sitting at the table.

"You're sure?"

Herman made like it was beneath him to answer the question and instead he remained stoic and sipped his beer. It wasn't his intention, but he looked mean. Laverne let the silence linger for a moment, smiled just a little and then emptied her glass of vodka in a single mouthful. She closed her eyes and appeared as though she was listening to something. Undoubtedly part of the act, thought Herman. Then he saw something disturbing reflected in the curved surface of his beer glass. It was two people coming up the sidewalk outside the bar. One of them, the woman, was not only immediately familiar, but she had the ability to stoke emotions in Herman that he was unable to contain. He wheeled about in his chair to get a better look at the couple. The woman was Margot. She had her hair down and she was walking with another man and having a laugh with him. She was beautiful when she was laughing. The guy that she was with wasn't all that handsome. He was shortish, wearing a shabby suit, and had a big ugly nose. But still, he didn't like the way she was looking at him. A jealous rage shot through him. Was Margot two-timing him? She and the mystery man disappeared from view and by the time Laverne opened her eyes back up, Herman was boiling mad and couldn't contain it.

"Is everything alright, Mr. Glüber?"

"I said call me Herman."

"Is everything alright, Herman?"

"It's fine. Let's get this thing underway."

"Before I start to deal, is there anything that you want to get out of this reading? Anything in particular that you would like me to focus on?"

"What do you mean?"

"Well, many people are looking for guidance with their careers or their relationships. They may have questions about love or are wondering about people that they may be in love with," Laverne winked at Herman and his eyes bulged as he sat frozen, trying to conceal his thoughts. Was she talking about Margot? "Many people are looking for help with making decisions, or going through periods of change. Is there something that is on your mind at this time?"

"I'm sorry but I'm not sure what you are asking me here."

Laverne and Herman sat quietly staring at each other across the table, waiting one another out.

"I think you have a very strong wall around you, Mr. Glü-- excuse me. Herman."

"What's that supposed to mean?"

"I'm not sure. It's very strong so it's very hard to see through. But I worry that you have become so obsessed with this wall that you have lost sight of why you built it."

"Assuming this wall actually exists, why do you think I built it?"

"I don't know, Herman. But that may be the point. Because of this wall it is hard to know you. Because of this wall, the world can not get to you and you can not get to the world. It's as though you are stuck inside and everyone else is stuck outside. I realize that you have many interactions with people. But there is like a big black hole where tenderness should be. Do you know this word? *Tenderness*. Does it feel the same to you?"

"I thought you were a fortune teller, not some kind of hack therapist." Herman was on the defensive, particularly because Margot had specifically requested more of this *tenderness* in their relationship and he treated her like she was speaking in tongues. "Just turn a card over already."

Laverne kept eyeing him for a moment and then she relented and peeled the top card off of the deck and laid it down.

Herman glowered at it.

It was the Devil.

Lupita's Dog

During her moon, Lupita often had a hard time. The heavy flow, accompanied by cramps, was so bad that all she could do was lie on her side in a fetal position like a baby and try to pay attention to the television. She had cold sweats, an uneasy belly, and wasn't sure why she was watching what she was watching. From the icon in the lower left-hand corner of the screen she could see that it was the finals of the NCAA field hockey tournament. The plaid-skirted Demon Deacons from Wake Forest had a tenuous one goal lead over the pig-tailed (and also plaid-skirted) Clemson Tigers. There were four minutes left in the match and the Tigers seemed to have all the momentum. She reached for the plastic-lined garbage receptacle and threw up a little bit of the orange juice that she'd been sipping. When she stopped retching, she rested her forehead on the back of her hand and stared at the TV. Why was she bothering with a bunch of white girls chasing a ball around a grassy field, their movements restricted by having to hunch over and keep two hands on a little club. Qué juego tonto.

Her mind kept going back to the meeting, back to that pathetic performance of hers. What was supposed to be a chance to give a voice to a big, hard-working family that had no voice, devolved into a dull side-note that was nothing but a waste of time.

The Frenzels had been good to the migrant workers at Summerwood Farms, but they had an old-world aloofness to them and left their staff and their orchard unprotected. It was vital to get the relationship with the new ownership off to a good start. And what had she accomplished? She didn't get Herman or his buddies to sign the agreement that she brought. She didn't even know what happened to the document with everyone's signatures. They whisked it away to a back room and forgot about it entirely. Even she forgot about it. Well, she didn't exactly forget about it but she did forget to ask for it back. What was she going to say when she got back home? She failed.

Herman, the local guy who was supposedly about to move out to Peshastin to start running the orchard. He was a hoax. She was sure of it. He had barely acknowledged her during the meeting and avoided her eyes the entire time. He had reasons to be awkward in front of her, after she had so blatantly rejected his advances back in Leavenworth. He had definitely told her things that weren't true. How many things? That was the question. In some ways she kind of liked him. The truth was that she was sad. And horny. And if Herman had knocked on the door of her shitty motel room just then she would have invited him in just to see where things went.

Lupita was sick, and bored. Then she was cramping again and running to the toilet. After that she felt better. For the past couple of hours, the nausea had been coming in waves. Suddenly it was gone. Her belly relaxed at last, and her temperature came down to normal. She drank a glass of cool water. Her head didn't hurt anymore. And her blurry vision cleared up. In an instant she shifted from being repulsed by the thought of food into being ravenously hungry. So hungry in fact that every type of food that came to mind turned into a powerful craving and she had to stop herself before senselessly using what little money she had to buy potato chips and candy from the vending machine in the motel's parking lot, which gleamed underneath a billboard advertising a marijuana dispensary. She told herself to slow down, and that she could probably afford to go out for a cheap dinner, but first she had to get into the bath. She found a grimy rubber stopper and started filling up the shallow tub with hot water.

While the tub filled, she picked up the remote control and switched over from the post-game comments after the field hockey match—Clemson had come back and won—to a music station that was airing a documentary about Madonna. Lupita danced around the room to a performance of "Like A Virgin" from the Fox Theater in 1988, while peeling her clothes off and tossing them onto the bed. Her singing was a little behind the lyrics. She didn't really know the song.

She did a naked leg kick and the hiccup with Madonna but she didn't sing the chorus because her phone lit up with a picture of her cousin Rosalie's eyebrow piercing.

"Hola Rosie."

"I'm glad you're feeling better," Rosalie was known amongst her own people as a bruja, the Frenzels called her a clairvoyant. A traveling new age scholar once labeled her an empath. To Lupita, she was just a very intuitive cousin from which she couldn't hide a thing.

"I've only been feeling better for like five minutes."

"I know. I was waiting to call. I hate talking to you when you're all depressed."

"I wish you were here."

"I wish I was there too. Fuck. I never get to go anywhere. How did your presentation go? It flopped didn't it? Still, at least you got to go to the city for a couple of days."

"So far on my trip to the city, Rosalie, all I've done is look like a stupid puta in front of a bunch of rude businessmen. It doesn't feel like a vacation."

"I'd probably take it I'm so goddamned bored. Tell me about Herman. How was it when you saw him?"

"There's like nothing to tell, Rosie. I wouldn't exactly say he acted like he'd never met me. But he didn't pay any attention to me. He might have told me to 'speak up' once."

"What an asshole. Qué típico. Tries to sleep with you and then no se recuerdo que tu existes."

"It doesn't matter, Rosie."

"Pinche cabrón."

"Si, lo es," Lupita closed her eyes for a moment and let it all just float away.

"Y que pasó con los Frenzels? No, les importamos?"

"They make it seem like they do care, Rosie. They buy into all the crazy promises about stuff that the businessmen are going to do once the deal goes through but those guys could easily be lying. They've got all sorts of lawyers. It doesn't make any sense that Herman would want to move out to the orchard. Not when you see him here. He's different. He's really a city guy. I don't get the feeling that he cares about any of the things that he says that he cares about. I think that he just cares about money. Que va a pasar, Rosie? You're the one who always knows this kind of shit. Are they going to cut the trees down? I can't even tell." Lupita laid back on the bed and stared at the ceiling. Rosalie was quiet as well. "And at this point the papers have all been signed. The orchard doesn't even belong to the Frenzels anymore. Herman and his buddies can do whatever they want with it. I feel so bad, Rosie. I feel like this is all my fault. Maybe if I had slept with that asshole none of this would have happened. Qué puta. Arruiné todo."

"No arruinaste nada, prima. Todavia no lo esta terminado."

"Que dices?"

"Que hay esparanza. Yo no creo que nada ha terminado. Tengas que pelear, prima. Tienes hambre, no?"

"What does me being hungry have to do with anything?"

"No se puede hace nada con hambre."

"Si, tengo hambre! Quiero ir al mercado para dulces y sal. Quiero puerco. Quiero helado. Quiero comer y despues quiero acostarme in esta cama deprimida para una semana."

"No lo hagas, Lupita! Escuchamé. Yo se que has sufrido mal suerte. Pero todo va a cambiar pronto, te prometo. Asi que no te quedas en el cuarto asi."

"Y dondé voy, Rosie? Tengo veinte dolares y poca gasolina."

"Tienes bastante. Escuchamé, prima. Tengas que buscar una casa de bistec."

"A steakhouse? Did you not just hear me, Rosie? I have twenty bucks. What am I supposed to eat at a steakhouse? La sopa? Pan libre con mantequilla? They wouldn't even let me through the door with the clothes that I have with me." Lupita got up from the bed and sat down in a vinyl chair beside the barred window that opened only about three inches. The air coming through the gap tasted different. There was a weighty tang that hadn't been there before. The scent had been so foreign for so long that it took her a moment to recognize it as rain. The one window that the room had looked out at an aquarium supply shop and the western sky, but she avoided getting close to it. She was still naked and didn't want to give anyone a glimpse. The sun was low and it was still bright and hot but the temperature and the barometer had to both be falling quickly. When she looked up it was as though the sky had been separated into two halves. One half was the tranquil blue color that had marked the end of every day for almost as long as anyone in Washington could remember. The other half of the sky was a mass of vivid pink and gray clouds, dark, and quite beautiful with the sun's rays bouncing off its monstrous underbelly. The clouds were also laden with water, coming in low, and covering the city like a lid.

"Prima, todavía estas?"

"Si, estoy aquí."

"I know you brought the nice black Lulu yoga top. Just wear that with your Guess jeans."

"You want me to go out looking for a fancy steakhouse, on a Friday night, wearing jeans and a yoga shirt?"

"You're in Seattle, Lupita, not New York City. No one will care. And you need to wear your boots. Not the flip flops. You've got a lot of walking to do."

"What exactly are you trying to talk me into here, Rosie?" Lupita had picked up a bottle of screw-top Merlot at the convenience store the day before. She was finally feeling well enough to have some and poured a third of the bottle into a paper cup and had a sip. It was sour and needed to breathe for a few minutes to be drinkable.

"No estoy segura, prima. But something is happening and someone needs your help. It might be the Frenzels. And your relationship with Herman is not over. Maybe you should call him."

"I don't even know his number, Rosie. He gave me one when we met but it turned out to be the office line. I called it once and got his secretary; she didn't even put me through to him."

"You need to go find him then."

"Rosie, Herman Glüber isn't the man for me."

"No, he isn't. But you still have to go and find him."

"Even though he isn't the man for me, I have to peel my bitchy, crampy, yucky ass out of a room that I at least have to myself, with a television that I can watch whatever I want on, take a bath, and then go out looking for him at a steakhouse, when I only have twenty bucks. That's what you're telling me to do? Did you have some vision of Herman buying me dinner? If he wanted to take me to dinner, he easily could have invited me when I saw him earlier."

"I don't have any vision of Herman buying you dinner. I agree that he is a scoundrel. He is not the man for you."

"Are you sure?"

"Yes. There is another man for you."

"Un otro hombre? Que buenas noticias. What does this other man look like, Rosie?"

"No se. Pero tiene un buen perro."

"A dog? Now you want me to go out looking for Herman Glüber, and a man with a dog."

"Yes. Go have fun. And save the orchard."

"Sabes que va a lluviar?"

"Si, you're going to need an umbrella."

"I actually have one in the trunk. Is it raining over there?"

"Ya no. Pienso mañana." Just then the television came back to life all on its own and an advertisement for a mattress with adjustable firmness settings started blaring across the room. Lupita stood rooted to the shag carpet floor, the phone pressed to her ear and her eyes bulging out. "Que pasa, prima? Alguien esta?"

"No. The television just came on by itself. I must have stepped on the remote or something," Lupita's words trailed off. Her explanation was thwarted by the fact that the remote control was in plain view, still on the nightstand where she had left it. She lunged for it so that she could at least turn the volume down but the power snapped off again before she could reach it. Rosalie was quiet on the other end of the line.

"Que pasó?"

"Something is on the television?"

"Que dices, Lupita? There's always something on the television. Forget about it."

"No, Rosie, I'm mean there's something *on* the television, like, crawling across the screen. Yuck! There's like twenty of them."

"De que estas hablando, Lupita?"

"Dios mio. Son insectos.

Volkswagen Buses

Every vehicle traveling east over Interstate 90 was outpacing the lime green Volkswagen bus that puttered its way up the pass at a steady fifty-two miles-per-hour. That was just fine with the driver, Saint Stephen Rheese. The 1700 cc motor had just been rebuilt and was purring nicely. Saint was driving barefoot, and keeping a rather obsessive eye on the oil temperature gauge. It was a steady climb in third gear up to the summit, and it was hard to keep an air-cooled engine cool when the air temperature was pushing triple digits east of the pass. Saint's bloodhound, Moe, was sitting shotgun and painting the driver with his hot breath.

The back of the bus was loaded with blue duffels that were full of one-hundred-twelve pounds of vacuum-sealed bags of fresh marijuana. There was also a carton of extracted products like shatter and hash oil cartridges. Even though marijuana was legal to produce in Washington, the haul in Saint's bus was produced under the radar and ultimately bound for the east coast or Texas where it was worth a whole lot more money. His job was to get it all to his contact in Seattle, pick up the loot, and bring it back over the hill to Kettle Falls. What happened to it after that he didn't much care.

It had been a long time since Saint had been on a run. And even though he had promised himself that he would play it safe on the drive, he loved smoking weed in the van. He grabbed a chubby joint that he had pre-rolled and left in the ashtray in case he changed his mind and lit it up with the tall flame of a dollar store lighter. Saint drove as well or better high than he did when he was sober so there wasn't much risk, and because the VW bus was only capable of speeding in school zones. Saint took a long drag to get the joint going and exhaled a big plume of white smoke into the already pungent interior of the van. If the cops pulled him over with this load, being stoned would be the least of his problems.

Despite being sealed up the weed stank, in a good way. It was a new hybridized variety called El Diablo that hadn't even hit the streets yet. One of the parent strains was famous locally: a G-13 hybrid developed in the early nineties by students in the botany department at the University of Washington, known colloquially as the UW or Graybud by those who knew it well—because the white frost that caked the dark green of the plant's leaves made the nuggets appear gray. At the time it tested as having the highest THC content ever recorded, twenty-one percent, a figure that got blown away in the past couple of decades as hobbyists and professionals continued tweaking marijuana's genetics in their hermetically sealed indoor laboratories. Every once in a while, Saint and his buddies would have a reverent moment of silence in honor of the godparents of kind bud, Ronald and Nancy Reagan. If they hadn't clamped down on outdoor production with those 'Greensweeps,' pot smokers might still be stuck with lightweight ditch weed instead of taking the show indoors to see what the plant could really do. Uncontrollable variables suddenly became highly manipulable variables. The other parent strain of the El Diablo was actually brought up from Mexico. It was the pride of a hot shot teenager known as Jardinero, who smuggled the seeds—as well as himself—over the border in a cargo box on the roof of an SUV with Texas plates. He called it Oaxaca-96. The cross was mind-blowing, like kryptonite covered in snowflakes. Saint took another long pull off of the joint and coughed so hard when he exhaled the expansive smoke that his eyes watered. Then the dog released a poisonous air biscuit.

"Jesus fucking Christ, Moe," said Saint while he tried to roll the windows down and then realized they already were down. "Fuckin' A it's hot." A sign said that it was only three more miles to Snoqualmie Pass and Saint gave the dashboard an encouraging pat. "Come on, girl," he said. He glanced into the side view mirror and noticed a police vehicle approaching quickly from behind. It lingered behind the bus for a moment—maybe running the license plates—and then pulled right up alongside. Saint kept the Joint down by his legs, hoping the officers wouldn't see the smoke wafting up. There were two cops in the car, both in aviator sunglasses. After a moment the one in the passenger seat gave Saint a thumbs up, but with a questioning look on his face. Saint—not wanting to raise the joint up to where the cops could see it, took his hand off the wheel and gave them a thumbs up with a big grin and the cops sped off up the hill in front of him.

It was really hot. The joint that was burning in Saint's hand was damp from finger sweat and stuck to his lips when he smoked it. The heat was on so that it would take some of the hot air out of the engine compartment and keep the new motor happy. Once Saint got the bus to the top, he'd be able to take it out of gear and let the engine cool as it coasted down. The oil thermostat was climbing steadily up from one-hundred-sixty-five degrees. The red zone began at one-eighty. One-ninety was certain to blow gaskets. Saint had his iPhone propped up beside the speedometer and he saw the screen light up with a text from his buddy Colin.

How's the bus running?

Saint Stephen always considered it to be bad luck, or at the very least rude to discuss the bus while it was in earshot. He wouldn't do that to a person and he liked his VW bus better than he liked most people. It had more personality than most people. It was forty-five-years old. It had the benefit of experience. Having just acquired a heavy buzz, and being already unreasonably superstitious about his bus, he wound up putting a lot of thought into whether or not he should answer the message. Colin knew that the most recent engine rebuild happened under precarious circumstances. But he should also have known not to ask Saint Stephen about it while he was on the road. What the fuck was the matter with his friend? Had he lost his mind? Was he trying to make him paranoid? Because that was what was happening.

The engine rebuild was done just outside of Spokane by a suspect mechanic whose name was Classified. Which isn't to say that some people with security clearance knew it and others deemed less trustworthy did not. The mechanic's hippy parents actually named him Classified in a attempt to be funny. Classified Panky was on the dude's birth certificate and he wore that name like a badge of honor. His garage was surrounded in scrapped cars. The inside of it was part hoarder's den, part saw mill, and part auto repair. There were heaps of greasy tools and a rusty lift operated with a hand crank. The only organized feature of the space was an Ikea shelving system with a chronological arrangement of every issue of the porno rag Plumpers since it was first released in 1979. Saint got stuck with Classified cause Classified was a friend of Gretta's. And Gretta was the one who fronted Saint all of the weed inside the van. She was kind of generous that way, but failing to return with her money could be lethal. The last person who stiffed her wound up cross-eyed and limping on a foot turned ninety degrees the wrong way.

"Aw, fuck it," said Saint. He took a quick glance at the oil temperature gauge and it registered somewhere that the needle was climbing but his brain—now under the spell of El Diablo—juxtaposed it with the speedometer and he chalked it up as good news. He was picking up speed. Except he wasn't picking up speed. Most of the way up the hill from Ellensburg he had maintained that steady fifty-two miles-per-hour. The bus had decelerated to thirty-five and it was struggling to stay there. A pair of cyclists were pedaling their way up toward the summit. Saint overtook them so slowly it was as though he was on an only slightly faster bike. He gave them a friendly wave and they looked back at him with that kind of vile disgust that bikers reserve for people who rely on gasoline engines. The guy in the front actually shouted something at Saint but he couldn't hear what it was over the music and the hum of the engine. Truthfully, the engine was no longer humming. The noises that it was making were more polyrhythmic at that point but still not really alarming enough to attract attention. Saint took another drag and held the smoke in his lungs while he laid the spliff in the ashtray, gripped the steering wheel with his knobby knees, and picked up the phone to respond. When he exhaled the van filled up with smoke. Visibility was temporarily short and Saint forgot that he was even driving.

Good almost at top of pass

Saint fired the text off, put the phone down, and picked the joint back up.

The little air-cooled motor was fighting hard for every foot of elevation. And with every foot the sky got more beautiful. All afternoon it had been the color of a western scrub jay. As the bus got closer to the summit, the sunset and the horizon came into view and shot the blue sky through with oranges and golds; but there were also grays, violets, and colors that were close to black. The sun and stars had traded off the sky for so long that what Saint was looking at appeared like a mythical creature that had been spoken about but not seen for thousands of years: clouds. The top half of the sun was still visible above the lowland forest, but barely. Above it loomed an angry looking expanse of cumulus and the air got instantly cooler. To Saint's left he could see the idle chair-lifts that serviced the Central Summit ski slopes in the winter. The slots of grass between the trees were all brown and the tips of the branches of the parched forest sagged in an unnatural way. The engine whined a little less and an odd smell started getting into Saint's nose. It wasn't the weed. He looked at the dog, who barked at him.

"Sorry, Moe," he said. "I shouldn't blame everything on you. That doesn't smell like a dog fart, I know." Funny thing was that Saint Stephen didn't remember seeing any clouds to the east but when he looked in the side view mirror there was a similar nasty plume swallowing up everything that he could see. Cars and trucks were literally disappearing into a billowing white mass and he thought that he could make out the sound of horns starting to blare from inside of the cloud. The road bikers—presumably still pedaling up the shoulder— were invisible. "That's fucking weird," he said to the dog.

Then the phone screen lit up with another message from Colin.

Cool bro once you're over the pass you're home free

Saint smiled at the message. But when he reached for the phone so that he could reply his eye caught the reading on the oil temperature thermostat and this time he read it right. The needle was pinned all the way over. Two-hundred-fifty degrees or more. He had the pedal all the way down but he was losing power.

"Home free my ass," he said, as the smoke thickened inside the bus and the bloodhound—with his ultra-sensitive nose—- sought shelter from the smoke by Saint's feet. Luckily the bus had already crested the pass.

Saint turned the key to the off position and let it start to coast down the mountain. "Fuck, fuck, fuck," he shouted to Moe. "I don't deserve this. Not now."

Saint was only making the drive to help his mom out of a jam. She lived in Leavenworth and had been working as the head receptionist at Summerwood Farms for more than two decades, since just after her husband died in an avalanche trying to do a winter crossing of the Pickett Range in North Cascades National Park. Her name was Dolly Rheese and she and her husband Dave—before he froze to death—were huge fans of the Grateful Dead. That's how Saint Stephen wound up with his name. He was conceived in the parking lot outside of a concert, at some point after a show in 1987. Dolly could remember that the Dead played 'Saint Stephen,' that night. She could just never remember what city the show was in. Saint had a sister, six years younger than he, named Althea. A few years back Althea got married to a wind prospecting thug from Moses Lake named Vincent, and Dolly had to remortgage her land up the Chinquapin to pay for the wedding. Even though real estate was going up, Dolly had to remortgage again to pay for the lawyer that handled Althea's divorce. Althea had to move back in with Dolly. By that time Althea had a daughter named Frances and the wind-prospecting ex-husband was belly up and drunk off his ass somewhere.

The little girl, Frances, was an adorable kid but she also had respiratory issues. She needed a very expensive operation to open up her nasal passages and Dolly took care of the insurance deductibles, was down to nothing, and she didn't know what was up with her job. The old couple that she had been working for forever were finally retiring and the orchard was about to come under new ownership. She thought that she'd be getting all kinds of overtime as the business transitioned to the new owners but Dolly had been complaining that they were non-existent and that there was suspiciously little to do. Saint was supposed to be cut in ten percent for being the mule on the pot run. He was counting on over twenty-thousand dollars he was going to give straight to Dolly, minus a few expenses.

He hoped that one day he and his sister would have their shit together enough that Dolly wouldn't have to worry about them. Maybe they could even get their shit together enough that they could take care of their mom when she got older, so she could rest and quit trying to set him up with Lupita—the smart, cute, and funny señorita that she was always going on about.

With the engine off, the billowing cloud started to dissipate and angry motorists were emerging from it and mean-mugging Saint as they passed him on the way down the hill. Many of them were yelling and flipping him off but he ignored them and kept his eyes on the center of the road. Saint kept the motor off for the most part. If there was a slight incline, he put the key in the *on* position, popped the clutch and gave it a little gas to get over the hump. There was very little compression but the oil temperature had come down enough that at least when he put it in gear it wasn't just cooking the oil right off. It was critical that he didn't wind up marooned with all the contraband on the side of the road. The bus didn't lock up that well and he was bound to draw the attention of state patrol officers soon. Saint wasn't a cop-hater like a lot of his friends were, but he did consider state patrol to be a particularly nasty breed.

The nearest town was North Bend and he decided that it was either get there or die.

He made the exit ramp while the bus was taking its last gasp. If it stopped there was no way it was going to move again. At the last possible moment, the traffic light at the bottom of the ramp switched from red to green, as though Saint's angels had flipped the switch, and he managed to nurse the bus into the back of a Safeway parking lot in second gear. The last time he shut the key off there was a loud clunk in the back, like something heavy and metal just fell off of the engine and was rattling around on the pavement. Saint cursed Classified Panky for his shoddy work but he couldn't blame him entirely. If he hadn't stopped looking at the temperature gauge he could have pulled over before the engine overheated. He slumped his head on the steering wheel and tried to come up with a plan. Moe licked his face and Saint actually managed to laugh.

"Holy shit, buddy. We made it."

Saint clipped a leash to Moe's collar and the two of them stepped out for a little fresh air.

Saint had been wearing pretty much the same outfit since the beginning of the heat wave: Sanuk flip-flops, a pair of double-front beige Carharts with the legs chopped off just below the knee, aloha-shirt completely unbuttoned, pair of polarized sunglasses either on his face or dangling from a cord around his neck, and a beat-up old Volkswagen baseball cap that said

'Drivers Wanted.' He had long brown hair that he kept pulled back into a pony tail. And even though he did a lot of hanging out and beer drinking, he was a relatively healthy eater and had always enjoyed the benefits of a high metabolism; though the love handles were beginning to set in. The familiar balmy warmth was giving way to some decidedly chilly air.

"Damn, Moe. Maybe we should've brought a sweatshirt or something."

It was true that Saint wasn't always the best prepared. In fact, it had been a much bigger issue for him over the course of the last two years, since Bonnie left him. Saint and Bonnie had been inseparable since they sat next to one another in psychology class in high school. They had this fantastic teacher named Dr. Curran, who wound up having a very profound effect on them. Dr. Curran once delivered a lecture that he called the 'Nineteen Rules for Living a Well-Adjusted Life.' The doctor was sensitive to Einstein's Theory of Relativity. Even when it came to relationships. He said that it was poor form to ask people if they were happy because to be happy required—even if this wasn't obvious to the conscious mind— that someone else be unhappy. It was therefore better to use the term well-adjusted. Saint couldn't recite the entire list but he remembered a lot of it and put it into practice as often as he could. Some of his favorites were: try to have friends of all different ages, never discuss money with people who make a lot more or a lot less than you, jealousy's ability to be unattractive is nearly lethal, people like to talk about themselves, ask people questions and pay attention to their answers, learn the art of controlled social-drinking, and become a great lover. The doctor probably could've expanded more on the last one and he once hypothesized to the class that sex is better for women than men simply because if you use a finger to scratch the inside of an itchy ear, the ear winds up feeling better than the finger. He was a little weird but highly impassioned and enthusiastic.

Bonnie got a job offer in Philadelphia after graduating from WSU and Saint just couldn't bring himself to make the move with her. He visited a few times and he didn't dislike the place. He just felt disoriented without snow-capped mountains around. The closest ocean was in the wrong direction. The Northwest was Saint's end of the rainbow. And leaving felt too much like spiting the higher powers. His trees were Douglas Firs, big Western Red Cedars, and dry-side Cottonwoods. The Columbia was his river and the craggy snow-capped ridges were his craggy snow-capped ridges. Saint couldn't leave. Not even for Bonnie. Their break-up was drawn out. Bonnie was as addicted to having Saint in her life as he was to her. Eventually enough things happened to them when they were apart to fill up some of those holes. Or at least that was true in Bonnie's case. She told him that she had a new boyfriend. That was nearly a year ago. They had only spoken once since, about an overdue utility bill.

Saint had been celibate since the breakup, not intentionally or because he wasn't attracted to other women. He was just friendly and aloof. He never wanted to take advantage of anyone and he just kind of lacked the killer instinct that guys who got laid all the time seemed to have. He was fine that way. If something happened it happened. But he wasn't going to be a slave to his libido. He didn't have to be. Maybe it was the end result of spending every waking moment of his adult life under the influence of tetrahydrocannabinols. Which was also fine. One of the only things that Saint was certain that he believed, was that marijuana was good for the world. He thought that the world would be more relaxed if more people smoked it. He also thought that the ones who already smoked it needed to learn to smoke it better. He harbored a particular resentment for the plant's association with laziness and stupidity. That was a false mythology that he blamed on the contemporaries of Cheech and Chong. To Saint, the marijuana experience was about collapsing into the present moment, and then bursting with ideas. His ideology encapsulated perfectly in the license plate frame on the back of the bus that read 'I'd Rather Be Here Now,' and almost as perfectly by the bumper sticker to the left of the plate that read 'Dog is my Co-Pilot.'

The wind shifted and the warm air was suddenly being sucked up the mountain and the temperature dropped further. Saint shivered and his belly moaned. He knew that he had a lot of shit to deal with but he couldn't really see dealing with any of it until he got some food into him and Moe. He looked at the Safeway, which had a Bank of America branch and a Starbucks inside. He looked back at the dog.

The bloodhound had been going everywhere with Saint since it was a puppy. It knew exactly what was going on and didn't like it. The inside of the bus was still smoky and it was hard to breathe. Plus, there was a murmur of starlings flitting about the parking lot that looked worthy of chasing. Saint went about rolling up the windows most of the way, leaving cracks for Moe, and getting the bus as locked up as possible. He plucked a checkbook from the glovebox and put it in his back pocket. With the driver's side door open he looked at the dog. "I've got to figure out a way to get us out of this," said Saint.

The CEO

Fruit from backyard citrus trees and a whole bunch of other random crap was stuffed into a cardboard box that had been wrapped in about a quarter mile of duct tape. The box was sitting underneath the marble console in the entranceway to the luxury high rise condominium where Duncan Klevit lived alone in the penthouse. The box was from his grandmother Mabel. She sent it up to him from her place in Florida. Besides the fruit, there was a letter in an envelope which he decided not to read. Mostly Mabel just rambled on about conspiracy theories, UFO's and the plight of her pet chickens and Duncan wasn't in the mood. It had been too long a week. There was a plastic pink flamingo in the box, a coffee-table book with photos of orchids, a ceramic mug decorated with drawings of brightly-colored thongs, a pair of lemon-yellow bathing trunks, a white linen fedora with an alligator skin band just above the brim, a pair of alligator skin boots, and a matching alligator skin belt. The boots were ugly, but his size at least. And no doubt fashioned by Mabel's new husband, the Cuban airboat captain and hack-cobbler, Joubert Cleophat.

Duncan was raised by Mabel and even though he'd have been lost without her, he always thought of her the way he thought of everyone else: as being in his way. The familial association came with some embarrassing side-effects that he was often at a loss for how to process. She'd always been kind of a floozy. But the older she got the more it seemed to ramp up. To the point that he was forced to consider his grandmother to be an octogenarian slut. It seemed like just yesterday that she was married to that squat Texan who had lost all ten of his fingers in a mining accident. Duncan couldn't remember his exact name, only that everyone called him Palmer. The two of them used to have a business that rented dune buggies somewhere outside of Houston. But all of his toys were trashed in the big flood. What the fuck ever happened to him?

He closed the box up and deposited his wallet, keys and phone into a blown glass bowl that he kept on the console. Odd, he thought, that his phone hadn't rung for a while. Duncan had been expecting to hear from the escrow firm that the sales numbers were recorded. It was getting late on a Friday. It should've happened already. It was possible that the message came through and that no one at the office thought to share the information with him. In that case someone would have to be fired. He cracked his knuckles and wondered if he should worry or start making some calls about it. He decided instead that everything was fine, and that being in close proximity to Mabel's package had nudged him along through some foggy terrain, past the point where healthy concern morphs into unhealthy paranoia.

Duncan went into the bedroom with its glass wall overlooking the Puget Sound and swapped out his work clothes for a velour Puma warm-up. He was a big fan of basketball, especially college basketball. He made the team at Arizona, which was a near impossible feat for an un-recruited player. He was mostly known as a scrappy forward and a good defender who was seldom brought in off the bench, but as a senior he finally started knocking down consistent three-pointers and averaged about fifteen minutes of floor time per game. He sunk a buzzer beater against UCLA on their way to a Pac Ten title. He was also part of a colossal defensive collapse when the team lost to Santa Clara in the first round of the NCAA Tournament.

He sat down on the couch with a cold Stella Artois and threw his feet up on the suede ottoman. It was an energetic twilight with strong gusts of wind. A pillar of gold stretched across the choppy surface of the water toward the setting sun. Silhouettes of cranes that offloaded cargo at the port looked like a herd of brontosaurus on the move. Shipping barges, ferry boats, and smaller sailing vessels were sounding their horns as their paths crossed, racing to their harbors. A small pod of killer whales wiggled its way north just below the surface and Duncan saw one of them breech. For the first time in forever it looked like a storm was coming in.

He turned on the television for a little bit of low-maintenance company. A White House spokesperson was on, mounting a convoluted defense of the flagging attempt to build a border wall, which had been renamed a trellis, since construction was halted by a circuit court judge after only a two-hundred-foot stretch had been raised in East Texas. A stretch that was quickly overtaken by bougainvillea. He flipped through the channels and landed on a basketball game on ESPN Classic. They were replaying the NCAA Championship game from 1986, when Never Nervous Pervis Ellison and Louisville beat Duke. It was late in the fourth quarter and Coach Krzyzewski called a time-out and the show cut to a commercial for a psychic hotline. The psychic's name was written across the bottom of the screen, Madame Laverne Korzha de las Bulgarias. Along with phone number and a flashing banner that said 'First Minute Free.' Madame Korzha had an endearing European accent and she looked like she might have come from old world mystics but she had a drawn-out face and her feathered black hair was too perfect to be real. And there was something about her throat. Something decidedly not feminine. "Looks more like Mr. Korzha to me," said Duncan. The commercial morphed to a diptych or split screen, one side showed the psychic sitting behind a wooden desk with a phone on it, the other side showed a woman seated on a print love seat in a midwestern looking living room, complete with diaphanous white curtains and shelves lined with little league baseball trophies. The woman looked like she probably had some kind of disease or affliction for every letter of the alphabet. After listening to a little of what the caller had to say, the camera angle switched to a bird's eye view of the psychic dealing from a deck of tarot cards and interpreting their meaning in a very general sense. Her enhanced pale cleavage looked like it was moonlit. Back to the diptych: a look of relief washed over the caller's face as the banner *$4.95/minute* scrolled across the bottom of the screen. Almost three-hundred an hour, he thought. Not bad. In the final few seconds of the commercial the camera panned out to show the psychic's storefront and Duncan swore it looked like a block that he recognized. The kook was set up in Seattle. It was a revelation that gave Duncan something like an idea that was more accurately described as an urge. He couldn't stop thinking about that neck of hers. There was something strange about it, and that he wanted to probe it for the presence of an Adam's Apple with the sharp end of his necropsy knife. The television psychic, Madame Laverne Korzha de las Bulgarias, was a little high-profile in comparison to the victims that he tended to go for, but if he waited for the right moment that shouldn't matter. It was already a foregone conclusion. When he thought about capturing her and removing her head, his penis began to stiffen. Imagining the encounter brought him to a swift and disappointing climax and he cursed himself and resolved to do better later on. His normally unshakeable self-confidence waned slightly as he walked to the bathroom to clean himself up. Hoping he didn't get any on the velour, bemoaning his inability to control his phallus.

To the staff at Cronkey, Mitchell and Wolfe, Duncan was a very mysterious figure. He was known for being cut-throat and he was able to justify it by adhering to an almost incomprehensible standard of professionalism. No one there knew anything about his private life, could claim him as a friend, or knew what kind of family he came from. No one ever saw him eat or drink anything. He certainly didn't smoke. He never got a cold, went on vacation, stunk up the john, or repeated himself during a meeting. He was a solitary man. Mostly. He did occasionally crave company. And unfortunately for his company, Duncan needed them to be dead.

The coffee table in front of him had a mirrored surface and there was a secret button on the underside of it. Duncan pressed the button and the surface slid forward and gave access to a velvet-lined compartment that contained a silver box. He had to twist the body of a gilded snake counter-clockwise, and then enter a six-digit code to release the locking mechanism. Inside of it there was a human skull.

Duncan never had a second thought about missing out on a career as a veterinarian. Though he retained a psychotic loyalty to the success of his first real business venture back when he was an intern, when he made himself some seed money by chopping off heads. To him the universe looked like patterns repeating themselves on different planes. What his firm had done that day felt to him very much like the decapitation of an animal, or a human, and it was going to work the same way that the industry of trafficking body parts did. It cost money to keep something alive. But once something was dead, its components acquired value, and the maintenance costs evaporated. It was how he was going to make big money off of Summerwood Farms, by cutting off its head. And then cutting up everything else; selling every single piece for as much as the market would bear. It was satisfying to him and on some level he felt like he was restoring a crucial balance that held things together. But it wasn't the kind of visceral satisfaction that came from sinking his knife into a soft throat, and hinging the head backward.

Duncan leapt up to fetch his humming cell phone from where he'd left it on the console. It was one of the members of his banking team, Benjamin Plotnick.

"Ben."

"Duncan, we have a problem."

"No one has called to tell me that the sale numbers have been recorded."

"Because they haven't."

"Why not, Ben?" Duncan kept his words steady and slow even though his temper was flaring.

"The documents never made it over to escrow. Something happened to the bike messenger. He was struck by a vehicle. It's pretty serious. I don't know if the kid is going to make it."

"To escrow?"

"Duncan, the kid might be dead."

"The bike messenger is not our problem. Where are the documents that he was carrying?"

"At this point we have no idea. Escrow called us when they were getting ready to close to say that the sale documents never got to the office. And the messenger service couldn't get the kid to pick up his phone. We had Linus, since he always rides his bike to work, ride over to escrow. You know, trace the route, see if he could figure something out. And that's when he saw the emergency crews and the kid laid out on the pavement."

"Did he ask anybody where the bag was?"

"He tried asking the cops but they weren't really having it. He said he didn't see the kid's bag laying around anywhere."

"What about the car that hit him? Maybe that driver picked it up."

"Doubtful. It was a hit and run."

"Jesus Christ, Ben. It was downtown on a Friday afternoon at rush hour. How the hell was there a hit and run?"

"Yeah, I know. It's all over Twitter right now. The vehicle that hit the biker was one of those rolling billboards that you see. It was for the energy drink company called RocketFuel."

"What happened to the driver?"

"Abandoned the car and took off running."

"Shit. Did you call Herman? Where the fuck is Herman?"

"We've been calling him like every ten minutes but he isn't picking up. Not sure where he is. Any ideas, Duncan?"

"What about Loven? Did you try him? He and Herman are probably together."

"I'll call him right away."

"You know what, Ben. I'll call Loven. Fuck. What else did escrow say?"

"Escrow's done for the week. Buttoned up and left half an hour ago."

"Make sure someone stays at the office."

Duncan put the phone down and massaged his temples. He could feel something burning in the center of his head, like an evil seed that had just split open and begun to grow. Duncan was fated to live forever alone because of the extraordinary intensity of his control issues. It had been a while since something slipped from his grasp and left him feeling the need to impose his will over other human beings. This wasn't the result of someone clever getting a leg up on him. The situation with the missing sales documents was the product of base human stupidity and ineptitude.

The universe felt off balance.

Something had to happen.

It had been years since Duncan had taken a victim. The last time, in fact, he was still living on the east coast. Her name— odd that he actually remembered—was Doris. She was a member of the longshoreman's union and had just pulled into the Port of Newark after a seven-month leave. He met her in a bar in Hoboken, left after a single drink, and then tailed her later on in a black panel van. When she entered a deserted alley behind Rector St. he jumped out of the van and injected an intramuscular sedative cocktail into her gluteus and then forced her into the van through the open sliding door. She was inebriated and disoriented but still a longshoreman and during the scuffle, while the drug was still dispersing through her capillary system, she managed to fold two of Duncan's fingers backwards and snap them. Which so enraged him that he actually killed her by bludgeoning her skull against the floor of the van before the drug even came close to rendering her unconscious. It wasn't his preferred style. He tended to like things to be cleaner than that.

He wrapped Doris's corpse in a blanket and drove the body back through the Lincoln Tunnel and to a warehouse in Brooklyn that he leased under the name of a dummy corporation with no ties to him personally. It was a two-thousand square foot space with a garage door so that you could pull in and unload cargo without anyone watching. The space was formerly occupied by a sculptor who had gone mad, and then bankrupt. A three-ton block of Italian marble that the artist had begun carving into the likeness of a giant cane toad was still anchoring a corner of the space. When his dummy company took over the lease, they agreed to taking on the responsibility of selling it or having it moved but he had never gotten around to it.

A lever served by a piece of three-quarter inch metal conduit turned on a bank of halogen lights that hovered over a stainless-steel table. On the table he would put a layer of clear plastic to make the clean-up easier and then he would lay the bodies out and secure them at the shoulders, waist, and ankles with trucker straps. Duncan wasn't into torture. Normally he made it to the table with his victims still alive and unconscious. He would finish them off by hooking their feet and hands up to a marine battery that put out seventy-two volts of cranking power. It was enough to stop their hearts in a matter of seconds. Then he would move on to trying to slake that unquenchable thirst that he developed in veterinary school in Arizona. He would use the same custom-made necropsy knife that he owned for many years to disarticulate the head. More often than not, he wound up fully erect and capable of masturbating as the souls of his victims leaked out through their open throats.

The bodies were of no interest to Duncan but he did have to get rid of them. His preferred method was to cut the corpse into manageable-sized pieces, place them in plastic garbage cans and cover the bodies with lye. A process that was made possible by the five-hundred CFM exhaust fan that the sculptor had installed. If anyone ever asked, he would just say that he was making soap. No one ever did.

He would trim all of the soft tissue that was easy to access off of the skull. What was left got dropped into a large cauldron to boil while he went and poured the toxic remains of the bodies into a concrete pipe that led to the Hudson River. It took a couple of hours to boil the head clean and the smell of it was like tomato soup. It made him hungry. Once all the brain matter and the skin were dissolved, he would dry off the white bones that remained and let his fingers caress the forehead and slip into the eye sockets, penetrating the hollow cavity behind. He liked the teeth without the distraction of the lips. He liked the mouth without the vile tongue lying in it. He wasn't drawn toward things that were squishy or warm. He preferred them cold, ossified, and smooth. It put his mind at ease.

Despite not having taken a victim since moving to Seattle, he was prepared. Mostly he went back and forth between his condo, the basketball court, Arnüd's French Bakery, and the Smith Tower. But he had also procured an industrial space on W. Marginal Way, just a bit south of the West Seattle Bridge. It was a stone's throw from the perfect place to get rid of his victim's bodies, the Duwamish River. It had everything that he required already inside. There was a new stainless-steel table, straps, a fresh battery and leads, good lighting, garbage bins, lye, and a sound system. Duncan liked to listen to classical music while he worked. Not having christened the space hadn't mattered to him so far, he was fine just knowing that it was there.

Just knowing that it was there was fast becoming insufficient. He needed to bring the space to life, with death.

He needed to kill the psychic.

Tarot

Glimpsing Margot on the arm of another man right before seeing the Devil card had made Herman a little fidgety, he ran his fingers through his heavily moisturized curls, causing them to appear matted, dry, and fluffy. It was something that he had mostly trained himself never to do but it was also a nervous twitch. A few deep breaths after that he started to recover his poise and his bullishness as he sat through the explanation of the meaning of the card.

"You see how that the Devil is drawn on the face of the card? He is alone, and in a position of dominance with the respect to the man and the woman who are shown here with no clothes on, and in chains. But there is also a lot of trickery that isn't immediately obvious here. The Devil is petty, and overly addicted to the material world. The naked couple only looks happy because they are deceived by the Devil's promises. They are like he is, drunk off of their quest for base desires. It is interesting to me to think about how one develops into having the Devil come up as their central card. It suggests to me that there was some sort of powerful influence over you when you were a boy. I don't believe that you were born to be devilish, Mr. Glü—Herman. I believe that you were talked into it by someone. Someone who misled you by telling you that you were always right. Do you have twin?"

"What do you mean do I have *twin*? Like a twin brother?"

"Yes, something like this."

"You are a terrible fortune teller. No, I don't have a twin."

"Hmm," Laverne looked like she almost didn't believe him. "That's odd," she said. "I can see someone intersecting with your life. He is close to your age and totally different than you, but complimentary. I expect you would get along. Are you expecting any visitors? Like someone from across the mountains," she squinted like she was trying to bring something into focus. "Someone with a dog."

"A dog?" Herman didn't want any hair on his suit. "No way."

"Then you must have been an only child. And this voice that influenced you, it must have been one of your parents. Since you are young boy, I think that this was most likely then your mother. Tell me, Herman, are you only child?"

"If you throw enough spaghetti at a wall, eventually something will stick. Yes, I'm an only child. I also, as you have accurately predicted, had a mother. Let's move this thing along, okay. I don't want to be here all night."

Laverne obliged and started dealing out the cards quickly. When she was done, the arrangement looked like the following: The Star card was laid over top and perpendicular to the Devil. Moving around the Devil in a clockwise direction, there was the Emperor, the Eight of Wands (upside down), the Queen of Wands, and the Three of Pentacles. There were four cards in a row to Herman's right of the cross. Starting at Herman and moving toward Laverne, the were the Fool, Death, the Knight of Swords, and at the top of the row was the Seven of Pentacles.

"What is it now?" he asked with a bit of his own showmanship, sensing the drama again and assuming that since it was all part of an act that he might as well play along with it.

"I suggest that you pay careful attention to this reading, Mr. Glü—Herman. The first two cards are from the major arcana. If nothing else, this indicates that there are many forces at work here that are beyond your control. Major changes await you."

"What kind of changes?"

"Big life changes. Spiritual changes. The kinds that you would never predict. I see someone you look up to turning into a monster. And there is someone else as well. Someone you dislike but for no good reasons. I think this person is going to save you."

"Save me how? Am I gonna become a Hare Krishna, you think? Should I get the boys to come over here so we can all sing Kumbaya?"

"I can see that you think that this is funny, Mr. Glü— Herman. So far, I am not myself finding things in this reading to be laughing about. This second card is your opposing factor."

"She's my opposing factor? She looks pretty harmless to me."

"It is not her job to harm you. Her job is to be beautiful, complete, pure, and honest. The woman on the face of the Star card is content. And the reason that she is content is because her life has meaning and I think that this is the essence of what opposes you. This search for meaning. I feel like your successes have been mostly, how you say, like on the top of the water?"

"The surface?"

"Like this, yes. On the surface. Covering your wall, like wallpaper. This may have something to do with the wall that is around you."

"There's no wall around me."

"But you're so defensive about it. I think that you have deceived yourself into thinking that the wall protects you. Instead you are held back."

"Held back? That's a good one, *sveetheart*. If this is what you want to call held back, then I'll take it. Do you have any idea what kind of a week I've had? Just this afternoon I closed a deal that is going to make me more money than most of the idiots in this bar will make all year." Laverne shook her head back and forth, clearly negating something that he was saying. "Let me guess," said Herman, feeling like he was getting the hang of the schtick with the fortune teller, "there is a *pwoblem* with the deal?" he said while laughing, and mocking Laverne's accent.

"There is a problem with the deal," she said.

"Bullshit," said Herman, but without the intensity he was looking for. They did gamble on sending the docs to escrow with the bike messenger but the numbers had to have been recorded by then. It was after six o'clock. True, he hadn't heard any confirmation from the office yet. But they probably did call. He just hadn't looked at his phone in a while. He wanted desperately to look at it and confirm that everything was fine. At the same time, he was concerned that doing so would somehow validate Laverne's prediction, or at the very least make it look as though he was actually falling for her crap.

"If it makes you feel better, Mr. Glü—excuse me. Herman. You may check the messages on your phone now."

"Why? There's no point. Everything is fine."

"If you don't look now it will be nagging at you for the rest of the reading. Better just to have a look." Herman seized his phone like a rabid maniac and began furiously scrolling through all of the missed texts and calls.

"I'm only doing this to show you proof that the deal that we signed today is all buttoned up, and that your fortune telling skills could use a little refining." Herman saw that he had missed six phone calls from the office and one from Duncan. "Shit," he said before he could stop himself. "I need to take a break for a minute and make a couple of calls."

Herman started to stand up and he was suddenly slapped hard across the face by a female hand that did not belong to Laverne. It was a serious blow from a trained martial artist using the knife edge of her hand and he saw stars and was temporarily disconnected from his surroundings. He fell back into the chair, shook his head back and forth a few times and looked up at his attacker. It was a stripper from Kittens Cabaret that he had stood up for lunch earlier in the summer, her name was Jazzmin.

"Fuck you, Herman," Jazzmin said. Then she snatched his phone from his hand, plopped it into the pint of beer that he was drinking, and then poured the entire contents of the glass onto Herman's lap. "Careful, sister," Jazzmin said to Laverne, although she seemed to be reconsidering the word *sister,* at the same time she was using it. "He's a real asshole." Jazzmin was in a short emerald green dress, had a purse hanging from her neck by a tiny silver string, and was extremely well-balanced on her high-heeled shoes. Petit as she was, she still seemed to loom over the table as Herman groped around on the floor for his phone. "I'd say that you need to learn to take what comes your way in this life, sister. But I think you already know that." Then she did an erotic spin and slid away, taking the arm of a man with thick eyebrows who was undoubtedly about to part with a princely sum for some quality time with her. Herman picked his phone up. It was completely dead.

"Shit," he said looking at it. He was suddenly confused. He wanted to maintain his arrogance but six calls from the office and one form the boss were hard to push out of his mind. There were texts too. At least one from Duncan telling him to call right away. He thought about grabbing Loven or Dmitri and getting them to see what the hell was happening. But they were deeply engaged in conversation with a couple of paralegals that they had met a few weeks ago. Loven had his tie around his brow like a headband and was proposing some kind of cockamamy toast in gringo Spanish. All four of them had shots of tequila they were about to throw back. Herman couldn't have them making calls to the boss in their condition. If there was a problem, Duncan would be furious with all of them.

"There's nothing that you can do about it now," said Laverne.

Herman was torn. He told himself that Duncan was most likely just calling to congratulate him. He called the cocktail waitress over and borrowed a bunch of napkins to mop up the beer in his lap and ordered another round of drinks for himself and Laverne. "Just tell me about the rest of the cards."

"This card," she was pointing to the Queen of Wands, "represents your unconscious influences. This, I believe, is your mother."

"Why?"

"Do you see the sunflower that she is holding? It always turns toward the light. That is because this influence is hopeful, or maybe, how do you say, optimistic. Even if it is sometimes misguided. Was your mother smothering or, suffocating or something like this?"

Herman didn't like the feeling of being psychoanalyzed by an Eastern European kook, even if she did have a sexy pair of legs. He had a flash fantasy of the two of them getting back to his apartment later and behaving like some kind of ancient, eight-limbed pleasure monster. Once the fantasy evaporated, he was left with a weird and undeniable feeling. He actually wanted to talk about his mother. He did have an intense relationship with her and no one had ever asked him about it. He was overrun by a stew of emotions that he was unaccustomed to. He choked and fought back tears with muscles that he wasn't used to using. One tear slipped out from the corner of his eye, rolled down his cheek and fell onto the Queen of Wands. Laverne smiled.

"There you are," she said.

"What?" said Herman, impatient and irritated. Something inside of him seemed to have just been unlocked. Things were being let out and he couldn't control them.

"I can see you now."

"I've been sitting here the whole time."

"I'm talking about your wall, Herman. Some bricks have fallen out. I can see through it now."

Herman had to use the sleeve of his jacket to dry his eyes. He took a deep breath and tried to get back to being condescending and mean. It was a struggle. What she was saying about his mother, even though it wasn't much, was true. She smothered him. His dad ran a hardwood floor refinishing company and was always at work. His mother devoted herself to raising Herman completely. She took him to and from school every day of his life. Or at least until he was sixteen when he got his Camaro. She was his tutor, and she was his biggest fan whenever he was out on the ice. Hockey was a big part of Herman's childhood for a long time. Every single early morning practice and every single long road trip for a game, his mother was there. Standing in the bleachers with her earmuffs on. Cheering. On the ride home she always told him that he was the best player out there. After he did well on an exam, she always told him that he was the smartest student in the school. It wouldn't be that far from the truth to say that Herman's mother spent his entire childhood blowing up his ego like a balloon. Young Herman learned to crave his mother's approval and he let his opinion of himself be influenced by her opinion of him. He grew up sort of thinking that they were the only two people in the world that mattered. Fuck, he suddenly thought. How long had it even been since he had phoned her?

Herman, self-absorbed as he tended to be, assumed that without him to take care of that his mother would settle into a ho-hum life on the couch waiting for him to visit or call. But to his astonishment that wasn't the case. His father died unexpectedly after falling from the roof, and Herman's mother started tapping into their savings and spending it on big experiences. With some of the girlfriends that she found playing mahjong, she went to France and Greece. He wasn't even sure where she was. He had a vague recollection of her telling him that she was making a summer trip up to Banff. But the summer was over.

He stared to think Laverne was reading his mind. The feeling was so intense that he wasn't even sure if he was thinking or saying things out loud.

"The next card is about your past," she said. And the word *past* was like a bittersweet dagger to the heart.

Herman normally hated dwelling in the past. Now he was stuck there and he didn't really want to leave; even the embarrassing way that his mom used to brush his hair when he was a kid felt endearing.

"It is the Three of Pentacles and it normally signals a job well done," said Laverne, looking disappointed.

"Finally," said Herman. "Something that makes sense."

"I suppose it makes sense. Normally this is a very positive card."

"Are you trying to tell me that it isn't positive now?"

"It worries me only because this card appears in the past. If it were your present or in your future it would be different. What I think that it means, Herman, is that you will have to find way to let go of all that. You must find new way."

"A new way to what?"

"Just a new way. Maybe for everything. I think your life, Herman, is about to begin again. I know that it can be frightening. I know that transitions are hard. But you can take what you have learned in your previous life and let it help you in the future. Do you want to have children, Herman?"

"Hell no."

"Is a shame. I am thinking that you would make a very good dad." Herman just stared back at her as though he was accused of having a tail. "The next card tells us something about your future, but not your certain future, just a potential future. In the Emperor I see the differences between how you are seen and how you see yourself. Your version of yourself is much like the Emperor that we see on the card here. The Emperor is practical and authoritative. His upward pointing scepter is a symbol of his aspirations. And the rams that flank his throne remind us that his dominance has been acquired through war."

Herman was leaning on his elbows and looking at this card in more detail than the ones that came before. He needed it. So far during this reading he had seen his sort-of girlfriend out on the arm of another man, realized that he missed urgent calls regarding work, had his cell phone destroyed and his pants soaked by a stripper that he had made the mistake of disrespecting, and had the inner workings of his relationship with his mother exposed.

"It is very important now, Herman, to understand what lessons are contained in this card. Even though the Emperor is warlike and aggressive, he possesses also a calm maturity that is the essence of how he retains his kingdom. He is responsible, and logical. The Emperor adheres to a set of ethical standards that is very high. I think that this is what this card is really telling you to do. You need to determine what is right and what is wrong. And after you do that you become like the Emperor, practical and logical. I think that if you can do this, though it will be very hard, that everything will be okay. I see that your loyalty lies in the wrong place. You are looking up to the wrong person. Maybe someone who is not good. Or maybe is just the money. Herman, please listen to me. There are many things that are more important than money. The Emperor is wealthy, Herman, but not because he takes advantage his people. The Emperor is wealthy because he cares."

"I care."

"Yes, Herman. You care. The truth is that we all care. It is impossible not to care at all. Even caring about nothing is caring about something."

"You really are a woo woo."

"What is a woo woo?"

"It just means a new-agey nut job like yourself. I'm sure that most of your friends qualify."

"This is not my country, Herman. Sadly, I do not have friends."

"Maybe I could be your friend. I think that you should reconsider having dinner with me tonight." Laverne smiled and then averted her eyes from Herman's.

"Thank you again for the offer, Herman. I can not eat dinner with you tonight."

"But you'll be here tomorrow?"

"I will try, Herman," she didn't seem annoyed, just sad.

"I thought we had a deal," pragmatic as Herman's little plan was, it was clearly making Laverne uncomfortable to discuss it.

"The next card describes your future. But not your distant future. It's about the immediate future. It is about what will happen next. You've got the Eight of Wands in this position but for some reason it is upside down, which is a bit terrifying, or at least it may be for a little while. The spears that are normally headed for the sky are headed for the ground. You will need to dodge them to make it through this night."

Herman was getting used to the extreme and sudden predictions of massive change and calamity. The fear factor, if there ever was one, was wearing off.

"This thing about the Eight of Wands being upside down," asked Herman, "is that something that you learned early in fortune-telling school, or was that part of the advanced curriculum?"

"This is not funny, Herman. This is very serious."

"It doesn't look serious."

"I wonder what your opinion will be in a few hours, she paused, "I recommend you keep your friends by you tonight. You may need their help."

Herman was already squeamish about being anyone's official friend and acquiescing to the idea that he might need anyone's help was laughable. He rolled his eyes and then flicked his fingers in such a way as to indicate that he was about at the point of blowing the whole reading off.

"You just ran back behind your wall."

"Stop with the wall, already. What's the next card about? Please tell me that we are close to done here."

"The next card is at the bottom of the staff. The staff is the masculine portion of the spread and it is to designed to balance out the female portion."

"We could sure use some of that right now, wouldn't you agree?"

"No. I don't agree. I think that this has been a very masculine reading so far," her voice was gravelly and down an octave. The shift freaked Herman out.

"Who the fuck are you?"

"What difference does it make right now who I am, Herman? These are your cards. I didn't choose them."

"What's the card at the bottom of the staff mean?"

"It's your self-image."

"It's a fool."

"What were you expecting?"

"Something more regal."

"But the cards have a sense of humor," she pointed out with a smile. Herman wasn't laughing. "The Fool card is never so bad as it seems, Herman. Sometimes it is good to be the fool."

"I don't see myself as a fool. This is garbage."

"What is garbage?"

"All of this. It's nonsense. I can't believe that I am still sitting here listening to it."

"You don't need to go back to building your wall just because you drew the Fool card. Look at what the Fool does. He steps off of the cliff. Not because he is an idiot who has no idea that he is walking straight into his doom, but because he has faith. Faith means letting go, Herman. And it is the exact opposite of belief, which means to hold on. Look at how his face is turned up. The Fool has a close relationship with God. He is not absurd or moronic. He is special. He is chosen. In this way I think that we can understand why the card is here. You see yourself as special. You think that you are chosen. And the cards seem to agree that this is true. The question is: what were you chosen for? This, I think that you do not yet know. This, I think, is what you need to find out."

"What's with the dog?"

"I am glad that you ask this. The dog is a very important feature of the Fool card. The dog follows the fool with the same blind faith that the fool puts in God. I think it means that people will follow you, Herman. This is why your responsibility is very great. But there is also something else here that is very important."

"And that is?"

"The dog."

"I thought that we just talked about the dog."

"Yes. But then I was talking about the metaphorical meaning of the dog. I also see an actual dog. Do you have a dog?"

"No. I don't have a dog. I don't like dogs."

"Are you sure?"

"That I don't like dogs?"

"That you don't have a dog."

"Is that a serious question? Is something the matter with you?"

"Maybe you should get a dog."

"You want me to be a dad, and get a dog. This is starting to feel like one of those speed dates. Are you sizing me up as marriage material? Cause you're gonna be disappointed if that's the case."

"I don't agree. Somewhere in there is a good husband for someone, and a dad. And I also think that you might enjoy having a dog more than you think. The wall around you, it is quite possible that a dog might fail to notice it. Dogs are very intelligent this way. It is also possible that you won't feel the need to keep a dog on the other side of the wall. A dog might help you take the wall down. The twin that you say you don't have, he is also close to his mother. And I believe that he has a dog. I also can see that he takes good care of his dog and that his dog takes good care of him. I see your twin as having very little money. But at the same time, he is richer than you. It may be that he is richer than you because of the dog."

"Hypnotism isn't going to work on me."

"Did you know that people with dogs live an average of ten years longer than people without dogs?"

"What kind of psychic leans on statistics? Do people with two dogs live an average of twenty years longer than people without dogs? I think you've stumbled onto something big here. Better keep our voices down."

"You like to take serious matters and present them as jokes."

"I can see what you're trying to line up here. You're trying to plant this crazy idea in my head that I would be so much better off if I had a dog. Then tomorrow, some dude who looks my age and vaguely like me is going to come around trying to talk me out of a thousand bucks in exchange for some flea-ridden mutt and you think that I'm going to jump at it because of this fucking reading. No chance, *sveetheart.* I don't fall for this kind of crap. I never do. But I will admit to admiring your persistence. I can see how you might have a lot of sway over weaker-minded people. If you are interested in getting out of this kind of low-level scamming and getting yourself a real job, we should talk. People like you are convincing."

"What kind of person am I?"

"You keep it up. And that's what always winds up convincing people. If they don't believe what you're telling them just keep telling them. Eventually they'll come around. I've seen it happen a million times."

"You are talking about people falling for your lies. Am I wrong?"

"What difference does it even make? I didn't think that was even a part of the conversation that we are having. You are dealing in lies here yourself."

"I'm not dealing in anything, Herman. And the cards do not tell lies."

"Oh wait, I'm a fool, who can't get anything done. What do I know? What's the next card about? The way I see the world?"

"Not a bad guess, Herman. The next card is about the environment. It is about things that are external to you. It is representative of the things that you can not control." She sat still and let Herman absorb her words. They could both see the face of the card she was referring to. It was Death. Herman shifted in his seat and tried to look away but he failed. True fear spread through him but was gone as soon as it arrived. It was ugly and stank. The stink lingered.

"There is your regal king, Herman." He stared at the card. There was a lot happening and it was hard to take in. "The Death card is given the number thirteen."

"These things are marked," said Herman, trying to discredit the legitimacy of the deal.

"You do not have to be afraid of the Death card, Herman."

"I'm not afraid. I just think this is bullshit is all."

"Death is like the Fool. Easy to misinterpret. Death does signal change. And as I told you before, people are always afraid of change. Death can mean different things to different people. This is why we have four faces on the Death card. So, we can see how the different characters look at death. Tell me, Herman. Are you afraid to die?"

The question rocked Herman as much as having to think about his mother. Death was one of those topics that he avoided. Sure, he was aware of the inevitability of it. His dad had died and he had to go through the whole business of picking out a coffin for him with his distraught mother and finding a plot in a Tacoma graveyard where they could stick him in the ground. But he didn't let himself really feel the loss. He didn't exactly ignore it either. He circumvented death's abstraction by filling up his mind with other stuff to think about. It occurred to him, maybe for the first time, that he was almost always engaged in some amount of looking ahead. He had very few moments in which he bathed in the *here and now,* or felt content. It got him wondering what contentment even meant. Did other people experience it? Contentment and happiness. They weren't the kinds of things that made for good conversation at bars or cocktail parties. Being forced to define the terms also meant being forced to ascertain whether a person was doing what it took to attain them. And usually they weren't. He found it suddenly odd how something like happiness, as a topic, had such a profound ability to steer thoughts to such dark places. While he was thinking about it, something very strange happened.

The lights flickered and then one of those bugs, just like the ones that were crawling across his computer monitor earlier, fell from the ceiling and landed on top of the Death card. It was on its back, with six feet desperately grasping for a purchase they could never get. Like a turtle that had been flipped over onto its shell. It had fuzzy amber-colored chest hair and its back end was comprised of six horizontal segments that were white and gray. It had piercing and sucking mouth parts that were moving wildly, ready to devour anything that its little bug teeth could latch onto. Between the two horns on its head was a blue spark that extinguished after a moment.

Then it died.

*   *   *

"I just need to get it together before my Parkour class," said Loven, right before throwing back a shot of Johnnie Walker. He was unafraid to mix all sorts of liquor in his belly.

"When's that?" asked Bev Houghton. She and her pal Clare Sobedecki were the two paralegals from the Houghton Group that Loven and Dmitri were drinking with. They were both single and liked to party. Neither was particularly attractive but they were fun and friendly. It was well known that Loven was happily married and the girls never crossed the line with him. Dmitri had allegedly taken Clare home one night last spring but there were several bottles of Wild Turkey involved and no one had a clear idea of what really happened that night.

"It's not until Sunday afternoon at 5:30. But I've got to be fully hydrated and ready to work hard. It's pretty intense."

"Parkour is for sissies who've been ostracized from the skateparks," said Clare. She liked to needle Loven.

"It is not," Loven was getting ruddy-faced. Despite his endurance and enthusiasm when it came to intoxicating himself, he had an allergy to something but he wasn't sure what it was. The result was an excess of red blood cells surging through the vascular system in his face, affecting his color. "It's the perfect intersection of strength, explosiveness, agility, creativity, and concentration. And on top of that, it's minimalistic. It was the first form of recreation."

"According to who?" asked Dmitri.

"What else could it have been?" Loven shot back. He sounded like he was wasted and nearly in need of being ushered home. "Cave men could Parkour in their bare feet. I know they didn't call it Parkour. It probably had some name that sounded more like grunts and clicks but they were doing it. I know it."

"How do you know it?"

"Because it's in my blood," Loven's phone started buzzing in his pocket and he fished it out to have a look at who was calling him. It was Duncan, calling from his personal cell phone number. Not something that happened very often. Loven excused himself again to the narrow hallway in front of the bathroom to pick up the call. "Hello," he said, doing a terrible job of trying to be sober.

"Loven. It's Duncan."

"What's up, boss?"

"Is Herman with you?"

" ... "

"Loven?" Duncan shouted.

"Yeah, boss?"

"Are you drunk?"

"No, boss."

"You sound like you are sloshed. I'm looking for Herman. Is he with you?"

"Umm. He's here. But he's a little busy right now."

"With what?"

"The famous Madame Laverne Korzha de las Bulgarias is reading his tarot cards."

"Loven, I am warning you. This is not a good time to be playing games. We have a serious situation on our hands and I need you to get your fucking head together. We've been calling Herman all afternoon and he isn't picking up his phone."

"What's the situation, boss?" The mention of the situation, whatever it was, sent a bolt of adrenaline through Loven that helped him straighten his head out.

"I'd rather talk with Herman. What the hell is he doing, Loven? If he's busy hitting on a woman I need you to interrupt him and put him on the phone."

"I, umm...I wasn't kidding, boss. He's getting his tarot cards read."

"His what?"

"His tarot cards. We met this woman who's on the television. She's got a phone number or a hotline or something where people call her up and she reads their fortunes or some shit but we just met her at the bar. She was kind of fucking with Herman and now she's reading his fortune. They're here. You want me to go get him?"

"What did you say her name was?"

"Madame Laverne Korzha de las Bulgarias is her made-up name. She's a wacko but she seems like she's good at what she does. She's been reading Herman's cards for a while now."

"I think I saw one of her commercials today during a basketball game."

"It's possible."

"Tall and thin, with long black hair? Accent like she's from Romania or something?"

"That's her."

"I thought that she was in drag," Duncan said. Loven stood spying on Laverne from the hallway near the bathrooms. He had to pin himself to the wall to let a man pass who had just come out of the men's room adjusting his belt.

"Holy shit, Duncan. I think you're right. I don't know how I missed that."

"You mean Herman doesn't know?"

"I don't think he knows. He *was* hitting on her. Should I go get him?"

"Yeah, go tell him to call me right now. We need his help getting out of a jam."

"What happened?"

"The documents from the sale this afternoon never made it to escrow."

"I thought that Benny took them."

"Benny was in a hit and run accident after he left the office today. He's in critical condition in the hospital, and the messenger bag that he was carrying the documents in has vanished into thin air."

"Holy fuck. What do you want us to do, boss? Should we go look around somewhere?"

"I'll get somebody else on that."

"Do the Frenzels know?"

"They do. I need Herman to keep them calm."

"What's the plan?"

"Have Herman call me. Do not let him leave with the fortune teller, Loven."

"I won't."

"And don't get too drunk for fuck's sake. I'm going to need you guys this weekend. Tomorrow we are supposed to be firing the staff of a company we don't even own."

"I understand, boss."

Duncan ended the call.

*   *   *

"This is an omen," Laverne said.

"What kind of an omen."

"In many cases the Death card just means change. But sometimes it means something more literal."

"Like what?"

"Like death. Someone is going to die."

"Are you telling me I am going to die now? That's a little intense. Don't you think?"

"It may not be you, Herman."

"Who else could it be?"

"Me."

"You?"

"I am a part of this reading, Herman. Perhaps it is a good thing. After death comes new life."

"So now you're saying that you are going to die?"

"It is not certain. I think that it will be either you or me."

"One of the two of us is going to die? When?"

"Very soon. I think this night."

"'I'll give you one thing, Laverne, or whoever you are. You aren't shy about your predictions." If Herman were being truthful, he would have had to admit to being a little bit afraid for his own safety.

"I see a baby being born."

"Is one of us going to have a baby tonight as well?" As quickly as Herman had shifted toward considering the possibility of his own imminent demise, he shifted back to feeling like the reading was steeped in the whimsical and nothing more.

The waitress finally showed back up at the table with a fresh beer for Herman and another vodka for Laverne.

"That took long enough," said Herman.

"Sorry, we are slammed right now."

"You think you'd be as slammed if people knew how filthy this bar is? Look at what just fell onto our table from the ceiling?" Herman pointed at the bug.

"Cool," said the waitress. "Are you having your tarot cards read?"

"No, I'm getting my car waxed. What the hell does it look like we are doing?"

"My mom always warned me about people who answer questions with questions. She said that they are hard to communicate with."

"Just get this bug out of here before I call the health department."

"I'm sorry, sir," she said as she leaned over the table and gently plucked the bug's body off of the Death card with her fingers. Her tone was a little patronizing. "I'm sure it was just a random bug. Might have to do with how hot it's been lately. Poor guy was probably just looking for somewhere to get away from it and found his way in here. Is there anything else I can bring you two?"

"We're fine," said Herman, shooing her away. "Anything else you want to tell me about the Death card?" Herman drank half of the pint of Manny's he ordered in one big glug. It tasted fantastic. He was amazed at how much he needed that drink of beer. It calmed his nerves. Laverne didn't mess around when she drank. She picked up her glass of vodka and tipped her head back as she poured it into her mouth. Herman watched her throat as she swallowed the liquor and there was something horribly disturbing about it but he couldn't exactly pinpoint what it was. He was a businessman, not a biologist. Whatever it was, it wasn't exactly sexy. She was starting to remind him a little of Gene Simmons from Kiss and he cringed the next time he looked at her. She smiled and it pissed him off.

"One of the things that this card is telling you to do, Herman, is to stop resisting things out of habit. You need to let more influences into your life. And not just influences that are your own age. You need to let the wisdom of the young and the elderly into your life." Just the suggestion creeped Herman out. He didn't like babies because they were needy and gross. He didn't like older kids cause they either talked too much or were too hard to relate to. And old people, those he really tried to avoid thinking about. Probably because they served as a constant reminder of what was coming up next: decrepitude. Couples like the Frenzels, they were on their way out. And it wasn't worth letting them bog all the time down. It seemed more efficient to Herman to just get them out of the way so that the younger generation could get on with running the planet. But then again, he was going to have to come to terms with getting older at some point. Maybe even some point soon. As

Herman followed that train of thought it started occurring to him that he was terrified of death and that the admission led to his being able to see across a whole other dimension. He saw everything that he had ever done and would do, moments strung together across time. He had been ignoring the passage of time and had left himself totally exposed and vulnerable to the merciless power of it. He was losing his connections to the past. He felt completely unmoved by what he saw. And he was sowing very few seeds that would exist in the future.

Herman had some art, some money, and a nice car. It dawned on him then that Margot was trying to do something that there weren't many people queuing up to do. Which was to try and love him. It had never before occurred to him to let her. He could even consider loving her back. It was all so terrifying. And Laverne must have been able to see the terror. She actually smiled at it.

"I can see you again, Herman."

He knew what she meant and he didn't egg her on. If he wanted, he could develop his relationship with Margot in ways that he had never considered before. They could go steady, or whatever the adult equivalent of that was. Not marriage. Something a little less intense. But still, along those lines.

"On the face of the card we can see how the different characters confront death. Your skeletal king is up on his horse and his expression is sullen. His status is bound to earthly things, like his power. And he is afraid because death robs him of all that he has. The skeletal king confronts death poorly, but I sense there is something about the horse that he is riding that is pertinent to your reading. I'm not sure what it is. Do you know someone who goes by the name of 'Horse?'"

"I sure don't," said Herman without giving it much thought. The truth is that he did.

"Hmm," Laverne didn't look convinced. "The priest is in communion with God. Instead of fearing death he welcomes it like a friend long expected. The young woman turns her head away. She too is afraid, but also sad. She knows enough to know that death comes to her at the most bitter of times. Before she was allowed to fully develop into someone or something that can accept death gracefully. But she accepts it nonetheless, implying a maturity beyond her years. The child is naive. He doesn't even know what death is. He gives it flowers. It would be best if we could all view death like the child does. Only the child knows how to steal the trauma from death. And this is how it should be. Death always brings new life and change. And that those changes are often positive is confirmed by the shining golden sun."

Herman closed his eyes. He was tired. It had been a long week but that wasn't it. Since starting the reading, he had been saddled with an unexpected avalanche of thoughts and emotions to sort out. He could barely process any more. He was still thinking about his mother. He was worried about the status of the deal to buy the orchard, he was wondering about this alter ego of his with the dog, he was second guessing the meaning of success and happiness and wondering if he was successful or just the butt of an elaborate joke that he'd been playing on himself. And he was definitely under the reader's spell. He could barely fight it any longer. There were two more cards and the thought of learning what they meant was exhausting. But his whole identity, at least in his mind, hinged on his ability to get to the end of things. It was how he closed so many deals. It was how he got to the top of Annapurna. It was how he finished the triathlon and how he sank the eagle putt at Pebble Beach. It was his trademark: finishing.

"The Knight of Swords.," said Laverne, with a turn toward the upbeat. "This is a good card. It is in the position in which you look for guidance, or something that has been overlooked. The knight comes dressed in blue, because he is emotional and sensitive. Things that you are not letting yourself be. Even though, Herman, it is my opinion that you want to be more emotional and sensitive than you currently are. The knight is coming to help you, I think. The knight is dreamy, caring, and loving. The knight will not be fooled by the wall that surrounds you. The knight will see through."

"Am I expecting this knight to be a man?"

"It is hard to say. I am feeling the knight more like a presence coming into your life. And this presence may be embodied in one person or several people. Possibly too from a dog. If I was you, I would be looking, not so much for a person who is like a knight, but anyone or anything that is trying to help you. I am afraid that if you reject the help that is being offered to you, that things will not go well. But if you are wise enough to recognize it and to accept it, that you will soon be arriving at that place that you are trying to get to."

"What's the last card about?" Herman asked.

"The last card will tell us how things will turn out, Herman. But that discussion will need to wait."

"Why?"

"Because now we have to go."

There was the sound of something being smashed as a woman standing nearby let go of a martini glass, and then a deafening shrill. "Something just fucking bit me!" She was screaming because another one of the bugs had fallen from the ceiling and landed in her auburn bob. And then another fell on her shoulder and she screamed again. The consistent screaming was followed by a shower of sparks.

The televisions started cutting in and out for a few moments while the ceiling lights flickered. It was as though the inside of The New Luck Toy had turned into a strobe lit rave.

Then the power shut down completely.

A ceiling panel fell onto the bar, scattering glass about and soiling Jordan's well.

Some of the happy hour crowd retreated underneath the tables with their drinks.

Everyone else started running for the door.

What it Takes to Survive

Having the bus legally parked between two parallel white lines at the back end of the Safeway parking lot was such a relief that Saint wished he could light one up and blaze in the van with Moe before shopping, even if it was noxious inside. But it wasn't possible. It was a Friday night and the store was busy. Everyone seemed to know that rain was blowing in because there was a sense of urgency amongst the shoppers, who were wheeling their buggies out to their cars with hasty footsteps and heads slung low. Like they all had a destination to race to before it was too late. Saint had places to be but he wasn't going to be getting to them. At least not soon. He scanned the parking lot and there were no vehicles like his. It was mostly full of mid-sized SUV's and lifted pick-up trucks covered in dirt. No one around here was going to be able to help him with the bus. And even if someone could it wouldn't matter anyway. He didn't need something minor like a fuel pump. He needed another complete engine rebuild. It would take weeks, at best. He needed another car and had a brief fantasy about being a more complete type of criminal, the kind that is always decisive, authoritative, and packing an intimidating weapon. He would simply take his 44 magnum out from inside of his aloha shirt, point it at the head of a tech nerd out fetching Advil in his wife's minivan, and then watch as his hostage transferred the contraband from the bus to the minivan with the smell of loose stool wafting out of the back of his trousers. After which Saint would either leave the man behind, kidnap him, or kill him. It really didn't matter. The important thing was that he would be back on his way to the city with the weed in a very small amount of time. This wasn't the type of plan that suited a person like Saint. He was squeamish about confrontation, had a natural aversion to hurting people, and he'd never in his life held a gun, much less fired one. The person most likely to end up with poop in their pants was him.

Saint didn't know anyone who lived in the city and his contact was a guy that he'd never met before and Saint was pretty sure the dude didn't have a car. The obvious solution was to rent something. With a rented car Saint could get back on the road in a safe vehicle and still deliver. He'd be late, but he could still deliver. The problem with this idea was coming up with the requisite documentation and funds to procure the car. Saint was pretty strapped. There was a lone ten-dollar bill in his wallet. His bank account had something in it. He couldn't remember exactly how much. But he knew it was less than a hundred bucks. Saint also carried a Mastercard with a two-thousand-dollar limit but he wasn't sure what the balance stood at. Since he knew that he couldn't pay it off he didn't let himself look, he just paid the minimum charge and got on with his life. He thought about whether or not there might be enough room on the card to fit the rental car fees and the security deposit. It was hard to know. If there was it would be close.

It was a lot to think about and the poor air quality inside of the bus had rendered Saint lightheaded and confused. Plus, he was starting to get a headache and his mouth was so dry that he couldn't have conjured up a drop of spit. Neither him or Moe had eaten since around noon. Since they were stranded in the lot of a grocery store, they at least had good access to food. The problem, once again, was money.

Saint thought about calling Dolly for a loan and then decided immediately against it. This trip was supposed to be about helping his mom out of a jam. It would have been better to get thrown in jail than to have to call his mom up and tell her that he is just another dysfunctional adult that she needs to burden herself with taking care of. Fuck that. He had another option. It wasn't a great option. But it was at least an option.

Saint had grabbed an old checkbook from the glovebox that had been riding around in there for at least a decade. Maybe more. There were a few checks still in it that were tied to an account that Saint had closed a long time ago, after a brief period that he spent doing construction in Missoula, Montana. Saint had to leave Moe in the toxic van. "Sorry buddy," he said to the loyal dog as he stepped outside. "I'll be as quick as I can." Saint turned and looked back at the bus as he was walking away. The air had gotten thick and moist. Visibility was diminishing and the light from a lamp in the midst of the parking lot was reflecting off of the smoke that was still pouring out of the engine compartment and encapsulating the vehicle. Moe crawled up onto the driver's seat and draped his head over the steering wheel.

The banking branch inside of the Safeway was closed but he just wanted to use the ATM machine anyhow. He had a little trick in mind for picking up some extra cash in the short term. It wasn't exactly a trick. It was more like a totally stupid thing to do that was going to come back and haunt him. But it did have the potential to keep him afloat for one more night. The first thing he checked after swiping his bank card was the balance. He wasn't sure what it was because he really didn't use the card much. Difficult as it was to pull off, Saint still conducted nearly one hundred percent of his affairs in cash. He never got comfortable with the idea that people could track him and profile him based on an analysis of the things that he purchased. They would know where he was and when. Just using the ATM that night cemented his presence in North Bend at precisely 7:32 in the evening. It was a dangerous but necessary thing to do. His balance was seventy-seven-dollars. Better than he was expecting by about thirty bucks. Which felt like making money. It didn't take the pressure completely off but it helped. Next Saint wrote himself a two-hundred-dollar check from the defunct back account in Montana and deposited it in the ATM. He knew that the bank would make a hundred available for immediate withdraw. By the time the check bounced early the following week Saint would be swimming in money and he could easily bring the balance up above zero. It worked. And in a few moments Saint was receiving one-hundred-sixty cash dollars from the machine that only dispersed denominations of twenty.

Flush with the money, he loitered around the front of the store—doing some of what passes for research in the modern era—on Google. There were three rental car agencies in town but they were all closed for the night. Hertz and the Enterprise both seemed too corporate for Saint. He brought up the page for a smaller outfit called Rent-A-Wreck. They advertised cars starting under fifty bucks per day. He'd take his shot with them when they opened.

Since he wasn't going to be able to get out of North Bend until the morning at least he was going to need to stretch his money to cover a shitty motel. There wasn't any space to sleep inside of the van. He searched 'shitty motels' and found a few that might work. He'd make the calls after shopping. As well as the call to the dealer in Seattle who was expecting him any moment with the weed.

He started lollygagging up and down the aisles, pushing a plastic shopping cart with a stuck front wheel. He didn't have anything particular in mind other than something for the dog and enough for himself to survive on. Saint was a vegetarian. In the produce section he picked up a few pounds of carrots and some very late season Rainier cherries that were on special. He picked up a tub of sun-dried tomato humus, a fresh mozzarella sandwich (bumping up against the expiration date), a bag of Tim's Cascade Jalapeño potato chips, a pint of Cherry

Garcia ice cream, a tray of Fig Newman's, two large bottles of Arrogant Bastard Ale from the Stone Brewery in San Diego, a twenty-five pound bag of inexpensive large-breed dog food, and a nylon donut for Moe to chew on. The he remembered something critical. The shampoo bottle in his shower had been empty forever. He swung by the hair care aisle and picked up a large bottle of Vidal Sassoon that was on sale. He would have to lug it around for a while until he got home but at least he would have it. Before checking out he second guessed his beer choice and went back to the cooler to switch out one of the Bastards for something more local. But he couldn't bring himself to put one back. He just added one more to his selection. It was a bottle of IPA from the Elysian Brewery and it was simply called 'Hop.' It had an alcohol content of over nine percent, and the bottles were discounted down to $6.99 so long as the shopper had a Safeway Club Card, which Saint had. He shopped there all the time.

One of the things that Saint noticed, as he waited in an endless check-stand line, was that all of the Safeway stores that he knew of were notoriously hard to get out of. They tended to have very few tills open, even during busy times. There was never any help roaming the aisles if you were having trouble tracking down the Knudsen Juices. And the folks who ran the registers and bagged the groceries seemed to have incentives built into their contracts to go as slow as possible and to have the same conversations with every customer. It was finally his turn after a heavyset man—who was showing so much ass crack that Saint had to take shelter in a current issue of People Magazine—got all of his hot dog buns and industrial-sized condiments back into the cart. Normally Saint couldn't care less about famous people but he had gotten himself invested in the week's cover story. It was People's sexiest man alive issue and there was a candid interview with the winner: the two-time academy-award-winning actor, Lucky Soul. Saint didn't want to have to spend the balance of the night wondering how the mega-star took care of his incredible skin. A fact that the interviewer kept hinting would be revealed by the end of the article. Saint added the magazine to his pile of purchases and said hello to the acne-covered teenage male drone—obviously not adhering to the film star's skin advice—that appeared to be somewhere in the middle of a thousand-hour shift behind the register. There was bagging help also but she wasn't very efficient. She was old and boney; covered in make-up that was applied with an unsteady hand. Like a poor man's Joan Rivers. She was so slow and frail that she looked like she could throw her back out lifting her tea cup. She kept her eyes fixed mostly on the ceiling as she double-bagged every single item by itself.

The last item to have scanned was the dog food. Saint had to help the kid who was working lift it up so that the belt scanner could read it. The hand held scanner with the bungee cord on it must have had a bad connection because it had a lot of electrical tape wrapped around the spot where the bungee cord connects to the gun and a small index card said 'out of order' in script that was inconsistent in size and very hard to read.

"Looks like we got some rain coming in finally," said the kid with the acne.

"Sure does," said Saint.

"Got your hatches battened down? I don't even know what that means," the kid accidentally spit on Saint while he was talking. Saint pretended not to notice even though it landed squarely on his chin.

"What do I owe you?"

"Seventy-one dollars and eighty-five cents," said the kid.

"That can't be right," said Saint. After which the two of them just stood there staring at one another while Saint felt the pressure of the deep line of people that also wanted to check out and go home. "I think that you forgot to scan my club card."

"Are you Saint Stephen Rheese?" asked the kid. Saint didn't say anything. He was thinking that it was a totally unprofessional move on his part to now have his whereabouts confirmed and time-stamped because he was trying to save himself a few dollars at a grocery store. He hoped the lapse in judgment wasn't going to come back to haunt him. "Because it looks to me like it has been scanned and your discounts have already been applied." Saint looked like he was just standing there dumbfounded but he really was trying to think quickly about what he should do next.

"Seems high," Saint said, as he extracted his wallet from his back pocket.

"Would you like to put some items back, sir?"

"No. I wouldn't like to put anything back," snapped Saint. "I just don't see how it got up over seventy dollars so fast."

"Those fancy beers you like really add up," said the kid. It's true that Saint was in the middle of spending a large percentage of the only money in the world he currently had access to. But it was also true that the money was insignificant compared to what he was going to make as soon as he made it to Seattle. With the right tilt of the head one could see Saint as having reasons to celebrate, and he really didn't appreciate the condescending tone that the pock-faced kid in the red apron was taking with him.

"They're not that fancy," said Saint, as he forked over four twenties.

Saint could barely remember what he'd even bought. Joan Rivers had separated his order and packed it into a whole landscape of white plastic bags. Saint had to cock his left forearm and start hanging all of them off of his wrist. When he had them all on his arm, he rolled the bag of dog food onto his right shoulder. It was an awkward and cumbersome load. The beer bottles were already clanking together and threatening to explode and he hadn't even walked anywhere yet.

"Do you need a cart?" asked Joan.

Saint was kind of miffed at the suggestion. He didn't see why he would have needed a cart, but he was also glad that the old lady had said something kind of friendly. "I'm fine. Thanks. But I would like to know where the Mt. Si Motel is. Do you know that place?"

"You're not one of those crazy fans of the television show, are you?"

"What show?"

"Twin Peaks."

"A little before my time."

"Ever since the new ones came out, there's been a whole 'nother wave of wackos coming through. Most of them call the motel by its other name, 'The Blue Diamond.' It's just a little north of here, where the road that you're on out there hits the road that runs along the base of the mountain."

When Saint emerged from the grocery store it was into another world. A biting gust of wind out of the north had whipped up a cyclone of fast food wrappers and it had gotten so cold that Saint could feel his balls shrinking. A thin rain was making all of the cars in the lot appear darker and cleaner. He put his bags down and the dog food in the covered alcove in front of the automatic sliding doors, took his cell phone out of his pocket, looked up the number for his contact in Seattle, and gave the dude a call. Every time Saint absentmindedly took a step backwards the doors opened up and he felt like someone was sneaking up on him.

"Jah."

"It's Gretta's friend. Saint Stephen."

"You downstairs, mon?"

"I'm not. I had some car trouble coming over the pass."

"What is it you are telling me, mon?"

"I'm not going to make it tonight. I'm broke down in North Bend. It looks like I can get a rental in the morning. Man, I'm really sorry about this." Saint was nervous and pacing around while he talked. The automatic doors opened again and Saint lost track of the conversation.

"Is she safe?"

"Is who safe?"

"Your passenger, mon."

"Yeah, she's safe. She's safe for tonight."

"Where at?"

"In a parking lot in North Bend but it's well-lit and the store's open twenty-four hours. Nobody will mess around with it."

"I don't like this. How come you not make sure that your car is in good condition?"

"I swear I did. A friend of Gretta's just rebuilt it for me before I came over here."

"Eye not know about cars, mon. Plus Eye not know you. Starting to get suspicion."

"Hey man, this sucks for me too. It's not like I was meaning to break down. I think it's going to be fine though. It looks like some of these rental agencies open pretty early. I bet I can be there by breakfast time tomorrow."

"By what time?"

"Breakfast time. Ten at the latest."

"Is too early, mon."

"Ten is too early?"

"Yes."

"How about eleven?"

"No. It is still too early, mon."

"Do you have work or something?"

"No."

"Eleven is too early because you are still going to be sleeping?"

"Yes."

"What time do you get up?"

"You can come in the midday."

"Like after noon?"

"Yes."

"Alright. Sorry about all of this. I should have been there by now. I'll see you sometime tomorrow afternoon."

"Do no disappoint, mon."

Saint put the phone back in his pocket, loaded all of the plastic bags back onto his arm, put the bag of dog food back up and onto his shoulder, and stepped out into the wet night. He had to duck his head so the wind didn't strip him of his ball cap. He skirted around the edge of a Toyota Tundra pulling a horse trailer, and then he saw something that he wished that he didn't see. There was a police cruiser parked beside his bus and two cops were circling his vehicle like they were practicing a Chinese fire drill. Saint ducked back behind the horse trailer, trembling, trying not to let his bottles clang together. And from where he was crouched downwind, he could hear the two officers talking. There was a senior officer with an expansive waistline. The other one looked young and pretty green. Even though he was red. He had thick red hair and his cheeks were spattered with a densely packed array of matching freckles. He didn't seem to know what to do with his hands so he kept moving them from his pockets to his belt.

"Stupid hippies," Saint heard the older cop say. He thought that he was sunk for sure. They were gonna lock him up and toss the key away. His best friend, Moe, was going to need to be re-homed, because he'd be dead long before Saint gets out of prison. Dolly would lose the house and end up living underneath a freeway overpass beneath route 97; only coming out to beg for change when the weather is good enough and starving the rest of the time. His sister would wind up a crack whore or worse, and her daughter a ward of the state; destined to live out the rest of her childhood being bounced between Republican leaning foster parents who don't remember her name, only the day of the month when the benefits check arrives.

Saint kept watching the two cops circling the van and looking in the windows. Moe was sitting up on the driver's seat watching the officers but he wasn't barking or acting defensive. Despite being a bloodhound, he wasn't aggressive or threatening. Moe was a lot like Saint. He was a pretty nice dog. The red-haired cop stepped up to the vent window on the passenger side door and did something that only Volkswagen enthusiasts know how to do. He swiveled the little triangular window open and then reached in through it all the way up to the armpit. Just enough to grab the lock button with the tips of his fingers and then pull it into the open position. Couple more donuts and that young cop might have had to have that arm amputated. Getting it out was a lot harder than sliding it in. When his arm was free, he opened up the door, let Moe out, and gave him a nice scratch behind the ears, telling him he was a good boy and that everything was going to be just fine.

"He seems like he's okay," said the young cop. The older one just stood there on his thick legs. There was a roll of cellulose that folded over the black belt that he had cinched up around his waist, completely cutting off access to his gun. He was in short sleeves and no hat, chewing on a toothpick. He didn't seem to notice the weather at all.

Saint did. His teeth were chattering. And he was feeling so skinny and hungry that his ribs were cold.

"We have to cite this idiot when he gets back," said the old cop. Saint stepped out from behind the horse trailer and hurried up to the officers, making a big dramatic thing out of un-hoisting the dog food from his shoulder and letting it land on the ground with a whoosh.

"Is there a problem officers?" asked Saint. They two cops stood there looking at him but Moe came right over to say hello.

"Is this your vehicle, sir?" said the younger cop. Saint didn't answer, he just nonchalantly pet the dog. Saint had an uncle that ran with the Hell's Angels who used to warn him about giving any information to cops.

"We got a dozen reports," started the old cop, "of a vehicle matching this description, being operated by a fellow matching your description, emitting smoke from the engine compartment and creating a major visibility hazard coming down off of the pass this afternoon. It's a miracle that we get to be down here saving your dog instead of on ninety with state patrol clearing a big pile up of metal and dead bodies because a tractor trailer jackknifed behind you. I thought all of these damn hippie vans were in the scrapyard by now anyway. Son, do you have any idea how much trouble you could've caused?"

"I'm sorry, sir. It wasn't a great decision, I know. I just thought that if I could get into town here that it would be so much easier to get the bus fixed."

"This is your vehicle?" Saint was cornered. He had to say it was. "Half an hour goes by, and we get another report, about a dog being locked inside of a smoking vehicle in the parking lot of the Safeway. Again, the caller described you and your vehicle. You want to tell us what's going on here, son?"

"It's nothing. I was on my way to Seattle when I started having engine trouble on the pass. It's totally broke down. I'm going to have to stay the night and deal with it tomorrow."

"You know anyone who lives around here, son?"

"I don't. I was thinking that I'd have to get a motel."

"Shame you can't sleep in the camper," said the younger cop.

"Now why's that, Arlo?" said the older cop.

"Well for one thing it would be against the law to loiter in the parking lot of the grocery store, even inside of a vehicle. But the other thing is that the inside is completely stuffed with duffel bags. What have you got in all those bags, Mr.—sorry, I didn't catch your name?" That same uncle who rode with the Hell's Angels was pretty specific about never telling cops your real name.

"Franklin," said Saint.

"Mr. Franklin? Or Franklin?"

"Franklin," said Saint.

"What's in the bags, Franklin?"

"Just clothes mostly."

"Clothes?" said the older cop. "That's a lot of clothes. Especially for a hippie."

"What were you doing in the Safeway, Franklin?" asked Arlo.

"I was shopping for food. The dog and I are hungry."

"And thirsty," said the older cop, using the toe of his patent leather shoe to draw attention to one of the bottles of Arrogant Bastard Ale that was sticking out of one of the plastic bags. "How are these fancy beers anyway? You see they don't really pay us police officers enough to drink that kind. We tend to stick with the local canned stuff like Oly and good old vitamin R."

"Do you want one?" asked Saint.

"Are you trying to bribe an officer of the law, son?"

"No. I'm not. Forget I said it. You can't have one."

"Where are you planning on drinking all of this beer at, Franklin?"

"I just said I need to get a motel room. I was thinking about the Mount Si Motel. Do you guys know that place?" Saint was trying to play it cool but he was so cold he was barely holding himself together.

"Friday night. Could be tough. Did you make a reservation?"

"I didn't. Like I said, I broke down. Wasn't quite planning on spending the night. Do you think I could leave the van here until the morning?"

"You want to abandon the vehicle?"

"No. I don't want to abandon the vehicle. I just need some time to figure out what to do with it." The two officers looked at one another but didn't say anything. It was evident that they had the power to help Saint out if they wanted to but they probably hadn't decided yet.

"Arlo," said the older cop, "why don't you give a ring over to Winnie at the motel and see if there's room for Mr. Franklin here." Then he turned back to Saint. "You know, ever since that TV show started again the motel has been pretty full."

"Is it nice?"

"Oh, it's nothing special. Probably worse because of all of the popularity the place gets from being on the show. Hasn't been updated in quite some time. And they can get away without keeping it all that clean. People will come and take rooms anyway. It's not even cheap."

"What's it run? Do you know?" Saint was hoping to hear something like thirty dollars.

"Not sure but I bet it's up to eighty or ninety. Might be a little less if you've got AAA. Are you cold?"

"A little. I'm fine."

"Why don't you put on some of the clothes from one of those duffel bags you're carrying?"

"I'm fine. I'm not really cold," at this point Saint's nuts were the size of raisins and his nipples were hard and burning. A little bit of viscous snot started to fall out of one of his nostrils.

"Does your dog get along with other dogs?"

"Moe?" said Saint. "Sure, he's real friendly." As soon as Saint said this, he realized that it was a mistake. The police cruiser that was parked beside his van had rear windows that were tinted nearly black so he had no idea if anyone or anything was back there. But there was some pretty obvious lettering on the side of the vehicle that said 'K-9 Unit. Stay back.'

"That's good," said the fat cop, "because we've got a dog in here that loves saying hello to other dogs. She's a working girl and unfortunately winds up spending most of her time in the back seat of the cruiser." He pushed on a remote-control button that was in his pocket that unlocked the rear doors. Then he opened the vehicle up and let out a tan and black German Shepherd that was big enough to take up the entire back seat. The dog had an enormous head and even though she seemed to have a gentle disposition, she flashed a lethal set of teeth. Rivulets of saliva were streaming down form her lower jaw and soaking the hair on the underside of her chin. And at least a couple of unsightly blue tumors were attached to the top of her head between the ears, there were a few more at the tops of her shoulders.

"Name's Alice. She's an old girl as you can see. Eyesight is starting to go. But that nose of hers can still smell marijuana a mile away." Saint's sphincter got so tight that it would have taken a high-powered impact drill to get in there. Alice and Moe had arranged themselves nose to butt and were swirling slowly about like a furry yin yang. "Yeah, she's still good at her job. Even though it's basically obsolete at this point."

"What do you mean?"

"Now that the marijuana is legal, she smells it in practically every car we pullover. Makes the whole *probable cause thing* a little messy since people are allowed to have it anyway. It's tricky cause we still get a lot of people trying to take the marijuana out of the state to places like Montana and Chicago. If we have an eastbound driver that looks suspicious, we still use her a little bit." Moe was sniffing around at the base of a dead birch tree in the middle of a parking lot island. There were half a dozen similar islands in the lot, all with dead birch trees in them. Alice's nose was drawing her toward the bus. She was clearly on to something. Moe had apparently found the spot that he was looking for. He squatted and took a large dump. It was just upwind from the bus. Arlo emerged from inside of the police cruiser with information but as soon as he stepped out, he screwed his face up and winced in disgust.

"Tastes like someone just took a shit in my mouth," he said.

"Mr. Franklin's dog just took a crap right over there."

"I hope that you've got something to clean that up with. I'm not sure what it's like where you come from, Mr. Franklin, but here in North Bend we clean up after our animals."

Normally Saint was completely unprepared for incidents like that one. But at the moment, thanks to Joan Rivers' less fortunate twin, he had plastic doo-doo bags in spades. He pulled out the pint of Cherry Garcia ice cream, and set it on the bumper.

"What are you planning on doing with that?" asked Arlo. Saint assumed he was talking about the poop. He picked it up with his hand, protected by the bag, inverted it and then tied the handles in a knot to keep the stink at a minimum.

"I'll look for a garbage can for it," he said.

"I'm taking about the ice cream. There's no freezers in the rooms at the motel."

"Oh yeah," said the fat cop, "what did Winnie say?"

"Someone just cancelled seventeen. It was good timing when I called. They're getting a lot of people just stopping by right now but they'll hold it for our friend Franklin here. She even said she can give you a discount on it since she is already keeping the deposit from the folks who cancelled at the last minute. There will be an extra charge for the dog though." It's a good thing Saint's sphincter was so tight because his stomach was starting to feel frothy and his bowels were threatening to release. He would have given anything to be somewhere warm for ten minutes, to be able to use the john and put something in his belly. "How's that sound?"

"Sounds good," said Saint. Alice was really casing the bus now. The big German Shepherd was slowly encircling it with her nose pretty much stuck to the chassis. "I'll just walk on over there in a few minutes."

"Nonsense," said the old cop. "There's nothing on the radio right now. We'll give you a lift over there."

"So, you think I can leave the van here for the night."

"Arlo, why don't you go on inside the store and let Kacey Poppins know that Mr. Franklin here is going to need to park his van in the lot for the evening. I don't think that she'll mind."

"Sure thing, Kip" it was the first time Saint got to hear the older officer's name. "Say," said Arlo turning to Saint, "what are you planning on doing with that ice cream."

"I was just going to eat it later. It's gotten so cold though, I barely want it anymore."

"Be a shame to waste it though."

"You want it?"

"I'll grab some disposable spoons while I am inside. We can share it on the drive over to the motel."

"Get me a coffee too, will ya?" said Kip. "It's been a while."

As Arlo walked off, Kip popped open the trunk of the police car and started piling in the dog food and Saint's groceries on top of a full-sized spare tire and next to a pair of twelve-gauge shotguns.

"Alice sure has taken an interest in your van," said Kip to Saint, once all of the groceries were in the trunk.

"Yeah, I'm not sure why," said Saint.

"Have you got yourself some marijuana in there, Mr. Franklin?"

"No sir," said Saint. Way too fast and formal to be convincing. Kip froze and studied Saint's face for a moment.

"Sure, you don't, son. I expect you'll at least want to be grabbing yourself something else to wear out of that van of yours. You look like you're about to catch your death out here."

"I'm fine," said Saint. "I don't feel like unpacking anything. I'll just take a shower and these clothes will be dry by the morning."

"Now that doesn't make a whole lot of sense. Does it?"

"What?"

"Why you'd rather freeze than get yourself something warm to put on."

"I'm really not that cold."

"Not that cold, huh. Or maybe you're not being honest about what you've got in them duffel bags. Mind if I take a look inside one of them?"

"There's no reason for you to do that," said Saint, trying hard to channel his motorcycle riding uncle, who'd have sooner shot the cop then let him have a look at was he was carrying.

"I think there is."

"What do you mean?"

"I've got a marijuana sniffing dog, a veteran of the force, that just made your vehicle. I can cite you for reckless endangerment, and I can cite you for animal abuse," officer Kip delivered the series of threats in a soft, steady tone. It was hard to tell if he was trying to be intimidating or if he was going for deadpan humor. In either case, he had inched so close to Saint that the two men were now standing nose to nose.

"I'm not doing anything wrong, officer. I swear. Just having a hard night."

Officer Kip pushed his hips forward. Saint could feel the cop's belt and his Billy club pressing against his thigh. He was also pretty sure that the cop had a hard on. And that he was pressing it into Saint's crotch.

"Feel my balls," Kip whispered into Saint's ear. Saint was fairly certain that he had heard the officer correctly. They were standing in the middle of the parking lot in the pouring rain. The way the police cruiser was parked at an angle to the VW van, it was actually kind of private.

"Pardon me?" Saint said. The officer put his lips right up to Saint's ear.

"Reach down, and feel my balls," he said. "Do it and I'll let you go." Saint pulled his head back and looked the officer in the eyes. He was expecting to see the face of a menace. A man who was using the power of his position to take advantage of a total stranger. A man who probably had a history of abusing innocent motorists. But that isn't what he wound up seeing. He wound up seeing the face of a man who was abandoned and lonely. The face of a man who was struggling to find a place in world that was moving on without him. Saint was also glad that, if he touched the officer's balls, he wasn't going to have to show him the inside of one of the duffel bags. If he had to open one of the bags, he could wind up touching all sorts of balls that he didn't want to touch. So he did it. He reached down and cupped officer Kip's testicles gently in his palm. Kip closed his eyes and relaxed. Creepy as the whole thing was, the guy looked momentarily happy. And Saint drew some satisfaction from being able to provide that. It was one of those moments that seemed to last forever and was simultaneously over in a flash. Arlo was hustling back across the wet parking lot with Kip's coffee in one hand and three plastic spoons in the other. Officer Kip backed away from Saint before Arlo got too close and it was instantly as though nothing had ever happened.

"You sure that's all you need, son?" asked Kip, as though they were in mid-conversation. "You don't look too well-prepared. Maybe a tooth brush or something." Saint did have a toiletry kit buried at the bottom of one of the duffels but he had no idea which. If he could have grabbed one thing from the van it wouldn't have been that though. It would have been a handful of weed to smoke after his shower and his feast at the motel.

"I'm good," said Saint.

Officer Kip had to put Alice on a leash and pull her away from the bus. Arlo picked the ice cream up off the bumper, peeled the lid off, and helped himself to a heaping spoonful.

"This stuff is really good," said the young cop, eating Cherry Garcia by himself in the rain. "Who wants some?" Kip didn't say anything and Saint shook his head. Arlo just kept on eating. "What kind of engine you got in there?" he asked. Normally Saint liked talking VW's but he was soaked and freezing and dying to get out of there.

"1700 cc pancake," said Saint, hoping that the description would be too technical for the young cop and that he would just forget about it and they could all just pile into the police cruiser.

"You run digital points?" asked Arlo. Saint's heart sank when he realized that the cop actually had the vocabulary for this conversation.

"Nah," said Saint, realizing he was potentially about to open up a big can of wax, or at the very least get himself drawn into a pointless debate, "I still run the mechanical ones."

"Me too," said Arlo.

"You've got a bus?"

"'69 Karman Ghia. Totally stock. You got the full camper rig inside?"

"Nah," said Saint, "It's the more like the Weekender. Those other systems take up so much space. I like the extra sleeping room but that's about it. I don't need to cook inside the car."

"I agree. Keep it simple, shithead. That's what I always say. You sure you don't want a few bites of this? It's really good." The ice cream had gotten soft since Saint bought it and it was pooling at the corners of the officer's mouth. He wiped it off with the sleeve of his navy-blue uniform. Behind him, what seemed like a single ray from the setting sun snuck out below the cloud cover and splintered into a rainbow that danced across the sky and faded quickly to black.

"Did you see that?" asked Saint.

"See what?" Luckily Saint was with it enough to realize that answering could cost him the scant amount of credibility that he had with the two uniforms. He clung to the memory of the colors and let the conversations drop.

The officers and Alice finally took off once Saint, Moe, and all of their crap was inside of the room they had procured him at the hotel. The air inside of the room was damp and stuck. It smelled like cat piss. There were short curly hairs of different colors on the toilet seat. The cleaning staff had done a cute triangular fold with the toilet paper roll but they had completely neglected to wipe out the shower stall. And someone had left their enema bag hanging from the towel rack. Fortunately for the motel management, Saint wasn't a big complainer. He scooped up all of the stuff that wasn't his and laid it outside the door to the room. Then he stripped down to nothing and turned the shower water on until it was scalding. Then he backed it off some, until it was ice cold. After that he couldn't seem to get it to run hot at all. He lathered himself up with the complimentary shower gel, gutted out a quick cold rinse, and then dried himself off with one of the low thread count towels.

Moe was still working on devouring a galaxy of dog food that Saint had laid out on the carpet for him. Saint turned on the television and sat down on the edge of the bed. The set was tuned to Jeopardy.

"I'll take painters and planets for three-hundred, Alex."

"The name of the artist who depicted Saturn devouring his son."

"Who is Francisco de Goya" said Saint. His mom took a class in art history when he was little and he used to help her study. He flicked to another station. There was a baseball game on. The Seattle Mariners' ace had just coughed up a home run ball and they were now trailing by a run in the bottom of the fifth inning.

Saint used the edge of the nightstand to pop of the cap off of one of the Arrogant Bastard Ales and had himself a big drink of it. Then he opened up the Jalapeño chips, and spent a bunch of time alternating between eating the chips, drinking the beer, and watching the baseball game. Occasionally doing all three at once. He farted and it smelled just like the chips. He thought about huffing it back to the bus to get himself a joint for tonight and one for the morning but it was kind of a ways, the weather was nasty, he had no extra clothes, and the more he drank the lazier he got.

The game was droning on. Saint didn't even like baseball. Halfway through the mozzarella sandwich he realized that he could look for something else. On one of the movie stations he stumbled upon a marathon of the X-Men films and settled on watching those. He opened the Fig Newman's. After a close up shot of Magneto the film cut to a lengthy commercial for an eight-hundred number where a sultry Romanian sounding psychic was waiting to read the caller's tarot cards or use her crystal ball to predict the future.

"Are you lost along the way? Are you searching for your true love? Are you making less money than you would like? Call now and let me help you keep from making terrible mistakes that could sabotage the rest of your life," the psychic had an endearing accent and seemed to stumble a lot over her verb tenses but her message was very convincing and seemed as though it was being delivered directly to Saint. "I will use the ancient power of the tarot to understand where you are at in your life, where you need to be, and what you must do to get there. Please call now, the advice that you receive may be the most valuable that you ever get," she pronounced all of her V's like W's, "and the first minute of counsel is free." First Minute Free was flashing in across the middle of the screen in big purple letters. Beneath that, in much smaller print and in a swirling hard to read font, it said that additional minutes cost

$4.95 and that the charges would appear on the caller's cell phone bill.

Saint was vaguely aware of the dangers of getting caught on the phone too long with one of the fast—sometimes slow—talking con artists. But he was certain that this Madame Laverne Korzha de las Bulgarias was legit and that he wouldn't need much more than a minute on the line with her to get the counsel he needed. He was the ultimate client; lost along the way, with a floundering love life and money problems. He grabbed his phone and dialed the number: (800) B4I-S2L8.

"Hello," the voice on the other end of the line matched the voice from the television commercial perfectly.

"Hello," said Saint, burning several precious free seconds.

"How are you, Mr. Rheese?"

"How do you already know my last name?"

"Names, Mr. Rheese, are, how do you say, are like *Zee low hanging fruit*," the words all came from the back of her throat like phlegm.

"They are, aren't they?"

"What can I do for you, Mr. Rheese? I can sense that you are on something like a mission."

"I am on a mission," said Saint, tilting up from his slouch to a sitting position. "What can you see about it?"

"That it is more complicated than is immediately obvious."

"In what way?"

"Your intentions are good, but the universe has other plans for you."

"Is that why I broke down?"

"Precisely. It is also why you must keep going."

"To deliver?"

"That is correct, there will be a delivery."

"Will I get paid?"

"I can see that the riches will be coming to you. Do you have a financial advisor?"

"A what?"

"Someone who helps you make good decisions with your money."

"Like a fairy?"

"..."

"Nevermind. Do you know a good financial advisor? I'm about to come into some money."

"There will be a lot of money."

"Are you reading my tarot cards?"

"Not yet. Your energy is very powerful. So far the cards have not been necessary."

"Do you think the cards will tell us something more?"

"The cards are always very interesting, Mr. Rheese."

"What would it cost to do just like, a short reading?"

"Short readings typically take only ten or fifteen minutes. But what they reveal, spans decades."

"What if I do just the beginning?"

"The beginning of a reading provides a snapshot of where you are at in your life, Mr. Rheese."

"Do you have a sense of that already?"

"I do, Mr. Rheese. I sense that you are sincere, loyal, handsome, tall. Am I correct?"

"I think so. My big question is, do you think that I could be even taller?"

"Than you are now?"

"I'm just having some fun with you. I know that I'm done growing."

"Spiritual growth is never done, Mr. Rheese."

"Are you telling me that *you're* still growing too, spiritually?"

"I am, Mr. Rheese. Spiritually, I grow every day. Talking to kind people like yourself, it nourish my soul."

"And what exactly is the soul? I've always wondered that."

"The soul is all of those parts of you that is not lashed to your skin and your muscle and your bone. The soul is the part of you that reacts to life on a cosmic level. Take, for example, what you are doing now. You are on a trip, no?"

"I am on a trip."

"And this trip is to help someone that is very important to you, no?"

"It is."

"Is it to help a friend?"

"Not exactly."

"Someone in your family, then?"

"Yes."

"Your sister?"

"In a roundabout way."

"Your mother, then?"

"Exactly. You're good."

"What you are doing for your mother, it is dangerous, yes?"

"It is dangerous."

"Your bravery is admirable, Mr. Rheese. Your mother is lucky to have you, and your sister."

"That's amazing that you know I have a sister."

"You are very open, Mr. Rheese." As soon as Saint said this someone from the room next door stepped out for a smoke, which caused Moe to take a pause from eating and the tags on his collar jingled as he kept his suspicious gaze focused on the door.

"Let me ask you something, Mr. Rheese."

"Sure."

"Do you have a dog?"

"I do. How did you know?"

"Mr. Rheese?"

"Yes?"

"Would you like me to tell you about how I first became a psychic? The story has to do with a dog."

"Am I going to get charged for this part?"

"It won't take long. And I think that you will find that it has a lot of relevance to your, delivery."

"You know that I'm trying to deliver something?"

"Oh yes, Mr. Rheese. It is very clear. You are about to be a part of a very special delivery."

"Damn right, I am."

"But what winds up being delivered may not be that which you expect."

"What else is there to deliver?"

"Many things."

"Like what?"

"Mail. Babies."

"I'm not trying to deliver mail, or a baby."

"I didn't say that you were trying to."

"Which is it going to be? Mail, or a baby?"

"A baby."

Cursed

Inside of the lobby of the El Gaucho steakhouse, there were several couples waiting for tables as well as a husband and wife who had brought along their toddler who was flying a replica Boeing 727 toy plane between and around everyone's legs. Most of the hungry people were avoiding eye contact with one another, looking at their watches or trying to pretend that the little kid and his toy and all of the accompanying sound effects weren't annoying as fuck. None of them had a reservation obviously and they were indubitably wondering if dinner at El Gaucho was in the cards for them that evening, or if it might not be more efficient to just bag the whole steak idea, grab a hot pie from Belltown Pizza and shlep it on back to the condo. On a more typical late summer evening that would have been an easy trigger to pull. A night consistent with the current pattern would have meant a balmy, dry twilight. The relentless heat of the day would finally be dissipating. Even seventy-five degrees of late had been sweet bliss by comparison. Being outdoors after sunset was practically mandatory and it sure seemed as though the city had dispensed with its open container laws or the mayor had instructed law enforcement to look the other way because it was no longer possible to swing a dead cat at sunset without hitting someone walking around nursing a cold beer or a glass of chilled white. Not that night though. The rains had shown up and it felt already as though they had never left. A stiff wind was whistling out of the northeast and the raindrops were so heavy that they seemed to bounce back to waist level after impacting the surface. It was a mess out there. And no one really seemed to have their wet weather gear handy.

Herman, Loven, and Dmitri were part of the crowd in the entryway. Herman was shifting his weight nervously from foot to foot as he crashed from the cocaine high and fretted about the status of the deal to buy the orchard. Herman was feeling helpless without being able to use the phone that the stripper destroyed. He was going to need one right away to be able to communicate with Duncan and the old couple and he almost left the restaurant as soon as they entered to find a store that was open. But he didn't do it. He could have at least borrowed Loven's phone and returned Duncan's call. He just wasn't up for it yet. After the emotional reading he was having a hard time thinking about much other than his mom and Margot. He would have preferred to be sitting down to eat with Margot— and the kid if that's what it took—but he was having a hard time making short term decisions and he chalked it up to being starving. He was going to eat a steak. Then he would move on to solving other problems; both small and large. Because of the humidity spike and the fact that Herman could no longer keep his fingers out of his hair, his silky curls had reverted to the texture of a Brillo Pad, a nickname he wore for a brief period of his youth at Sunday school classes. And his suit, stylish as it was, was soiled below the crotch and buttoning the jacket barely helped.

Herman and the boys were without a reservation, but that normally didn't matter. The head chef—a veritable hippopotamus of a man named Tipton Glacier—was also from Tacoma, and had played on the same ice hockey teams as Herman when they were adolescents. In fact, not only did they play together on a club team called the Mighty Lions and later for their high school, they were two parts of a three-pronged offensive attack squad that Herman used to brag was a plus 250 over the course of their career. Herman played center, had the most goals by far, and made sure that everyone knew it. Herman may have been a cocky son-of-a-bitch back in his playing days, but it was also true that he was a brilliant skater and that he was always around the net. Tipton played left wing and he was much larger than the other kids. No one wanted to go into the boards with the big guy. If the puck was in the corner, Tipton was coming out with it. Over on the right wing was Ork, David Orkin, Herman and Tipton's former childhood pal; two-time-academy-award-winning actor Lucky Soul to some. Ork's forte was hanging back around the top of the face-off circle. He was quick side to side and good at keeping the puck in the zone. Plus, he had a wicked wrist shot. Herman, Ork and Glacier; they became known as the HOG's line. They used to hate to come off of the ice.

Things with the HOG's line fell apart in their junior year at Mount Tahoma High. Tipton was almost too big to play anymore. He got winded easily, and was put off by coach Paul, who used to routinely bang his head against the boards or keep the team on the ice skating until at least one person puked; and he was preoccupied. The big guy had already heard the call from the food business. Most of his afternoons were spent pouring over cookbooks in the library and transcribing recipes. He was already cooking dinner every night for himself, his parents, and his eleven siblings. Ork was ready to give up hockey as well, but not the Puck. He landed the lead role in the school's rendition of 'A Midsummer Night's Dream,' and never looked back. Herman was aware of his talents as a hockey player. He stuck it out for a little while but quit soon himself. It was more of an uphill battle without his wingmen. Plus, he had also unearthed a new obsession: money.

The restaurant always held a few tables in case a high-octane political figure, athlete, or rock star decided to come in unannounced. Herman never had any problem convincing Tipton or Roxanne—the hostess who sported a luxuriant coil of red hair that stretched all the way down to her waistline—to let him have one. That night Roxanne was in a floor length scarlet gown and her hair was French-braided—not as long as usual. Herman didn't manage to get his hands on those coveted tables because of any kind of loyalty that Tipton felt towards him. There wasn't any. Tipton, in a private moment, might tell you that he'd always hated Herman's guts. But he also didn't want Herman to cause an obnoxious scene in the restaurant. It wasn't at all beneath Herman to start complaining at high volume, touting his accomplishments and diminishing the efforts of everyone around him. Tipton and Herman were anything but friends. But they had spent a lot of time together in sweaty locker rooms and for that reason it's fair to say that Tipton knew Herman well. Herman never spent much time thinking about other people. Although that was changing as he thought more and more about Margot and her son.

Roxanne and the rest of the staff treated Herman with their typical professional charm but that was a facade as well. He was incessantly demanding and needlessly critical. But a big tipper. Which fit in well with the whole point of working at El Gaucho: separating rich people from their money. Even if waiting on Herman was an exercise in humility and baseless contrition, his companions were usually funny and friendly and they made him more bearable. The hostess knew the drill. She was just about to lead Herman and his two friends to the last open table in the dining room, a four-top right against the glass window overlooking the sculpture park and the Puget Sound, when a nervous-looking Tipton came rumbling out of the double doors leading to the kitchen. He was in checkered pants, wringing out his fists on his apron, and a few locks of his battleship-gray hair had escaped from his towering chef's hat. He squinted at Herman as though trying to place him, whispered something into Roxanne's ear, and then hustled back to work.

Herman was peeved that Tipton didn't even say a proper hello to him. He was Herman Glüber, former hockey star turned entrepreneur, poised to claim the entire northwest as his kingdom. He was insightful. Didn't Tipton remember Herman telling him, on the day that he quit the hockey team, that if he quit, he'd never get out of the kitchen. All these years later and Herman was still right. Herman could never wrap his head around the fact that Tipton wanted to be in the kitchen.

"Sorry, boys," said Roxanne, "special guest is coming in. We need that table. There are a few open stools left at the bar. It's the best that we are going to be able to do for you tonight."

"Special guest," repeated Herman. "Who?"

"I can't say, Herman," said Roxanne, still holding the menus. Then the phone at her hostess station rang and she had a short conversation that was inaudible over the noise that the diners were making as they ate, and the piano music that was being played by a man in a tuxedo that looked a little too tight.

"Can you believe this?" said Herman. Both Loven and Dmitri were smart enough to duck this rhetorical question. Roxanne hung up the phone.

"Should I lead you to the bar?" she asked. Herman snatched the menus from Roxanne's hand.

"I know where the bar is," he said.

The last three open stools were in between an older couple—who were deep in each other's eyes and halfway through a bottle of Bordeaux—and a single gentleman who had a glass of neat scotch in front of him that was untouched. He was rather skittish and impatient looking. His gaze kept bouncing back and forth between his watch and the front door.

On the way to the bar Dmitri took his phone from his pocket and tripped and fell after looking at the messages on his home screen. "Fuck," he said as he was going over. Loven had to pick him up off of the floor.

"What's up, Meech? Forget how to walk in English?"

"I've got to step outside and check my voicemail. I'll meet you in a few minutes."

"What should I order for you?"

"Something strong," Dmitri peeled himself away.

When they arrived at the barstools Loven tapped Herman on the shoulder and inclined his head toward the bathrooms. It dawned on Herman that a lot of time had passed since the last toot of the cocaine that he had taken. And that it could be a contributing factor to the waxing sensation of nervous agitation that was threatening to engulf him. He didn't get a table at the restaurant, a quack fortune teller had all but torn him a new asshole and freaked him out by predicting that one of the two of them wouldn't survive the night, and that he should be expecting the arrival of some kind of bizarre hex. A vindictive stripper had destroyed his cell phone, and he had just learned that the deal that he had spent most of the year putting into place had gone off the rails at the last possible moment; but that was only the last couple of hours. Overall it had been a good day. He didn't really have reasons to be as pissed off as he was feeling. He was supposed to be out celebrating. The deal was still done and the business about the missing sale documents was a minor technicality. It made sense to blame the cocaine. Which didn't mean that he didn't want more of it. When Loven got back he would hit him up for another bump. For the moment, Herman was left alone with Ed the bartender and the man ignoring his scotch. That man wasn't dressed like anyone else in the restaurant. His clothes were clean and pressed but only because they seemed brand-new; and were more appropriate for being on walkabout in the Australian bush than a fine dining establishment. Herman quietly scoffed at the fact that they even let people in wearing Ex Offico shirts in offensive bright blue colors designed to attract exotic birds. The ones with the SPF built into the fabric. At least the guy wasn't in stretch pants and flip-flops with a yoga mat slung over his shoulder, and trying to call it Smart Casual.

"Evening, Herman," said Ed, while setting down a coaster in front of Herman. "What are you having?"

"Pour me a glass of that '85 Malbec, will you?"

"Celebrating?"

"Trying."

"Sorry to disappoint you, Herman, but we poured the last drop of the Malbec during lunch today."

"You've got to be kidding me, Ed. I've been dreaming about that wine all day."

"Might be dreaming about that one for the rest of your life, my friend. It's not an easy vintage to come by. You want to try—"

"No. You know what, Ed?" Herman had a sudden hankering for something unusual. "Fuck the wine," he said, "I'll take a Santori on the rocks."

"Wish I could, Herman, but we are out of it. There was a structure fire last night at the warehouse that brings us our liquor order. Hardly any of the downtown restaurants got their shipments today. We are pretty bare bones tonight. If you like I could get creative with—"

"I don't want you to get creative, Ed. You are absolutely killing me right now," Herman squeezed his eyes shut. He was annoyed as hell and couldn't think. Partly because of coming off of the blow. But also because of being low blood sugar and having a hard time tuning out the din of the other diners, and the piano player, who was tickling out an insufferable instrumental rendition of the 'Girl from Ipanema.' He twitched and seethed and then resolved to keep it simple. "Can I at least get a goddamn beer?"

"Manny's Pale, Elysian IPA, Elliot Bay's Chocolate Stout, or a Coors Light?"

"Who the hell drinks chocolate stouts at this time of the year?"

"You'd be surprised."

"Just pour me a Manny's, Ed."

"Sure thing, Herman."

It was deafening in there. The windows were shut and the air conditioning system was running but the rain stroking the glass wall on the west side of the building sounded like an advancing battalion. Everyone entering the restaurant at that point was wet and the place had acquired a tropical steaminess. While he was waiting on his beer, Herman had his eye on the front door. It swung open, and in walked a man with whom Herman was quite familiar. The man's muscular handler was protecting his perfect hair with an umbrella. His entourage consisted of the muscle, a Middle Eastern looking woman in an American looking business suit, and a taller gentleman in a tastefully mismatched three-piece with slicked back hair and a lot of flashy accessories. One of which was a heavy silver ring with an orange stone set into the middle of it. His jacket was purple. His silk or rayon button down was bright yellow. He still had his sunglasses on, even though it was pouring rain outside, and it didn't even look pretentious. This guy could have fit right in during a fashion exposé in Rome. Upon closer inspection Herman noticed that the man in the fancy suit with the sunglasses on was Asian. It was hard to tell at first because he wore his facial hair in Elvis style chops. If he was in the mood to stereotype, he'd have said the guy had Chinese Mafia written all over him. But what would the mafia want with Ork?

The noise inside of the restaurant morphed from grating and random to soft and pointed. Despite the captivating appearance of the mafia dude, almost every set of eyes in there turned to the leader of the small pack that had just stepped in from the sopping dusk. Muted whispers ricocheted off of the walls. There was a temporary pause in the clanging of forks and spoons. No one sipped their drinks. The staff all stood rooted to their stations. Then the kitchen doors opened and a giant strode across the landscape of frozen faces to greet the party with nothing but the sound of the piano as his background music. This time Tipton looked like he had all the time in the world. One sentence was being repeated in the dining room like it was an ancient Hindu mantra: "Hey look, there's Lucky Soul."

Herman didn't know how Tipton addressed the actor. He said something into his ear, then they shook hands and hugged. He may have called him Lucky, or David. Herman was fairly sure that he didn't call him what Herman would've called him. Which was Ork. After which he would have reminded Ork that in their sophomore year in high school Herman scored more goals than he and Tipton combined. Before sitting down the bullshit actor made a big thing out of holding everybody up so that he could sign the fuselage of the little kid's toy airplane while the kid stared at him all bug-eyed from the floor and wondered who the guy was who was defacing his stuff. Herman watched, being eaten by envy, as Tipton led the actor personally to the last open four-top in the restaurant, the table that should have gone to Herman. The view from it was so good, like floating above the waterfront on your own personal cloud.

"Rough night, mate?"

"Excuse me?" Herman must have been broadcasting the internal rage that he was feeling on his face because he had attracted the attention of the gentleman that was sitting beside him. He had an accent that might have been Australian, but polished, like he had been the beneficiary of a proper education or was part of some kind of aristocratic bloodline.

"You look like you're full of piss."

"Ed," said Herman, ignoring the man who was trying to talk to him, "where is my beer?"

Ed was working the tap but the beer was only trickling out and the pint glass was only about one third full. Then there was a sudden gurgle, the nozzle coughed and spat out a bunch of white foam.

"Sorry, Herman."

"Is that your new catch phrase?"

"I've got to switch out the keg." Ed disappeared behind a set of black double doors that led to some type of behind the scenes staging area.

Herman, with no one else available at the moment to be the sounding board for his anger, turned to the man beside him. "What's it take to get a goddamn drink in this place?" He said.

"Thank God for alcohol," the man said. "Not likely I'd survive this world without the stuff."

"Doesn't look like you're moving too quickly through your scotch."

"Just trying to stay sharp, mate. I'm sort of on the clock," he said before taking a baby sip of the liquor. "Saw you clenching your jaw at the bloke from the pictures. I take it you're not a fan."

"Who the fuck are you?"

"Name's Doctor Jodie Cavendish." He extended his right hand toward Herman.

"Herman Glüber. You don't look like a doctor."

"Why? Because I'm in field clothing and drinking in a bar?"

"Maybe."

"I'm not a medical doctor. I'm more of a researcher. Perhaps we are harder to recognize."

"What do you research?"

"My degree is in Environmental Science and I've spent the bulk of my life studying trees and the pathogens that affect them. Lately I've been concentrating on the international movement of fungi and insects."

"So, you're not a doctor."

"If there is something fiddling about in your unmentionable regions and causing you an itch, I don't want to hear about, it if that's what you mean."

"Ha," Herman laughed, less at the joke than the irony of what this tree researcher would think if he knew that Herman had just purchased Summerwood Farms, and was about to lay waste to nearly a thousand acres of mature apple trees, assuming the sale documents turned up. Since Herman was alone at the moment, and partially because he was carrying around some repressed guilt associated with not only the pending slaughter of the trees but all of the jobs that were about to be lost, he did something he almost never did outside of the context of working with clients: he asked the doctor a question. "So, who do you work for, a university or something?"

The doctor took another sip of his scotch before answering. "I did until somewhat recently. University of Minnesota. Although I am from British Columbia originally."

"So, you're a Canadian?"

"My wife is from the United States so I have dual citizenship now."

"But you're out of teaching?"

"I am."

"Blackballed?"

The doctor laughed. "No, mate. Just a few months shy of being eligible for tenure I made a very risky move and left my post. I was offered a chance to work as a consultant on a project that was pitched as being far more charming than it initially turned out to be. Although I hasten to say, in the last couple of weeks it's become a sight more interesting."

"How so?" The doctor demurred and looked away from Herman, toward the table where Lucky Soul and his company were shrouded behind their menus.

"You really don't like the actor do you, Mr. Glüber?"

"Kind of presumptuous, don't you think?"

"Am I wrong?"

Herman didn't answer. He'd already given enough rope to psychics for a Friday, but this guy was quite perceptive.

"I don't blame you," the doctor went on. "That last award that he got, it should have gone to Steve Carrell."

"You didn't mention who you are consulting for," asked Herman, and the doctor laughed again. "Did I say something funny?"

"Not really, mate. If you care to know, I was until recently working for the government of the United States of America; tracking a problem in this region that is extending beyond trees. Do you notice it's been a bit warm of late?"

"What stooge doesn't realize that?"

"Well, there are plenty of stooges who don't realize the repercussions of it."

"Such as?"

"Such as massive populations of pathogens and insects that are normally kept in check by cold weather are flourishing year-round."

"The trees are in danger?"

"We are all in danger, Mr. Glüber."

"Kind of morbid, don't you think?"

"I wish I had a more hopeful message. I have seen some things in the past few days I never thought I'd see."

"Sounds like you've been binge watching 'The Walking Dead.'"

"I'd recommend laying in some supplies."

"For what?"

"For keeping yourself amused, Mr. Glüber. I'm going to make sure I've got plenty of scotch and books to read."

"Is there a storm coming in I don't know about?"

"That's a good way to put it."

"You want to fill me in on a few details, doc? Your doom and gloom speech is lacking substance."

"Alright, mate. In the late nineties I was part of the first wave of scientists to confront the proliferation of the Asian Longhorn Beetle and to develop large scale plans for dealing with its eradication. And that earned me something of a reputation. Twenty years later we seem to be on the cusp of a similar, potentially even worse problem." Herman's wild hair, and big white eyes that kept darting around the room, but consistently back to the doctor, prompted him to continue. "An unknown length of time ago, I suspect about four years, there was a small village called Ganhe in Inner Mongolia, between Ulanhot and Hulunbuir. It was a quaint hub of motorcycle-riding sheep farmers and there wasn't a lot of technology there anyway but cell phones were popular like they are everywhere and the towers that service the area went offline. The Chinese sent in their engineers who failed, for a variety of reasons, to solve the issue and were returning to China proper with stories about insects that were eating the power cables."

"Sounds like Star Wars."

"Pardon."

"Just sounds like science fiction. Insects eating power cords."

"Nothing outer space about this problem, mate. This is pure stuck on planet earth biological catastrophe."

"What's it got to do with you? I thought that you were a tree guy."

"The first wave of Chinese engineers to come back from the region also told stories about a particular species of the genus *Betula* that was standing dead. They took photographs and some of those photographs found their way to me. That was around the time that a group of Chinese nationals contacted me in conjunction with members of the American intelligence community."

"Is any of this supposed to be a secret?"

"No. At least I don't think so. That was the last I'd heard about it for a long time and I assumed the issue was either dealt with or bumped down some priority list to the point that my help was no longer required. But that isn't what happened at all. In fact, what happened was so thoroughly devastating to the modern way of living that the Chinese did what they do best."

"Which was?"

"They built a wall that surrounds the entire region, closed it off from the rest of China and Mongolia, and renamed it Deadland."

"Could I get killed for what you are telling me?"

"By this time tomorrow, Herman, what I am telling you will be common knowledge."

"You went over there?"

"I did."

"And what did you find out?"

"The shorthand version of what I discovered there was that an unusually hot stretch of weather, led to the proliferation of an aggressive species of insect called *Agrilus anxius*. It feasts on species in the genus *Betula,* loves warm winters, and has become quite common in this area in the last decade or two. When the insect had devoured all of its favored food source in the region, the population cross-bred with a similar insect and the offspring was a new beetle that somehow had the ability to derive nutrition from being in close proximity to sources of alternating current, both low and high voltage wires, as well as fiberoptic cable. It's truly quite remarkable and I suspect the capacity to feed this way works something like photosynthesis but tests need to be run. Eventually the new species of bug converged in massive numbers upon all of the electrical and internet service cables that it could find. The new insect, discovered by the Chinese but officially first described and named by yours truly, is called *Agrilus suprema*. So far it has no common name in the West."

"They don't eat through the cords?"

"Well, they are insects, Mr. Gluber."

"What's that mean?"

"That as a species they are sometimes capable of amazing feats, but as specimens they are not thought of as being discerning, and don't always act in their own best interests. They become so numerous and ravenously hungry that eventually they do wear through enough of the protective coating around the cables that they cause a short circuit and cut off their own food supply. But up until that moment their behavior is remarkably similar to a shark's. Once one of the insects starts getting pumped up and propagating from exposure to electrical current it's like the smell of blood in the water. The critters gather and multiply with such reckless ferocity that they eventually create a mechanical disruption and cut off the flow."

"They're just dumb bugs."

"I think it bears mentioning, Mr. Glüber, that there are plenty of human beings who also behave in ways that undermine their own self interests. You might even say most of them."

"Doesn't sound like you think that the bugs are the actual problem."

"Despite their incredible and unprecedented ability to conduct electricity without frying to a crisp, I'd still say they're a symptom."

"We're the problem?" said Herman.

The doctor finished his scotch and shoved the empty tumbler toward the other side of the bar and stared off into the void.

"You know, a ton of beetles started falling out of the ceiling of the last bar I was at. Do you think that we are starting to get those around here?"

"Let's put it this way, Mr. Glüber: in the Pacific Northwest there is a large population of trees in the genus *Betula*, you probably call most of these birches, that are nearly dead from a massive infestation of *Agrilus anxius*. The weather has been unusually hot, the winters fairly mild, and the area is obviously replete with the kinds of power lines that the insects like to congregate near. You have the presence of the host that the insects favor as well as the conditions that they thrive in. All it would take would be the presence of *suprema* and the conditions would be ripe for a population explosion that could cripple the entire northwest, maybe even the country."

"*Suprema* sounds intense. I like it," Herman said as he reached into his jacket pocket, withdrew a tin of Altoid's, and opened it up on the bar. The two insects that he had plucked off of his computer monitor earlier in the day to show to Ethan were in there next to about a dozen wintergreen flavored mints. "Does this look like them?" The doctor glanced over at the bugs but he didn't pick one up.

"That's them."

"How can you tell?"

"Flat head. Two iridescent red stripes on the thorax. Short horns that curve toward the midline that carry the current. The more *suprema* evolves, the more the horns are curving in. I can see it happening already."

"You don't sound surprised to see these."

"Oh, I know they're here. Frankly, I am a little surprised, and even somewhat impressed that you have two of them in your pocket."

"I found them crawling across my computer monitor this morning and kept a couple to show my girlfriend's son. How did they get here?"

"The region that they were discovered in is under quarantine and U.S. intelligence has been watching it for several years and there had been no movement whatsoever across the borders. In or out."

"Until recently?"

"Until recently. It is believed that someone who has a residence close to here commissioned something from this quarantined region in Mongolia, known as Deadland, to be shipped to the Port of Seattle. It wasn't legal but the shipping container passed through the old village of Ganhe and traversed most of Deadland on its way to the pier in Beijing. The government watched it happen with satellite imagery and I followed the container through the zone," he leaned in close to Herman to whisper, "under cover of course. But we weren't in any kind of a position to do anything about it. It is possible that some of the bugs hitchhiked over with the container. But it's not out of the question that a similar mutation happened here on its own since the conditions are so similar."

"How could the Chinese let that happen?"

"That's a ridiculous question, Mr. Glüber. You obviously have not traveled to China. With that kind of iron-fisted free-enterprise, there's really nothing that can't happen. In fact, I'd be less surprised to find out that this was a designed biological attack, masterminded by someone in the orient."

"Like who?"

The doctor shrugged. "Maybe Genghis Khan."

"Why would Genghis Khan want to conquer America?"

"I'm not a conqueror so it's hard for me to say."

"And who is the asshole who paid to have the container moved?"

"We aren't exactly sure, Mr. Glüber, but we have a pretty good idea. The purchase was made using an alias. It hardly matters now anyway."

"Is the person you suspect in this restaurant right now?"

Again, the doctor demurred, and Herman let his vision drift across the restaurant toward his chosen nemesis. A man who probably never gave Herman a second thought once his film career took off. He didn't need to hear the answer.

"That mother fucker. What are you going to do?"

"If I could get that bloody statue from him and give it to Steve Carrell I would."

"I mean about the beetles."

"There are things that can be done. The Mongols have found a way to live in harmony with them. But as a rule, they are a far more disciplined people than you Yanks. They know how to suffer and to do without. If I were a betting man, I'd say the word 'civilization' will be omitted from the English language within the week."

"They multiply that fast?"

"My plan is to go east first, and then north. Maybe to the Yukon territory. I've always wanted to see it. Fetched myself a new parka at the REI this morning. Lovely store."

"Kind of a cowardly response, don't you think? I thought that you were a special consultant, working for the Americans. You're just going to run back to Canada."

"What's wrong with Canada?"

"We ask that question a lot in the United Sates?"

"Amusing. Since you seem curious, I am rendezvousing with a highly capable friend tomorrow on the other side of the mountains. When I leave here, I'm driving the rental car out over the pass. Plenty of room if you would like to join me."

"Do I look like the type pf person who gets in a car with a total stranger who is suggesting that the world is about to end?"

"Frankly, it's hard to tell what kind of man you are. You seem like the kind of bloke that is rather at home in a place like this. All the same, you look like you could use a bath, and something fresh to wear. But there's hardly time for that. Though I doubt anything I say will convince you. Tell you what," Jodie took a business card out of his wallet and started writing on the back. "That's my phone number, though I wouldn't count on it working much longer. If you change your mind and decide you want to save yourself, try giving me a call. Just don't wait too long."

Herman accepted the card and tucked it into his own wallet. For a moment the two of them sat in pensive silence until Jodie broke it with a philosophical question.

"Do you know what the curse of being a human being is, Mr. Glüber?"

"Call me Herman. And no, I'm not aware of this curse."

"It's that we are conscious of time. We need to be constantly making amends for our pasts and making certain that our futures are loaded up with the promise of pleasure. If we have these two things, then we can be in horrific pain in the present moment and still happy."

"I'm not following you."

"I know where this lovable and perishable life is headed, and I wish that I didn't. I wish that my mental faculties were sufficient to enjoy this single malt and nothing more. That I didn't have to be constantly plagued with remembering every mistake that I made, and constantly anxious about a future that has never looked anything but bleak to me."

"Little heavy, don't you think?"

"Time in and around Deadland passed slowly. I did a lot of thinking, and a lot of reading while I was there. Have you ever heard of Alan Watts?"

"Is he a philosopher?"

"Of sorts."

"What does he have to do with the bugs?"

"Nothing. And everything. Can I give you a piece of advice, Herman?"

"I'm not promising I'll take it."

"Learn to live in the present moment. It's really all there is." The doctor got up to leave, took a twenty-dollar bill out of his pocket, and left it on the bar.

"Hold on a second. What happened to Deadland?"

"What do you mean?"

"Is it gone?"

"It's perfectly fine."

"But the people left?"

"They stayed."

"Did they figure out how to get rid of the bugs?"

"Yes, but they never did anything about it. They decided instead just to let them be."

"But they got the power on?"

"No, Herman. The people in and around Deadland sacrificed their relationship with electricity and the bug population collapsed in the absence of its food source."

"They had to revert to a primitive way of life."

"They could have cut the host trees and switched over to direct current. The bugs are attracted to it but not with the same kind of vigor they express in the presence of AC. It's not a guarantee but there is a possibility the bug population wouldn't thrive in the presence of a DC grid but months of testing would have to be undertaken and there just isn't the time for it. Perhaps Edison was right and Tesla was wrong after all. Either way, the people of Deadland decided that getting the power back up wasn't worth the effort. They are back to using oil lamps and cooking over fires. I don't know I'd label it primitive though. Some might argue that they evolved."

"Why can't we do that here?"

"What?"

"What you just said. Cut the trees down and change over to another power source."

"I just told you, the logistics of what you are suggesting are too massive to undertake in the little time that is available. So much of what surrounds us is sucking down alternating current it's like water going over a waterfall. It can't be stopped. And also, because the beetles, or some other insect, will adapt its habits to make use of the alterations to the power grid and the lights would likely remain off but for new and equally complicated reasons."

"Where exactly are you going?"

"Over Snoqualmie Pass," said the doctor, rising up from his seat.

"Yeah, but I thought you were working for the government, tracking that asshole actor?"

"The government relieved me from my position today. The glimpse of the actor was for the sake of my own self interests. But at this point, I really must be going."

"How did you know Lucky would be here?"

"Colette's Lover tipped me off. And that, you might get killed for knowing."

"Have you considered going back to Deadland?"

"You know I have, but I'm just not willing to go alone. Eliza is out there somewhere and I'd like to find her before I do anything."

"Is she going to be with you when you flee north?"

"I'm not inclined to get my hopes up. I don't even know where she is. I'd obviously be delighted if she made the rendezvous point as well."

"Who did you say you are meeting out there?"

Jodie stepped close to Herman so that he could speak quietly. "Please don't say anything to anyone, but I am being collected by a friend of mine. He might be the only person on the planet that can circumvent this and maybe try to implement a solution."

"This guy have a name?"

"Nevil Horsetrainer. Good bloke."

Another name that had the ability to make Herman sick. Whatever the fuck a *bloke* is, Herman was fairly sure he wasn't a good one.

"Perhaps we will see each other again, Herman Glüber."

Jodie left and Loven showed back up and sat down on the stool that the doctor had been keeping warm.

"Where were you?" Herman asked, feeling honestly relieved to see that he was back. Independent-minded as Herman was, on that particular evening he was beginning to feel inexplicably safer when Loven was nearby. It was an odd sensation. Herman didn't really have buddies, let alone wingmen.

"Who was that guy?"

"Another kook. So far tonight I've been had my head split open by a psychic and a spy and I can't seem to get a fucking drink in this restaurant. Hey, can I go in there and hit that vile of yours again?"

"Sorry, Herman. I dropped it into the shitter. No way I was going fishing for it. It was ruined anyway."

"Fuck."

"Tell me about it. That eight ball was Colombian and cost me two-fifty. I can call my guy and line up some more."

"You probably should," Herman sounded desperate.

Loven popped his phone out to make the call but he forgot what he was doing when Dmitri reappeared, with his suit sopping wet and his hair all pasted down to his scalp.

"What happened to you?" said Loven.

"Something is up with my nephew. He left a bunch of messages on my phone. He was very upset and swearing every other word. I think that he was in an accident."

"Know where he is?"

"I don't. On one of his messages I swear he said something about trying to make it to Canada. But that's ridiculous. I don't think he knows where Canada is."

"North. I'm fucking starving," said Herman.

"I'm stucking farving," said Loven, "how do we get some food over here?"

"I could use a drink," said Dmitri.

"Good luck," said Herman. "I think that Ed won the lottery and quit in the last ten minutes. He's supposed to be switching out a keg but I swear he is brewing the beer first. We've at least got to get a food order going," Herman popped up from his barstool and drifted toward the dining room where he managed to intercept a blond waitress wearing orange lipstick and a metal stud through her eyebrow. The labor shortage in

Seattle had obliterated any notion of a dress code, even for the staff at Gaucho.

"Hey," said Herman, grabbing onto her sleeve so she couldn't run off. "Can I place a food order for the bar? Ed's gone off to Alaska or something."

"I'm not supposed to take food orders for the bar," she said. Herman's edginess and the fact that he was starting to smell may have startled her. It wasn't typical of Gaucho on a Friday.

"It will be quick. I promise." End of the world or not, Herman was going to eat first.

"Fine," she said, agitated. She withdrew a pen and a pad from her apron.

"I'll take a filet of the Wagyu beef, salad with bib lettuce and fingerling potatoes." The Wagyu beef filets at El Gaucho were imported from Australia and went for $225 a plate.

"Been a run on the Wagyu," as she told Herman the bad news, he watched a sommelier stride past with a bottle of the '85 Malbec and uncork it for Lucky's table.

"Son of a bitch."

"It isn't my fault, asshole, if all of these little shits who work in tech want to eat expensive steaks."

"Sorry. I wasn't talking to you."

"Then who the fuck were you talking to?" she was quite mean and direct.

"What about the chateaubriand?"

"Maybe. Tipton said we were running low."

"What do you know that you have?"

"Pork chops. And there's plenty of the sage chicken with cream sauce." There were few things that Herman hated less than white sauces on his food.

"I don't want either of those. Can you just wrangle me a nice steak? I don't care what it costs."

"What about your friends?"

"Two burgers. No mayonnaise," he waited while she wrote it down. "Any idea where Ed got off to? It's hell getting a drink in here tonight."

"Threw his back out moving a keg. Our backup is coming but he was fishing when we called him. He has to get home and shower first."

"Who's pouring drinks?"

"We were going to have one of the busboys do it, then Roxanne remembered he's only nineteen. The manager will be there to cover shortly. Why, you looking for a job?"

"I'm just thirsty."

"Just sit tight and we'll get someone over there soon."

"How do you want the burgers cooked?"

"Rare."

She vanished into the kitchen and Herman slunk back over to the bar.

Loven's eyes were so red that it was like looking at a photograph of him taken with a shitty camera. He had plenty of energy though. He was talking so fast that it was impossible to penetrate the stream of words coming out of his mouth. He was drilling Dmitri with some pseudo-profound rant that was somehow rooted in the Simpsons' episode in which Homer coats his stomach in candle wax so that he can eat Guatemalan insanity peppers and goes for a hallucinatory romp with a spirit guide in the form of a coyote. Dmitri was glazed over. Not even nodding along with the story. He looked preoccupied and sullen. Something was heavy on his mind. Loven was finally bringing the whole long convoluted speech about the cartoon around to some kind of salient point that you really had to be on cocaine to appreciate. It was still a ghost town behind the bar. Herman needed a change of scenery and excused himself to the bathroom but no one was paying him any attention.

On the short walk to the john Herman realized that he not only needed the change of scenery but also to sit on the throne. That blow of Loven's—good as it was—could easily have been cut with some laxative, and he'd been pinching one off since lunch time because he'd been so goddamn busy. Maybe that fucking doctor was onto something. If you're so busy that you can't even remember to take a dump something has to be wrong. There was no one in the bathroom when he got there and the first thing he did, considering how his night was going, was to make sure that there was sufficient toilet paper. Inside of the luxury stall there were two shallow wicker baskets. One with several extra rolls. The other with a fan of magazines. He dropped his cashmere trousers to his ankles, settled himself on the seat and started thumbing through the latest issue of Golf Digest. He couldn't believe how badly he had to go. His stomach was hurting from it, and he was a little embarrassed that he was about to destroy Gaucho's bathroom.

Then there was a problem that was hard to define. Herman had always prided himself on being a good pooper. He had logged countless miles along fragile rivers and way up above tree line where it was often hard to find a good place to go, or to get into a comfortable position, and it was never once a problem. Herman was such a robust eater and so active that nothing but a smoothly functioning intestinal tract was familiar to him. Everything always moved right through. It was never a problem. Suddenly it was a problem. He was seated on a top of the line Bemis comfy in a luxury stall in a five-star restaurant and nothing would release. He pushed. Nothing happened. He pushed a little harder and still nothing happened. He started getting the willies and pushed really hard. So hard in fact that his eyes began to tear and his sphincter started to prolapse; meaning that part of his small intestine was coming out instead of the fecal matter but Herman had no idea. He only knew that it felt wrong. Like his insides were being shoved into a solid toxic mass that refused to budge. He was getting a mean cramp in the pelvic zone and some of the blood vessels in his face were threatening to burst. Herman was worried. Even though he still wasn't ready to believe that there was some kind of black magic monkeying with his evening, he was starting to get a creepy notion that the two-bit prophecies of the tarot card reader were more than just coincidence. He could feel his face flush and he sweated.

The first thing that he had to do, if he was going to shit or accomplish anything else, was to get himself to relax a little. Herman was so unaccustomed to anxiety that he didn't have a methodology for dealing with it. Knowing that he needed to come up with one was adding to his minor bout with terror. The possibility certainly existed that, through some bit of cosmic treachery, that he had allowed himself to be influenced by some of the information and advice that he had been getting. That he was actually feeding the cycle of fear and self-doubt that had led him to his current predicament and that if he could just recapture control of his confidence, he could put an end to the sequence of frustrating and tedious crap that had been happening to him. The way out was to reattach his focus to self-confidence and achievement, as opposed to insecurity. He took a deep breath and let himself off the hook. He tried to take the doctor's advice and just be in the moment. If he wasn't even trying to relieve himself anymore then he couldn't exactly fail at it, could he? He was just going to be and to let things happen. And while he was being, he figured that he might as well read something. Golf Digest was running a story about housing prices adjacent to pristine destination courses, like the one that Herman was about to develop. The article was occasionally separated from itself by up to a dozen glossy pages of advertisements.

Herman turned the page to an ad for Ford pickup trucks with a long-legged brunette in a bikini reclining against the windshield. Her hair looked liquid. And unlike most of the photos that you see in dentist-office-waiting-room sports rags, the model had her legs spread. Not a lot. Just a little. But enough. Enough to make Herman want to buy a Ford. And enough to get The Herminator's attention as well. It only took a couple of seconds before Herman's pale boner was sticking straight up into the middle of the stall.

The erection at least softened the muscles around Herman's anus and the need to defecate was no longer so severe. It also posed a new problem. The Herminator didn't go down easy.

And thoughts of crawling up onto the hood of the Ford truck and turning the model—who looked a lot like Laverne and inside of his imagination became Laverne—over and sliding into her from behind were starting to coalesce. Maybe tugging on her hair so her little pleasure moans mingled with a tinge of real pain. In Herman's head he was slipping the panties off of the fortune teller as he played with himself. Herman was stroking himself with his right hand. He had the magazine laying down on the floor where he could glance at it if he needed to but he didn't really need to anymore. His eyes were tightly shut. Laverne was on all fours on the hood of the car and Herman was crawling up on top of her and even though the fantasy was his, it was intruded upon by a shadow. The shadow lay across the hood of the car beneath them and it was cast by a huge cock that was dangling down from between Laverne's legs. It stretched all the way from her waist to where her knees were. Laverne held the windshield wipers in tight fists. Herman had one hand on her shoulder and one on her hip and he was driving the Herminator into the tight slot between her thighs. She let go of a wiper, reached back between her legs, behind her huge cock, and took a hold of his balls.

"Anybody in here?" someone shouted. It sounded urgent. Was the restaurant on fire? Herman snatched the magazine from the floor and draped it over his penis like a hat. His heart rate shot up to about 500 BPM. He could feel that there was a cool draft in the room from the door being open. Then he heard someone letting go of the door and walking inside. The wooden soles of their shoes clicked on the tile floor. The door shut softly on its pneumatic hinge and Herman could tell that whoever had entered the room was hunched over and scanning beneath the stall doors for sets of feet. "Anybody in here?" said the voice again. Softer this time. Herman knew that his Salvatore Ferragamo loafers were completely visible.

"I'm taking a crap," said Herman. "Is there some sort of a problem?"

"We just need this room clear for a few minutes."

"Why?"

"Lucky Soul has to piss."

"Fuck that asshole," Herman mumbled inside the stall.

"Excuse me?"

"So why doesn't he just come in and piss?"

"Parasympathetic nervous disorder. Makes it hard for him to go if anyone else is around. Lots of guys have it. I don't. I could piss in front of anybody."

Herman wanted to tell the bus boy to tell the actor to hold it but he was a little too beaten down for the confrontation. "Just give me a second," said Herman. He stood up and put his pants back on.

*   *   *

Herman was terrified of the idea of running into Ork on the way out of the john so he kept his head slung low and his eyes down. Herman had a crooked nose. It was broken during the overtime period, when Herman, Tipton and Ork's bantam league team beat the Puyallup Rodeo Clowns and won the league title. Herman went back on the ice and scored the game winning goal after his nose was broken. It was a legendary story, considering he was only twelve when it happened. He still wore the crooked nose with pride, another badge of honor decorating his head. It gave him an excuse to keep telling the story to girls. Usually they thought that the nose was cute. And the story was magic. Sort of. It's easy to love a winner so you could hardly call that magic. Either way, Herman had gotten a lot of mileage out of the deal with the nose, but with his hair and suit all fucked up looking, the broken nose came off more as a deformity than an endearing quirk. Ork would definitely recognize it and he couldn't afford to let that happen. Not when he was drenched in sweat, constipated, famished, parched, and trying to conceal a painful erection.

By the time he got back to his barstool twenty minutes had passed and he had accomplished exactly nothing. Dmitri and

Loven had beers but they didn't order him one. Loven had a white foam mustache. Allegedly a bartender had been there. But there wasn't one around to take an order from Herman.

"Sorry, man," said Loven, "we weren't sure what you were having." Herman was so thirsty that he considered swiping Dmitri's beer from him. Loven's was practically gone already. But he couldn't bring himself to do it. He couldn't even grovel for a sip. At least the waitress was coming over with the food. But she only had two plates on her tray. Both meals looked suspiciously like sandwiches.

"How did it go with the steak?" asked Herman.

"Not good," she said. "We've still got more than fifteen tables to turn over tonight and Tipton says everyone is ordering steak. Thinks it must have something to do with the article that just ran in the Times. The one about the status of the ocean water and all the chemicals that the fish are carrying. We can't sell anything that swims anymore." She put the burgers in front of Loven and Dmitri.

Dmitri immediately popped the top bun off of his and inspected it. "Got any mayo?" he said. The waitress gave the stink eye to Herman.

"I'll be right back with some."

Loven was cutting into the middle of his burger with a knife. "Honey, the chef forgot to cook this," he said.

This time the waitress put the heel of her boot on Herman's big toe and rocked until all of her weight was on his foot while she smiled and picked up Loven's plate and told him that she'd have the chef cook it well and bring it back.

"What about me?" said Herman.

The waitress turned and looked over her shoulder. "We still have the chicken," she said.

"Just bring me one of those burgers, please?"

She may have nodded before walking away.

Herman sat, tortured by the aroma wafting toward him from Dimitri's burger, unable to figure out a place to focus his attention, his eyes darting all around the room like there was a disco ball or something. He was untethered and skittish.

The waitress reappeared with Loven's burger, still sizzling, and mayo for Dmitri. He immediately opened the sandwich up and started slathering it on. After his first bite it started oozing out the sides and down his chin. It was disgusting and Herman suddenly remembered that he had intended to enact a new personal policy of only going out for food with Dmitri that was consumed with chopsticks.

The revolting image of Dmitri and the mayonnaise dripping like it was catapulted Herman back in time to one of his repressed memories from elementary school, where he watched his classmate Randy Matson load as much mayonnaise as humanly possible onto the two hoagies that he would eat every day for lunch. In fourth grade Randy was a slim, quick, and a star on the soccer field. By sixth grade he was obese, no longer an athlete, stricken with cold sores and chronic pink eye. Herman swore it was the mayonnaise that did it to him.

"Did you call your buddy about the blow?" Herman asked Loven.

"Shit. I totally forgot. I'll call him right after we eat."

While they were talking the waitress snuck up behind Herman and laid a plate down in front of him. A burger, basically burnt, drowning in mayonnaise, with a mesclun salad on the side.

"Fuck," said Herman. He spun around on his barstool so he didn't have to look at the plate and gazed out across the dining room. At the far end of the restaurant, he could see Lucky Soul and his group sitting with their food and their wine glasses. The muscle and the brains were locked into a private conversation. Ork was leaning against the back of his chair, and staring right back at Herman. It wasn't clear if the stare was blank, or if there was a hint of recognition in it. Herman thought he saw a mean smile begin to form on Ork's face. And then the actor looked down at his plate and helped himself to a piece of succulent meat. "I've got to get out of here." He took a hundred-dollar bill out of his wallet, dropped it on the bar and started heading for the door.

"Are you going to eat that?" asked Dmitri, pointing at Herman's sandwich. When he saw that Herman was leaving, he stuffed as much of it as he could fit into his mouth and chewed it while putting his jacket back on.

Outside it was straight up dumping rain. A November kind of rain that only took seconds to soak a person through. The streets were plugged with cars because everyone had forgotten how to drive when it was wet. Since it had been so long since the sky had washed the roads, a sheen of oil had built up and it was unusually slick on the surfaces as the two incompatible fluids mixed underfoot. Herman thought about summoning a cab but he needed to clear his head. He wasn't concerned about the rain. He started marching south. Moments later, Dmitri and Loven emerged from the restaurant and started zig-zagging through the raindrops toward Herman, trying to catch up.

None of them noticed the young Mexican girl standing outside the entrance, taking shelter under an umbrella with alternating gray and white panels. They moved along having no idea that Lupita was following them, twirling her umbrella, and doing her best impression of an uninterested pedestrian.

Barbie

Jars of cherry-picked nuggets of premium marijuana strains were neatly arranged and labeled in a gun locker that stood open in a corner of the loft. Inside there was also a shelf stacked up with canisters of live resin and shatter, a beaker full of extracted THC thinned with a glycol solution, a Ziploc bag stuffed with wafers of bubble hash and a half-kilo block of old school Blonde Lebanese. All of the smoking paraphernalia was at the bottom of the locker. There was a triple-percolating glass bong with a bonafide piece of a meteorite embedded in the tube, a sting ray shaped bubbler that was part of the dab rig, a torch and an old soup can full of sixteen penny nails, three glass pipes of varying sizes—all of which were too caked with black resin from overuse to be functional—and a quiver of one-hitters. There was also a shoebox containing paraphernalia for the paraphernalia: metal pokers, pipe cleaners, rags, a few Bic lighters, dental hygienist tools, and a surgical spoon. The inside door of the locker had a photograph taped to it of Peter Tosh squatting in the middle of a field of ganja, exuding unapologetic confidence. When Barbie walked in through the front door of the loft, Kenovan was rooting around in the locker, pulling out the supplies that he needed for his twilight smoke.

"You is all wet, mama," said Kenovan. After setting the dab rig down on the coffee table, he fetched a beach towel and then wrapped her up inside of his bony black arms. Barbie was very pregnant. She hadn't been keeping track of the weeks but the baby seemed fully developed and was starting to drop. "What is this?" Kenovan asked.

Barbie had a bag slung over her shoulder and resting on her hip. It was one of those kinds of bags that bikers always carry, made of thick rubber, folded over and clamped at the top so that the contents of it would not get wet.

"Just something I picked up," she said, after scooching up onto her tiptoes to kiss him back.

Kenovan was a Rastafarian whose parents had emigrated to New York City right before he was born. And he grew up in such a tight knit circle of Caribbean families that it wasn't immediately obvious that he was an American. He was well over six-foot, favored boots with thick soles, and the mound of dreadlocks on his head added a few more inches to a foot depending on whether they were coiled up or not. Barbie on the other hand, was so short she could barely get on the adult rides at the amusement park. Her belly and boobs were big but that was it. Everything else had stayed tiny. She had a blonde bob and blue eyes.

The loft that they lived in was in a building on Western that was slated for demolition. The city had already condemned the structure but the owner was still allowing a few artists to occupy the place for under the table cash deals while the project that was going to take over its footprint was frozen in permit reviews. Kenovan was a musician, the loft space was perfect for him and while he was going to hate to lose it, he wasn't really known for thinking all that far into the future. The pending demolition of the building didn't translate as stress for him. He played bass in a ska band and spun vinyl at parties. Kenovan's prize possession was a pair of Cerwin Vega speakers so large that he could only fit one of them at a time in the freight elevator. When he took them to parties, he had to rent a flatbed trailer and tow them behind his '68 Dodge camper van.

"What is inside the bag, mama?"

"I'm not sure."

"Did you steal it?"

"It was going to get left."

"Eye don't understand."

"I don't either, baby. I was just walking to my pre-natal yoga class—there was a sub for Zen neZ, which is worrisome—then I saw a really bad accident happen. Someone who was in a car that looked like a spaceship ran a light and hit a bicycle rider. The spaceship crashed into the front of a restaurant and the driver just got out and started running. I don't think that anyone was able to stop him. It was really scary."

"You sure that this is not a dream, mama?"

"It's not a dream. I've got the bag right here. This is what the biker who got hit was carrying."

"Did the biker die?"

"I don't know, baby. He bounced off the front of the spaceship and went way up into the air. He actually went all the way over the top of the car and landed on the street. And his bag went flying another way and landed right where I was walking by on the curb. The bike was flattened."

"Did the police come?"

"I'm sure that someone called them. Lots of people rushed over to help the boy out but no one was paying any attention to the bag. I just picked it up and took it. I don't know why."

"You should be more careful, mama. You have big baby in your belly and Gretta's guy is coming with the shipment. We can't be having no cops snooping around here. Did anyone see you take the bag?"

"I don't think so. The biker looked up for a moment and we saw each other, but then he put his head back down on the ground. I don't think that he will remember anything. He might not even survive, baby."

"Eye no like the sound of this, mama. Hopefully the biker will live. Eye don't want you to have to see a man die before our baby come into the life. Come here," Kenovan wrapped her up again in his long arms and gave her a squeeze.

"Sorry, baby," she said. "I don't know why I took the bag. I just couldn't help it. It was like something was telling me to do it."

"Then something was telling you to do it, mama. We should look at the inside. Maybe it is filled up with the money."

They didn't find any money in the bag. They found a pair of wet ankle socks that smelled like dog. There were three cigarettes left in a pack of Camels, a ring of keys, an iPod with ear buds, a wrinkled nylon wind-stopper jacket, and one of those Velcro straps that bikers use to peg their pant legs so that they don't get caught in their chains while they pedal. There was also a thick cardboard folder with the name Mitchell, Cronkey and Wolfe embossed on the cover. Inside of the cover was a stack of the kinds of documents that made Kenovan question his literacy. He had no attention span for legalese. He put on some King Tubby and went back to setting up the dab while Barbie kept flipping through.

Kenovan lit the butane torch and started heating up the glass bowl mounted on the outside of the bubbling sting ray. He wanted it up around 900 degrees. He checked the temperature by seeing how close he could get his hand to it. When it was how he liked, he let it settle and started scooping some of the live resin out of a canister with the sharp end of one of the nails. Barbie was sitting down on the love seat that they had found on the curb just last week with a *free* sign on it. It wasn't very comfortable or clean. She could tell that what she was looking at were the closing documents that transferred ownership of Summerwood Farms and all of its related assets to a Seattle based firm called Cronkey, Mitchell and Wolfe. The sale was dated that very same day. She had heard of Summerwood Farms before. Their apples were all over the place and the juice that they made was always being advertised during the afternoon talk shows that she liked to watch. Still, she couldn't see how there was anything useful in there. At least as far as she and Kenovan and the baby were concerned. She could have looked up the phone number for the company whose name was on the folder and asked them if they wanted their documents back. They probably did. But she was feeling lazy. And it was late on a Friday. Maybe she would look them up on Monday if the baby still didn't come. She kept the iPod for herself and then repacked the bag the way it was, kicked it deep underneath the bed, and then returned to the love seat next to Kenovan.

Kenovan touched the nail to the side of the hot bowl and twirled if deftly around so that all of the resin would come in contact with the hot glass. The inside of the sting ray gurgled and filled with a dense smoke. Kenovan inhaled slow and even, then he covered the bowl with the cap of the resin canister so that he could force out every wisp. When he exhaled it was a giant white plume that had a yellow tinge to it. But that was because of the warm spectrum CFL bulb that hung naked from some squiggly wires that descended from the rafters. Kenovan set the sting ray down on the coffee table, which was really just a piece of quarter inch plywood precariously balanced on four mismatched milk cartons. The plywood had a poster of Bob Marley smoking a a long cone-shaped spliff protected by a piece of plexiglass. He sat back and let the buzz wash over him.

"Isn't the pot coming soon?" asked Barbie. Kenovan seemed like he was drifting through another dimension.

"Not tonight," he said once he finally found his way back to his body.

"What do you mean? I thought Gretta said it would be here tonight."

"The guy phoned and said that his car is broke down. He can not make it until tomorrow."

"Shit. Where's he broke down?"

"Not sure, mama. Said that he could be here in the morning."

"Not too early, right?" Barbie was a person with lot of specific attributes. She was optimistic, resourceful, upbeat, open-minded, didn't ever run fast, didn't wear shorts or skirts, watched a lot of TV, believed in the existence of elves, ate a lot of canned food, and needed to sleep in. She was big fan of Joyce Carol Oates, a way above average roller-skater, and had seen every single episode of the television series 'Lost' twice. Not an easy feat for someone her age. She wasn't known for being moody or nervous, but she sure wanted to see the pot deal over and done with before the baby came. And she had a little bit of a queasy feeling that was connected to this friend of Gretta's being late with the weed. Once it showed up Kenovan was going to need to be gone for a few hours dealing with it. Big loads got shuttled up to one of his cousins who lived just north of the city. There they would repack it and load it into trucks that were going to New York. Kenovan didn't even get his cut of the money until it got back safely from the east coast. That's just the way it went. At least he didn't have to drive it there. By the foot of the bed was a brand-new duffel bag from the Army/Navy; soldier issue, olive green, with a hundred thousand dollars in cash in it. None of the money was Kenovan's. He was just the courier. If all went smoothly, he would come out of the deal with about fourteen thousand. Not bad for an afternoon's work. But it was going to be a month or more before he got paid. In the meantime, they were squatting in a condemned building with no furniture to speak of, a bare refrigerator, and a fantastic stereo system. Barbie was not a big complainer, but a little bit of money would have been nice. If the baby agreed it said so with a ferocious elbow to the bottom of the ribcage, followed by something that may have been a shoulder wriggle. Space was severely limited within the womb. "Ow!" she shouted.

"Is restless, mama?"

"Is biting I think. It won't stay in there much longer, baby."

"Eye know."

To say that Barbie's baby was due soon was as technical of information as there was available on the subject. She hadn't been to the doctor and had received really nothing in the way of prenatal care. She did attend a birthing class offered by an old doula with gray dreads that hung to her feet and a tender disposition. She was disappointed that Kenovan would not attend the classes with her. But it wasn't because he didn't want to go. He was just too self-conscious about being the tall black Rasta who had put the baby in the little white girl to be able to sit there in a room full of expecting couples and open up about the birthing process and being a father. It was fine. Kenovan could do a lot of things the other men in that room would never be able to do. And he was really interested in everything that was talked about in the classes and had Barbie fill him in when she got home. He even did some of the exercises with her for being able to stay with the breath during the contractions. They did them while clutching ice cubes to simulate what enduring a contraction was sort of like. Or at least they did until the freezer broke.

The birth didn't worry Barbie at all. She was a devoted naturalist and had a relaxed faith that her body would know exactly what to do when the time came. And she did have someone lined up to deliver the baby. She was what you would call a lay midwife and Barbie had taken a few prenatal yoga classes from her. She was a native of the big island of Hawaii named Agnes but she preferred to go by the palindrome Zen neZ. According to Zen neZ she had delivered between nine and twenty—the range was unnerving—healthy babies while hiding out in the jungles of the Napali coast with a bunch of feral hippies. Her cell phone number was written on a piece of paper that was stuck to the front of the refrigerator with a free magnet from South West Plumbing. On the magnet there was an image of a friendly plumber with a name tag that read 'Bob' waving—presumably at a customer—from the back of a very well-supplied and organized plumber's truck. Smug as he was, Barbie kind of liked Bob. He dealt with shit and it was a comfort having him around.

Kenovan took Barbie's hand, raised it to his lips and gave it a soft kiss. They didn't realize that Barbie was pregnant until she was around five months along. And Barbie figured that Kenovan was probably going to freak out about it. It was already too late to have an abortion even if they had wanted to. He didn't though. He shocked her by being glad. He'd been right there for her ever since, ready to be a dad. His reaction kind of contradicted everything that her mother had told her while she was growing up in the trailer outside of Savannah. She used to stand in front of the kitchen curtains, the ones with the flamingo print, smoking Pall Malls, ashing in the sink and warning Barbie about the uselessness of men. But Barbie was starting to think that her mom had just made bad choices or had bad luck or something. She and Kenovan should have been terrified of having a baby together. Neither of them had any experience with kids. And while Kenovan had a few cousins in town, they didn't have the kind of family network that makes taking care of a baby any easier. They were both young and unestablished. But it didn't matter to them. They weren't terrified and they didn't really mind not having much to work with. It made things less complicated. Barbie already had the only plan she really needed. She was going to breastfeed her baby and carry it everywhere.

"Want to watch movie?" asked Barbie, picking up the remote control and switching the set on. She had just dropped by the kitchen for a reheated burrito stuffed with steamed kale, ginger yams, grilled tilapia and grated cheese. She had it on a snack tray in front of her, along with a bowl of pretzels and a wedge of lemon cake. Kenovan and Barbie had pretty good cable service that was spliced off of the feed that the welder who lived on the bottom floor sprung for. Kenovan didn't respond to Barbie. The set was already tuned to a baseball game. Barbie was vaguely aware that Seattle had a baseball team but she didn't know its name and she didn't care for sports so she switched to Northwest Cable News where there was a breaking report. A female correspondent wearing a lot of make-up and a serious expression stood nodding silently at the camera, her eyes slightly downcast, one hand holding a microphone and the other holding an ear bud in place. The banner across the bottom of the screen introduced her as Alyssa Herder. She was hunkered underneath an umbrella with the station's logo on it, in front of the Cinerama movie theater. The entrance was blocked off with yellow caution tape and there were several individuals in white hazmat suits coming and going through the main doors. The in-studio anchor introduced Alyssa as being first on the scene for the Seattle Beetle Invasion.

"Thank you, Margaret and we aren't talking about Ringo and Paul here. In fact, we haven't even confirmed that the insects we are currently dealing with are even technically beetles. We do know that they are propagating in mass and being found in just gigantic numbers at some of the buildings in the downtown area. The Cinerama movie theater had to be evacuated during a double-feature of Rob Zombie horror films. You can see that some of the patrons behind me are dressed to, well, kill." Right on cue, one of the movie fans who was missing an eyeball and had the handle of a dagger sticking out of his neck bullied his way into the shot. "One woman who I spoke with was at the gastro-pub The New Luck Toy for happy hour and she said that the bugs started literally pouring out of the ceiling. As if the sprinkler system had come on and started spraying bugs out of it."

"Have the bugs been biting anyone?" asked the studio anchor.

"They don't seem to bite as much as they just sting; or what people I've spoken to, who have had contact with the beetles, describe more like electric shocks. And several of the buildings that have reported infestations have also had power outages and issues with the fiberoptic communication lines. Here at the Cinerama the beetles actually managed to short-out the projection system."

"Do the authorities think that the beetles or whatever they are might be chewing on the power lines?"

"It's a little too early to say anything definitively, Margaret. I can tell you that the fire marshal has reached out to the entomology department at the University of Washington and that—" Barbie switched to a movie station that was airing a marathon of the X-Men films. While it's true that Barbie had a thing for tall black guys, it was also true that she had a thing for Hugh Jackman-shaped white guys with claws instead of fingernails and gaudy sideburns.

"What do you think?" said Barbie.

"About what?"

"Do you want to watch the X-Men?" Kenovan stayed still and stoic while the gears of his mind turned and locked.

"Na," he said. Then he took the remote control from Barbie and turned the set off. With his big hands he grabbed the waistband of her Love Pink sweatpants and slid them down and off of her ankles, along with her panties. "Eye gots a better idea."

Retirement

Knots were forming at the top of Hartmut's calf muscles and his back had a tendency to ache when it rained. It was a side effect of being thrown from the back of a horse when he was a teenager and not having had the patience to let it heal properly. He handed his pickup truck off to the valet at the entrance to the Edgewater hotel and the walk from the curb to the elevator took a dog's age. The Frenzels had just returned from a downbeat celebratory dinner at Canlis overlooking Lake Union. Once they were back in their suite, Hartmut didn't even take off his hat before disappearing into the bathroom. He ordered the dry-aged duck with beets, molé, and sunflower seeds, but it wasn't the fault of the food. His IBS flared up after absolutely everything. Renata ate the roasted chicken Sabayon with artichoke, fermented carrots, and a side of forest mushrooms. She still had half of it with her in a paper bag that was neatly folded over at the top. Renata was one of those small eaters that always saved room for a slice of cake. Although after dinner at Canlis she had the banana mousse and a glass of champagne. They made an ambivalent toast to their retirement, all the money that they now had, and not having to get up every morning to confront the myriad peculiar problems that come along when you manage a large fruit orchard, processing facility, and a big workforce. They were trying to be happy but they were in unfamiliar terrain. Hartmut had some half-baked plans to pick up a twenty-foot watercraft with an outboard Evinrude motor and use it to pull some fish out of the Columbia River. Renata had been looking at investing in one of those long-arm quilting machines and setting it up in the basement so she could crank the quilts out at ten times the pace and help her girlfriends with theirs. She was nervous about it though because it would mean spending a lot of time on her feet, standing on the hard, concrete floor, and her planter fasciitis hated that.

At their core the Frenzels were sad. It wasn't so much the letting go of the orchard and getting older, it was that they both wished that they had someone that they could hand the business off to, so they could stay at least partly involved, and so it wouldn't have to feel like in the end, the only reason they did all the things they did was for the money. Handing off the reins like they were felt too much like dying, without the being dead part. It was merciless. They never wanted to sell their life's work to strangers. They wanted to be able to gift it over to family. But the Frenzels were rendered permanently childless when a devastating miscarriage at twenty-seven weeks left Renata unable to conceive afterward. That was in 1969, and they resigned themselves to never being parents. But later in life, when the idea of ever having a child had fallen way off the radar, one came their way. In many ways she was perfect, but she was also perfectly awful. And the fact that for the last ten years they have had no idea where she was loomed heavily on their hearts, and refused to let them ever experience a truly peaceful moment.

Her name was Ophelia and she was the grand-daughter of Hartmut's brother Martin. She was a whip-smart kid who had a childhood that was riddled with tragedy. Her mother abandoned her when she was just a toddler. The mom had addiction issues and was rumored to have run off to join a cult of some sort close to the border of Texas and Louisiana. No one ever went looking though. She was abandoned again a few years later by her father, who died of pancreatic cancer in an adjustable bed in the living room of Hartmut and Renata's farmhouse. After Martin was gone, there was nobody but Hartmut and Renata to look after Ophelia, so they adopted her.

She was nine-years-old at the time and already smoking Winstons.

The smoke in the young girl's lungs didn't hamper her athleticism though. She excelled at tennis and skiing. And her grades in school were impeccable, even after her attendance became spotty. She was a good driver, partially because of all the experience she gained stealing Hartmut's truck since she was barley a teenager. There was a rumor in the valley that before the end of high school Ophelia had had sex with a hundred different boys, and at least a handful of girls. Hartmut and Renata did their best to block that rumor out. Which was especially hard after they caught her one night, buck naked behind the cider press with little Sammy Bakungan and José. The Frenzels resorted to denial because they were inexperienced parents and had limited tools in their toolbox. By the time they became the legal guardians of the young girl, Renata's mothering instincts had diminished and gone mostly dormant. Hartmut was always at a loss as to what to do with her. He was too logical, and Renata was too much of a pushover. The only things that the old couple could think to do to gain some control over her was to threaten her with taking her things away—which they never followed through with—or promising to buy her things or give her candy if she did behave—which they always followed through with even if she didn't behave. They didn't realize that the best way to raise her was by setting a good example for her follow. They weren't capable of being confident role models. They were desperate and lost, but they also cared deeply about her and tried all of the things that they could think of to do. Ophelia was too beautiful for her own good, drawn to trouble, clever, and relentlessly energetic. Not knowing where she was for so long came with a helping of incessant shame and terror. Shame that they had failed as her guardians and lost her. Terror at the thought of all of the horrible things that could have happened to her.

Renata sat down in a leather armchair and threw her stockinged feet up on an ottoman that resembled a black bear cub. It was one of the features that made the classic Seattle hotel that they were staying in come off more like a Montana hunting lodge than a place that was literally built on a pier that hovered over the salt water. She heard the toilet flush but Hartmut did not emerge from the bathroom. It would be at least another flush or two before he would. The gas fireplace in the room kicked on and cozied the place up and Renata was surprised at how nice the warmth felt. It had been so hot and sticky lately, all the way up until dinner. By the time they had finished their desserts it was rainy, windy, and cold. She turned on the television set. It was tuned already to The Wheel of Fortune and Renata made a quick study of the puzzle. "Public Enemy Number One," she blurted out, even though there was nothing but the three E's and the R to work with. Then the suite's telephone rang and Renata jumped up to get it. Neither she nor Hartmut had consented to getting a mobile so far. Unlikely they ever would at that point.

"Hello."

"Renata. It's Omeed." Their lawyer was calling from a cheaper hotel that he was staying at up in Lynnwood.

"How are you, Omeed? Staying dry?"

"I am. Can you believe this weather? One minute it's the Bahamas, the next minute it's the North Pole. How was your dinner?"

"It was tasty but the portions were a little small. Where did you go?"

"My favorite. The Old Spaghetti Factory. No issue with the portion size there. Had to loosen my belt twice. And then I took it off entirely."

"How many bowls did you eat?"

"I lost count. There's something about the marinara at that place. I can't get enough. But listen, Renata, this isn't the reason I'm calling. There's something that's happened that I need to tell the two of you about. Is Hartmut handy?"

"We just got back from the restaurant. He's indisposed. Should we call you back?"

"No. You can just pass the message along. Although I am warning you that this isn't very good news. The numbers from the sale of Summerwood haven't recorded and the money hasn't budged. I've been on the phone with the staff over at Cronkey, Mitchell and Wolfe all afternoon. It seems as though the bike messenger that was hired to deliver the sale documents to the escrow offices was struck by a vehicle. He was badly injured and the documents that he was carrying have gone missing."

"Oh, my lord, Omeed. Is the boy going to be okay?"

"I don't know, Renata. He was taken away in an ambulance. Someone from the firm called down to Harborview where they took the kid, to see if they could get a hold of him and figure out what happened to his bag, but there was no way of getting through. It sounds like he is in surgery and probably being moved to intensive care after that."

"We have to send flowers. Do you know his name, Omeed?"

"His name is Benny Greene."

"I'm going to contact the hotel desk right now and have them put me through to a florist."

"Renata, I'm not sure what this means with respect to the sale of Summerwood. If those documents don't turn up, we may have to stay in the city and re-sign on Monday."

"We can't do that, Omeed. We have to be at church on Sunday morning. Hartmut already said that he would help set up chairs for the luncheon afterwards. And I'm supposed to be helping Dysa make cookies for the rotary club on Monday afternoon."

"Let's just hope that they turn up then, Renata."

"And that the young man who was carrying them is okay. I'm sick about this, Omeed."

"Me too."

"Do you think he's going to be okay?"

"The biker?"

"Yes. Benny Greene."

"I'm not sure, Renata."

"I'm going to pray for him."

"Good idea, Renata."

She hung up.

Just after the toilet flushed again and Hartmut materialized. "Who was that?" he said.

"Omeed. Hartmut, there's been a terrible accident."

"What kind of accident?"

"The young man carrying the closing documents that we signed to the escrow firm was hit by a car. It sounds like he's badly hurt. He might even die. We have no idea."

"Heavens, no," said Hartmut. "Where is he?"

"In the hospital having an operation. We need to send something."

"We will. Right away. What happened to the documents?"

"They're lost."

"Lost?"

"Lost."

"This is a problem."

"It could be a sign."

"What kind of a sign?"

"A sign from God. What other kinds of signs are there?" Renata was starting to bawl and rooting through her purse for a travel pack of Kleenex.

"Okay, love. It may be that he is going to be okay though, right." He put his arm around his wife.

"Omeed said that we might have to stay until Monday to re-sign, and go through it all again. We can't, Hartmut. We can't miss church. And I don't want to have to go and sign away our orchard again."

"It's alright, love," Hartmut massaged her neck and shoulders for her. "I'll give Omeed a call and see if we can figure something out. It will all be okay." He reached for the phone so that he could dial Omeed's number but the phone started ringing before he could pick it up. "Omeed?" he asked.

"Excuse me?" responded the caller.

"This isn't Omeed?"

"Who am I speaking with?"

"This is my hotel room. Who am I speaking with?"

"Apologies, sir. My name is Detective Cavalieri. I'm with the Pima County Police Department in Arizona. I am trying to track down Hartmut and Renata Frenzel. I was given the number of this hotel by their housekeeper," he paused while he rooted around for the name, "Celiné Ochoa Perez. Is this Hartmut?"

"It is," said Hartmut.

"Who is it?" asked Renata. Hartmut put his hand over the mouthpiece.

"It's a detective from Pima County Arizona."

"Oh my God," said Renata. "It could be about Ophelia."

"What should I do?"

"For God's sakes, Hartmut, talk to him." Hartmut took his hand off the mouthpiece.

"What can I do for you, detective?"

"Mr. Frenzel, I have some news regarding the disappearance of your dependent Ophelia Dreiss."

"Yes," said Hartmut.

The officer took a breath. "We've located her body, Mr. Frenzel. I am afraid that she is no longer alive."

Hartmut put his hand back over the mouthpiece. "She's dead," he said to Renata, who started sobbing uncontrollably. Hartmut gave her his hand and she squeezed it tightly. "Where did you find her?" said Harmut, back to the detective.

"Her bones were discovered in a shallow grave on a piece of public land in the Coronado National Forest. It was actually two twelve-year-old boys who found her. They were attending a wilderness survival camp and digging a trap when they found the remains of some old blankets with human bones wrapped up inside. But it was our people who fully excavated the site once the counselors called the police."

"Did she look like she suffered?"

"That is a hard question to answer, Mr. Frenzel. Her body was in the ground a long time. We haven't determined the cause of death yet. But we do feel like Ophelia was murdered, Mr. Frenzel."

"Because someone took the time to bury her?"

"Yes. But also because of something else that we learned after we exhumed her body."

"What was that?"

"That whoever buried Ophelia, Mr. Frenzel, also separated her from her head."

"What?"

"There's just no other way to say this, Mr. Frenzel. There was no skull in the ground. And it appears to have been removed from the body prior to burial. I'm very sorry to have to give you this news."

Hartmut sat down on the arm of the chair that Renata was sitting in. Shocked.

"What is it, Hartmut?" she asked. He covered the mouthpiece again.

"Someone cut off her head."

Renata snatched the receiver away from her husband.

"Detective, this is Renata Frenzel. Would you please tell me what you just told my husband?"

"Mrs. Frenzel. My name is Detective Cavalieri with the Pima County Police Department. I just informed your husband that the bones of Ophelia Dreiss were discovered in an unmarked shallow grave on public land in the Coronado National Forest. And that there was no skull with the rest of her bones."

"Where is it?"

"The head?"

"Yes."

"We don't know that, Mrs. Frenzel. I'm very sorry for your loss. We think that the best thing to do at this point is to focus on figuring out who committed the crime against Ophelia."

"Did you find any other clues?"

"We didn't find anything like a murder weapon if that is what you are asking but there are some leads that we are following up on."

"Well, what are they?"

In the background Pat Sajak was going through a smarmy commiseration with a guest that had just gone from $5000 to Bankrupt in one horrific spin, and then segued into a commercial for erectile dysfunction. Renata fumbled with the remote until she found the mute button.

"I'm sorry but I'm not really at liberty to say, ma'am. At this time, it remains an open investigation."

When Ophelia went missing, she was living in Tucson, Arizona. She had barely made it through high school and gotten a diploma. Her grades were fine but her attendance record was abysmal and she got herself into major trouble with the school after lighting a Roman candle in the boys' locker room during the homecoming football game. There was a bunch of smoke damage, the locker room had to be repainted and the game had to be stopped and the stands evacuated. The police and fire department responded as though it was a terrorist attack and the Frenzels had to make a huge donation to the school district to have the charges dropped. She also had an arrest record for urinating off of a freeway overpass and for being pulled over at sixteen-years-old going well over a hundred in a forty-five-miles-per-hour zone with a blood alcohol content of 1.4. Principal Nathanson let her graduate mainly to be rid of her. The Frenzels convinced themselves that a change of scenery could save her and talked her into enrolling in Pima County Community College and moving to Tucson. They drove her there themselves and rented her an apartment close to the campus. Her first semester went surprisingly well. She put up a B plus average in four classes and was showing some real interest in business logistics. Just into her second semester she dropped out. She even had the bursar's office refund her tuition in the form of a check made out to her for just over two-thousand dollars. She withdrew two-hundred dollars of that money right away. The remaining balance had been sitting in her checking account ever since gaining small amounts of annual interest. One of Renata's unhealthy obsessions, since Ophelia's disappearance, was to check the account's balance daily, hoping that it would be suddenly drawn down. But it never was.

"Do you have any questions that I can answer for you, ma'am? I know that this is very difficult news to hear."

"I apologize for not having been here to accept the call earlier, detective. It's been a hard day for us already."

"I'm sure it has, ma'am." The detective stayed quiet for a moment and waited for Renata to collect herself. She closed her eyes hard and swallowed.

"What happens next?"

"When we know something definite, we will get in touch with you. And of course, we are assuming that you will be wanting to transfer the body for a proper burial."

"What do you think the chances are that we will get to bury her with her head?"

"I honestly don't know, ma'am."

The Killer's Private Dick

Leftover rigatoni and Dungeness crab from the Seatown Snackbar sat in a paper box on the granite island counter top in Duncan's kitchen. He had barely touched it. He was too busy ranting about the incompetency of the bike messenger service to an old acquaintance of his, a private detective named Hal Baranoff.

"I swear, Hal, I'm thinking about buying that bullshit company, and sending those freaks over to Siberia where they can learn what it means to do some work, and not just ride a goddamn bicycle around all day. I can't believe that idiot failed us."

"Doesn't exactly sound like he failed you, Duncan. You just told me the kid was hit by a car."

"He isn't a kid, Hal. He's almost my age. And his only mission was to carry a small bundle of papers across town and he screwed it up. It wasn't even a car that hit him. It was a rolling advertisement for RocketFuel energy drinks. Of all the things not to see coming. These bikers. RocketFuel is probably the cornerstone of their diets."

"Do you know if the kid is dead or alive?"

"I don't. Whether he is dead or alive is his own problem. All I care about is what's in the bag that he was carrying."

"Can we back up for a moment here? You haven't even told me what *was* in the bag that he was carrying." Hal was an ex-cop who had been working in the private sector for most of his career. As a private sleuth he was pretty typical looking. Overweight from a lot of fast food and sitting around in the front seat of cars. His mop of curly brown hair was fighting its way out the underside of his porkpie hat. He wore a beige trench coat that went down to his knees. In the breast pocket of the coat he carried a spiral notepad and a blue Bic pen. Hal and Duncan knew one another from college. They were both members of the same fraternity at the University of Arizona, or The Zone, as they had referred to it since.

"This afternoon we signed the closing documents that transfer ownership of Summerwood Farms and all of its assets over to Cronkey, Mitchell and Wolfe. Ever heard of Summerwood?"

"The ones who make the apple pie pockets?" Hal had picked up a small mountain's worth of Summerwood's fruit pie pockets at the Quiki-Mart over the years. They were one of the main culprits that contributed to his shapeless mass. The trench coat didn't help either. It made him look not so much dressed as tarped.

"I hate to break this to you, Hal, but the last run of pie pockets from Summerwood has already been cranked out. The only stuff of theirs that we are interested in is their land, their fleet, and some of the processing equipment. It's all getting divided up and sold off."

"What about the trees?"

"Cutting them down next week. Herman's supposed to be putting together a team to take care of it. I think he's still hunting for some way to get a little more money out of all the wood so we don't just have to burn it all."

"What about the apples?"

"I'm talking about the apple trees, Hal. Are you going 'round the bend?"

"I didn't say the apple trees, Duncan. I said the apples. I'm no orchard keeper, but I'm pretty sure that apples are picked in the fall." Duncan just stared back at Hal.

"We are not doing anything with the apples, Hal. We are just going to let the birds have them."

"Not worth bringing in one more harvest?"

"Are you thinking about a new career, Hal? Trying to nose into investing?"

"I'm just curious to know if anyone has motivation to make these documents go missing. I'm not trying to squeeze your shoes here."

"In order for the developer to make use of the winter we need to get some concrete work done and some new roads blasted through the property. We can't put that off for the sake of dealing with the apples. Herman is going to get the trees cleared next week, and the bulldozers are slated to start tearing out the root systems and regrading on the tenth. If we are lucky, the developer will have three or four weeks to excavate and to pour. If it doesn't work out, they are going to lose half a year."

"Where is Summerwood Farms?"

"Their orchard is in Peshastin. It spans both sides of the river and has a power substation sitting on it that is on a state-owned easement, but the facility is run by Bonneville Hydro. Their transmission lines traverse the site and follow the river. So, we have them to deal with but they haven't made a peep so far. Summerwood Farms also owns a bit of property in Cashmere where they keep their motor pool and an office building in Wenatchee as well."

"Any groups out there opposing this plan of yours to cut down the orchard?"

"Almost no one knows about it. The locals are all aware of the sale but they think that we are going to keep the orchard running and be making improvements. We had to put up Proposed Land Use Action Signs that show where the first round of new buildings and ingress/egress are going to be. Supposedly the footprints are for a new bunkhouse for migrant workers, exercise facility and medical clinic, but changing the functions of those buildings is a simple matter. Peshastin's a pretty small community and we have an inside guy on the township's board that is buddies with the local congressman. We have confirmation that this project is going to be green lit as part of the state's new push to present itself as being friendly to business development. But we haven't publicized it yet. Our biggest hurdle is the old couple who technically still owns the farm, the Frenzels. They marketed the farm with an airy contingency of not cutting the orchard down but they didn't have sense enough to write it into the deal. And every time we reiterate that once the sale goes through, CMW obtains all decision-making power with respect to the land and the business, they are not phased. We are of course expecting a little pushback at the beginning just because no one is comfortable with change. But we also feel like the locals are going to come around on this one. The new resort and the construction of the adjacent development is going to create a lot of year-round jobs for the people who live there. Not just work for part-time transients who don't even pay taxes. It's beautiful country out there. And the apple trees are taking up a lot of space that people could be using."

"Do you think it's possible that there was a leak?"

"I guess so but I doubt that's what happened."

"How come?"

"We made it all the way through the signing of the paperwork. If the internet didn't go down this afternoon, all of this would be over. If someone wanted to sabotage the deal, they pushed it pretty far."

"You're convinced that this is an accident."

"Bad luck."

"Back in the Zone you once told me you didn't believe in luck."

"I did, didn't I."

"Hmm. Tell me more about what happened today. What are the Frenzels' names?"

"Hartmut and Renata."

Hal wrote the names in his little book.

"It's kind of a unique situation. The farm has been in their family since the 1800's but they don't seem to have any kids or nephews or anyone to leave the thing to. We had them over to the office today to sign the closing documents. They were fine. Kind of like they always are. You have to repeat everything for them a hundred different ways and they need to eat about every five minutes. What should have taken an hour took a grueling three but we got it done. When it was finally over, we sent the documents to the escrow office with the bike messenger so that they could record the numbers from the sale. But the documents never made it to the escrow office."

"Do you know the name of the bike messenger who picked up the documents?"

"Benny Greene."

Hal wrote it down. "Is that what you normally do with sale documents? Send them with a bike messenger?"

"No. As a matter of fact we have never done that with closing documents before. The procedure is to transfer a digital copy to the escrow office and their agent keeps the originals. Which, by that point, are kind of a formality because they have all been uploaded. But not today. Today we got fucked over by the never-ending construction in this town. Plumbing crew or something pierced one of the fiber-optic lines that services the tower and we had no internet or fax available. This is a perfect shit storm isn't it, Hal?"

"I kind of like all the construction going on in this town."

"What the hell for?"

"I'm out and about all day. If I need to use the head somewhere, I just look up and find a crane that is being used on a job site. Then I follow it to a Honey Bucket the way a leprechaun follows a rainbow to a pot of gold."

Duncan stared at Hal, his face ghostly white and disoriented. He wasn't accustomed to having to come up with solutions for the type of banal problem that Hal was proposing. He didn't even find it funny. He simply couldn't relate. Hal got back to business.

"Have you ever used that bike messenger before?" Hal asked.

"Benny? We use him for shit all the time. Normally he's very good."

"Did you see him personally today?"

"I watched Allison from Talon Escrow hand him the folder with the sales documents myself. I even saw him tuck it into his hip bag and get on the elevator. His left pant leg was rolled up like it always is."

"And that was the last that you saw of him?"

"Yes, Hal. That was the last I saw of him. I tend not to follow the bike messengers to their destinations. I have enough to do."

Hal remained stoic while Duncan let his emotions weave together with the facts. "When did you first find out that the documents were missing?"

"After I got back here. Not long after six."

"Any idea where the accident occurred?"

"Fourth and Battery. Sounds like the biker was northbound on the one-way and the billboard that hit him was traveling west."

"Was it really a billboard?"

"No, actually. It was a PT Cruiser built out to look like a rocket ship. It wound up smashing into the dining room of a noodle place that was closed at the time. We had Linus go down there to do some recon. He texted me this picture." Duncan showed Hal the screen of his phone. There was a photograph of the rocket's back end. One wheel was way up in the air. There was shattered glass all over the sidewalk and the area was cordoned off with yellow caution tape. Hal jotted down the license plate number. Duncan opened up the refrigerator for another beer. He offered Hal one but he declined. Hal had given up drinking after his last divorce and Duncan knew it.

"What happened to the driver of that vehicle?"

"We don't know. Word is that he fled the scene."

"Maybe with the messenger's bag?"

"I suppose it's possible."

"What else did Linus find out?"

"Nothing."

"Did he try asking the biker?"

"Sounds like he tried but the cops and the paramedics had the kid walled off."

"Was the biker talking?"

"I'm not sure he was breathing. I don't think that he was talking."

"There are a bunch of businesses down at that intersection. Lola is on the corner, there's a Bed Bath and Beyond. Lots of apartments. Did he ask any questions?"

"You've met Linus, Hal," Duncan drank the neck of the beer and set it on the counter. "He's a pimply faced little turd who probably cheated his way through Dartmouth. I'm surprised that he can remember what floor to tell the elevator operator to take him to. I'm sure he didn't ask any questions. That's what I need you to go down there and do."

"I'll call the station first and see if the biker's bag didn't wind up in the evidence room."

"Thanks, Hal."

Hal checked his Timex wristwatch and Duncan could see that he was wearing the gold commemorative bracelet that the two of them had earned during their last year together in The Zone. They had organized a wildly successful—depending on how one tilts the head—charitable fundraiser through their fraternity house. They convinced fifteen teams full of members of the Greek community to get sponsors and participate in a Cannonball Run to raise money for a variety of debatably good causes. The race started and ended on campus in Tucson. In between, each team had to collect a certificate of arrival from a station close to the Canadian border in northern Michigan and bring it back with them to the campus. Two teams had to bow out with blown motors. Three teams had arrests for DUI slow them down, but only one person served any real jail time. A Tri-Delt sorority sister flipped a Nissan 370Z on a farm road in Iowa and skidded past several acres of corn on the roof.

Everyone else made it to the finish line but none as fast as Duncan and Hal, who were driving a navy-blue Sterling, which was basically an amped up Honda Accord but with harder to obtain replacement parts. DJ Shadow spun records at the party after the race, which lasted for the better part of a week. Hal got laid, which was a rare occurrence in The Zone. She was a freshman from Peoria, Illinois who wanted to study the molecular structure of polymers. She was pretty rough on the eyes when the sun was out, but at night with the right buzz she seemed cute enough. Luckily for Hal it was night when she cornered him in the phone booth. And he was roaring drunk.

There was such a massive financial windfall attached to the charity fund raiser that people tended to forget pretty quickly about the tragic mishaps that it spawned. A research clinic in North Carolina working on a cure for emphysema got a check for twenty-seven-thousand dollars. A hundred new TX-91 calculators were gifted to the Tucson public school system. An eleven-year-old paraplegic living in the Buena Vista Trailer Park got sent to a real Texas Rodeo. An occasion marked by a framed photograph of the limp, lanky kid being balanced by his terrified-looking parents and a grinning cowboy on the back of a three-thousand-pound bull. The fraternity house got a new roof. And Duncan, Hal, and the fraternity's treasurer Edmund Loosestring, each received a few thousand dollars in cash and instructions not to mention anything about that part to anyone ever. Plus, the embossed commemorative gold bracelets, which was still a part of Hal's daily ensemble. Duncan didn't have any idea where his was, if he even still had it.

"I'll put a call in to the hospital as well and see if I can get an update on the biker's condition. I'm assuming they took him to Harborview?"

"They did but that's a dead end. We already tried calling there and they said that they will only give out information to family members."

"I may have better luck. I'm sure that the RocketFuel car is registered to the business but I'll see if I can get the name of whoever was driving it. If I don't turn something up, I'll start nosing around down at that intersection. Somebody had to see something."

"It worries me that some crackhead just absconded with it. It's not the best part of downtown to leave something lying around on the road. A half-eaten Big Mac is a hot commodity around there."

"That may also be the best thing that could have happened. Getting a stack of paperwork back from an addict will be cheap." That reminded Duncan that Hal was going to need some street money to work with. He withdrew a copper money clip from the jacket pocket of his Puma jump suit and gave it to him. There was fifteen thousand dollars in the clip but there were several fives and tens on the outside. Duncan knew how Hal liked a billfold to look. If he had to grease someone, he didn't want to start waving Ben Franklins at them right away. A typical junkie in Pioneer Square would sell the bag for enough to get one fix. Maybe two if he had some skank hanging on him.

"Whatever it takes, Hal," said Duncan, making intense eye contact so that his old friend would be able to see how serious he was. Hal put the money safely away.

"What's the issue with just bringing the Frenzels in to re-sign the deal?"

"I'd rather not see it come to that. There are already reasons to be worried about them backing out. They're not like most of the people we buy companies from. They don't have their eyes on the future. They're always looking backwards these two. It's like they don't even care about the money or what they can do with it. They're all concerned about the people who've been working for them and their legacy in Eastern Washington. Herman has been stringing them along forever on this one, really pushing the boundaries of corporate fraud. The old couple is under the impression that Cronkey, Mitchell and Wolfe are going into the apple producing business. When they find out that we are going to mow the trees down and have a developer breaking ground on a new golf resort with a year-round indoor water park they're going to fill their adult under garments. Having to re-sign would be more than unprofessional looking. It might make this whole thing fall apart. Hal, this fish is hooked, reeled to the surface, gaffed, and in the boat. If it flops out now, we are total assholes and deserve to lose it."

"Where's Herman at? Sounds like this is his baby."

"His phone isn't working and I had to track down Loven just to find him. He's at a bar, getting his fucking tarot cards read by some kook from the TV."

"What for? Is he worried about something?"

"He should be, and if the card reader is any good the freak will hopefully tell him that."

"Where's he at?"

"I didn't ask. I'm assuming that they just went out drinking after the deal closed and met the card reader somewhere. Loven's supposed to have Herman call me as soon as he's done but it's been nearly a fucking hour."

"Sounds like they are both in hot water."

"Herman's a loose cannon, Hal. He's been gloating about this purchase all along. Way too cocky and sure of himself. I like that he is aggressive but he looks at everything through the same lens. He's a blockhead. And I'm pissed at myself for allowing him to get us over-extended here. If this thing falls apart, we are looking at a lot of wasted time. And it's going to be my ass that gets chewed out by Cronkey."

"Those guys really exist?" Hal was aware of the running joke around the office about the three gentlemen, or women, that the firm was named after. No one who worked at the offices had ever met them. Except for Duncan supposedly, who was the CEO of the business and the sole liaison to its absentee ownership.

"Very funny, Hal. Yes, they exist. And they are not very understanding with people who manage their money poorly."

"Do you think that there is any way that Herman could have had a role in the documents going missing?"

"What do you mean?"

"I mean does Herman have any reason to benefit from the deal not closing."

"I haven't thought about that. I don't think so. He stands to do pretty well on the commission. He's been counting on the money for months even with the deal on shaky ground. I really don't think so. At worst he'd get too drunk to be able to deal with any responsibilities."

"Would that be like him to do?"

"Not really. He's an asshole who only thinks about himself. But he doesn't drop the ball. This is the first time that I haven't been able to get him on the phone. And I agree that it's suspicious that I talked to Loven over an hour ago and Herman still hasn't called back. What's your angle here? Sounds like you think this might not have been an accident."

"I'm not ruling anything out. And I am not as knowledgeable as you are about all the legal stuff here. Are you worried at all about getting hit with a lawsuit from the Frenzels once you start cutting the trees down?"

"There's been a lot of conversations about that. Even though Herman keeps filling their heads with bullshit promises the old couple and their lawyer haven't asked for anything to be confirmed in writing. They are a part of that generation that still thinks that looking a person in the eye and having a firm handshake are things that you can take to the bank. Herman at least keeps reminding them that once the deal is signed, Cronkey, Mitchell and Wolfe will have the autonomy to do whatever we want with it. Even if it means modifying verbal agreements. That part of the deal is in writing."

"What about their lawyers? Seems like they should be advising them differently."

"Their lawyer is a major genetic mishap. The Spartans would've tossed him off of a cliff the moment he was born. Looks like a Pakistani crossed with a grouper fish."

"Sounds like grouper fish make better sandwiches than they do lawyers."

Duncan walked over to the glass wall that overlooked Seattle. "There are a lot of idiots out there, Hal."

The private investigator took that as his cue to leave. He let himself out while Duncan just kept staring out the window at the city below. There was someone down there waiting for him. Someone whose name was Laverne Korzha de las Bulgarias. For a few minutes Duncan engaged in a meditation technique that he had learned by accident while riding the subway in New York City a long time ago. He was alone and without anything to read and there was a discarded Utne Reader on the seat next to him. He checked out an article that seemed about as generic and hokey as everything else in that rag, promising inner peace or stability or something. It was called The Path Technique and it asked its participant to close their eyes and meditate on a spiral. Duncan didn't remember anything more specific about the article than that. But he developed a practice from it and he retreated to that practice during moments of unbearable mental noise and stress. There was a lot of lingering mental residue from the work week and Duncan needed to put it away if he was to function as his best self. At times such as those he was keenly aware of the need to be precise. He started at the outside of the spiral and let his eyes follow the soft blue curves of it as they tightened around the spiral's cold center. When he got there, however long it took, he kept his thoughts trained on that center until the rest of the world fell away. Soon the only thing that he was aware of at all was the purified air in the condominium drifting lazily in and out of his lungs, him putting zero conscious effort into the activity at all, simply noticing it and leaving it at that. Once he had attained the absolute calm that he sought he went back to his wardrobe. Comfortable as the Puma jumpsuit was, he couldn't risk getting it soiled. Plus, it was important that he didn't draw any unwanted attention to himself. He kept a special outfit for those kinds of nights. It was the outfit of every man and it made him impossible to see and even harder to remember; size 31x34 Levi's 505 dungarees in classic blue, long sleeve black cotton jersey, Seattle Seahawks baseball cap, hunter green Helly Hansen rain slicker, and some slip-on Blundstone boots.

He took the elevator down to the parking garage, tapped a button on his keychain and the door of his 2017 Tesla Roadster opened automatically for him. He wanted to drive around downtown but he couldn't do it in the sports car. Even in Seattle the new edition of the Roadster turned a lot of heads and that was the last thing he needed. He drove up north along the waterfront to a private lot underneath the Magnolia Bridge where he kept his special-occasions vehicle, still yet to be broken in. It was a windowless van in the same gray as the rain. A 2015 with very low miles that he bought for cash off of a general contractor named Aldert Hessel, who was moving his family back to Amsterdam. Duncan had actually left the van registered in Aldert's name. An 'I'm Ready for Hillary,' sticker eroded on the passenger side of the rear bumper, providing the absolute perfect cover. Duncan left it there even though it made his skin crawl.

He hadn't used the vehicle in so long that there was a build-up of pollen and dust on the windshield that smeared and caused a wicked glare. It was nothing like the Tesla. It was cold inside of the cavernous van and the big Ford engine took a long time to heat up and warm the interior space. Duncan tended to think of himself as being tough. But he sometimes wondered if he was tough enough to go to work every day at six am in a cold cargo van. He knew that many of the guys who did that for a living even worked outdoors. It was an almost unimaginable plight, like something that was only fathomable for the members of a much lower rung on the ladder of civilization. But it did force him to turn the lens on his own role within the territory of the civilized. What rung on the ladder did the reclusive serial killer occupy? The same one as the corporate CEO he assumed; the uppermost. He didn't think that he shared much of anything at all with common men. His ilk were the polar bears and orca whales of the world. Duncan was an apex predator, and he needed a meal.

While the van rumbled and hissed and organized its rhythms, Duncan did a quick search on his phone for the fortune teller. It took a little bit of digging to get past her website's primary goal, which was to get people to call in to her psychic hotline. On the blog of a local birdwatcher Duncan discovered that Laverne had a storefront in Belltown where she saw clients and did in-person readings. The birdwatcher gushed about how her tarot card reading was all about witnessing something rare and special and it preceded—by only two months—the sighting of a Hudsonian Godwit feeding at a mudflat near Ocean Shores. Duncan got the address that Laverne worked out of and drove south thinking that he should probably do the world a favor and kill the birder too.

He pulled the van into a loading zone at Fourth and Lenora and let it idle for a moment. He could see the neon signs that wrapped the Cinerama movie theater from where he was parked. They flickered in an unsettling way and then shut off. Droves of people were spilling out of the theater and fanning out across the streets in the rain. Many of them dressed in macabre attire. It was more like watching an army of the undead pouring out of a whole in the ground than watching people walk out on a film. It was strange, but rather than dwell on its origins he chose to appreciate the distraction.

The mob seemed like it was going to head mostly south so Duncan pulled the van out of the loading zone and went north on fourth, which felt upstream because of the crowd. In a block or two it was quiet and the city seemed like it had already gone to sleep even though it was still early on a Friday night. No one was on the sidewalks, which made sense because of the rain. But it was true as well that many of the buildings were uncharacteristically dark.

He looped back on Second via Broad Street and drove through a few more dark blocks before crossing Wall where the lights at the Cyclops were at least on. There was another loading zone that was empty and he pulled in on the west side of the street in front of a small business wedged between a sushi restaurant and jewelry store with the windows barred. It was Laverne's shop and he could see her inside, seated in an elegant wooden chair stained black. She had an array of cards laid out in front of her on an expansive table that matched the chair. The customer was a black woman, with hair that was separated into innumerable thin braids that reached down to the middle of her back.

The vehicle in front of Duncan's van pulled away and he was able to slide into a legal spot that he could watch the fortune teller from. The rain kept pouring down and made him feel invisible. He switched the radio on and caught the back end of a news report about an army of bugs that was breeding at an alarming rate and taking out a lot of the city's power grid. Duncan felt a moment of kinship with the bugs. Perhaps that insect too belonged amongst the Orca whales, polar bears, and Duncan Klevits of the world. No reason an apex predator should have to be large. When the report segued into a commercial for a television liquidation superstore, he turned the radio dial and alighted on a classical station playing the Goldberg Variations. From the glove box he withdrew a pair of leather gloves, black and well worn. Then he withdrew the old necropsy knife from his veterinary days, and checked his reflection on the side of the sharp blade.

Eccentric Friends of Zen neZ

Mass hysteria and panic ensued when the assembly of horror movie fans were forced to evacuate the Cinerama as the bugs shorted out the power. There wasn't much in the way of authority nearby to help. It was already a busy night in Seattle. The Eagles were in town for their final farewell tour and eighteen thousand fans were packed into the re-remodeled Key Arena singing 'Peaceful Easy Feeling.' Fans of the band would be the some of the last to find out that during the show the rains had come back and an exploding population of hungry insects was threatening to shut the entire city down. Peace and Ease were on their way to being Dead and Buried. Two weather related car accidents involving fatalities were already under investigation. One was on I-5 close to the entrance to the West Seattle Bridge. The other was on Denny Way and involved a pedestrian that was also a renowned violinist from a touring symphony company. On top of that, a higher than usual percentage of police officers who had been required to work the busy late summer weekends had requested off and fled town with their families looking for a little R&R before it turned full blown autumn and wet all the time. So when the bugs rained down from the ceiling of the Cinerama movie theater and several hundred fans of Rob Zombie's horror films—most of which had shown up in costumes reflecting their profound love of blood, guts and general sadomasochism—spilled out into the streets, there simply weren't a lot of officers on duty or even on call that could react. The crowd was moving south on Fifth Ave. like a small hurricane. Couples on first dates, families with young children, and weekend warriors who had just gotten up from their naps and headed out for a night on the town, all fled to the other side of the street when they saw a mob coming.

The mob was both terrifying and terrified. Seattle wasn't really a hub for violence and most of the people in the crowd had come in from smaller Washington and Oregon towns and didn't know the city at all. They were lost and confused by all of the tall buildings and concrete. And many of them, despite harboring a television level affection for watching other human beings endure pain and die, were so frightened by the sudden appearance of the insects that they could barely function at all. Anger, frustration, fear, trauma, disorientation, disappointment, drugs, and cheap liquor were all fueling a strange party that wasn't sure what to do with itself. There was a cacophony of devilish laughter, murderous screams, threats of torture, and then someone announced a hunt for a sacrificial lamb. The crowd was instantly soaked when it left the theater. The gutters ran pink as the rain dissolved the fake blood and ran it toward the storm drains, which already sounded like Hell's Canyon and were close to overflowing. A short old man in a dirty brown union suit tore a garbage can off of a lamp post and held it high above his head. He had a stringy, Amish style gray beard but his upper lip was shaved smooth. To most of the people in the streets that night he was unfamiliar but to some of them he was known as Masochistic Mitch. With the garbage can he smashed the windshield of an Audi wagon and the car's alarm started to blare. About half the crowd unleashed a joyous scream at the sound of the alarm. The other half was trying to stop shivering and coming to grips with the lifetime of nightmares about insects that awaited them. Because of the bugs, something had erupted at the horror movie screening that no-one was anticipating: true horror.

After a couple of blocks of rollicking and screaming the energy of the crowd either fizzled or was extinguished by the pouring rain. Many of the disoriented movie fans had exchanged their wild hoots for uncontrollable teeth chattering and were suddenly mired in the very complicated puzzle of trying to figure out where they had left their vehicles. Friends who had driven in to the city together were clustered and providing support to one another as they walked around arm in arm looking for landmarks; or safety. There were a lot of wet cigarettes being smoked. There was also a lot of crying, especially amongst the girls, who could handle watching a film of one of their own bleed out from small slashes while being tied to a bed post, but couldn't endure the thought of a tiny six-legged critter hiding somewhere in their hair, waiting for the right moment to sink one if its microscopic fangs into the nape of its victim's neck.

There was a couple that drove up together from Oregon and the two of them had a love for the films that they had come up to see that ran at a creepy depth. They dressed in character, and called themselves The Devil's Rejects, after the title of the second film. Prior to the show, and during, they had been hitting a stash of well-refined mephedrone, otherwise known as bath salts. In combination with alcohol, mephedrone was known to cause serious psychotropic effects. The man was the one who had procured the salts. He was technically a senior citizen, who stood a full head above anyone else that encircled him, wearing a soggy wife-beater and a denim sarong. His face was painted to look like a scary clown. The paint got scarier as it thinned out and ran. Blue eyebrows exaggerated into giant arcs that stretched up to his receding hairline and also dripped down into his eyes. The cowgirl he was with called him Daddy. She had hair that was curly and golden and stretched all the way from the sides of her Stetson hat down to below her waist. She was wearing shredded blue jeans that revealed a lot of her long legs and almost all of her ass. The jeans rode so low on her hips that they looked like they could fall off at any moment. Diamond hard nipples were visible through the skimpy black halter top she had on. Her belly button was pierced with a silver skull. Hard to believe that she was able to function as a phlebotomist at a pediatric clinic earlier in the day. Whatever name her parents had given her was long gone. That night she was Baby. And Baby couldn't feel the cold or the rain. When the theater was being evacuated, Baby was in a stall in the ladies' room injecting a spoonful of the bath salts into her arm using a needle that was fresh at the beginning of the evening but had already been passed around a bit. Nothing about the crowd stampeding toward the exits registered with her. She was sitting on the toilet, in the midst of letting the post-injection bliss wash over her, when one of the insects fell from the ceiling above her and landed on her breasts. In her mind it was the size of a large prawn and it stared her down until the lighting in the bathroom suddenly failed and the insect disappeared down her shirt. Since then she had obsessively run her hands over her own skin, trying to find the body and make sure that it was gone. She kept unbuttoning her pants and sticking her hands inside of them to feel around, which was giving the clown an erection.

"Run rabbit, run!" Someone screamed in the distance.

The old clown tried to grab a handful of Baby's ass, but she slapped his arm away and went back to methodically searching every inch of her skin for bugs. It wasn't helping that all of the raindrops clinging to her skin felt like individual crawling things that were threatening to cover every inch of her.

The clown—on most days, a famous OBGYN with a private practice in Salem, Oregon, who had delivered exactly 9,999 babies during his storied career—had adopted the nom de guerre of Captain Spaulding, and was trying to get Baby to calm down.

"I don't think there are any of them on you, Baby, but if you like I'll strip you down and have a thorough look. Make sure they didn't get into any cracks."

"You won't see them," she snapped. Then she took off her Stetson hat and started scratching her head like a hippie with lice. "This isn't just about one goddamn bug, Daddy. This is one of those, fucking, what do you call them?"

"A Pestilence."

"That's it," she said as she kept scratching. "It's a fucking pestilence. It was sent by the devil."

"He's mad."

"At us? Why at us?"

"Because we are the rejects. I know it sounds fucked but when you get rejected by the devil it's the same as with God. There has to be, like, retribution," said Spaulding. Baby put her hand down the front of her pants and clawed at her pubic region. "You want help with that?"

In Baby's zonked out mind the word *retribution* wobbled and circled her mind like a wild animal about to go in for a kill. Was Spaulding busting out some kid of ancient philosophical shit? "What the fuck is retribule, retra," she couldn't remember what the hell he had said. "How the fuck do we get rid of these things? They are all over me."

"They aren't all over you."

"Yes, they fucking are," she screamed.

"We just need to get you somewhere that you can take a proper shower and you will feel better. I've got a friend, somewhat of a colleague even, that lives near here. We will go to her place and wash up. Get some food. I'm starving."

"Have you lost your mind?" asked Baby.

On the other side of the street, the little old man in the union suit who busted the car window, and five wet cheerleaders with black and white pom-poms and big letter R's sewn onto their turtleneck sweaters, were making their way down the sidewalk with a few other boys who looked more like fraternity-bred hanger-onners than people who had just left the movie theater. One of the girls was without her pleated white skirt and was marching in just a pair of light blue cotton panties. The panties were sopping wet and her black muff was clearly visible. Her eyes were so hollowed out that she didn't appear to be taking notice of anything at all. Her friends, who were seated in the seventh row with her, saw her tear the skirt off when a whole pile of the insects fell into it. After that she seemed to scream without stopping to breathe for a full five minutes. At some point she went quiet and numb. Wherever she had retreated to, it was going to take a lot of therapy to get her back.

The small group stopped in front of a construction site where a new tower was being raised. Typical of the recent downtown building trend, the tower was going to have retail at the surface level, a few floors worth of office spaces, and then luxury apartments occupying the upper two-thirds. The building was nearly complete but the facade had not yet been applied to the lower levels so the building was surrounded by scaffolding which was wrapped in mesh that looked like industrial bug screening. One of the frat boys was carrying a pocket knife and he used it to cut into the mesh. Once he had a good hole started, his friends reached in and began to tear and shred until they had exposed a big enough hole for them to start streaming through. The cheerleaders stayed on the ground while the boys began to climb. The old man in the union suit was the fastest making his way up the wet scaffolding.

"What the fuck are they doing?" shouted Baby.

"Who fucking cares?" said Spaulding. "The bugs have gotten inside their brains and they are starting to act like insects. Do you see?" At that point there were about seven or eight boys clumsily making their way up the steel poles from plank to plank. Because they were still clustered together near the bottom, they looked like an army of ants advancing their way up the outside of the tower. The old man was spry, like a spider, and way ahead of them. "What do you love?" Spaulding asked, to Baby but also just out loud to the universe.

"Just getting fucked up and doing fucked up shit, Daddy," responded Baby with a similarly detached tone. She seemed to have forgotten about the bug was that was hiding somewhere in her clothes.

"Let's get out of here," said Spaulding, and he took her by the hand.

*   *   *

Herman didn't so much like being freezing cold and soaking wet as he was just happy to have something to distract him from the frustration; borderline torture, that he had endured at the steakhouse. He didn't mind that his socks were saturated and that every step he took was squishy. He didn't mind that the twelve-hundred-dollar suit that he was wearing would never recover, or that he looked completely pathetic. He was really just annoyed that Loven and Dmitri were still tagging along behind him, nipping at his coattails like insufferable minions with nothing more productive to do than to be witnesses to his misfortunes. He felt like he was going through an ordeal and he would have rather gone through it alone than with an entourage. He had his hands tucked up underneath his armpits and the suit jacket hiked up over his head to keep the rain kind of off his hair, and he walked without any destination in mind. His only intention was to clear the fog out of his brain, but in so doing he compromised his peripheral vision and failed to notice the homeless wino sitting against a brick wall with his legs stretched out in front of him. Herman tripped over the man's legs with his arms and head tangled up inside of his jacket and he wasn't able to break the fall. The first part of Herman to smack into the pavement was his face. His trademark broken nose was broken again. He could taste blood in his mouth that was trickling down from the nasal cavity. At least one of his teeth had been knocked loose. And his forehead sustained some sort of laceration or contusion because there was a searing pain above his eyebrow and blood dripped into his field of view and making it hard to see.

"Hey watch where you're going, man," slurred the wino. During the fall Herman inadvertently tipped over a brown paper bag and the remains of a bottle of Strawberry Banana flavored Mad Dog 20/20. "That was supposed to last me all night."

Loven found a five-dollar bill in the pocket of his trousers. He tossed it at the wino and stooped over to have a look at Herman.

"Shit, dude," he said. "You're messed up. We've got to get you to the hospital."

About twenty paces behind, Lupita had folded her umbrella and tucked herself into a doorway, where she could stay out of sight but still keep a good eye on what was going on.

"Dmitri," Loven was shouting at him. Dmitri was squeamish around blood and keeping his distance. "Get us an Über, already." Loven then removed his lucky paisley tie from his pocket and used it to staunch the blood that was pouring out of the gash in Herman's forehead.

"No Über's," barked Herman. He had a strict policy against ever using the ride hailing service because of the way that the company's name rhymed with his and he had a strange paranoia about people declaring that Glüber is arriving in his Über. But that was only the line that he told people. The cold truth was that in 2013 Herman met Ashton Kutcher at a party in Hollywood. Kutcher was trying to talk him into getting in as an early investor in the company. Herman declined. Financially it turned out to be a devastating call on Herman's part and he hated to be reminded of it. Loven looked at him like he was crazy for wanting to be so petty in the midst of a crisis, but quickly relented.

"Alright, Meech. Call a cab then."

Almost as if it were a magical chariot, an Orange Cab for hire emerged from the curtain of rainfall and Dmitri got the driver to pull over. At first the Arab driver refused to accept the fare because of how the men looked and all of the blood. Herman jerked out a billfold and gave three-hundred to the driver. Reluctantly the man looked at the money, and then up at the sky. In the trunk he had a green rug—which he probably used as a prayer mat—and he laid it out on the backseat before letting Herman get into the cab, talking all the time either to himself or to Allah in a language that was completely unfamiliar but decidedly submissive. Loven sat with Herman in the back. Dmitri sat up front, leaning forward in the seat and clinging to the *Oh Shit!* handle. Just trying to distance himself from the blood as much as the cramped space in the little Chevy Volt would allow.

"Where to?" said the cabbie in sing-song English.

"Closest hospital," said Herman.

"Harborview," said Loven.

"Very good, sirs. We have to take a bit of a roundabout way. I was just near there and there is a mob of people filling up the streets and there is a tremendous amount of traffic in that part of downtown."

"What is he talking about?" said Herman, who was getting woozy as he thought about all of the blood that was flowing out of him.

"I don't know," said Loven. "Could you just drive please?"

Lupita stepped out of the doorway that she had been hiding in and out into the rain. She was deflated. Things had been going so well. She was really starting to believe, after running into Herman and his friends outside of the steakhouse, that she was onto something. She had convinced herself that her cousin Rosalie was right, and that there was still something that she could do to protect the orchard. She was even expecting a young guapo to come walking around the corner any second with a dog on a leash to sweep her off of her feet. She felt dumb for letting herself get her hopes up. The truth was that she was a long way from home, broke, and standing in the pouring rain. She was about to turn around and start trudging her way back to the dumpy motel when something exploded.

It sounded like a gunshot, followed by the sound of grinding metal. She spun around and saw a small fountain of sparks coming from the front end of the orange cab. The car had plunged into a deep pothole that was hidden underneath a pool of dark water. The front corner of the car was stoved into the ground and it was possible that there was also a front axle failure or some shocks or springs had collapsed. Lupita didn't understand cars all that well. The driver leapt out and when he saw the damage, he buried his fingers in his greasy hair and started chattering away in his native tongue. The three businessmen exited the car. Herman still had Loven's tie pressed against the wound on his forehead. With his other hand he was gingerly pinching the nostrils of his broken nose to try and clot the blood flow there as well.

"Flat tire," said Dmitri. Which was both obvious and understated. The front bumper of the car was bent and the front quarter panel was crumpled as well.

"Fuck this," said Herman. "I'm walking." He tried to take off in the direction of Harborview but the cabbie got in his way and wouldn't let him leave. He was talking an incomprehensible blue streak and pointing wildly at the meter inside the cab. The guy still wanted to be compensated for the drop and the half a block that he had driven them. About four more bucks. "I just gave you three-hundred dollars," shouted Herman. But whatever English the driver had known was long gone. He was feverishly debating with them in a language that they didn't know one word of. He could have been making good points. He also could have been critiquing Lebanese cuisine, or pontificating on U.S.-Iranian relations. What was getting through, was that the guy wasn't going to shut up without being paid first. Herman looked at Loven and Dmitri. "Either of the two of you have any small bills?" Dmitri shook his head and mentioned that he never really carried cash.

"Sorry, Herman," said Loven. "I've got a few Benjies but I dropped the last of the small stuff I had on me to the drunk that you tripped over. I was planning on just hitting the ATM whenever we pass one. I need a little more cash for more guy if you're still interested. Oddly enough Herman was still interested, even though he had just sustained an injury that would make the act of snorting cocaine nearly impossible.

Herman peeled another hundred-dollar bill off of the top of his wad and handed it to the driver.

"I hope you have some change," said Herman. The driver looked at him patiently, as though there must be more information coming that would help him understand the concept that Herman was trying to introduce that was known as *change*. "Change," Herman said again. The cabbie continued to just stand there looking kind of bug-eyed but also agreeable. Herman's hard-headedness was waning as he continued to lose blood and his body temperature fell.

"He's asking you for some change," Loven piped up, trying to spook the cabbie back into understanding the way commerce works in America. For a moment it appeared to work. The cabbie didn't say anything but he did sort of seem like something had dawned on him and he shot back over to his vehicle and opened up the trunk. He didn't come back with change for the hundred though. He came back with a lug wrench and a scissor jack and wearing a big old grin like Loven had just offered to change the tire for him in the pouring rain. Herman grabbed the lug wrench from the cabbie and heaved it out into the center of the street and it clanged around for a second before coming to rest on the yellow center line.

"Keep the fucking change," said Herman, and he started off up the hill toward the east.

Loven and Dmitri fell in behind him.

Once they were a safe distance away, Lupita opened up her umbrella again and headed up the hill, staying about a block or so behind.

*   *   *

Even though it was a busy Friday night in the E.R. at Harborview hospital, Herman was an active bleeder and no one likes those patients to be sitting in the waiting room, especially the other patients. Herman was whisked through triage and into a private room with white curtains for walls with an efficiency that had so far eluded the preceding parts of his evening. The travel nurse, named Abud, wasted no time checking his vitals and installing an IV port in Herman's wrist in case he needed to be given fluids. His doctor looked scarcely old enough to operate a vehicle and couldn't have possibly plowed his way through medical school and a residency with a baby face like that. Because it was a teaching hospital owned by the UW, two stone-faced medical students in lab coats with clipboards hovered behind the young doctor, observing and taking notes but never intervening. The doctor cleaned Herman up with a sterile wipe so that he could get a closer look at the contusions. There was only one loose tooth, an incisor, and it was hanging on by a few thin fibers of gum tissue. That was going to have to wait until Herman could see a dentist on Monday but the young doctor promised to write Herman a prescription for something to help with the pain. The wound on Herman's forehead was still bleeding and the doctor gave Herman a piece of gauze so that he could apply pressure while he examined the nose, which was the part of Herman's face that had sustained the bulk of the damage. The doctor snapped on two fresh rubber gloves and set up a shot that he would use to numb up Herman's face. As he did so he asked Herman some basic questions to eliminate the possibility of a concussion. One of which was the status of the DOW Jones Industrial Average—not that random since Herman had introduced himself as an investor to the doctor—which Herman could actually answer within a hundredth of a point. He had been watching it carefully when he left the office. It ended the week way down because of the Maritime Report that was released earlier in the day. Herman, just in case, thanked a higher power for steering him clear of investing in seafood.

"Best to reset the nasal bone right away. So it doesn't heal crooked," said the doctor, partly to Herman and partly to the students.

"I already broke my nose once in hockey, doc, and there's already a crook in it. I don't mind."

"This is a bit more than a crook. Here, have a look," the doctor handed Herman a small mirror and that he could hold up to his face. He looked like awful. And the nose, which used to have a slight jog to the right, now made a sharp left and drooped. It looked something Picasso might paint.

"That won't do," said Herman.

"I didn't think it would," said the kid. "If we straighten it out right away there's a good chance it will heal up just fine."

"What's the other option?"

"Wait a few months until it heals and then schedule a rhinoplasty were the doctor can re-break the nasal bone and sculpt the area. You'll need to wear a face mask after and you'll have a pair of shiners for a couple of weeks."

"Shit. Have you done this before? You seem kind of young."

"I attended a whole bunch of these during my residency in Detroit. But, just being honest, this will be my personal first. People just don't punch each other in the face out here as much as they do back there. Don't worry though. I know the technique. And if it doesn't come out the way you like, there's always the rhinoplasty."

Herman was having a tough time making the call. His head was in pain, his thoughts were clouded and he wished that he had someone that he could bounce this decision off of. He wanted to talk to Margot but his phone was toast and he had no idea what her number was. She'd know what to do though. Probably because she was a mom. What he really wanted at that moment was to go home. But that wasn't what he did. "Okay, doc. Do it."

The doc put the needle into Herman's cheek to numb the region. Then he wrapped his fingers around the sides of Herman's head and used his thumbs to work on the bone structure of the nose, narrating all the while for the students barely younger than he. The enthusiasm of the overworked young students had clearly piqued now that they were about to learn how to reset a broken nose. Herman couldn't feel anything when the doc moved his fingers but there were uncomfortable crunching sensations reverberating inside his skull.

"Shoot," said the young doc. And not the kind of *shoot* that you want to hear from someone who is setting one of your broken bones or giving you a tattoo. The kid was in over his head. Because Herman's nose already had an unorthodox and somewhat compromised structure, it just buckled and more or less fell apart when the doc pressed on it with his thumbs. It turned out looking like a flaccid zig-zag or a lightning bolt that had worn out and gone limp before striking its target. Only upside at the moment was that it didn't hurt. Yet.

"What happened?" Herman was on the cusp of losing it.

"Oh, nothing," said the doc. Trying in vain to play it cool. The youngster had a fledgling bedside manner.

"Why did you say *shoot*?"

"Because the fracture is compound."

"Compound or compounded?"

"I think that at the moment it is fair to say that there is a compound fracture to your nasal bone and that a rhino is going to be inevitable. There is also a fear of internal bleeding and if your hematocrit is dropping, we need to know. We are going to have to keep you here and monitor your blood work every six hours for at least a full day so we can be sure."

"Bleeding where?"

"Inside the head."

"That sounds ridiculous."

"I'm sorry, sir. Doctor's orders," the unqualified, smug doctor that had just fucked up Herman's nose actually had the gall to smile. Like he was setting an indispensable example for his students.

"Let me see it." Reluctantly the doc handed back the mirror. "What the fuck, man? What did you do to my nose? It looks like it is trying to get off of my face."

"It's going to be fine, Mr. Glüber. But we are going to have to get you in to see a specialist."

"When?"

"Well, your injury is rather serious. I'll tag this as urgent and hopefully you can see someone this week."

"This week? I need some help now, man. Look at me."

"I understand that it is traumatic, Mr. Glüber. I can write you something for the pain. But no one in the E.R. is going to be able to set this for you tonight."

At this point the medical students were feverishly taking notes, trying to avoid seeming in any way involved.

"Should I be in one of those masks you were talking about? Fuck, man."

"That is not a good idea. It is going to swell up quite a bit I expect. What you need is Ibuprofren and ice. I'll write you a prescription. You're going to need to be extremely careful. Don't bump it. Sleep on your back. It may also be difficult to chew so think about eating soft foods for a while."

"Shit," Herman was in disbelief.

"Like I said, I'll write you something for the pain. There's nothing else that we can do tonight. A nurse will be along in a few minutes to get your forehead stitched up and take your first blood draw."

"Asshole. You can't—"

The young doc was probably freaking out a little bit himself. He wasn't going to hang around to be undressed by Herman. There were too many other patients that needed him and there was nothing else that he could do. He more or less ran for his life with his lackies in tow and left Herman stranded, with a numb face, still bleeding but just barely.

*   *   *

Loven and Dmitri were posted up in the waiting room. Dmitri was zoning out on the fish tank. Loven was sending some text messages. Trying to line up some more cocaine, when he got a text message from Duncan.

Loven. This is Duncan. Where the fuck is Herman? You were supposed to have him call me.

Loven got nervous. He had to respond though. "Hey, Dmitri."

"Yeah," said Dmitri without taking his eyes off of an angel fish that was diving down to nibble something off the bottom. On the other side of the tank, Lupita sat with her back to the two men, trying to look immersed in the most recent edition of People Magazine. Incidentally, she had the magazine opened to a photograph that a paparazzi shot of Lucky Soul parasailing somewhere in the south of France.

"I just got a text from Duncan. He wants me to have Herman call him. What do you think I should say?"

"What's wrong with the truth?"

"That a stripper trashed his phone, and that we aren't at the office helping out because we we went out for steaks instead, and Herman injured his face when he tripped over some drunk's legs and smashed his face on the sidewalk?"

"Yeah, that doesn't sound great. But you could tell him that we are at the hospital, and that Herman had an accident. It's going to be obvious on Monday. You saw Herman's face. It's not like it's going to heal that fast."

"How do I text that?"

"You don't. You've got to call him."

Loven was still wound up like a jack rabbit, high enough to orbit the moon, but also terrified when he thought about where his next hit was going to come from. His guy was being slow to respond. "Alright," he said. I'm calling him. Loven stepped away from the waiting area and had his conversation with Duncan outside. While he was gone, Lupita sat with her back just inches from Dmitri's. She was even listening when he released a quiet but hot fart that made it hard for her to keep her position on just the other side of the tank. In a few minutes Loven was back looking strung out and sweaty from the stress.

"We're in deep," Loven said.

"What's up?" Dmitri asked.

"Duncan says that Renata is already calling this an act of God or something, that maybe they should be rethinking the sale. Said he tried to get patched through to their room at The Edgewater but they're only willing to talk to Herman. Lupita dropped the magazine she was reading on the floor and had to bend over to pick it up. She let her hair fall all around her face and prayed that she wasn't being noticed.

"Fuck."

"Gets worse. Most of the termination letters for the staff at Summerwood are already stamped in the outgoing mail bin for tomorrow. If we don't get the sale docs back, we are going to be firing a whole lot of people who work for a company we don't own."

"Jesus Christ. Aren't the excavators supposed to start knocking the trees over Monday?"

"You know what Duncan just told me, Meech?"

"What's that?"

"That the vehicle that hit the biker carrying that documents was driving a RocketFuel advertisement car. Wasn't your cousin driving one of those earlier?"

"Are you being serious?"

"I am. Do you think it was him? He could have the documents."

"Alex? I doubt he has any paperwork. He has an aversion to paperwork."

"He might know where the documents are."

"He is also probably about to be arrested."

"Not probably, he is. We need to find him before the cops do. Can't you call him?"

"What did you tell Duncan about Herman?"

"I told him that he was in the Emergency Room at Harborview. It's as good an excuse as any. And like you were saying, his face kind of proves it at least. But he wants us to get Herman a message. As soon as Herman is done here, he has to get a hold of the Frenzels and convince them to come in and resign if we need them to."

"What about us?"

"He wants us back at the office doing damage control but the building is closed right now. There's some kind of beetle invasion happening and all of Pioneer Square is under fucking quarantine or something. This could get ugly, and you're still on the hook for spilling coffee on the young Mexican girl's agreement or whatever that was."

"Should we get out of here?"

"We should but not yet."

"How come?"

"There's nowhere to really go. I do have an idea though."

"What's your idea?"

"Let's leave a message for Herman with the front desk that he needs to call the Frenzels as soon as he can. Before the office reopens let's find these documents. I'm going to hopefully score a little something I could use. It may be a long night. Then I'm going down to where the accident happened to see if I can find anyone who saw anything. You try and find your cousin. If we get those docs before anyone else, we are going to be heroes. We'll be seniors in no time."

"Is anyone else looking for them?"

"Duncan has a P.I. on it. His buddy Hal. But Hal doesn't know that the driver of the RocketFuel car may have been your cousin. If we get the docs, I bet Duncan could even pull some strings to get the kid out of the country. He'd have to go back to fucking his sister but I assume that's better than a cell mate."

"You haven't seen his sister."

"Sometimes you make it sound like you come from pigs."

"We aren't all pigs. But there are some piggish ones amongst us."

Lupita's intrepid surveillance had paid off and she couldn't sit still any longer. She had to find Hartmut and Renata right away and get them the news. The way she got up from her chair all of a sudden and tossed the magazine onto a coffee table was a little too abrupt and she caught Loven's attention as she walked toward the exit. At the first set of double doors she chanced a glance back over her shoulder. Loven was staring right back at her.

*   *   *

Dmitri was tasked with finding his cousin and since the kid wasn't picking up the phone and he didn't have any leads, he figured he would just go and have a look at home. The apartment that they shared was a two-bedroom in a brick building at the bottom of First Hill and when Dmitri got dropped off in front, he could already sense trouble. There were lights on in several of the apartments but they would occasionally blink off and then back on, all in unison. Like the building was either trying to deliver a message, or going through some struggle of its own that leant it a human quality. It turned out to be more like a dying gasp.

The elevator had an 'Out of Order' sign posted on its doors and the light was out in the stairwell, so Dmitri had to climb the four fights to the apartment that he shared with Andre in the dark. It was easy to make his way up holding onto the hand rail, the troubling thing was the crunching sound coming from underfoot. In the blackness something had littered the floor and he could not see what it was, he only knew it had bad intentions. He had a terrible feeling Aunt Yaz would not want him to go any further but he ignored it and made the door to the hall as fast as he could.

The corridor was still lit by a flickering bulb and in the intermittent light he could then see that the floor was almost completely covered with the bodies of what looked like dead beetles. They were everywhere but they weren't moving. The proportions were biblical.

The door to his apartment was still locked and there was a similar distribution of bugs on the carpet inside. It smelled foul but that may not have been the bugs' fault. Andre's door was shut.

"Andre," he called out, but there was no response.

The inside of his cousin's room appeared ransacked but it was hard to tell if he'd been there. It was how he always kept it. One thing was for sure though, Andre wasn't in the apartment.

The inside of the building was louder than usual. A lot of tenants seemed to be stomping around, maybe packing up to get the hell out of there. The place was definitely uninhabitable.

Someone screamed.

The lights continued to flicker. Dmitri figured he should also grab a raincoat and leave, he just wasn't sure where to go. He was sure he had to piss so he went into the bathroom and brushed a dozen or so dead bugs off the seat. A couple of them landed in the bowl and started to sizzle and Dmitri didn't think that much of it but he should have. The building had a high voltage power feed that was shorting out and creating a ton of heat where it was located in a control room on the roof of the building. On a clear day or night, it would have been easier to see the smoke that was already billowing up into the sky. The control room also housed the high-density polymer pipe that delivered water to the building. The HDP pipe was big and in the control room it paired down into smaller copper pipes and an array of hot water tanks that serviced the units. The walls of the control room caught fire around the time that the bugs had the casing eaten off of the high-voltage two aught black lead that led to the main panel. The pipe that delivered cold water to Dmitri's unit was closest to the fire's center and it melted away. As the control room became consumed by a roaring inferno, a tower of bugs that had been feasting on the power current succumbed to the heat and fell, all scrambling on the backs of the other soldiers in their relentless army.

The tower of dying insects landed squarely on the breach in the pipe that fed water to Dmitri's apartment. In the moments before the building's power found its way to ground and conked out for good, the water that was available from the fixtures in his unit was charged with enough electricity to fry all the fish in the sea. As soon as the stream of urine from Dmitri's impressive cock struck the bodies of the beetles that were floating in the toilet bowl, the current arced back up through Dmitri's penis and instantly boiled all the water in the cells of his body. He exploded from the turgor pressure. There wasn't anything left of him but bones, a tuft of burnt hair, and a gross diffusion of soft tissue and blood sticking to the walls.

Tarantulas

Napa cabbage, Winesap mushrooms, and threaded bean curd were all being tossed into a frying pan on high heat. Margot was whipping up a little stir fry as a late dinner for herself and Ethan. She loved it when it was just the two of them together, but there was also a weight attached to it. A strange loneliness that was sometimes so unbearable that she had to lock herself into the bathroom and cry softly until it passed. The rice was just about ready to be fluffed. It felt like an entire week had gone by since she had the pho for lunch. Truth is that she was lucky to have squeezed a lunch in at all. The environment inside of the Zonama headquarters was fierce and absurdly competitive. It was the kind of place where you couldn't afford to lay off the gas at all, and too many people who didn't give a fig about corporeal needs like eating and using the lav. A flicker of weakness, incompetence, or even the hint of a personal life, rendered one's job vulnerable to the thronging millennials with their androgyny and their bow-ties. They were an emotionally fragile bunch but they had an incredible amount of endurance in the face of the rigors of corporate America.

Ethan, normally a big help in the kitchen, was seated at the table in the dining room rehearsing his science day presentation. He was a sixth-grader at the highly esteemed Bush School. It was kind of a pain in the ass for Margot to get him over there in the mornings, but convenient for his dad, who lived in a house on Lake Washington Boulevard, right next door to where Kurt Cobain was living when he shot himself in the head. Ethan didn't play for a single sports team. He did play chess though, and his conversational Italian was strong. He was so proficient with computer systems that he wrote a piece of software that regulated all of the various pumps, fans, heat lamps, and humidifiers that controlled the atmospheric conditions of the thirty plus terrariums that were stacked on shelves around the perimeter of the modest bedroom that he slept in. Over the course of the last few months Ethan had done something that was fairly difficult to do. He successfully mated a *Poecilotheria ornata*—a very dangerous species of tarantula. He was so precise in how he went about establishing the right breeding conditions that the mother spider produced a double-clutch of eggs, and Ethan had gotten more than four-hundred nymphs to grow into viable young tarantulas that were ready to find new homes. Each of them was living in its own small plexiglass cube with cross ventilation and vermiculite substrate. It may have been a little presumptuous of Ethan to assume that he was going to be able to find homes for all four hundred of his babies at Science Day. Had he thought to undertake a quick survey of average Seattleite's and their desire to be in possession of potentially deadly arachnids he would have realized that he had a better chance of getting rid of none, then all of them. Nonetheless, every single one of the miniature ten-gram terrariums was stacked inside of a larger Tupperware container with the lid off that was already lashed to the bottom of a hand truck with a modified trucker's hitch—a knot that his dad shown him how to tie.

Ethan cleared his throat. "A female tarantula needs to be fully mature and completely at ease if you are going to be able to mate her successfully. She should be between one and three months from her last molt, and very well fed. Most people feed their tarantulas pin head crickets because they are easy to buy. I like to try other bugs when I can find them and I've noticed that the Rocky Mountain Pine Beetle is a big hit. It's also in pretty good supply right now. Unfortunately, wait…" He was one of those kids that was so full of information that he was predisposed to veering off course. He made some notes on his page. "Umm. Okay. You never move the female for breeding. Always bring the male to the female. Usually, one and a half hours after sunset is thought to be the best time. Tarantulas are nocturnal, so I guess you could say that they like to do it best after they wake up." Margot couldn't help smiling when he rehearsed this part. Ethan was conceived in the morning and she wondered if this meant that the lethal female tarantula might be her alter-ego. She grabbed a jar of cumin and added a few dashes to the pan. "Tarantula breeding is very scary for the male spider. If anything goes wrong, the female is likely to eat him. Even if things go perfectly, and the copulation," Margot smiled again, since it's always funny to hear a little kid use the word *copulation*, "is a success, the male could still get eaten. I bred mine in the bathtub so the male would have more room to be able to run away after. Next I am going to describe how to handle the egg sacks and what to do when the eggs start to grow legs." Ethan could tell that dinner was just about ready so he picked that point to take a break.

"Are Alfred and Medusa all packed up?"

"Not yet, mom. I want them to be comfortable so I left them in their regular terrariums for the night." Alfred and Medusa were the parents of the army of baby tarantulas.

"Would you mind clearing the table? The food's almost ready."

The stack of paperwork accompanying Ethan's project was nearly four inches thick. For those who were interested, he had printed out numerous articles about *Poecilotheria ornata* breeding, and details about how they lived in their native Sri Lanka. The tarantula—also commonly referred to as the Ornate Tiger Spider—could develop a leg span of ten inches when fully grown. Medusa was about that big. Ethan had been taking copious notes during the entire gestation cycle, charting the progress of the egg sacks, and crunched the numbers every way that he could think of after the legs emerged from the sacks and the first instar phase began. He had used two incubators set at different temperatures, just to see how it would relate, if at all, to the progress of the nymphs later on. Before the first instar phase he patrolled the incubators daily with a set of sharp tweezers, removing the desiccated eggs that were doomed to fail—notable by their difference in color. Once the nymphs started molting regularly, he again patrolled daily with his tweezers, taking out the discarded skins quickly so that they wouldn't mold and create a toxic environment in the petri dish. Ethan set his stack of papers neatly on top of the Tupperware that all of the young tarantulas were stacked in.

He returned to the dining room where Margot's new kitten was climbing the drapes in an attempt to slaughter an unsuspecting horsefly that was bouncing off of the picture window. The kitten was mainly a bluish gray but its color points had a way of changing with the light. It lost its purchase on the frilly fabric and splattered on the hardwood floors. It was a funny little cat but spectacularly clumsy. It forgot about the fly and walked over to Ethan, who gave the pretty cat a scratch behind the ears.

"Hi, Dogwood," he said. The cat got its name in the early summer when the Korean Dogwood tree in the front yard was in full bloom. Margot and Ethan lived in a little house in the Central District that she wound up with after her divorce. It was only eight-hundred square feet and the lot size wasn't much more than that. But it was clean, easy to take care of, and paid off. It was also just a few blocks from downtown and its value was surging. Someday she would be able to swap it for a forty-acre horse ranch in her native South Carolina.

Margot laid out two bowls with rice on the bottom and stir fry on top, and a couple sets of chopsticks. She poured two glasses of water from the reverse osmosis filter, a full balloon of cabernet for herself, and then, because she was unconscious of how obsessed she was with her work, she picked up her laptop to have a quick glance at her email before sitting down to eat. Nothing in her inbox was all that interesting but she did notice that the number one thing trending on Yahoo was called the Seattle Beetle Invasion. She opened up an article and skimmed it as she fell into her chair. "Oh my God, honey."

"What is it, mom?"

"You have to read this."

Margot passed her laptop over to her son, who was sucked promptly into the article and forgot all about his food.

*   *   *

There was a lull in the rainstorm. Herman was on the street outside of Harborview, drinking in the damp air, and gazing at the gibbous moon that hung just above the sports complexes to the south.

The scene out there on the curb was borderline apocalyptic, while still being pretty much normal for a Friday night. Injured people were flooding their way into the E.R. Most of them looked like they were coming from a Halloween party that turned bad, but it wasn't close to Halloween. On his way out of the hospital Herman overheard a couple of nurses talking. They said that a protest group or something started climbing the scaffolding on the side of a building that was under construction and collapsed it. Now the E.R. was getting everything from severe physical traumas and corpses, to drug overdoses, and the whole gamut of psychological and psychosomatic issues related to and most likely caused by drug overdoses, shock, and exposure to trauma. A few wasted looking cheerleaders in sweaters with big letter R's sewn onto the fronts walked past him. The girls were draped all over one another and were having a difficult time keeping on their feet. One of them had lost her skirt and was only wearing panties. One of her arms was also bent in a direction that it clearly should not have been.

Herman leaned on one of the concrete pillars that supported the covered area over the ambulance circle and tried to think. He was in a frightful state, and stuck clinging to the pillar for balance. He couldn't move. A couple of paramedics were seated on a bench nearby, eating ramen noodles out of steaming Styrofoam cups and talking about a biker they brought in earlier who was hit by a car. One of them said something about needing a spatula to get the body off the street. For some reason the story sent a chill down Herman's spine. He thought about approaching the paramedics. He wondered if they meant Bennie. But there was no way he could bring himself to ask. They'd have dismissed him as a complete fucking nut job. His suit looked like something that he picked up at the Goodwill and then dragged through a puddle of fermented muck. The laceration on his forehead wasn't bleeding any longer. A purplish black coagulation had formed and it was unsightly but at least it was functional. There was a length of suture from his unfinished stitch job dangling in his field of view like a hair on the eyeball. His lower lip was swelling up even worse than before and it was hard to form words. The tooth ached like hell.

For the first time that Herman could remember he was considering admitting defeat. He wanted something to eat. He wanted to be able to sit on his toilet for a while, then take a bubble bath. Had he ever even taken a bubble bath before? Then he wanted to lie down in his bed and get some sl—. Right there Herman caught himself and snatched his mind away from the lazy drift toward surrendering the fight. He clicked over from that deplorable mode of self-pity to chastising himself for allowing the kind of thin-skinned bullshit that must be the thing that helped most people navigate their miserable days to find a way into his brain. He steadied his resolve and began to formulate a new plan. The need to get himself cleaned up was legitimate, but a little too dangerous to undertake straight away.

Whether the curse was real or not, it was definitely in his head. First order of business was to go home and get a shower and get on top of trying to deal with the Frenzels. He could at least do that from his home phone. Plus, he could chat with Duncan.

Trouble with that plan was that it was Margot who he wanted to see. On some level he was still infatuated with Laverne. She was exotic, but there was obviously nothing lasting there; which was normally perfect. And the giant schlong that dangled from between her legs during the ill-fated bathroom fantasy was lingering in his mind and turning his stomach and making him queasy. Girls like Margot weren't easy to find. She and the kid were all he could think about. He put some effort into dissecting his feelings on the matter as he dragged himself over to the curb to hail a taxi. He wondered what they were up to, Margot and Ethan. He also worried about what would happen if Margot found out about Laverne, or even worse, the stripper that ruined his phone. Did that mean that he cared or something? The mystic, clairvoyant, witch, whatever Laverne was; he wasn't really attracted to her. Pursuing her was more like a mission for him than a logical response to his feelings. Feelings. Fuck. Since when did he have those? As if he could encounter any more difficulties that night, he was starting to be saddled with complex feelings that threatened to cloud his judgment and mire him in a sticky emotional web. He had to get on top of what was going on with work but his *feelings* about the orchard were starting to conflict as well. A growing voice inside was asking him if he was doing the right thing. A lot of history and a lot of lives were about to be laid to waste. And for what? There was a yellow cab approaching and Herman put his arm up. With his free hand he patted himself to make sure that he still had his wallet, keys and phone. The phone was still dead but he had everything else and was pleased to at least not be flat broke by that point. The indicator lamp on the top of the cab switched from available to hired and Herman made eye contact with the driver.

Or so he thought. Herman stepped off the curb and the cabbie went sailing right past him so that he could pick up a small group of UW students that were huddled about twenty paces behind Herman wearing hideous purple and gold hooded sweatshirts. There was a crunching sound, like the tires had run over a box of cereal. Herman wasn't sure what it was at first. And then a viscous serpent of pain bit him in the foot and uncoiled itself throughout the entirety of his nervous system. The toes on his right foot had been pulverized, flattened, reduced to mashed bits of powder and cracked bones rattling around in sad sacks of skin.

He screamed at full volume as he keeled over backwards onto the cold, hard ground. It was an involuntary cry, announcing his agony to the night. Almost no one reacted. A bunch of the horror movie fans—the ones not injured when the scaffolding collapsed—were loitering nearby, smoking cigarettes and eating sandwiches from Jimmy John's, waiting on news about their friends. The mob had done a lot to desensitize the night. An injured white man, writhing and hollering on the sidewalk, was hardly a spectacle at that point. The cab driver pulled away with his fare. A couple of psychotic-looking street people continued an argument they were having about where someone named Jerome went.

Three of the hospital's custodians were taking their shift break and must have seen what happened to Herman and took some pity on him. They sauntered over and surrounded him where he was laid out on the ground, helpless. At first Herman thought that they were demons or wraiths come to escort him the rest of the way to hell. One of the men was as tall as a skyscraper. He blotted out the moon. His skin was blacker than the slice of night sky above him, his khaki uniform was unsoiled and meticulously pressed, and his mud brown eyes were stashed behind thick lenses set in wooden frames. The hung-faced white kid to his left was far shorter, and rotund. More like obese. He was trying to remove a booger from his nose. The fat kid's uniform was stained below his chin with what looked very much like tomato sauce, next to something else that was chalky and white, like bird shit. His pants were too long for him and he had a pair of gray Chuck Taylor's on his feet that were begging to be replaced. They were right by Herman's head, and wreaked of medicated foot powder. There was also an Asian dude with chopped hair. He was slight, but dangerous looking. He was the one who did all the talking.

"You are not looking good, my friend. You should let us help you into the hospital."

"No fucking way," shouted Herman. He was trying to use a No Parking sign to hoist himself back up to vertical, but the sign was wet and he lost his grip and fell back onto the ground.

"Okay, okay, man. Take it easy, man. We just want to help you out. Your head looks like it needs a few more stitches. And you aren't going to be able to walk on that foot, man."

"My foot is fine," endorphins of all kinds were surging inside of Herman. The pain was so bad that he couldn't tell it from euphoria. He was gone from his normal self, the pain had driven him to another plane of consciousness, one on which he wasn't injured, one where there no attachments to anything at all. It was a miracle he could even stay awake.

The custodians exchanged glances. The trio seemed to have some capacity for telepathic communication, at least amongst themselves. The fat one nodded at the other two and walked off. He used a magnetic key card to slip into the hospital through a windowless metal door.

"Where are you going, my friend? At least let us put you in a taxi."

"No fucking taxis," spit Herman. He was getting dizzy. His head felt really light.

"Okay, okay, my friend. No taxi. No taxi. Just tell me what we can do."

"I'm having a hard night as you can see. It would help me the most if you would just clear the fuck out of my way," Herman's words were harsh but meekly delivered. The nastiness was more like a strange habit that the body couldn't let go of.

"This is a hard night for you, my friend. But you trust me, no one knows hardship like us three. Moustapha here, it took him seven months to cross the Libyan Desert so that he could escape the genocide where he is from in Chad. Little Willie, that fat punk that just went into the hospital, he did three years in a maximum-security pen for something that his uncle did. And me, I used to have my own luxury karaoke bar in Palo Alto, but I lost it when that fucking recession hit in 2007. I used to go to work in a Nudie suit. Now look at me. I been trying to get back to zero ever since. We been around, my friend. You could use our help."

The metal door popped open again and Little Willie's silhouette appeared with a set of crutches in one hand and a paper bag in the other. In the bag he had some supplies for cleaning up the wound on Herman's head. Herman allowed it. Moustapha didn't finish Herman's stitches but he put a knot in and clipped the excess so it didn't look like one of his eyebrow hairs had gone rogue and stretched by six inches. Then, with a deft hand, he removed the medical tape and the IV port from Herman's wrist in one swift move. Little Willie cleaned the rest of the gash with a cotton swab soaked in alcohol, and then he covered the area with a neatly folded piece of gauze held in place with steri-strips. The gash continued to burn but in a way that felt oddly good, like being branded by a benevolent tribe. The former owner of the karaoke bar adjusted the crutches for a man of Herman's size and then did some showing off with them.

"I know how to use crutches," said Herman. "I used to play hockey." As Little Willie and Moustapha picked him up and got him stable on his good foot, their friend leapt off the ground, flipping all the way over into a handstand on the crutches, supported barely by his feet resting lightly against the hospital building. He flipped back over by shoving his feet off the wall and then handed the crutches over. "Thanks," Herman said.

"It's okay, my friend. It's okay, my friend."

"Why are you helping me?" Herman asked.

"Because, my friend, it is because you are an American man."

"What's that supposed to mean"

"This might not look so good to you but, where we come from, it's worse. It's worse."

Herman was confused.

"Open your palm," it was the first thing that Little Willie had said so far. His voice was a few octaves higher than Herman would have expected. Herman did as he was told, and Little Willie dropped three pills into Herman's open hand. One oblong, and two small white discs. "Eight-hundred milligram Ibuprofren and two oxycontin for the pain," Little Willie gestured for Herman to put them in his mouth and then handed him a liter of drinking water to wash the pills down. "There's a dozen more in this bottle." Little Willie tucked an amber pill bottle into the breast pocket on Herman's coat. Herman was feeling much better already. The pills had reinstalled Herman inside of his normal self. Albeit a more grateful self than usual. He almost felt like giving them a hug.

"Go get some rest. Go get some rest," the one who kept repeating himself clapped him on the back.

"I will," said Herman. "Thanks for the help."

When Herman crutched away from the hospital it was still during a lull in the storm. He had a particular destination in mind, and took off in the direction of the Central District.

*   *   *

Margot was still hungry after the sushi happy hour she was required to attend. She got her chopsticks onto one piece of chicken teriyaki before the entire dish was slaughtered. The selection of nigiri and sashimi remained mostly untouched since the news report that came out earlier in the week. There were still a few souls brave enough to eat the raw fish. Free sushi was nothing to sneeze at, even if it did shave off a decade or two off of life expectancy, and those were the perfect people to be eating it. At times, nothing seemed more on the edge of extinction to her than the Chamber of Commerce. She never made any connections at those events, but the food and drinks were still popular as ever.

Her bowl of food was empty except for a few saturated rice grains and a broccoli floret that she just couldn't bring herself to eat. Her glass of wine was reduced to a thin puddle. She put the bowl in the sink, uncorked the bottle and poured herself another full balloon, then sat back down at the table and watched her son who was still ogling the computer. Brief moments of nothing to do were so rare she wished that she could put the moment in a box and hang onto it. Ethan was still picking at his dinner. The news feed about the Seattle Beetle Invasion had captivated him. He was scrolling through tweets and articles, intermittently stopping to pinch another vegetable with his chopsticks. A lot of kids Ethan's age were big eaters—impossible to fill—but not Ethan. Something else seemed to always have his attention. Margot hated to interrupt him in the middle of something, especially if he was learning. But he also needed to eat and get enough sleep. She had just read somewhere that adolescents needed between nine and thirteen hours of sleep per night. Nine she could comprehend. But thirteen? That was most of the day. The people she worked with struggled to get that in an entire week. The reason for that being more the insane stress than an actual scheduling issue. Like a lot of her co-workers, she needed a full bottle of red just to shake the day off, let alone figure out how to relax.

Despite not being a very big eater, Ethan was growing fast. In the past year he had shot up a couple inches, and thinned out. His hair was longer than he had ever worn it before, he had taken to wearing a blue beanie everywhere, and pants with elastic cuffs at the bottom called Joggers. He was still nerdy, but he was also a little hip-hop. She wondered if any girls liked him yet. There had to be a few.

Dogwood leapt up onto the table and knocked over a glass of water, and that was the end of the relaxing moment. Margot got up to grab a towel.

"I'm full," said Ethan, pushing his bowl away.

"Are you sure?" Margot laid the towel down to sop up the water and cleared Ethan's plate.

"I am. Can I have ice cream?"

"Did you do your reading yet?" Ethan didn't answer. Which meant *no*. Ethan was an enthusiastic young scientist and excellent in math. In English he stunk, and it was very hard to understand why. It certainly wasn't any kind of attention deficit thing. He was picking up the Italian at an incredible rate, even if he couldn't write it very well. He could spend hours poring over data, and he had a reasonable tolerance for articles, especially if they were about bugs. But it was pulling teeth to get him to crack open a book and just read. His spelling was awful. And his reading comprehension was so bad that Margot had been called in for several parent teacher conferences over at the Bush School, where there was a lot of academic pressure. Ethan's teachers and principal were far more concerned about it than Margot was. He wasn't into reading. So what? He wasn't lazy. They always seemed to gloss over things, like the kid had just bred over four-hundred baby tarantulas, with no guidance at all besides the exuberant You Tube productions of charismatic entomologists. Wasn't the school impressed with the computer programs he wrote? She hated it when they were so discouraging. To her, Ethan was a youngster with everything going for him. He was cute. Maybe he wasn't going to be the next Hemingway. But Darwin wasn't out of the realm of possibility yet. All that being said, she had acquiesced to a plan to help him get the right half of his brain going. "You know you can't have dessert until you've done your fifteen minutes." Ethan was slogging his way through *The Graveyard Book* by Neil Gaiman.

"Can't I take tonight off? I need to call Marcus. I wonder if he and Jodie know about the bugs yet."

"You can call Marcus but after that you have to do your reading."

"Fine," said Ethan, as he dialed his friend's number. The two of them had met several years previous at a gathering of young entomologists in rural Georgia in the heat of the summer. For Margot, hanging out on the periphery of the week-long camp was torture. They were stuck more than forty miles of gravel road away from the nearest small town. It was too hot to stay inside of her cabin, and too buggy to leave the shelter of the mosquito netting. But the kids were in heaven. And it was at the camp that Ethan met Marcus Horsetrainer, nephew of the famous entrepreneur Nevil Horestrainer, and the two had kept up a correspondence ever since. Their correspondence included one of the gentlemen who was featured as the main instructor at the camp; a scientist teaching at the University of Minnesota named Dr. Cavendish. Although the kids had taken to calling him Jodie and they were chattering away with him on the email about bugs constantly. Marcus picked up right away. They were talking on speaker phone.

"Ethan," he said. "Are you guys alright?" Clearly, he knew about the beetle infestation.

"So far, but things seem to be happening pretty fast. The power is already out in a lot of the city.

"Can you believe there's a bug that eats electricity?"

"I know, it's really cool."

"It's also really scary. If you're not in the dark yet you are going to be soon. You should be planning on getting out of there."

"Out of Seattle? It's that bad?"

"That's what my uncle thinks. We are coming there in the morning."

"If it's so unsafe then why are you coming here?"

"Well, we aren't exactly coming to Seattle. We are going somewhere on the other side of the mountains. I heard that the military is setting up in an apple orchard over there that has a big electrical substation on it."

"Any idea what they plan on doing?"

"Sounds to me like they want to shut down the power to all of Western Washington, I guess to try and contain the bugs."

"Do you think that will work?"

"No. And neither does Uncle Nevil. There are just too many power sources around for them to cling to and too many people moving around this country to contain them like that. It won't do anything but doom the people who live there. Which is why you should be getting your stuff together to get out."

"Where should we go?"

"Come to the orchard where we are going, I'll text you the name of it when we get off."

"Does Jodie know?"

"He knows. He's been tracking the beetles since they left Mongolia."

"Mongolia?"

"We are pretty sure that's where they came from, but it hardly matters now."

"Does your uncle have a better plan than just shutting down the grid?"

"He said we need a more aggressive strategy but I don't think it's come to him yet."

"What about Jodie?"

As soon as Ethan asked that there was a loud explosion that sounded like it was a block or so away. Dogwood shot straight up into the air and then threw himself through the cat door and disappeared. The house shook and the lights flickered and went out. It got eerily quiet as the white noise from the pumps and the fans in Ethan's room shut down, but the connection with Marcus stayed live.

"What happened?" said Marcus.

"We just lost the lights. Sounds like a transformer blew up somewhere near here."

"You better go, dude."

"Text me the name of that orchard."

"I will. Ethan?" said Marcus.

"Yeah."

"Good luck. Be careful. Hopefully I'll see you tomorrow." They hung up.

"It's the insects," Ethan said it so emphatically that Margot could only assume that he was right.

"I thought that they were beetles."

"I think that they are a new type of beetle. Anyway, beetles are insects."

Margot pursed her lips and thought about the bold hypothesis that her son had already formed as she glanced out the window and could see that a piece of equipment at the top of one of the utility poles was smoldering and the entire neighborhood had gone dark.

"Here," Ethan opened up the flashlight feature of his mom's iPhone and passed it to her.

"Thanks," Margot used the light to help her find a few candles and a book of matches. She and some of her girlfriends had gone through a brief flurry of candle making, what must have been twenty years ago. Her collection of molds was still boxed up in the basement. She even still had a few tall cylinders and some pyramids that she had poured. They weren't really her style anymore. Too hippie. But they did the trick in a black out. She was in Ethan's room, lighting one of the cylinders and placing it on his dresser, when someone started pounding on the front door.

For anyone living in a gentrified, but still rather rough part of town, there's something really comforting about electricity. That imperceptible background hum of the appliances and all of the conveniences they bring. Easy to take for granted until it's gone. Which is totally understandable. Electricity might be the most symbolic of modern civilization's achievements. And light, while it has the tragic side effect of making the stars invisible, does tend to expose and neutralize those things that like to lurk in dark places. During power outages, there were hidden monsters that suddenly grew fangs and sprung forth. The pounding on the door kept up. Margot slipped into the kitchen and picked up a meat cleaver. She whispered to Ethan that he should go hide in a closet but he thought that she was being silly and he didn't budge from his chair. She double-checked to see that the back door was locked and then she crept along the wall beside the front door, staying low, with the meat cleaver in her hand. "Who's there?" she said.

"It's Herman."

"Herman?" she was stunned.

"Can I come in?" Margot undid the deadbolt, released the chain, and opened the door up. There was Herman on the other side of the screen, on crutches. He looked like he had been hit by a train.

"Herman, what happened to you?"

"Why are you holding a meat cleaver?"

"I didn't know who it was," she opened the screen door and held it for him.

"Could you put that thing down first? I'm a little leery of sharp objects at the moment." Margot passed the cleaver to Ethan who ran it back into the kitchen.

"Can I help you somehow?"

"Just hold the door." He levered himself up the front steps to the landing and squeezed past her. When he did so he surprised her with a light kiss. The curly hair he was so sensitive about was pasted to his head. His mouth was swollen, purple, and messed up looking—and he was talking with a lisp. But he didn't seem panicked. If anything, he seemed less concerned than he should be. The power of pain killers and adrenaline is hard to underestimate.

"Hi, Herman," said Ethan.

"Hey, kid," said Herman. "You mind if I sit down?"

"Were you in a car wreck?"

"Couple of them. Hey can I bug you for a glass of water. My mouth is really dry."

"Sure," Ethan went back to the kitchen to get Herman a glass of the reverse osmosis water.

Margot was having a hard time processing this version of Herman. He was always so polished looking. And normally he had this relentless sense of humor that was tinged with condescension and anger. He was a wreck, but he struck her at that time as being genuinely friendly. Plus, she hadn't been expecting him, and she was a big fan of surprises.

The rain had returned in the form of a fine mist and Herman—even though he barely seemed to notice—was dripping wet. She fetched him a towel and a fleece bathrobe. Ethan delivered his water and Herman drained the entire glass instantly and asked for a refill.

"You must be freezing," said Margot.

"I'm a little cold," Herman sat in one of the chairs that surrounded the dining room table and leaned his crutches against the wall. He took off his suit jacket and draped it over the back of one of the chairs. "Do you mind if I take this off?" he was talking about his shirt. Margot smiled. Herman unbuttoned his white Oxford and peeled it off of his skin. Herman was naturally lean. He spent a lot of time at the rock-climbing gym but it was more a result of his fortuitous Scandinavian ancestry. Normally his face was nice to look at as well. But not that night. That night it was gruesome. Especially viewed in the candlelight. There was a long gash in his forehead, stitched shut only on one side, the other side being held shut precariously with industrial looking band aids. His nose was obviously broken but the word that jumped into her mind first was *rearranged*. He looked battered for sure, but somehow the swelling and the vulnerability added a softness to his countenance that she had never seen before. It was endearing in its brutality. His lower lip was fat, and he was only wearing one shoe. Either he had lost one or abandoned it. Which had to have something to do with the crutches.

"Herman. Oh my God. What has happened to you?"

"Do you have anything to eat? I'm stucking farving. That's Loven's line by the way." Margot and Ethan both laughed and she got up to fix him a bowl of food. There was still plenty on the stove. "What were you two up to tonight?" Herman asked Ethan.

"You mean before the power went out?"

"The power is out?"

"You didn't notice?"

"I guess I did but I just wasn't thinking about it."

"I think it's the beetles."

"You know about the beetles?"

"They're calling it the Seattle Beetle Invasion. You've heard about it?"

"I was at a bar earlier when a whole shit-ton, excuse me, a whole gang of those bugs fell from the ceilings. They were in people's drinks. It was wild."

"That's got to be it. It's this new strain of insect that no one has ever seen before. Its population is exploding all over the city right now. They seem to like feeding on power lines and fiberoptic cables because they are taking out the electricity and the internet everywhere."

"It's terrifying," said Margot, poking her head out from the kitchen.

"Weird," said Herman, reaching into the inside pocket of his suit jacket. "This is actually the fourth time that these bugs have come up for me today. They were crawling all over my computer monitor this morning. I grabbed you a couple in case you might be interested." Herman withdrew the Altoids container from his coat pocket and handed it over to the kid, who set it on the table and made a quick round trip to his bedroom, returning with an illuminated magnifying glass. Margot set the food in front of Herman.

"You kept that for Ethan?" Margot's voice cracked when she asked.

"Yeah, why?" said Herman. He never would have realized that pocketing an insect for her kid would make her so emotional. Herman put his hand on top of Margot's. The gesture felt a little awkward but nice. Herman had never done anything like that before. "A couple of hours ago I met a scientist at El Gaucho that knows all about these bugs. We may be in deep shit here. Excuse me."

"It's fine. This is very cool," said Ethan while studying the insects. Margot wiped her eyes with her sleeve and looked over Ethan's shoulder. It was a fairly small and innocuous looking bug. But magnified, in the candlelight, it looked like a man eater. "Thanks for this."

"No problem. You want to know their Latin name?"

"You are aware of the botanical nomenclature?"

"I believe they are known as *Agrilus suprema*."

"Before the lights went out," said Margot, "Ethan was rehearsing for his Science Day project."

"Spiders, right?" said Herman.

"Tarantula breeding."

"Cool. You ever get bit?"

"I haven't."

"Don't you wonder what it would feel like?"

"The tarantulas I bred are *Poecilotheria ornata*. You don't want to get bit by one."

"Would it kill you?"

"Probably not. But you could lose a hand, or a foot."

"I may lose this foot here," said Herman, pointing at the foot in the sock, which was starting to resemble a club."

"What happened to it?"

"Cab ran it over. I have what I believe you call compound injuries. And the fluid that is pooling in my foot is unnerving, I've got to admit."

"Are you serious?" Margot asked. "Why aren't you at the hospital?"

"I was. They're a little busy tonight. I'll have to go back tomorrow."

"What is this?" Herman asked, looking at the food.

"Stir fry."

"What are these things?" he asked, poking at the bean curd with the fork.

"Threaded bean curd," said Ethan. "They're so good."

"What's it made out of?"

"Tofu. Right mom?" Margot was afraid to answer. Getting Herman to eat tofu was like getting a kid to eat Brussels sprouts. He shocked her again by shrugging and commencing to shovel the food down. He seemed incredibly hungry. "You eat like a bear."

"Ever seen a bear eat?"

"Umm, I guess not."

"You know I shot one once?"

"You shot a bear?"

"Yup."

"And killed it?"

"If I didn't kill it I wouldn't be sitting here right now."

"How big was it?"

"Full-grown male black bear. It was up in northern Michigan. Had a head bigger than you."

"Did you eat it?"

"Some. Most of the meat I gave away. You have to have the right kind of palette to like the taste of a full-grown bear. Well, basically you've got to be a hillbilly. It probably helps to be really hungry as well but even then, I don't know. You've got to boil the meat to remove the grease, then soak it in buttermilk for a few days to draw the toxins out. The flavor still winds up being pretty intense. And not in a good way. Your mom has seen the rug I had made out of its fur." Margot blushed. It was true that they had done it on a bearskin rug in his apartment. He laid it out underneath a plasma television screen that was running a video of a fireplace fire. But she had never heard the story about northern Michigan before. Honestly, since the fire was fake, she assumed the rug was fake too.

"What other big stuff have you killed?"

"Do you mean that metaphorically?"

"I'm not sure. What's a metaphor?"

"Think of it this way, kid. The dictionary is pretty thick, but it still doesn't have nearly enough words in it for us to be able to describe to each other what we think, and how we feel."

This had to be the first time that Herman had ever mentioned feelings in context. Who was this man who had suddenly shown up at her house? She was used to the tall tales. But well-developed ideas were not something that she associated him with. She didn't realize it but it was the pain killers that had him in a state where he was inclined to relax and open up, despite being in utter agony.

"What we do is we use metaphors to compare stuff," Herman was on a roll. "Think about this, if the president vetoes a law—you know what veto means?"

"I do."

"Good. If the president vetoes a law that is going to raise everyone's taxes, that's the same as killing a big thing. The law is the same as the bear. Do you see what I mean?"

"I think so," Ethan said.

"Herman," Margot butted in. "What happened to you tonight? You look terrible." Herman put the fork down and squeezed his eyes shut a couple of times, then let out a long slow exhale.

"I'm fairly sure I don't smell too good either. What do you think, kid?"

"You smell like a car full of skunks that crashed into a garbage truck."

"You think that's funny?"

"That's my dad's line."

"I'm in the midst of a run of bad luck," said Herman. "I'm not exactly sure what's going on. The day started off smooth. We signed the paperwork to purchase the apple orchard that I was telling you about. After that I went out for drinks with Loven and Dmitri. Next thing you know, I'm at The New Luck Toy having my tarot cards read when those bugs started falling out of the ceiling. Never even saw the last card. Since then, I've had a run of bad luck. I probably shouldn't be here."

"You were having your tarot cards read?"

"I was."

"By who?"

"Someone I met."

"A woman?"

"Her name was Madame Korzha de las Bulgarias. There's not a lot of guys out there reading tarot I don't think. She is on the TV."

"And then what?" Ethan said.

"Well, I couldn't get food, for one thing. Then I tripped over some drunk's legs and messed my face up. The cab that I was taking to the hospital hit a pothole and the tire blew out. The driver got like three-hundred bucks out of me and only drove me one block. I've obviously got a fat lip and a tooth that is going to have to be pulled on Monday. At Harborview I failed to get the wound on my head sewn shut before the place was overrun by freaks in worse pain than me. And then, as I was just trying to get home, a cab that I thought that I was hailing drove over my foot, resulting in some unknown level of structural damage. As you can see, I'm not getting much right now."

"You made it here okay," said Margot.

"That's true. This is like a port in a storm for me. I hope that the curse didn't follow me in. I'm sorry in advance if it did. I just didn't want to be alone in that hospital. They wanted me to stay all night and tomorrow looking for signs of internal bleeding. I just couldn't stay."

Margot squeezed his hand. "It's going to be fine," she said. "You're safe here." She was really digging his vulnerability. Dogwood burst back in through the cat door, bounded onto Herman's lap, and then slid off.

"Not a very sure-footed cat," said Herman. "It kind of worries me that the power went out before I came over. Maybe I should go."

"You don't have to go, Herman. It isn't your fault that the power is out. It sounds like it's these beetles or whatever they

are. And how bad is your foot? Can I see what it looks like?"
There was a loud thud in Ethan's room and Dogwood meowed
but they were all busy wondering what was inside the sock.

"I don't want to look," said Herman. "I know it's bad."

"Broken?"

"Definitely."

"How are you even functioning?"

"Some guys who work at the hospital gave me some strong
pain killers. I'd be in much worse shape without them."

"You should sleep here."

"I have to get home. My phone is dead. I need some clothes.
I need to use the john."

"We have a bathroom that you can use, Herman. And I can
find something for you to wear."

"Thanks, but the last thing I need to do right now is to start
dressing up in someone else's clothes. I want to feel like
myself again. I need to wake up at home. I'd take a ride though
if it isn't too much trouble."

"What's that smell?" said Ethan. He was right. There was an
offending smell. It was hard to notice initially because of all
the candles going and the thick air. But there was another
noxious smell that was settling in extra heavy. They were all
looking at one another in the flickering candlelight. When the
air got whiter and hard to see through there was the illusion
that it was natural. Dogwood shot across the floor and out the
cat door again, leaving behind an aroma of burnt hair. Down
the hallway there was a dense cloud of smoke wafting out of
Ethan's room and around the corner. The opening to the room
was suspiciously bright.

"Oh fuck."

"What, Mom?"

Margot had a fire extinguisher underneath the sink in the
kitchen. She pulled the pin on the way into Ethan's bedroom
and saw a clear Tupperware box that was already mostly
melted onto the floor. A pile of loose pages was giving rise to
tall orange flames and one of her candles lay on its side,

melting in the blaze. She emptied the fire extinguisher and put the flames out before it could spread to the dresser. None of Alfred and Medusa's babies survived.

The Third Seattle Beetle Invasion

Over an inch of rain must have fallen on Lupita while she walked. The storm was picking up again. This wasn't the typical enduring Seattle mizzle that the dry-siders were always joking about, this was more like being caught out on a trawler in the North Sea. She had dropped downhill from the hospital to the waterfront and the hotel that she was heading for was supposed to be just a few more blocks to the north, constructed on a pier that jutted out into the ocean. Not like she could see it. Just to the left of her was the seaside Ferris wheel. She could barely make out the deck where the riders loaded and unloaded. A heavy chain hung across it with a 'closed' sign dangling. The spokes of the giant wheel disappeared into the opaque rain cloud that was hovering above the water. The ferry from Bremerton had just docked and a modest amount of westbound traffic was disembarking, their headlights rendering the world a squat blur. A few pedestrians were huddled in the covered walkway that led to the receiving area for foot passengers but there was almost no one else out walking that night.

The exception being two figures coming at her, emerging from the curtain of water. One was a man. She could tell by the stride and the squareness of his shoulders. His head was cloaked beneath an oversized dark hood. He was walking a medium-sized dog on a leash attached to a choke collar. Normally Lupita would have given this sort of an individual a wide berth, but she was on a roll. Rosalie was onto something. The umbrella—even though it was on the cusp of being torn apart by one of the turbulent gusts that were rocketing off the water, had been coming in handy. She still hadn't eaten, but the trip to the steakhouse turned out to be massively productive. At the hospital she heard the ugly truth that she always expected was the case, that Cronkey, Mitchell and Wolfe was going to level the orchard. There was some hope that it could still be saved though. She had found out that the sale documents had gone missing. She was on a mission to tell the Frenzels what Herman and his partners were planning, so that they wouldn't make the mistake of resigning the deal. Or at least she was wishing that they wouldn't. The orchard wasn't hers but it was her home. She wished that there was some way that she could buy it but the twenty-dollar bill that she was still clinging to wasn't likely to cover the down payment.

Because luck seemed to be with her that night, Lupita was hyper-sensitive to men with dogs. Trying not to be corny about it, she had been scanning the landscape for canines. And because of Rosalie's prediction, she had been anticipating something like a dashing, single, young, attractive, construction foreman or something like that, to walk right up to her with some kind of a cute French Bulldog on a leash and casually ask her if she would like to come move into his two-bedroom near the light rail station and get married by an ordained hipster on the Harbor Steps. It seemed completely plausible. Lupita wasn't all that savvy when it came to dogs. She liked them but she was afraid of them. The only one she knew was Tio Rodrigo's Chihuahua, and it had bitten her on the calf the first time she met it. She was projecting the image of her construction foreman with the French Bulldog onto the visceral reality of the seedy man who was approaching with his muzzled Pit Bull. She reached out her hand as if petting the dog was something that the universe had already predetermined that she would do and that she was simply involved in the graceful pursuit of her own destiny.

The dog didn't see it that way. It was a defensive little beast with a hair-trigger temper. The dog perceived Lupita's awkward confidence as a threat to the safety of its handler. It exposed its teeth, lurched toward Lupita's fingers and snapped. Despite the muzzle, she would have lost them all if it weren't for the quick reflexes of the man hanging onto the leash.

They were in the glow of a streetlamp and Lupita could suddenly see that the dog didn't appear friendly at all. It was undernourished, all of its ribs were visible. But it was also ripped with muscle. From its teeth dripped a thick yellow drool and its head was covered with scars. It was a brindle with a white belly and only half of a tail. The man walking it pounced on the dog and squeezed its mouth shut.

"You crazy, lady? Trying to pet this crazy fucking dog."

"I'm sorry. I thought that he was friendly."

"Friendly? Hear that, Whitey? She thinks you looks friendly." Whitey kept flashing teeth and snarling while the man had himself a good laugh.

"Okay. Sorry again. You two have a good night," Lupita tried to walk on.

"Hey, you got any money?"

"Me? No," Lupita stopped and sounded completely unconvincing.

"Just a few dollars. Whitey and I are starving. You got him all riled up now. Getting riled makes him hungry. And being hungry makes him angry."

"I'm hungry too," said Lupita. "And I don't have enough money to feed you and your dog." She felt bad for them though. The man was soaked through and he was carrying a heavy pack. Everything that he owned might have been in it. Whitey was shivering even though he was still acting tough.

"We could all go to the McDonald's over there," the man pointed to the set of golden arches just past the ferry terminal, which at the time were still lit. "Whitey be happy to stay tied up outside."

From ten foot away Lupita could smell cheap booze on his breath. She was hungry, nervous, and in a hurry. She was having a hard time thinking straight but she was fairly certain that she wasn't supposed to go out for a fast food first date with a street person and his aggressive dog, no matter what Rosalie had predicted. She had a burning need to get out of there. There was important news to deliver to the Frenzels. But she couldn't just walk away and leave them helpless.

"I'll tell you what," said Lupita while she removed the twenty-dollar bill from her pocket. "Just take this. Promise me though that you will at least buy Whitey some dog food." The man took the money, jerked on the leash, and continued walking toward the south. He didn't even thank her.

*   *   *

The concierge at the Edgewater Hotel rang the Frenzels' room and they invited Lupita up to their suite. Renata came to the door and walked her in. Hartmut was subdued, nearly catatonic actually, in an armchair staring at the television. An ebullient weather girl was describing a low-pressure system that had been moving northeast across the Pacific and was settling in over western Washington and Oregon and appeared to have no plans of ever leaving. The ten-day forecast was for relentless rain. There was a half-eaten turkey sandwich on a room service cart.

"Would you like something to eat, dear," asked Renata. "We went to dinner earlier but Hartmut got hungry again. I don't think he's going to finish that though. Are you done with this, Hartmut?"

"I'm done," he grunted.

Lupita was too famished to be shy about it. She snatched up the plate and carried it over to the sitting area so that she could talk with both of them. She wasn't sure why but she sensed a pall over the room. The Frenzels had sold their orchard earlier in the day and she was expecting them to be in better spirits.

The weather segment of the news program that Hartmut was watching ended and the anchor introduced a field reporter who was standing under a gigantic umbrella with the Northwest Cable News icon on it and waiting for her turn to speak. She was standing at an intersection on First Hill near one of the hospitals. The traffic light in the background was out. A banner at the bottom of the screen said: Live Coverage of the Seattle Beetle Invasion.

"We're talking with Erin Salmanaca who is out tonight covering the Seattle Beetle Invasion," Harmut perked up when the news anchor said this. "So far the beetles have caused the evacuation of numerous restaurants and bars in Belltown. They appear to be chewing on the electrical cables and causing power outages. The Cinerama movie theater had to be temporarily shut down. Erin, what else can you tell us about the beetles?"

"That's right, Daphne. These insects are propagating at an incredible rate. As you mentioned, we've already seen closures in Belltown, Pioneer Square, and now it seems like the bugs have moved up to First Hill. Both Swedish Hospital and Virginia Mason Medical Center are running on auxiliary power. There are obviously a lot of critical patient issues due to the lack of power and the hospital staffs are working as hard as they can to clean up the incredible numbers of bugs that are falling from the ceilings."

"Are the beetles that they are finding still alive?" asked Daphne.

"I've got one right here, Daphne." The camera zoomed in on the field reporter's palm where she held a small insect that had a flat head and two red stripes that ran the length of its backside. "By the time they start pouring out of the ceiling they seem to be pretty lethargic. On their last legs so to speak. But we haven't been able to get any kind of confirmation on exactly what type of beetle, if it even is a beetle, that we are dealing with, or any details about its life cycle."

"Is anyone speculating about how the beetles are spreading, or where they might go next?"

"No one has answers, Daphne. Right now, we know that police and fire are struggling to keep up with call volumes, and Seattle City Light has all of their crews out trying to repair damage. The hospitals are very concerned about their auxiliary power systems holding up. If the bugs compromise those, the hospitals will be left without any kind of power. Right now, Harborview is the only downtown hospital that is accepting new patients. If you have a serious medical emergency it's the only place to go. But I understand that they are very busy. We are encouraging everyone who doesn't need to be out tonight to stay home."

"And what should people do if they encounter these insects in their homes? Should they call someone?"

"Right now, I am being told that entomologists at the University of Washington are convening to study the infestation and that there is a call center that is being set up but this is very new news and we don't have a number to call yet. Police and fire are asking that the lines are kept clear for emergencies only and that everyone else should just sit tight. It's the Seattle Beetle Invasion, there's never been anything quite like it, and we don't know when it is going to end. Back to you, Daphne."

"Looks like we caught all three," said Hartmut, smiling at Renata. She chuckled back at him.

"All three what?" asked Lupita. She was almost done with the half of a sandwich, warming up, and getting her strength back.

"Seattle Beetle Invasions," said Hartmut.

"I thought the newscaster just said that nothing like this has ever happened before."

"She's just young," said Renata.

"She doesn't know any better," said Harmut. "It all happened before she was born so she doesn't think that it's important."

"This is definitely the third time that Seattle has been invaded by The Beatles," said Renata.

"When was the first?" Lupita swallowed the last bite and dabbed at her face with a napkin.

"August 21st, 1964," said Hartmut. "Never forget it. It was our first big date."

"Hartmut got us tickets to see the Beatles at the Seattle Memorial Coliseum. We were at the night show."

"Couldn't hear the music at all," said Hartmut. "All the girls were screaming. For all I know, the Beatles may not have even played."

"It was awfully loud in there," said Renata.

"You were screaming too," Hartmut pointed out.

"I was enamored with them at the time. I got swept up in that devilish frenzy of theirs."

"It wasn't all that devilish, Renata. We had fun."

"The first time that we came to see them was fun. The second time still doesn't sit well with me," Renata sulked and blew her nose.

"What happened?" asked Lupita. She was hesitant about going off on a tangent when she had such potent information about their orchard that she was waiting to share.

"Renata used to have a bit of a crush on one of the boys in the band," said Hartmut, "that John Lennon fellow."

"It was more than a crush," Renata admitted, "I was infatuated."

"We used to have a deal that the only person in the world that she could leave me for was John Lennon."

"Was the second show terrible?" asked Lupita.

"Oh, we didn't go in to the second show," Renata said with a disproportionate amount of conviction.

"During the second Seattle Beatle invasion we came over to protest," Hartmut explained.

"Protest what?"

"That John Lennon fellow made a comment about the Beatles being bigger than Jesus and it didn't sit too well with the members of our congregation," said Hartmut. "We came over on a bus with a lot of other evangelical Christians that felt like the musicians were blasphemers. We tried handing out pamphlets and appealing to good people's sensibilities but we had a hard time getting anyone to listen. Even though it was August the weather was like today, awful."

"Do you remember that insufferable young man in the white jacket, Hartmut? He called me a 'nitwit' and spit on my shoes."

"What I remember most, darling, is mounting a new snow plow on the front of my truck on a freezing cold morning in 1980, coming into the house, and you telling me that 'John was shot.' I asked her 'John who?' but she couldn't say. Course I heard it on the radio a little later on. Renata didn't make a peep for days."

"I still get mad when I think about what he said," Renata's anger was half-hearted, maybe less.

"I don't think he meant it the way that people took it," said Hartmut. "He really wasn't a bad fellow. Renata mourned that boy for a long time."

"Can we stop talking about death please? It's been a horrible night. I'm not sure I'll survive any more of this," Renata was pleading. Lupita picked up on the fact that something else was afoot and she assumed that it must have had to do with the fractured deal to sell the orchard.

"Did you hear that the documents to transfer ownership from Summerwood to Cronkey, Mitchell and Wolfe have gone missing?" asked Lupita.

"We did, sweetheart," said Renata.

"We've been on the phone with Omeed," said Hartmut. "How did you find out?"

"Pure coincidence," said Lupita. "I was out looking for something to eat and I happened upon Herman and his friends from the firm out celebrating."

"You were celebrating with them?"

"No," said Lupita. "I just saw them while I was out. They didn't even see me. At least I don't think they did."

"You overheard them say that the documents had gone missing?" asked Hartmut.

"You were out with Herman? I don't understand, dear. Why hasn't he called?"

"Because he got injured."

"Herman too? This is all too overwhelming. How did you find this all out?"

"Like I said, I was following them."

"Like a spy?"

"I guess. Enough to overhear a few things that they definitely didn't want me to hear."

"So, what else did you hear?"

"Their real plans for the orchard after the sale is final."

"Which is to do what?"

"They're not even going to bring in this year's harvest," said Lupita. "They're firing everyone. And then they're going to cut the trees down. All of them."

*   *   *

Jodie had the rented Ford Escape's wipers on top speed and he could still barely see the highway in front of him. There were a lot of cars heading over the pass for a rainy Friday night and looking at their blurry taillights through the water was wearing out his eyes. He chanced removing his glasses for a moment and tried to rub the sleep away, then he lowered the window to blast himself with some cold, wet air. The radio was turned up loud and an old Thompson Twins song was playing. The repetitive chorus and the three-part-harmony were annoying him but helping to keep him awake which was more the point. A semi passed him and the water splashing off of the tires and onto the Escape's windshield rendered him completely blind. This kept happening over and over since he didn't have the energy to drive fast enough to keep pace with the traffic. He hollered a few times, figuring no one ever fell asleep screaming. Except for babies. Plenty of babies would go to sleep screaming all the time. The doctor was losing control of his thoughts. He was considering pulling off somewhere to look for coffee when the fuzzy reds and whites in the rearview mirror suddenly swirled with flashing blues. It was a disorienting change and Jodie sped up to get away, but the lights closed in on him and a loud voice came from a speaker on the roof of the vehicle behind him instructing him to pull over. It was the ruddy cops. He hadn't been traveling over the speed limit and he couldn't imagine what it was they wanted.

Jodie had to drift across two lanes to make it to the shoulder. He was fairly sure he wasn't supposed to get out of the car but no officer came to the window to write him a ticket. He watched in the rearview mirror as a couple of bodies shuffled around in the police car. Then the passenger door of the cop's car opened and someone approached the passenger side of Jodie's rental. It was a woman, and she was rolling a piece of luggage. All of his fatigue evaporated and tears came to his eyes. He unlocked the doors. She was the most beautiful thing he'd ever seen. Prettier than Deadland at sunset.

"Eliza," he said.

Whatever sensation of fatigue was plaguing him before the traffic stop had evaporated and given way to a steamy lust that was hot enough to thwart the cold of the night. Jodie tucked the rental car into a gravel turn out somewhere off the exit for the Denny Creek Campsite and he and Eliza did it in the backseat like they were a couple of high school sweethearts avoiding their parents. Eliza's heels and panties had been tossed up onto the dashboard, her skirt was bunched up around her waist, and she was leaning on the back of one of the front seats that they had tipped forward so there would be more room. Jodie was tall, and not particularly flexible, and in order to get himself into a position that would work he had to dig his toes into the crevice of the rear seat on the passenger side. With his left hand he had a death grip on the steering wheel. The right hand he used to alternately caress Eliza's breasts and to grab onto the short handle installed in the roof so the he could give his left hand a break. The position may have been awkward and reminiscent of teenage sex, but that didn't change the fact that Jodie was raised a British Gentleman who was both polite and aimed to please. Despite the endless amount of time it had been since he had last held her, Jodie saw to it that Eliza came twice before finally releasing himself inside of her. After that they fell asleep.

It was probably only twenty minutes, but it was twenty minutes of sweet rest like Jodie hadn't known known in far too long. It was a wonderful moment. But like all wonderful moments, it fled, and left behind it a wake of reality. A reality that was looking fairly grim, even for those in the know about the beetle infestation that was ravaging the Pacific Northwest and taking out the power. Even from where they were, tucked away on a forest service road, with the rain beating against the windshield, they could hear the traffic mounting eastbound toward relative safety. When Jodie left Seattle in the rearview mirror, he had it in mind to rendezvous with Nevil. But now that he was with his wife he no longer cared; he was sure she had another idea anyway. Eventually he caved in and broke the blissful silence that they both knew had to break.

"Where are we going?" asked Jodie.

"Summerwood Farms," she replied. Jodie wasn't a local and the name of the farm didn't really ring a bell.

"How come?"

"It isn't a farm actually, it's a fruit orchard."

"Are we going to become fruit pickers?" asked Jodie, half in jest, "that sounds bloody delightful. I'm sick as a dog with academia."

"I love you," she said.

"I love you too, darling," they kissed.

"But we aren't going there to pick fruit."

"I had a feeling we weren't, but I did enjoy the momentary fantasy. What are we going to be doing at this Summerwood Farms?"

"We aren't really interested in the farm or the orchard itself. But there's an airstrip nearby that we can bring teams into, there is a bunkhouse and cooking facility on the property to house and feed our people, and most importantly, there is an electrical substation on the property that we can use to deal with the little issue that we are having on the west side of the mountains."

"You mean the outbreak of *Agrilus suprema*?"

"That's right, my love. The bug you discovered is about to take down an entire major American city."

"Now let's remember, I didn't create the bug, I just found it. What's the plan to deal with it? Or am I not allowed to know now that I've been let go?"

"What are the options? We have to starve them."

"You're going to kill the power going over to the west side?"

"Right now, we are coordinating with Bonneville, Tri-Cities, and Skagit Valley Hydro to shut down the grid, unless someone comes up with a better idea."

"When is this massive shut down supposed to take place?"

"Tomorrow. At this point the focus is on getting the word out to the residents so that they are prepared and making sure the population doesn't spread in any other direction. Although it may be too late for that."

"What do you mean?"

"I just heard that the cables that service the electric trolleys in Vancouver, British Colombia have all gone dead and they haven't found a cause yet. It could be coincidental."

"Occam's Razor would say otherwise."

"Is there an alternative we aren't considering?"

"There are a couple of lads I'd like to consult with before you just cut the city off, which may not work anyway."

"Are these lads electrical engineers?"

"No."

"Are they scientists?"

"No. At least not on a professional level."

"Who are they?"

"Well, they're just lads as I said, but quite keen for their ages. One of them is my ceremonial nephew Marcus."

"You mean Nevil's nephew?"

"I do."

"Who's the other kid?"

"His name is Ethan and he is a friend of Marcus. And Ethan, more than any lad that I have ever known, understands insects and their motivation intuitively. If there is a solution that we aren't considering, it's probably in his head."

Bathing

Piloting her manual transmission Toyota Forerunner through the brutally wet night, Margot didn't say a word. It was a sad ride to be on but it was the right rig for the elements. Margot's late-eighties, mint-condition truck, was pretty cool. It had a removable hard top and a solid front axle. It was the first and probably only SUV that was ever worth a penny as an off-road vehicle. Margot shifted the gears and feathered the breaks like the truck was a part of her. It had a finely-tuned 22RE engine, a limited slip differential, new carburetor with a K&N filter, good tires, and on the wet roads it didn't shimmy a bit. She didn't even know how many years it had been since anyone but her had driven it.

Ethan sat sobbing in the back but he was under control. It sounded like he was in mourning. Herman's mood had soured. Sitting at the table and talking with Margot and her kid, he discovered a moment of peace and happiness. It was light. After the small fire everything got heavy again. He felt like he was an accessory to a crime that was going to alter the course of the boy's life. He was afraid that he might have somehow been a part of extinguishing the kid's spark. He could have been a great scientist, or an Emeritus scholar. But the genocide of the baby tarantulas may have steered him in another direction. Instead he might turn into one of those kids that wears his pants below his ass checks and hiked up boxer shorts beneath. Or one of those guys who gets by driving around with a neck brace in the glove box of his high mileage Hyundai, hoping someone with deep pockets will rear end him. It was also possible that Herman was just being overly paranoid and that the kid would prove to be resilient and get over it. It was hard to say. Kids confused him.

Neither Margot nor Ethan held Herman even partially responsible for the death of the baby tarantulas. If they were upset with anyone it was Dogwood the cat. But they blamed the Seattle Beetle Invasion, in a more abstract sense. Herman was the only one who really knew the truth. It wasn't the cat's fault. It wasn't Margot's fault for putting the candle where she did and it wasn't the fault of a random invasion of insects that like electricity. It was Herman's fault. He was being selfish. He never should have gone there. And it really stung him that he did. He felt horrible about it. It was possibly the lowest moment of Herman's life when they dropped him off at Belmont and Pine, near the entrance to the Terravita building where he lived in a one-bedroom luxury apartment. His normally taught and intentional complexion had turned hangdog and when he limply kissed her goodnight, he felt lost. In the glass door that led into the building he saw the reflection of a different man than the one that left earlier in the day. The one returning looked like life had just chewed him up and spit him out because it didn't like the taste.

On a footstool in his living room he sat down to remove his clothes. His suit was fucked. He never wanted to see it again. Before crutching over to the bathroom, he stuffed it into the garbage bin in the kitchen. His toilet looked like the promised land. Bright white and shimmering in the corner of the room. There was no line to be able to use it and there was no one around to hurry him up. Herman leaned his crutches on the wall, slipped out of his underpants and lifted up the lid. Yuck. It looked like he had neglected to flush the last time that he had used it. Either that or some other large mammal swung by and took a crap while he was out. The water was all yellowish brown, and there was a mound of feces nestled in the bottom of the bowl, iced with a layer of wet bath tissue. It smelled, well, like a carful of skunks that had crashed into a garbage truck. He tried to flush it down but that thing started to happen where the upper tank empties but nothing gets sucked down. The water started to whirlpool and rose right to the brink of overflowing and then stopped right there. There wasn't room in it for another drop.

"Shit, shit, shit," he said to himself. There was only one bathroom in the apartment. If he was going to void himself, he was going to have to dry dock it somewhere. Which was no issue on a trek but it wasn't something that he was willing to do on the floor in his apartment. He decided that he would have to fight it off until the exercise room opened up at five. In the meantime, he could just piss in the tub. Even that idea struck him as foul, but within the bounds of acceptable behavior, considering the special circumstances. Herman gripped the cold edge of the clawfoot tub and tried to arc a nice stream of urine over the side and into the drain. It wasn't easy because it was a deep tub, big enough for two in fact, and Herman had to stand on his tip toes to pull it off, which killed the broken foot and caused him to wince and moan. It didn't help either that the pain killers had diminished the muscle control in his pelvic region and that he physically couldn't push. It was perplexing to him and frustrating as hell. He had to piss so bad and all he could manage was to get a tiny amount of urine to dribble onto his balls and down his leg. Occasionally he would manage to get a spurt to land inside the wall of the tub. In the end he got just enough out to no longer feel like he needed a catheter and gave up. He laid one of his high thread count Egyptian cotton bath towels on the floor to sop up the mess that he made.

The attempt to piss, while it didn't go perfectly, was spun as a minor triumph for Herman. It didn't fail completely. And it gave him the confidence to take a shot at getting himself cleaned up. He used a cup that he kept on the edge of the sink to rinse the piss off of the walls of the tub, set the drain stopper, and started filling it up with water for a bath. Despite the tub being the couple's model, he had never actually used it in that capacity before. Most of the women that he entertained didn't spend the night, and took their baths at their own places. With the exception of Margot, who had used the shower once. A bottle of conditioner that she had forgotten was still hanging in the shower caddy. Herman regulated the temperature of the water until it was just barely too hot. He even added a few pumps of his liquid shower soap which, according to the label, was also ideal for bubble baths. Suds started forming in mass at the bottom of the cast iron tub. While it filled, Herman assembled his shaving supplies.

Herman liked his face to be clean all the time. It was a bit of a tricky proposition since he was prone to developing an intense five o'clock shadow that he assumed was the bi-product of an unusually high testosterone level. If he didn't get a chance to shave twice a day, then he reluctantly wore the scruff. In addition to all of the time that Herman had to invest into shaving, he also went through disposable razor blades at a breakneck pace. Just that morning he had loaded the last of his Gilette Mach 4 replacement blades onto his reusable handle. He'd have been lucky to get one or two more shaves out of it. The face that Herman saw in the vanity mirror was ghastly but once he started to lather his face up with an orange amber shaving cream that he liked, it turned into something that registered as normal, and comforting. He was left-handed and always started shaving the right cheek first. It was a habit that extended all the way back to his youth and was nearly impossible to fight off. As he dragged the blade upward against the grain of the hair, he could see the version of himself that he knew and loved emerging from under the muck. It was time to unveil himself to the world again. With the right side of his face done, he took one quick swipe across his upper lip and then put the blade below the tap to rinse out the hair that was caking it up. When he turned on the faucet the intense water-pressure popped the blade right off the handle and it disappeared down the drain. Herman wasn't even sure how it had fit through. He made a feeble attempt to snatch it from the foamy soup at the bottom of the basin but it was no use. If it wasn't lodged in the P-trap it was in the sewer with the alligators.

"Fuck," he said. There went the last blade. It would seem that after his moderately successful piss, that his accomplishments were not beginning to snowball. He was still stuck. Trapped behind enemy lines, with no means by which to find his way home. It nagged at him that he couldn't just finish one simple thing. He had a hunch that if he could manage to just complete one task, then afterward he could complete another. And then another. He just had to pick one to concentrate on and stick with it. See it through. Prove his mettle. No problem. He picked bathing.

"At some point, Herman," naked and alone in his own bathroom, Herman was speaking to himself, "we're going to have to step up and clobber this thing." It bears mentioning that this was Herman's first experience in referring to himself in the first-person plural and that the reference was accompanied by the idea that he had actually split into two separate entities with opposing ideologies. There was half of him that wanted to weep, surrender, curl up into a little ball and die. The other half—the half that retained control over the voice box—was fired up, pissed off, and was never going to cave in. If anything, Herman's angry half was at a slight advantage when it came to influence over the entire system, simply because of the weak half's tendency to cower, wallow in insecurity, and defer to the more emphatic opinion. "Get into the bath," he decreed.

Herman got into the bath, and it was far easier said than done. The clawfoot tub, which he had personally selected while the apartment was still under construction, looked as deep as the ocean. Anything but handicapped friendly. The crushed foot was of course too tender to bear even the slightest amount of weight. It wasn't even useful for balance. Herman had to keep it hovering and if he set it down, he had to set it down slow. He sat on one edge and leaned backward until he could grip the far side. It was scary but he pulled it off. Then he hoisted himself up over the topography of bubbles like he was an Olympic gymnast working his way through his pommel horse routine. He had a brief moment of glory, with all of the muscles of his upper body stacked and engaged, his feet extended straight out in front of him so that he formed a perfect capital letter L. Then his left hand lost its purchase on the slick enamel and shot out in front of him, causing his whole body to free fall into the water, which it turned out there was very little of. Since it was Herman's first official foray into the clawfoot he was unaware that the drain stopper was malfunctioning and letting the water seep out almost as fast as it flowed in. The bubbles had created the illusion of the water level being far higher than it really was. There were only a few inches in the tub and the water displaced instantly and did next to nothing for Herman when it came to cushioning the fall. A minor idiosyncrasy of Herman's physique was that his tailbone extended just a smidge farther than most. It took the brunt of the impact and a fresh bolt of pain fanned out from it in all directions, like it was the epicenter of an earthquake. His whole spine compacted. He could feel it in his jaw. He had to shift up onto the left butt cheek to get the weight off of the smarting tailbone, and the foot was under siege from the water coming out of the faucet, which was no longer hot at all. It flowed more like melted snow. With the help of a limp shot of adrenaline Herman managed to rock forward and shut off the flow. Then he laid back in the lukewarm tub—underneath the frothy cloud of soap bubbles— listening to the rest of the water seep out, and suffered. Everything hurt. He was cold. But he was also feeling oddly protected inside of the tub, like the way some dogs are more relaxed in their kennels, turtles find safety in their own shells, or ostriches that put their heads in the sand. The world inside of the tub was smaller, and therefore maybe more manageable?

There was the taste of salt on his tongue. He was crying. They were the first tears of his adult life, they came at thirty-eight years old, and they came when he was all alone, injured, and lying at the bottom of a cold bubble bath. It wasn't embarrassing though. It was cathartic. At least in the short term. He let the tears flow freely, until the angry half of him roused and applied the kibosh.

"What kind of sissy shit is this? Look at us." Despite the authoritative tone, Herman's angry half had lost some of its edge. The voice wanted to demand a full refusal of its fate. It wanted to spit in the face of its problems. It wanted to rally to the market—broken foot and all— for more razors. It wanted to finish bathing and shaving and get properly cleaned up, get the bones in his foot set, straighten out the situations with the various women who were on his mind, and replace his phone. The list was getting daunting and starting to seem impossible. Even Herman's angry half sensed the need to dial it back. "Alright, Herman," he was trying to sound reasonable, "let's see if we can get at least one fucking thing accomplished. The bath failed. Let's get a shave goddamn it." It was a modest enough sounding goal for a man of his ilk but one that required a lot of steps to complete. One of which was getting to the market for blades. There was a mini-mart close by that sold them and was open all night. He was getting way ahead of himself. If the goal was going to be to shave, he was going to have to break the project down into component parts. The first of which was to get himself out of the tub.

"Look," said whatever part of Herman retained some resolve. "At any point in time a person can make one of two choices," it was coming out like a gross oversimplification but there was the heartbeat of some potential there. "One is to surrender, and the other is to move forward. People are all ultimately going to land in one of these two groups. There's the group that gives up, and the group that endures. And it is pretty easy to see which group runs the world. All this bullshit, Herman, it's not a curse. It's an opportunity," there was the motivational kernel that he was looking for. "This is a trial. It's a brutal test but a test that we are going to pass. Hoist yourself up out of this tub. Wipe the fucking suds off of yourself. Let's go to the store and finish the fucking shave."

The pep talk wound up winning Herman's defeated side over. Using his two arms and the good foot for balance, it wasn't all that hard to get himself out of the tub. He was light years away from what anyone would call clean, but he was smelling a little less funky thanks to the lavender scent of the soap. His hair was barely moist. But it helped to create the sensation of all of it having been washed and rinsed. He slipped into a bathrobe that he had ordered from the Sleepy Jones catalogue and kept hanging on a hook behind the door, fastening the belt loosely around his waist.

The plan was to crutch his way over to the bedroom closet and put on some proper attire for a late-night trip to the mini market, on crutches, in what was pretty much a hurricane. On the way to the closet, his energy waned. The wall clock read 11:30 pm. The rain outside was coming down with an absolute vengeance and Herman's sectional sofa was calling out to him to take a load off, and maybe watch a little TV. The foot was in God awful pain and he was worried that trying to push it any farther could result in gangrene. Even Herman's angry half was too exhausted to put up any kind of resistance to the idea of sitting down. It suddenly seemed smartest that resting should *be* the mission. "We could just finish the shave first thing in the morning," was the compromise that was proposed out loud. Before plopping himself down on the couch, Herman took two more oxies from the pill bottle that Little Willie had given him.

When he flicked on the television set, he caught the tail end of the evening news. The smug in-studio anchor looked at the camera and told everyone who still had power to "sleep under cover tonight, folks. You never know what may be about to fall from above," then there was an immediate cut The Stephen Colbert show, which Herman tended to like. The episode set to air that night wasn't one that he could tolerate watching.

Evidently it was a rerun, because the announcer crooned that "tonight Stephen will be interviewing two-time- academy-award-winning actor, and recently dubbed People Magazine's Sexiest Man Alive, Lucky Soul." Herman hit the button to change the channels and started surfing through the stations for something else to watch. He arrived at a marathon of X-Men movies on one of the cable networks. It was the fourth film in the series which followed a complicated chronology. It was just beginning and Herman was keen on checking it out. He was actually a fan of the X-Men comics when he was younger and knew the characters well, but so far he had managed to miss every one of the movies. He was mainly a sports and stocks guy, but nothing seemed more appropriate to him than sinking into a good plot. The last thing that he needed was any more reality. Something escapist was perfect.

It worked.

At least for a little while.

By the middle of the film he was feeling warm and safe, thanks mostly to the pain killers. He was comfortable on the couch and the movie was dramatic and had sucked him right in. He was completely relaxed and enjoying himself at the moment that one of the rear legs on the sofa—which was brand-new and had been assembled by the Crate and Barrel delivery team just the previous week—decided to snap and the whole couch lurched backwards. "What fucking now?" he barked. The couch was so new that he could still smell the cologne the driver who brought it over was wearing. It didn't much matter though. He could still see the television and Crate and Barrel's customer service was pretty good. It wasn't a disaster. Just another thing to fix.

His nose was in as bad of shape as the foot. He just didn't need his nose for moving around so it didn't seem as critical to him as the situation with his foot, which, if he allowed his thoughts to go there, terrified him. What if it couldn't be fixed? He might not walk again. Something was itchy on his chin and he reached up to scratch it, noticed that it was a monster zit, and was then reminded of the fact that his face was exactly half-shaved and it pissed him off. On the screen, Beast went barreling through a wall, and then the picture froze. The can lights in the ceiling were already dimmed down low. They flickered and went all the way dark the same moment that the television shut down. The refrigerator stopped humming. And Herman noticed that the lights in the neighboring buildings had all gone out as well. The world had gone dark, quiet, and deathly still. Herman knew that he wasn't going to see the end of the film.

Even though he couldn't see them, he could feel the bugs closing in.

Labor

Quietly, in an old apartment building on First Hill, Captain Spaulding, some Goth teenager named Nina who was way passed out, and Zen neZ sat around a laptop computer on a knockoff Persian rug watching one of the movies that the Captain and Baby had driven up to see. Spaulding and Zen neZ had known each other for several years, having bonded during the lengthy delivery of a mutual friend's baby on a commune in the foothills east of Eugene. The two of them shared a common philosophy about childbirth, always tending toward the natural and trusting in the power of the female body to know what to do. Spaulding had just taken his skills to another level than Zen neZ ever would. She didn't have the discipline for all the schooling required to become an actual midwife, let alone a doctor. The actors in the film were snorting cocaine and having a debauched throw down on a Texas ranch. Zen neZ untangled her legs from the lotus position that she had them in and boosted herself up into a headstand and resumed watching the film upside down.

Baby wasn't watching the movie. She was in the dingy bathroom, using the light from her cell phone to scan her body for the presence of the vile insect with the red stripes on its back. She couldn't get a glimpse though. Every time she convinced herself they were gone and tried to go back to the living room she could feel one crawling on an ankle or between her shoulder blades and she would put the light back on and scratch herself like hell but she never managed to come up with a body that she could flick into the toilet or stomp on with the heel of her ostrich skin cowgirl boots.

Like most of downtown at that point, the power to the building was out. But the laptop's battery was charged and streaming the film off of a hot spot that still had sufficient bandwidth. Spaulding was getting a little melancholy as the night wore on and he could pin it to one of two reasons, or both: he was coming down off of his buzz, and before coming over to his friend's apartment he had found out an old friend had died. The term *old friend* didn't have the usual meaning in this case. The guy who died was someone that Spaulding only saw when the Zombie fans gathered and it wasn't like they had known each other all that long, the guy was just straight up old. Too old to be out gallivanting with a bunch young horror movie fans. But then again so was Spaulding. It was probably why they got along. His name was Masochistic Mitch, the old man with the gray beard, the one who smashed the car window with the garbage can. He was a crazy old kook. And if he was too old to be at the party, he was way too old to be scampering up that scaffolding the way he was. Masochistic Mitch had another moniker that he went by most days, Mudder Mitch. A name he had earned while making his living over the last several decades as a drywall technician. A skill that he retained—even continued to excel at— after rendering himself almost seventy-five percent blind from staring too long at the solar eclipse of 2017. He watched the entire astrological phenomenon with his naked eyes, never once looking away during the entire two hours it took for the moon to traverse the sun's path. Masochistic/Mudder Mitch lost his grip while climbing the wet scaffolding and rag-dolled his way to the ground. His head thudded off the pavement and a substantial pool of blood emerged from his ear but the injury could still have been secondary to something that happened while he was ascending—like his heart ceased beating after overdoing it with the bath salts, or the blindness finally caught up with him and he missed a handhold.

There were a couple of cases of beer open in the middle of the room but Spaulding wasn't in the mood to drink any of it. He was due for another fix and even though the party was small it didn't seem right to just boost up right in front of the everyone. He peeled himself off of the floor and made his way to one of the small bedrooms and shut the door. The flame from a small tea candle flickered on one of the shelves. There was practically nothing in there but a mattress, a skeleton that appeared stolen from some university's anatomy lecture hall, and a tapestry with a great big sequined elephant that wreaked of Nagchampa incense.

Despite the company that he kept and how he dressed, Spaulding was fastidious and had a reputation for being very well-prepared. Some quirkiness that his personality retained had to be from growing up in a house that wrapped the entire year around the celebration of Christmas. It left him with a soft spot for anything that resembled tradition. It was a Rob Zombie night. And tradition dictated that on Rob Zombie nights he liked to partake of the zombie drug. He was still sitting on most of what he had on him before the first movie started, back when Seattle was still in the grip of the heat wave. He sat cross-legged, facing a wall so he wouldn't have to look at the skeleton, and removed some supplies from a hip sack that he had on underneath his wet sarong. One of those supplies was a Petzl headlamp. He strapped it on above the smeared face paint and used it to illuminate his work zone. He unfolded a piece of clean cloth and placed it on the floor in front of him. On the cloth he laid a fresh needle, a vile of sterile water from the medical supply store, a nylon compression strap, a pack of cigarettes, cooking spoon, a butane torch, citric acid tablets, a pack of sanitizing wipes, and a small baggie of brown powder. He cleaned his hands, unwrapped the needle and used it to puncture the top of the sterile water container. Then he drew the water up and transferred it to the spoon. He poured about half of the baggie of brown powder into the spoon and then added one of the citric acid tablets. Bath salts— like heroin— are basic, and need to be mixed with an acid in order to completely dissolve in water. He picked the spoon up and lit the butane torch beneath it and moved the flame around for a few seconds until the water began to boil and the solution looked ready. He broke the filter off of one of the Marlboros that he smoked and laid it in the spoon. He drew the solution back up through it so that no insoluble material would make its way into the needle. The shot was all set and the clown laid it on the cloth while he rolled up one of his sleeves and flexed his arm a few times to get it warm. He clenched and opened up his fist, then he fixed the compression strap around his bicep and a nice blue vein revealed itself just below the elbow. Spaulding inverted the needle, tapped it a few times to get the air bubbles to rise, and then pressed on the plunger lightly until the fluid beaded up at the point of the needle. Pointing back toward his heart, he sunk the needle into the vein, released the compression strap, and then injected the drug.

People's reactions to bath salts tended to be widely varied, but hallucinations—especially hallucinations that had to do with dead bodies—were common. Spaulding left his shooting kit out on the floor in front of him and laid back while the drug dispersed itself throughout his body. He was staring up at the ceiling but he couldn't for long because the ceiling was lined with bats. The bats were huge. Bigger than seagulls and their high nitrogen feces was piling up all over the floor. The feces was bright purple. It glowed in the darkness. And the smell of it was so bad that his breath got stuck. He choked and fought his way to his knees. The faint audio from the film being played in the room on the other side of the door felt like it was blasting in his ears. It was the final scene and The Rejects were riding face first into a hail of bullet fire. He spun around, looking for an escape, and spied the skeleton.

It was then that Spaulding had the reverse of the typical bath salts hallucination experience, he took one look at the lifeless body of the bony doll and imagined it as alive and for some reason—perhaps it was the smarmy grin the skeleton wore—it filled with him with an uncontrollable anger and hatred. He brutally jerked it off its hangar by the skull and commenced smashing it against the floor. He didn't stop until every single bone was loose and scattered across the hardwoods. The sudden bout of violence in the bedroom sent something like a black angel rampaging out of the underworld and Zen neZ—empath that she was—received it like a jolt. Her neck went limp and buckled and she didn't so much fall out of the headstand she was in as crumple toward the floor into a lifeless ball that could no longer move a muscle.

*   *   *

A few blocks away, on the third floor of the abandoned building on Western, an urgent cry from the top of a stalled Ferris wheel found its way into the head of a slumbering Barbie and yanked her into a sudden and disorienting consciousness. She had been dreaming that she was eating funnel cake at a carnival. The baby rolled and laid an elbow or a knee against Barbie's bladder, which was perpetually full. She set her feet down on the painted floor and listened to the darkness. Because of the power outage, there wasn't any of that white noise that typically pervaded the city. No one was honking or whizzing by on the street down below. By her and Kenovan's bed there was a small window with a spider crack in it, secured with a duct tape cross. It was rattling in the wind. The rain was hitting the glass with so much force that she thought that it might be enough to shatter it the rest of the way. There was the low, steady rumble of a generator that was parked around the corner. But the machine may have been running out of gas because it was coughing and sputtering and fixing to die. There was also the slightly louder rumble of Kenovan snoring beside her. His big feet were sticking out from the bottom of the blankets. She could also hear dribbles of the dialogue coming up from the basement. The welder that occupied the bottom floor had apparently invited a few friends over to hang out in the dark wee hours of the night.

The noise was irritating and even though it wasn't that loud she had an idea that she might just stumble down there with a flashlight if she could find one and ask whoever it was if they could knock it off. While she was thinking about it the skin around the baby grew suddenly taut and the musculature in her abdominal zone got caught up in some kind of involuntary process, like her bodily functions, or at least some of them, had been hijacked. It subsided in under a minute. The belly loosened up and her insides stopped feeling weird and she waddled over to the bathroom to pee.

In the bathroom she peed some but she never felt like she could get all of it out. In the adjacent bedroom she heard Kenovan fart and the stench of it was just like Dick's Drive-In burgers. He must have stopped there while he was out doing errands without telling her. Barbie was a pescatarian with an aversion to red meat so Kenovan did his best to keep it out of her sight, which she normally appreciated, but in that instance the smell of the gas was enough to flip her stomach over. She was overcome with a wave of nausea and in a flash, she was on her knees gagging over the open toilet bowl. Nothing much came up but some spit and some stomach acid. The nausea passed for the most part and she shuffled back over to the edge of the bed.

Even though it had gotten cold, she was hot; sweating even as she took a drink of water from a mason jar. As soon as she climbed back in next to Kenovan the belly tightened again, a little firmer than the last time. She could feel it even down in her thighs and at the bottom of her buttocks. Which were damp and cold. She reached down in between her legs to check and see why that might be and she thought that she must have peed herself during the night and failed to notice. But that didn't seem right. Upon further investigation she found the sheets and robe not just damp but soaked through, and they didn't smell like urine at all. It dawned on her that her water had broken. It was time to wake her sleeping boyfriend and get the midwife on the phone.

Another Hole in Herman's Head

Rainbow-colored apples were dripping from the trees all over the lush orchard in Herman's dream when the sound of shattering glass shocked him out of the rejuvenating REM state. It was still pitch black and the room had grown chillier than it was when he fell asleep. He had pissed himself and he didn't even care. He was glad about it since he didn't need to go anymore, but it did leave him cold and wet. The storm hadn't abated in the least. It seemed to have redoubled its intensity. There was a draft. Something alive was creating a terrible racket in the bathroom. Herman was technically still in blinding pain. His thoughts were understandably cloudy and hard to form. His first instinct—which took a while to arrive— was that there was an intruder. The next thing that he decided was that he was sick of taking shit.

He was ready to unleash some fury and he wanted a weapon that was a little more functional than one of the crutches. Herman didn't own a gun so he settled on a nine iron from his golf bag in the hall. To get to the bathroom he hopped on one foot. Something was writhing and squealing inside. It was bleating like a lamb on its way to slaughter and thudding off of the walls. Herman jumped across the threshold with the club held high over his shoulder. He was lucky that he didn't plant his stockinged foot on one of the shards of glass that were covering the floor.

Whatever was in there was smaller than he had expected and its energy was waning. It was a shadow doing slow zig-zags across the floor. Like a sick raccoon or something. Herman put two hands on the club and brought it down hard. He missed badly and when the iron club struck the tile floor it sent a shock wave through his body so intense that he felt it in his ears. "Fuck," he cried out. When his teeth stopped chattering, he choked up and took a more modest swing and connected. Which, instead of slowing his foe down, caused it to speed up, and in a flash, it leapt and bit one of Herman's broken toes. "Fuck," he cried again. The next swing he took was in self-defense. He hit his foe three times before it backed up some and Herman could deliver the kill shot. He smashed it with the club and he kept smashing it long after all of its life had drained away. He still didn't even know what it was. He set the club aside and it was quiet again. Then he heard something ooze out of the thing's body and the smell—already horrible—became toxic and unbreathable. Herman buckled over and dry-heaved. Tears were pouring out of the corners of his eyes. And he was experiencing another side effect of the pain killers, everywhere on his body itched.

Eventually he managed to crutch back over to the kitchen where he kept a Mag Lite beneath the sink. He took it back to the bathroom to survey the damage, even though he really didn't even want to know.

In downtown Seattle there was a big population of overweight seagulls. The tourists tended to hang around on the pier in front of Ivar's feeding them their leftover fries. They were greasy birds, with a sense of entitlement. Most of them were resident Glaucous Wings. A particularly fat one had somehow rocketed through the double pane glass window in Herman's bathroom and landed on the floor. There were feathers and glass everywhere. His mother would have said that it looked like a war zone. Brown blood seeped out of the bird's neck and one of the wings was folded up on its back and looked to be horribly broken.

Herman was tired. And it wasn't lost on him that the bird was probably a messenger, sent from the underworld to interrupt his sleep. Either that it was just also addicted to the conveniences of electricity and the power outage had shorted out its navigational skills. It didn't matter. By that point he was too tired to sleep. It was three am. The hour of the tiger. The single hardest hour of the day to get up and confront challenges. The hour at which the true masters of the universe awoke to train.

"What should we do?" he said aloud. And then the warrior in him stepped forward and supplied a flat, one-word answer, "shave." And just like that it was decided. His life had been reduced to a singular purpose: getting a shave. And the reality of having just a singular thought in his mind was a massive relief.

It was such a powerful relief in fact, that it kept him on course, even when he discovered that his closet had turned into a field of missing buttons, busted zippers, and broken snaps. He couldn't come up with a pair of matching socks. But he got out the door anyway, in an old pair of navy-blue sweat pants with a silk screen of the mascot of the Delaware Fighting Blue Hens, and a Gore-Tex coat with the pit zips stuck open over a leather vest and a red fleece. He also wore a wool beanie with ear flaps. It looked like Armageddon outside and he wanted to be well-defended against the elements.

The storm drains were all overflowing. The sidewalks were manageable but the streets ran like rivers. By some miracle the block that contained the 24/7 mini-mart that Herman was headed to still had power and the store's Open sign was shining like a mirage. By the time he got inside, he was completely drenched again, he might as well have been swimming. The pain killers had really slowed his metabolism, and along with the constant itch there was a shiver that emanated from the marrow in his bones.

It was a tiny store that sold mostly candy and beer. But they carried Herman's brand of razors and even though the price was jacked up he bought the ten pack. This wasn't a situation that he wanted to run into again.

Behind the till there was a fat man teetering on an overburdened three-legged stool. Nearly everything about him was white. His white hair was thinning but long and pulled back into a pony tail. He had a white mustache and his white skin looked even whiter because he was wearing a white t-shirt and white painter's pants. The man was drinking a frothy beverage while he worked. If what he was doing could be called working.

"Man, you look like hammered shit," he said in a shocking falsetto followed by a pungent belch. "I thought I was ugly. What the hell happened to you?"

Herman balked at the white blob behind the counter. He never small talked with people unless they were clients that he was trying to bait or women he was trying to seduce. He blew off the rude personal inquiry and plunked the razors down on the counter.

"Alright," said the dude as he set his mug down on the counter. Herman could smell that it was beer that he was drinking, but there was something odd about it. "Just the blades?"

"Yes," said Herman. He had a twenty clenched in his fist already but he was also doing a lot of sniffing and trying to place the strange aroma from the beer.

"$20.70," said the clerk. Herman forked over the twenty. "That's not enough."

"What are you drinking?" asked Herman.

"Some of my home brew. You want some? It might just straighten you out."

Herman looked down at the beer and nodded. He was still thirsty. He was also hungry and the beer was dark. There were calories in it, that was for sure. The big man disappeared behind a bead curtain and returned with a mugful for Herman. Herman started gulping it down and letting it dribble down his chin. Like he'd been lost in the wilderness for months. It wasn't that good but he wasn't feeling picky. The beer was overly sweet and there was a distinct flavor—both distant and familiar—that he simply couldn't place. He found it to be both intriguing and nourishing and he kept guzzling until he couldn't guzzle anymore. But not because he ran out of beer. Herman's throat was beginning to close.

"What kind of beer is that?" Herman whispered as he dropped the mug down on the counter and wrapped his fingers around his own neck. He was already struggling for air and the aisles were starting to spin.

"It's kind of an acquired taste," said the brewer. "Do you like it?" Herman was powerless to reply. The dude misinterpreted Herman's reaction at first and started talking about the beer. "It's the world's first Peanut Butter Banana Cream Stout," came the proud announcement. Herman's knees buckled at the sound of the word *peanut* and he collapsed onto the floor, desperate for air. His face went blue.

The clerk finally recognized that his customer was in distress and rushed to his side. Herman's mouth was open and his tongue was protruding and dancing wildly about, like it had gone rogue and wanted to escape the confines of his mouth. His nostrils flared and his eyes were bulging and red. The swelling had divided his head from his heart. No blood was getting through. There was nothing he could do. He was as helpless as a baby chick. No one but the enormous and pale amateur brewer could save him.

"Looks like your airway is closing." With a surprisingly deft hand the dude tilted Herman's head to make breathing as easy as possible. "Peanut allergy?" Herman blinked and the dude seemed to count that as a yes. "You need a crike."

Herman could sense the man letting go of him. He was probably calling an ambulance. Herman didn't want an ambulance. He knew it would probably crash on the freeway with him in it and he would rather just die on that floor. Then he got to thinking about Margot and Ethan. It wasn't sitting well with him the way their night together had ended. He couldn't breathe, but somewhere inside of him there was an urge to keep fighting. Death tugged at him from behind and he willed himself away from it. It was all that he could muster. Like an obtuse angel the big man returned, though he hadn't called for help.

"There's no time to get you to the hospital so we are going to do this right here," he said. From the shelves of the store he had collected some supplies. He produced a pocket knife with a ceramic blade. It was white, like everything else about him, and sharp. He uncapped a bottle of rubbing alcohol and got a cloth damp so that he could sterilize the neck. "Don't worry," he said. "I was a medic in the Iraq war. That's where I lost my pigment." He located Herman's Adam's apple, goosed it upward, and started a vertical incision just beneath it. Herman's peculiar, half-shaven face helped him determine where the mid-line was. He avoided the arteries as he laid his weight on the tool so that it punctured the chrycothyroid membrane. The blast of pain that traveled through Herman was mitigated slightly by the trickle of oxygen that came with it. The clerk was kneeling on Herman's chest so that the patient couldn't move. The snow cloud of a man withdrew the blade of the knife and in one smooth motion replaced it with the body of a Bic pen that he had sawed off at two inches like a shotgun. The intensity for Herman was like having rats nibbling at every neuron. Stinging hellish pain swirled in him and mixed with euphoria as his lungs were allowed to fill with clean air and the toxic carbon dioxide was released. Herman was in shock, but alive, and subconsciously looking for the muscles that would allow him to suck air through the pen. Out the corner of his eye he could see that the clerk had gotten a medical kit open and was working on cleaning and dressing the wound.

"Try to relax," he said, "I've got to run to the drugstore for an EpiPen." With that, he darted off, placing a small cardboard sign on the door that said 'back in ten minutes' and locked it behind him.

Herman was left staring at the ceiling, channeling all of his available attention to pulling air slowly through the narrow tube and pushing it back out. It's what his physical reality had been reduced to. Herman the business tycoon, hockey player, or ice climber couldn't save him from the effects of a dose of that wretched legume. He felt himself drifting away and was disappointed. He had no pride anymore. All of his accomplishments and acquisitions were being dwarfed by a cold sense of solitude. If he sucked his last breath through that pen he wondered if anyone would care? His mom maybe? Loven? He'd like to think that Margot and Ethan and even the tarot card reader Laverne would care but there wasn't any real proof and they probably didn't. He wasn't really good to anyone. He made a silent resolve to change that. If he ever managed to get up off of the mini-mart floor.

As the regrets and desperate thoughts were wafting through his brain and he was laying on his back staring at the ceiling with his wet clothes leaching water into what was becoming a sizable puddle on the floor, he noticed something small and black disengage from one of the fluorescent light fixtures, increasing dramatically in size as it fell through the air. From the two red stripes on the insect's back he could tell instantly that it was *Agrilus suprema.* It landed on his face, crawled up onto the tip of his nose, and engaged Herman in what felt like some kind of creepy intra-species Mexican stand-off. But the bug could do whatever it wanted to him. Herman couldn't move. The wicked little creature looked enormous as Herman gazed at it down his nose, the breather tube looming behind the vile critter like a flagpole. The bug then reared back a little onto its back legs and delivered a small but visible electric shock, hot enough to fry one of the hairs in Herman's nostrils. The bug leaned back for round two and Herman was bracing for what was coming next. He was thinking something on the order of a lightning bolt. He shut his eyes and resigned himself to what he believed was going to be the bitter end of him when the big man came barreling through the door, followed by a gust of wind. The bug lost its purchase on Herman's nose and tumbled to the ground. It wasn't far off but its eyesight was poor and it wasn't quick to return. If it was going to deliver another bolt it would first have to find its way back.

The amazingly proficient albino medic was back to work, taking the wrapper off of the EpiPen. The bug's fate was sealed when he rocked backward onto his heels and crushed it with the sole of his white loafers. He gave the top of the pen a counter-clockwise twist to load it and then drove the needle into Herman's upper thigh. All of his constricted vessels relaxed at once and Herman was left in a state of temporary ecstatic bliss. Very temporary. The situation was still miserable. But sweet breath had returned to him and was bypassing the tube now. The air that had tasted humid and foul through the pen turned sweet like honey.

The clerk found a Navajo blanket that smelled like wet dog to place under Herman's head while he recovered. He even removed the breather-tube with an experienced yank and laid a butterfly bandage neatly over the wound.

"We need to get you to a hospital," he said. Herman couldn't speak yet, but he managed to convey a *no* by shaking his head lightly. The medic, despite the whiteness and the falsetto, came off as a dude's dude and had some respect for Herman's wishes. He was also riding a personal high after just saving a man's life, ignoring that it was his homebrew that nearly killed Herman in the first place. "So, no hospital?" he reaffirmed, lounging on the floor beside Herman, basking in the diminishing anxiety of the scene. Herman shook his head again. He was restful, and at the moment he was undeniably grateful to the big white man. Not for saving his life. Simply for being someone there to define his plight and to absolve at least a part of the loneliness that he suddenly felt that he carried like a cancer. "Is there anything I can help you out with, man? You seem to be having a real rough time."

"I just need some razors so that I can finish shaving," he whispered.

"Alright, man," the dude said. "But first you have to let me finish sewing up your face."

*   *   *

There was something on the curb outside of the entrance to Herman's apartment that would have made him cringe, had he seen it. It was a black Honda Element, idling with its lights off. The Sirius XM receiver in the car was tuned in to the Yacht Rock station at the request of the rider in the back. The vehicle's windshield had the Über emblem on the driver's side, the rider in the back was Loven, and he was in a good mood.

He had slipped out of the hospital waiting room earlier in the evening on two missions and he had accomplished them both. He had a fresh eight ball of cocaine, neatly packed into a tiny Ziploc bag, and for the past several hours he had been using his keys to dip into the stash and take little toots since he had dropped the vile and spoon that he normally liked to use in the toilet at Gaucho. Christopher Cross came on the radio and sang about being caught between the moon and New York City. Loven couldn't imagine the moon ever being visible in Seattle again. Without the wipers on, sitting in the idling vehicle was like sitting on the inside of a fish tank. It was a night fraught with darkness. Loven squinted into it and studied what he could see, which wasn't much. He was patient because he was high, but he was becoming less so as the minutes passed and he wondered if the driver would notice if he removed his bag and had himself another hit of the powder. In his mind he kept playing and replaying the moment that he was sure was coming up, the moment when he would find Herman, help him get his head straight with a nice thick line of cocaine, and start plotting how to salvage the deal to buy the farm. The irony of his own thought train was not lost on himself and sent his head spiraling off into dangerous terrain in which it was forced to consider its own mortality. Loven glanced at the driver, and thought that he could hear him snoring softly. He started fishing his keys out of his pocket, as quietly as one can maneuver a set of keys, and when he looked back up, he saw something tilting its way awkwardly through the darkness and the rain. It was a man in a sopping wet sweatshirt, using crutches to lever himself slowly up the sidewalk. In his hand he had a small paper bag that was soaked through and beginning to tear. At first Loven chuckled when he saw him. Then the bag's bottom tore out, a package of something fell on the sidewalk, and a can of what may have been shaving cream started rolling away down the hill. Loven's chuckle morphed into more of a hysterical laughing fit that ended once he realized that the man that he was looking at was Herman. He knew he should get out and help him and he tried but he had neglected to undo the seatbelt and he had to fumble with it in the dark to get it to release. Then he realized that the last thing he needed to do was soak another perfectly good bag of blow so he took a careful moment to seal the top and place it in the dark, and hopefully dry, recesses of his jacket's inside pocket.

Loven's moment of hesitation was costly—for Herman. In a feeble attempt to lean over and recover his lost items the crutches shot out from under him and he wound up splayed out on the pavement, face down, like a duck that had just crash landed on its way in after a long flight from a distant pond. He might have never summoned the will to get up if Loven didn't suddenly appear above him, grab him by the armpits, and lift him up so that he could lean against the side of the building, his weight resting on the good foot. Loven wanted to pick up the sundries and the crutches that his friend had just dropped and help him inside but there was something about the way Herman was looking at him that was sending out a different kind of signal, like he needed help but of a different sort.

And then Loven saw Herman do something unexpected. He was crying, and not the whimpering sort of tears that are sometimes possible to choke back, it was like a dam inside of his friend had been destroyed and every memory from his entire life was gushing forth in the form of tears. The tears were flowing from Herman's eyes at the same pace the rain was falling from the sky. Herman tipped away from the wall and toward Loven who enveloped him in his arms, keeping him upright and at the same time delivering the kind of cathartic hug that Herman had probably been needing for years. They stood there like star-crossed lovers, caught out in a romantic Parisian squall. But that couldn't be further from what they really were. Herman was just a guy who was too proud to admit that sometimes he needed someone to lean on, and when he finally discovered it, he was too terrified to disengage. It was different with Loven, he had always liked Herman. He liked most people, and he was happy to have found a way to help.

Eventually Herman pulled himself away, slightly embarrassed looking but not too bad.

"You alright, buddy?" asked Loven. Loven wasn't known for being the most perceptive but he could tell that something had happened that transcended everything Herman normally spoke or seemed to care about. This was no time to talk business.

"I'm in a bad spot, Loven. I'm a sham. I don't know what to do, Loven. I almost died an hour ago, maybe it would be better if I did."

"Enough of that crap," said Loven, bringing Herman in for another hug. "Wishing this life was over is a coward's desire, and that's not you. You're a soldier, and you are going to soldier on."

"To where?"

"Into the now, my friend." Loven let the unusually Zen comment that had just slipped out of him linger proudly in the air a moment. "Let's go get you cleaned up.

Morning Breath

Steppenwolf started blasting out of the shitty speakers on Hal's alarm clock. He swatted the snooze button with his doughy fingers. It was 5:30 in the morning and the rain was still sluicing across the window panes. He rubbed the sleep from his eyes and was offended by the smell of his own breath, and the taste when he licked his lips. The covers on the bed were all twisted up like a thick rope from all the tossing and turning that he did in the night. They weren't even covering him. Yet he was drenched in sweat. For those reasons, and more than a few others, Hal tended to be depressed in the mornings. He was a big, sweaty man. He didn't sleep well because of his overactive mind. He didn't feel well because he didn't pay attention to taking care of himself. Plus, Hal would rather not have been waking up alone. He shut off the alarm clock— still inside of the nine-minute snooze window—and found himself on his big hairy feet, slipping into a terry-cloth bathrobe. For company he turned on the television to catch the morning news and discovered that KIRO had temporarily relocated its team to another studio since the power was out at their usual building on Dexter. There was a high death toll from the previous evening. A shootout between police and a pedestrian downtown had a lot of unanswered questions swirling around it. The suspect did not survive and there wasn't any description of the motive because there wasn't any time. The anchors had to get to the top story of the morning—what was practically the only story of the morning—that Seattle was going dark, block by block, thanks to an outbreak of a mutated insect, that had a peculiar ability to feed off of electrical currents. The bugs would convene and breed and feed and eat until they shorted out whatever powers source they were working on devouring and then moved on to another. City officials were scrambling to predict the bug's next moves as the dark circle that started downtown widened and began consuming some of the outlying neighborhoods. By that point SODO and Pioneer Square were militarized zones, the waterfront was still open but for how long was questionable. The new tunnel along the west side of the city had to be closed because the ventilation system and the auxiliary lighting had failed. First Hill was half in the dark. Capitol Hill, the University District, and West Seattle were still clinging to a little bit of precious voltage and the millennials who were on top of the situation were using the opportunity to charge their devices. So far, there were enough cell towers still functioning to keep service steady but the bandwidth traffic was inching toward unsustainable levels as locals engaged in desperate communications with loved ones outside of what was now being called a National Emergency Zone. All flights between Asia and North America had been grounded. All flights in and out of Sea-Tac airport and Boeing field were stopped completely. Because of the severity of the situation and because of all the unknown variables surrounding the mysterious mutated insect, the National Guard had put up barriers north and south of the city on Interstate 5 and west on 90. No one was allowed to come in and any vehicle traveling out of the zone was doused in an unknown, but presumptuously lethal insecticide. The summation of a short interview with an F.B.I. Agent named Dr. Jody Cavendish, was that the situation was essentially hopeless. Hal had to admit that it was a fairly intense realization to wake up to. But since Hal lived alone and had no one to discuss the situation with, he elected instead to ignore it and concentrate on what he was getting paid to do, which was to recover Duncan's lost sale documents.

It's not exactly true to say that Hal lived alone. When his last marriage ended, he wound up with the dog. A red Australian Shepherd with blue eyes and no tail, who went by the name Copernicus. Copernicus was passed out on the couch when Hal lumbered by to get the coffee going. The lazy dog lifted a single eyelid—its way of saying *good morning* by exerting as little energy as possible. Hal nodded back at Copernicus.

In the kitchen he realized that he forgot to put his groceries away after he came in last night. A half-gallon of milk was sitting on the counter, covered in beads of sweat. A half-gallon of vanilla ice cream had melted into a sticky mess that found its way onto the faces of the lower cabinets and the painted plywood floor. The pound of Arabica beans that he picked up was sitting in the midst of the melted ice cream like an island. The strong sweet smell was jarring and not at all what Hal was craving. He wanted bitter. Luckily there were more than enough salvageable beans toward the top of the bag. He put a few spoons' worth in the grinder and then got a pot going. It started to brew and his mood improved as he used a few dishtowels from below the sink to mop up the ice cream.

Ice cream had been a bit of a thorn in Hal's big broad side and he was tempted to interpret the whole melting business as a sign. But he couldn't. Atheists weren't permitted signs, just cold realities. For years Hal was a heavy drinker but he had managed to give it up for the most part. He at least didn't keep liquor in the house anymore. And it had been almost fourteen months since his last cigar. The vanilla ice cream vice was new. He had been eating it every day for—he couldn't recall. At least a few months. Maybe close to a year. On rare occasions, when Hal was looking at himself in the mirror, he thought that he was starting to look like a bowl of vanilla ice cream. He tried to tell himself it was at least better than the booze, and all the smoke. Even though it might not have been. It was at least cheaper, as far as vices went.

Hal had money problems. Three ex-wives drained practically everything that he made away from him and he was endlessly bitter about it. They all left him for better-looking men, with better careers. They all lived better than he ever did. He had never been unfaithful or cruel. Though he admits that *cruel* is subjective. He was just tough to live with. His job tended to distract him and keep him out of the house for long stretches of time. He never vacationed. Plus, he was usually slovenly, and women get tired of that. Hal was capable of coming off as handsome, if he decided to put in some effort. His frazzled gray hair was kind of fun looking when it wasn't being squashed down by the porkpie hat that he always wore. If he shaved with an actual razor and got the knot on his tie straight, he could look good. He was a very patient listener, moderately charming, and his short career in law enforcement and almost twenty years as a private sleuth had loaded him up with stories that he was exceptionally good at telling when he was in the right mood. He was just rarely in the right mood. Most of the time he was pretty frightful to look at. Nighttime Hal was a snoring, sweating, and farting animal. He woke up breathing fire, unable to conceal his shapelessness and funky smell. He was gross, and too preoccupied to make any real changes. He was too busy being a detective.

Hal's teeth were ochre from the decades of cigar smoke and the middle two along the bottom had a dramatic overlap. He brushed way too hard and his gums were badly recessed. He stood in the bathroom and cleared the big chunks of wax from the insides of his ears with a Q-Tip. In the distance he could hear the coffee pot gurgle its cue that it was through brewing. He shaved with a loud electric razor that he received as a Christmas gift from wife number two back in 2001. When he was done, his face was still sixty-grit sandpaper. Good enough for Hal. He wasn't kissing anybody.

His plan was to get in to see the messenger in the hospital as soon as visiting hours began. A contact of Hal's that worked at hospital admissions gave him the room number that the biker

Benny Greene was occupying. It was in the ICU, and technically nobody but family was allowed in there. But Hal knew how to navigate the hospital better than the Chief of Staff. And he had a way of being invisible, despite his large size.

Picking out what to wear was always a breeze for Hal who only owned three versions of the same outfit: unflattering, un-pleated brown slacks, off-white button up shirts with a size twenty-one-and-a-half inch neck that he wore tucked into a pleather belt, and three Shitake-colored polyester ties that he plucked off of the sale rack at Men's Wearhouse. He was just finishing up buttoning his cuffs when someone started pounding on the front door.

It had been so long since Hal had a visitor that the lazy red dog actually sat up to see who it was. Probably wishing it was Dianne, coming to save him from his boring life of sleeping on the furniture in the gumshoe's grimy man-cave. Dianne was Hal's latest ex, the one who named the dog Copernicus after they rescued him from the pound. She was a physics student when she and Hal married. The two of them found some solidarity in their shared belief that there was no God, only what she called *motion*, and Hal called *clues*. Dianne graduated and left Hal without warning when she was offered a graduate residency at UC Berkley. Hal knew that she was shacking up with the department head, waiting another fourteen months until the alimony payments expired so that she could get married again. He just couldn't do anything about it.

Hal threw open the front door of the fixer-upper that he bought fifteen years ago—which was still a fixer-upper. Standing between the two coat-racked rhododendrons that flanked the front door was a friend of Hal's, a homicide detective that worked for SPD, named Adrian Campbell.

"Morning, Hal. Sorry for dropping by so early."

"It's no problem, Adrian. I'm just getting going for the day. Got a fresh pot on. Why don't you come in and join me for a cup?"

"Won't say no."

The rain had started to let up just a bit and there was the idea of a bright spot somewhere in the eastern sky. Copernicus came over to say hello and have his head scratched by the visitor while Hal fixed the coffee.

"What's going on, something to do with these bugs?" Occasionally Hal and Adrian got together to play cards at the casino, but he knew there was no way this was a social call before seven o'clock. Adrian stopped petting Copernicus and took a sip of the coffee.

"Not here about the bugs, Hal. Sure is an interesting curve ball to be dealing with this morning, especially considering everything else that's going on. Damn that's good. Kenyan beans?"

"Arabica. Sorry, I don't really have any bagels or donuts or anything."

"I'm good," said Adrian. "I've already had two anyhow. Missed you on Thursday night." Adrian had invited Hal to a Texas Hold 'em tournament but Hal couldn't make it because he was on a stakeout; trying to get photos of a city councilman committing statutory rape with a sixteen-year-old softball pitcher being recruited by one of the big Florida universities. He tailed them to a hotel by the airport but he didn't get any shots juicy enough to close the case.

"Couldn't get away. Sometimes this job has no respect for a man's needs. Or his time. How'd you do?"

"Lost. Came down to Bart and I at three in the morning. We both went all in. I had two pair, jacks high. Not a bad hand but he laid down a full boat and left with the whole kit and kaboodle. Nearly three large. Asshole even had the nerve to call in sick the next day."

"Bart writes traffic tickets for a living. He'll put that money back in your pocket next week."

"Let's hope. Man, this coffee's good."

"You still haven't told me what you're doing here so early. I gather it ain't to whine about Bart taking you to the cleaners."

"Nah, Hal, I'm here in an official capacity. It's been a crazy morning down at the station. You been watching the news by any chance?"

"I have, power's out nearly all over it sounds like?"

"You're lucky that you've got power over here. May not last long. We've got outages everywhere. Seems to have something to do with an insect that is feeding on the electrical cables or something."

"Sounds like a movie."

"Wish it was. Traffic is all seized up everywhere. Things are a mess. There was a shooting incident before dawn that's getting some press right now. Mostly because a reporter got the whole thing on videotape."

"Tell me."

"Last night two officers opened fire on an unarmed man who was walking north up First Ave. in the middle of the street. Looked like he was dragging a dead body by the feet but it turned out to be just a mannequin. Although I think it's fair to point out that it was a naked female mannequin. Possibly even one of those dolls you're supposed to put your pecker in and pretend it's the real thing."

"You do that?"

"I'm a happily married man, Hal," as he said this he peered around the house as kind of a tongue-in-cheek gesture. Looking for the presence of a woman he knew he wouldn't find. "You on the other hand."

"If this is a sales pitch, Adrian? I'm not interested."

"Take it easy, Hal. This all doesn't have to do with why I'm over here. I'm just filling you in on why we are a little understaffed today."

"Did the guy dragging the body die?"

"Oh yeah. They put sixteen rounds in him and they never even gave him a chance to surrender. He was dressed up like some kind of goblin or something, which obviously isn't a crime, but it ain't like it's Halloween. He went to the Cineramama to see a double-feature of horror films that got cut off when the power went out. Who knows what the dude had been doing since getting kicked out of the theater. Turned out to be a road crew foreman with no priors. Blood test was pretty interesting. Be easier to name the drugs that we didn't find in his system. Still, he wasn't driving, wasn't holding, and wasn't really doing anything wrong."

"Was he black?"

"Underneath the mask? Thankfully no, turned out to be a white guy. Twisted fucking world that we live in. We are having such a hard time reducing incidents with the black population that the chief has practically ordered us to kill a few innocent white people, just so the statistics balance out. In some ways the chief is glad it happened."

"Law enforcement isn't always what it's supposed to be is it?"

"'Is it ever, is a better question."

"Are you on this?"

"I'm not. I got something else that came across my desk yesterday that I been working on. Something that you might be able to help me out with."

"What's in it for me?"

"You're private and I work for the department, Hal. I'm sure you'll think of something."

"Does that mean that I have you in my back pocket?"

"The visual makes me a little squeamish, but yeah, something like that."

"Shoot."

"I'm supposed to bring in a local hotshot for questioning about a girl who was killed over a decade ago down in Arizona. Her body was just discovered by some kids on public land."

"Who's the suspect?"

"The CEO of a firm with an office in the Smith Tower. It's called Cronkey, Mitchell and Wolfe. Suspect's name is Duncan Klevit. Ring a bell?"

"Why would you think that I would know him?"

"Because you were fraternity brothers at the University of Arizona together." Hal was sort of immune to shock and barely reacted. "Do you know who I am talking about?"

"I do know him. I just—how did you connect him to me?"

"The investigating officer down in Arizona sent his file up to me. He's on his way to Seattle and he's looking for some help bringing him in. We know where he works and we have someone over there but that whole area is closed off because of the insects and we are having a hard time finding out where he lives. We think that it's possible that he has an alias or that his residence is under the name of a business that he owns. So, we started looking for family or friends that could give us a lead but the guy doesn't have much blood out there and he's got no social presence online at all. To be honest, the way that I connected him to you was pure chance. I was looking at one of the photographs in the file that was sent up. It was of a few members of the brotherhood and I recognized you in it."

"Are you implicating me in something here?"

"Not at all. I just want help bringing the guy in for questioning."

"What kind of evidence do they have against Duncan?"

"I'm really not at liberty to say. Do you feel like Duncan might have been capable of killing someone?"

"After twenty years of this, I no longer put murder past anyone. Can you at least tell me who the victim is? Maybe it was someone that I know."

"Alright, but you can't share this information."

"I promise you, Adrian, this has nothing to do with anything that I am working on."

"Victim's name was Ophelia Dreiss. At the time that she went missing she was a community college student down in Tucson but her family is from the eastern side of the state. They own Summerwood Farms. Big apple orchard out in Peshastin. You know her?"

"I don't," said Hal. And he didn't. At least not personally. But he found it pretty interesting that her name was tied to the documents that he was supposed to be looking for.

"Do you know where we can find Duncan?"

"This is a little tricky for me, Adrian. I don't know anything about this. And I've known Duncan for a long time. He's also a client of mine."

"This is a murder investigation, Hal. We are going to find him and bring him in eventually. Just give me an address. No one will ever know where I found it. If he's innocent, then he can explain himself during questioning."

"Wait a second. Is he being charged or are you just trying to question him?"

"There is a warrant."

"The evidence is pretty solid?"

"Seems to be."

"Adrian I've been to a house that he used to rent on Queen Anne plenty of times but he was planning on moving to a penthouse in one of the new downtown high rises, and I think he's been in it for a little while now. His office is in the Smith Tower. He likes to meet there." Hal understood that cops were some of the world's best natural psychologists and it was dangerous to lie to the man.

"Like I said, I know where his office is. But it's closed today. The elevators are way out of commission, and the fire department is ordering everyone out of the high rises that are without power. Where was this house on Queen Anne?"

"It was on the backside overlooking Lake Union, I can't remember the street, but it wouldn't matter cause he's gone from there anyway."

Any other idea where he might be?"

"I honestly don't know," said Hal. Adrian looked skeptical.

"You know where he likes to eat?"

"I know that he swims in the mornings."

"Any idea where?"

"One of the nice pools."

"You got a phone number for him?"

"Email."

"Any idea when you are going to see him next?"

"I don't."

"When is the last time you saw him?"

"Adrian, Duncan and I went to college together and I do some work for him from time to time but we aren't what you would call friends. I am pretty sure that he keeps to himself a lot. At least that's who he was when we were in school. I know that some of the business deals that he has been involved in traverse some ethical gray areas but I'm not paid to be a philosopher. I don't know anything about any murders from when we were in Arizona. I run extensive background checks on people that he is either thinking of getting into or is already in business with. That's it. We don't hang out. I know that he swims. I also know that he's a good basketball player and sometimes he plays in pick-up games but I am not sure where. Look at me. I don't do basketball."

"Me either," said Adrian. "Let me ask you this. If we were to apprehend him, do you think we should consider him dangerous?"

"Duncan might be dangerous in some ways but he's not going to be dangerous to you. At least I don't think so."

"You don't expect him to be armed?"

"If he carries a gun, I am unaware of it."

"Thanks for the coffee, Hal," Adrian was working his way back toward the door. It was still early but there was plenty of work to be done. "Are you sure that you don't know where he lives?"

"I really don't, Adrian. I'll see you at the casino one of these nights."

"If he contacts you will you call me?"

"It's unlikely he will."

"But if he does?"

"Alright."

Adrian left and Hal put Copernicus on a leash and walked him around the block so that he could sniff the bottom of some of the chain link fences that he liked and take his morning crap by the street sign at 33rd Ave S. He forgot to bring anything to pick it up with so he just left it. Like usual he was going to leave the dog at home for the day but for some reason he changed his mind and decided to bring him. He never barked in the car. It had been so hot for so long that taking dogs anywhere in cars felt like a thing of the distant past. But the weather had clearly turned. It wasn't just wet, it was brisk. He could spend a few hours in backseat of the car in the hospital parking lot. Visiting hours started pretty soon, and Hal's top priority was to get himself up to the floor where the biker was in Harborview. He was the one person Hal was sure he knew what had happened to the bag. It was the only sensible place to begin looking.

The Farmer's Plate

Totally hung over, Saint rallied from the motel bed early and made his way over to Ugly Duckling Automobile Rentals, who was willing to set Saint up with a car, and only required a deposit of two-hundred dollars. He held his breath and prayed to Jesus, Buddha, Allah, and all thirty-six-million Hindu gods as his Mastercard miraculously authorized the transaction. He left with a late nineties Impala. It had a mismatched quarter panel and a couple of bullet holes in the driver's side door. More importantly, it had a very large trunk with lots of room for the weed on top of the spare and the lug wrench. He didn't tell the agency that he had a dog but doubted that it would have been an issue anyway in that car. The vinyl seats were already weather-beaten, cracked, dry, and adorned with half a dozen duct tape crosses.

He drove the big V-8 back over to the parking lot of the Safeway where his beloved VW sat like a corpse begging to be resuscitated. "I'll come back for you," he said to the van. Then he transferred the duffel bags to the trunk of the Impala and drove back to the Mt. Si Motel where Moe was waiting for him in the room. The dog got up to say hello like he always did, happily shifting his old tail from left to right and giving Saint a few dry licks on his palm. Despite Saint's brief occupation of the motel room it was a complete disaster and he wasn't exactly sure why. He must've been eating in bed because the wrapper from the Fig Newtons was sticking out from underneath a pillow. One of the bombers that he was drinking tipped over onto the carpet and there was a very strong smell of stale beer, although the stain that it made was hardly visible because of all the stains around it. For some reason he spread the shower curtain out on the floor. He may have meant for the dog to sleep on it but the dog slept in the reclining chair. He found the television remote in the bathroom sink. It was all a mystery. Saint didn't remember going to sleep. The lamp next to the bed was still shining because he never turned it off. He had a dim recollection of seeing Lucky Soul do a hilarious interview with Stephen Colbert. People Magazine had recently dubbed Lucky the Sexiest Man Alive and Stephen was pretending to get uncontrollably horny the whole time they were talking.

Saint started to feel a twang of guilt as he assessed the situation in its entirety. He had been getting drunk, binging on crappy food, and passing out a lot lately. He knew that he should have been eating better, drinking less, and reading a book every once in a while. For weeks he had been toting a novel around. Something somebody loaned him. It was a thin piece of science fiction by Robert Heinlein called *Have Spacesuit Will Travel*. He hadn't cracked it. Moe licked his hand again. The dog didn't think any less of him. Saint appreciated how simple and pleasant it was to make the pooch happy.

"Must be why people love dogs so much," he muttered to himself as he knelt down and puts his knuckles inside of Moe's floppy brown ear. With his other hand he gave him a good scratch under the chin. "It's easy to make them happy. Whereas making people happy is nary impossible."

Saint rehung the shower curtain, rinsed off, and put the same clothes back on. He was feeling fresh and better about himself. He tidied the room up some and left a few dollars for the maids. The new, old car was gassed up and ready to go. He managed to squeeze the bill for the motel room onto the Mastercard as well so he still had a little bit of cash to work with. If nothing else went south he could be dropping off the stash and picking up his money in a few hours. He decided—as he always did—that the perfect time to smoke a joint was right then. He had grabbed a few of the joints he had rolled ahead of time while he was at the van and fired one up and smoked it.

At first, he felt great.

When he left the room, he was stricken with paranoia.

He mistook a gang of bushtits congregating in a nearby maple for spies. He let himself get too relaxed again. He had been sitting around thinking about nothing like nothing mattered when he had forty-seven pounds hung out to dry in the trunk of the car in the parking lot. He needed to get his game face back on. Saint took the sunglasses that were dangling from his neck and placed them over his eyes—despite the lack of any semblance of sun. Then he took the hat that Big Wave Dave had given him out of his back pocket and fixed it on top of his head. With the hat on, he was ready to drive.

Once he was back on the highway Saint couldn't help being in love with America. Where else could a hippy pull a battered rental vehicle up to a broken-down Volkswagen bus, transfer a dozen large duffel bags of marijuana into the trunk of a rental car, and then pull away without anyone making a fuss? The bus had a note on the dash that said: Please Don't Tow. He hoped it was going to be effective.

It wasn't ten minutes before hunger struck again. He had plenty of time but he was very low on money. The mission, however, was close to succeeding. He could afford to pull over and blow some of his cash on a meal. He parked at a diner adjacent to a gas station at one of the Issaquah exits and ordered the Farmer's Plate with a mug of coffee. While he waited for the food, he put in quick call to Kenovan. Just to give him an update.

Kenovan didn't pick up. There was a message in his Caribbean drawl, "I not available now, mon. Please to leave a message. Irie." After the tone Saint told Kenovan that all was well. He was back on the road and that he should be arriving pretty soon.

The food arrived. It was that fast. The Farmer's Plate was actually two plates. One plate had a stack of hot flapjacks. At the top of the stack a thick chunk of butter was melting from the bottom up. The other plate had four very runny, sunny eggs on it. There was a mound of greasy potatoes mixed with diced red peppers and onions. There were two sausage links, three strips of bacon, and a slice of pork roll. The gum chewing waitress called him Sugar. She brought a side of sourdough toast and refilled his coffee.

Saint was no farmer. He surrendered a third of the way through and had the leftovers boxed up for Moe. In the parking lot the dog polished off the food in about three swallows. After his breakfast Moe took a colossal dump in front of the sliding door of a burgundy mini-van with a handicapped sticker on it. Saint didn't have anything to clean it up with so he quickly loaded the dog up into the Impala and zoomed away.

Steely Dan was on the radio as Saint pulled back onto the freeway. Steely Dan was the first band that Saint had ever seen at the Gorge Amphitheater on the Columbia River. He remembered the "Do it Again" opener but nothing else from the set. He vividly remembered dabbing at some solution of psychedelic mushrooms and honey that was inside of a plastic squeezable bear with a lid for a hat. He remembered a flock of pterodactyls pouring out of a hole in the night sky and having to run for his life. The only other thing he remembered was waking up twenty miles from the venue, naked except for a green army blanket, and that he had wound up in the company of a toothless logger who was cooking a rabbit over a spit. The guy's old Dodge pickup truck had a license plate that read TRE-KLR.

The speakers in the Impala were surprisingly good, despite the run-down interior of the vehicle. The dashboard was badly degraded from ultraviolet rays. Once black, it had faded to gray and was full of white spider-cracks. But the thing ran like an antelope. Saint wasn't used to the speed. He liked it. He could actually drive in the left-hand lane. The drivers in front of him tended to bail out because they thought that he was a cop.

He could have sailed into the city in less than half an hour but he had drunk three, or four, or some other number of cups of coffee with breakfast. It was hard to tell, the waitress materialized to refill it after every sip. There were ways of thinking of it as just one big cup. However much it was how bad Saint suddenly had to piss and as soon as he got the car up to speed, he started slowing it down and exiting on the next ramp. It was a pretty rural looking exit with no signs indicating services were available anywhere. He couldn't have waited anyway. Saint pulled the Impala over right on the side of the exit ramp, scooted around by the passenger door, and unzipped his fly to go beside the car. What he was doing was pretty obvious but it wasn't like anyone could have seen his yang the way he was situated. Unfortunately, the car was pointed uphill and what amounted to a small creek of acrid urine mixed with the rainwater and flowed back down and around Saint's flip-flops. Not much he could have done about it. He barely cared anyway, it just felt so damn good to piss. He didn't really notice when Moe slipped out the driver's side door of the vehicle, which Saint had left open.

*   *   *

Nigel Bernick—lifetime long haul trucker—was on the home stretch of a run from Bismarck to Seattle pulling two full trailers of petroleum. It wasn't his first trip into the city but he didn't know it by heart and his GPS started fritzing on him about twenty miles out. He'd been listening to the news as he barreled west and the story about the power outages in Seattle and the little bugs that were causing them had gone from seeming like a joke to suddenly there being talk about sending in the National Guard, possibly even quarantining the region. Nigel was a little hesitant to even head into what sounded like an absolute mess but dispatch was having none of it. If there was going to be a quarantine, they wanted him to deliver his cargo and get the hell out of there. He was slated to pick up the first of the season's apples on his way back through Wenatchee and get them to a Safeway distribution center in Milwaukie by Monday night. There wasn't any room for error and Nigel couldn't afford to get lost on his way in. Technically the GPS was working alright but so many of the streets between him and the port where he was headed were either shut down or so clogged with traffic that the device kept trying to reroute until it seemed to buckle under the weight of its own programming and was trying to redirect him onto highway eighteen. Which made no sense. He canceled the navigation and started typing the address of his destination into the onboard computer again. Something he knew he wasn't supposed to be doing while driving, but he had to get it done before getting any closer. He took his eyes off the road for just a second and almost rode up and over the rear end of on old Mazda 323 hatchback in cherry red. That's when he decided to take the next exit and pullover and get his shit straightened out before he traveled any farther. He was still looking more at the computer than he was at the road as he descended his way down the banked exit ramp. He knew that he needed to bear left and he looked up in time to do so. What he also saw was a beat-up Impala pulled over on the shoulder, and a big brown dog leaping out of the driver's side door and disappearing under the front of his rig.

Benny Greene

Underneath a fire exit sign in one of the stairwells at Harborview hospital, Hal stood, trying to look natural, waiting for someone from the other side to open the door. When a nurse came through from the other side, he flashed his counterfeit security badge at him and made like everything was routine and there was nothing to worry about. Mostly he tried to make his moves when it was the doctors coming through the doors. They tended to be lost in their own little worlds while the nurses still noticed what was out of the ordinary. Hal was thinking about his meeting with his friend the cop. Whether or not Duncan was guilty of murder wasn't of particular concern. What seemed obvious to him was that, if he was going to make some money off of Duncan for retrieving the missing sale documents that transferred ownership of Summerwood Farms to Cronkey, Mitchell and Wolfe, he was going to have to do it quickly, before Adrian could track him down. At least it seemed like the police department was about to burst at the seams, due to the beetles. Chances are they weren't going to be able to put many uniforms on it.

The door to the stairwell popped open and a rabbi gave Hal a solemn nod and descended. It was Shabbos and the holy man was likely disinclined to ride the elevator. It was a lucky break that got Hal into the intensive care ward where Benny Greene clung to life in room 642.

In the hallway in front of the room was a woman who was audibly crying and whose face was buried in a wad of tissue paper. Her hair was a shoulder length mop of ringlets, golden with dark roots. Probably extensions. In either case it was all matted down above her left ear. She surprised Hal by coming right up to him and collapsing against his ample shoulder. He maintained a cool professionalism, holding her by the elbow and letting her have some time to compose herself. He couldn't see her face because it was buried in her hands. She let out a sound that could easily have been confused with a giggle. Hal wasn't sure if she was in mourning, relieved, or simply overwhelmed and falling apart. In a minute she calmed down enough for Hal to risk saying something.

"This is Benny Greene's room, right? Are you his mother?" Hal pointed at the door to the room which had swung shut.

She took a step back and sized Hal up, wiping tears away from the corners of her eyes with her thumb.

"This is embarrassing," she said. Hal pegged her as being somewhere around fifty and single. Professional appearance and demeanor, like she ran the front desk at a dentist's office or something like that. She was wearing black jeans and a tight turtleneck sweater that looked good on her, even though she obviously slept in it. She had a necklace on over the turtleneck with a Star of David on it and Hal wondered if the rabbi who let him in was there to see Benny.

"Not at all, mam," Hal gave her as warm of a hug as he could muster and the handkerchief from the inside pocket of his trench coat. She used it to wipe away the tears and some phlegm. With her high heeled boots on she wasn't much shorter than he was.

"How do you know Benny?" she asked, oscillating between her own personal pain and mild suspicion of the pudgy man loitering in the hallway outside of her son's hospital room.

"From work, mam. How is he?"

Hearing that he was a work acquaintance soothed her and she leaned back into him. Hal noticed her scanning his fingers for a wedding ring. It was good timing because a nurse in mint scrubs approached with a tremendous bouquet of flowers that was just delivered for Benny and Hal looked like immediate family. Could even have been the hurt boy's dad.

"These just came for Benny," said the nurse. Hal had the eyes of an eagle and he saw instantly the envelope that was tucked into the arrangement had Benny's name on it. Just below that it said that it was from Hartmut and Renata Frenzel. He asked the nurse if she would kindly set the flowers by the outside of the door.

"Are you one of the people from the messenger company?" asked Benny's mom. She was looking a little better at that point and continued to be skeptical of Hal even though she'd already soaked his lapels with her tears. It was smart of her to keep her guard up. It only took a second of looking at Hal to know that he hadn't been on a bicycle in a long time. If ever.

"Yes, mam. I'm the accounts manager, Dean Horowitz." Hal extended his hand toward Benny's mom. It was a strange gesture, the handshake, considering they had already hugged a couple of times.

"Gladys Greene," she replied. Her handshake was meek. Her fingernails were long and painted to match her hair.

An awkward silence followed the introduction. Hospital sounds were blending in the background. There was an orchestral overlapping of beeps and clicks at a variety of volumes. Rhythmic hissing. The sound of curtains being drawn. Hurried footsteps. Hushed conversations.

"We're very sorry about Benny's accident, mam. May I ask how he's doing?"

"It's hard to say," said Gladys, getting choked up again. "He broke more than ten bones. I can't tell you the names of most of them. I know that his ribs are broken. I know that his ear is badly damaged because of how his head is wrapped. I know that his eyes are swollen shut," Gladys was gurgling the words out. She put Hal's hankie up to her nose and snorted into it. She was looking down at the floor. Hal chanced draping one of his gorilla arms around her shoulder. Luckily, she seemed to appreciate it.

"Thank you," she said, looking up at Hal with eyes that were red and irritated. "I haven't been touched in so long." Hal knew that people got vulnerable in the midst of trauma. He stayed professional. Consoling but not taking advantage.

"Is he awake, mam?" Hal felt he'd earned enough credibility then to start trying to get some information. Gladys shrugged her shoulders.

"It's hard to say. He can move his head some. I think I heard him say my name when I first went in. But he's on so many pain killers now, I can't even tell if he's in there," she continued sobbing and laying her head against Hal's chest.

"What are the doctors saying?"

"That he's young and tough. That he has a good chance of making it. But I'm afraid they're just saying that to make me feel better. I know that they're worried about internal bleeding, and blood clots. I know they're worried about brain damage. They had me call Rabbi Rose and see if he could come down here to say a prayer for him. Why would they ask me to do that if he's going to be okay? He's going to be okay, isn't he?" Gladys lost control of herself again. Tears were pouring out of her and she was gripping Hal's lapels in tight fists to keep from falling to the floor. Hal hung in there with her. He was patient. All good sleuths were patient. He stayed right there with her while her son's life hung in the balance and she tried to get a grip on her own body. It took her some time but she recovered again. She wiped her face off again. She looked lucid again, and also appeared to have regained her mild suspicion of Hal.

"I need a break for a few minutes," she eventually said. "I need to use the restroom and stop by the cafeteria for a bite of something. You can go in and see him."

"Are you sure, mam?"

"It's fine, though don't expect him to say anything," she laughed sarcastically as she gazed down at the bright white floor. "He loves that job, you know? The bike riding."

Hal nodded. "They all do, mam. They're warriors."

"I don't know how he does it. Taking classes at the community college and studying all night. Being on that damn bike all day in all kinds of crazy weather. Do you know that he wants to be a geologist one day?"

"I do, mam."

"He should be glad to see someone from work," her tiny smile had only the faintest trace of hope in it. "Go on in."

Gladys turned away from Hal and walked off down the hall, and then she stopped and came back to him. He gave her a moment to formulate her words, but they never came. Instead of saying anything she reached behind her neck and undid the clasp that was connecting the chain with the Star of David hanging from it. She had Hal open his palm and she put the star and chain in it. Then she took a pen and a small notebook from her purse and scribbled her name and phone number on a slip of paper. She placed it on top of the star and then closed Hal's fingers around them. Then she turned and walked away again. Hal listened to her footsteps getting quieter as she turned a corner and exited the ward through a set of double doors. He put the jewelry and the number in his pocket, wondering if he just witnessed her forsaking her God. He was surprised but expected that he may wind up calling her.

He picked up the bouquet of flowers. It was a wide arrangement containing almost every type of flower that Hal knew of; tulips, roses, gladiolas, mums maybe, plus a few that were complete mysteries. He opened up the handwritten card that was with the bouquet and skimmed it quickly.

Dear Mr. Greene,

We are so sorry to hear about your accident and we are praying that you have a speedy and thorough recovery. If there is anything that we can do for you please let us know. The documents that you were carrying at the time of your accident concerned the sale of our company and we are devastated that you have been injured while in our service. The documents that

were with you continue to be very important and we would be
willing to offer substantial compensation for their safe return.
Again, our thoughts and prayers are with you.
    Sincerely,
    Hartmut and Renata Frenzel

There was contact information for the Frenzels at the Edgewater Hotel. Hal put the note in the pocket of his trench coat.

Inside of the room Hal found Benny awake. Though the boy's eyes were hardly open, he was sure that Benny was tracking the bouquet as Hal set it on the window sill, and then Hal as he settled himself into the leather armchair beside the bed.

The bed was flanked by monitors. Hal had a perfect view of the EKG screen. Benny's pulse was steady and slow. Only fifty-five beats per minute. It was no wonder. He was an athlete. Hal could see the muscles rippling underneath the thin cotton hospital gown. There was a wide strip of gauze wrapped tightly around the boy's head. It was tinted pink from the initial bleeding. It covered the ear as Gladys said, or at the very least the flat region on the right side of Benny's head where an ear ought to have been, and curved upward across the eyebrows. Benny had his mom's hair, tight healthy curls. Perhaps Hal was wrong about the extensions. Unfortunately, much of Benny's had been crudely shaved off by emergency room technicians. Benny's entire face was purple and red, like a beautiful sunset. His lips were swollen and broken. The bottom one had two sutures holding it together. His front teeth were all either cracked or gone. Benny's torso was being immobilized by a plastic shell tightened with laces. His left arm and his left leg were splinted. He could move his neck though. He cocked his head ever so slightly toward Hal.

"Who are you?" Hal had to lean in close to be able to hear Benny's whisper.

"I'm a detective, Benny. Are you feeling up to talking?" Despite the condition of his face, Benny managed to make the international gesture for *what else do I have to do?* "I'm sorry about your accident. You bikers are a tough lot. I'm looking for the bag that you were carrying when the truck hit you. It seems to have disappeared from the scene of the accident." Benny didn't move or say anything so Hal continued. "There were some pretty important documents inside of that bag. And there are several people who would pay a lot of money to get them back. If you can help me find that bag, I can see to it that you and your mother receive some of the proceeds." Still no reaction from the kid. "Do you have any idea what happened to your bag, Benny?" At that Hal could see that Benny was nodding. He whispered something that Hal couldn't quite make out so he had to ask him to repeat it.

"Stolen. It was stolen," came the faint declaration.

"It was?" said the detective in a keenly interested tone, the kind of tone that always got people to keep talking. The kid barely but clearly nodded. "Did you see who stole it?" Once again Hal picked up on Benny's invisible nod. "Can you describe them?" Another nod. Hal produced a small spiral notebook and a pen.

"Pregnant," said the kid. And Hal had to make sure that he heard him right.

"You're saying a pregnant woman stole your bag?" Benny nodded. "Can you tell me anything else about her?" He nodded. "What?"

"I know who she is," the words coming from Benny's mouth were muted but clear.

"Is she a friend of yours?"

This time Benny shook his head. A subtle but definite *no*.

"How do you know her?"

There was a long pause before Benny spoke again, like he was gathering his energy.

"We met last week. At a child birthing class. I was there helping my cousin Tina. Her husband's in Afghanistan. She needs me. I have to get out of here. The baby is coming soon."

"And this other woman, the one who stole your bag, was in the class with you?" Benny nodded. The peaks on the EKG monitor weren't quite as tall. His pulse dipped into the forties. "Do you know her name?" Benny's head didn't move at all, but Hal could feel him nodding from somewhere deep in there. "What is it?" asked Hal, putting his ear right up to Benny's lips.

"Barbie," the kid said as his pulse dropped into the thirties and an alarm started to sound. Benny's head rolled off to the side. Limp. Like his spinal cord was hanging on by a thread that just gave way. There were no more beeps coming from the heart monitor, just an urgent monotone. The green line at the bottom of the EKG monitor was flat.

Like a cat burglar Hal slipped out of the room and into the seldom-used staircase that he liked. A posse of worried individuals in scrubs and paper hats streamed into Benny's room. One of them was rolling a cart with the electric paddles mounted on it. Hal could hear someone shout "clear," as he started to descend the stairs. He doubted that the doctors would be able to revive the biker. It felt like death was lurking nearby.

The Ex-Mrs. Joubert Cleophat

Vainglorious individuals like Duncan Klevit get out of bed early. On most days, by the time eight am arrived, Duncan had already been waiting hours for the rest of the world to wake up. That morning was different. Duncan never went to bed the previous evening. His mission kept him busy until the wee hours and when it was completed, he was too plugged with adrenaline to go back to his condominium to sit in the quiet. Instead he switched out the van for the Tesla once more and drove over to the gym where he went for a two-mile swim followed by a kettlebell routine, stretching, and then transcendental meditation.

When he finally returned home there was a lot that he needed to shower off and he adjusted the water so that it was extremely hot. He left the exhaust fan off so the steam stayed in the room. After his shower he used a tweezers to pluck a rogue hair protruding from his earlobes, shaved with a fresh razor, and applied a layer of vitamin D enriched skin hydrating lotion.

In the bedroom he unwrapped the plush towel that was around his waist and selected some clothing for the day. In his underwear drawer there was a fresh package of briefs by the Italian designer Andrés Svevo. He opened the package and slid a pair on, along with a pair of straight cut Ralph Lauren jeans, and a button-down that was custom made by a tailor he liked who came over twice a year from Bangkok. His belly was rumbling and his feet were cold, so he put on some wool socks and cruised out into the living room, spreading open the drapes along the way.

The cloud layer was still stretched ominously to the western horizon but the rain had backed off for the time being. A stiff wind was still whistling in off of the sound and the birds were surfing on the updrafts, holding their positions without having to flap their wings. Duncan's building hung on to power throughout the entire evening and he had forgotten about the Seattle Beetle Invasion. To him, the day appeared to be proceeding like any other Saturday in Seattle. People were walking to and fro in their bright colored jackets from the REI store. The amphibious Duck vehicle had a full load of passengers and was making its way north up 99. And the croissant that he had sent up every morning from the French bakery he liked called Arnüd's arrived just like it always did.

It would have been an exaggeration to say that Duncan liked the owner of the French bakery that he frequented, but he did have a certain amount of respect for the man. His bakery was so authentic that Arnüd insisted that the entire staff speak to their clientele in French only; a blistering colloquial French at that. The policy precipitated a lot of confusion, nonsensical dialogues over botched orders, and lots of arguing in crude sign language over the money. It was a true French experience as opposed to an American exercise in the obtainment of food. Luckily for Duncan he became fluent as a high school exchange student living in Paris. His plain croissant was always dropped off outside the door to his unit at seven am. The croissant was packaged in a paperboard box tied with blue twine that was sitting on the console in the entryway next to the morning paper. The package from Grandma Mabel in Florida was still open beneath the console. The alligator skin boots were sitting on the top of all the other stuff.

Instead of taking the croissant and the paper right over to the breakfast nook, Duncan decided to give the boots a try. What the hell? He was already in stocking feet, and the boots seemed to have some potential. Duncan couldn't quite tell if he found them hideously ugly, or just so out of place in Seattle that their sharpness was eluding him. They did seem to be well made. They had a cherry wood sole and a lot of precise decorative stitching in the vamp. He grabbed the right one by the bootstraps and pulled it up until the heel popped down into place. It felt pretty good. He pulled the left one on and went for a little walk around the condo. The fit was perfect, and Duncan had strange feet. They were narrow and long, with incredibly high arches. If anyone knew that it would be Mabel. He liked the sound that the boots made as he strode around in circles. There was something commanding about the way the wood soles struck the wood floor. He also liked the added height. Duncan was already tall, but he liked the idea of being even taller. The added inch-and-five-eighths that the heels gave him could come in handy. He decided to keep wearing them while he ate.

Alongside the croissant, Duncan liked to have two ounces of paper thin imported Spanish ham, a pint of vegetable juice, and a single espresso. He had it all laid out in front of him, and had just opened the newspaper and read the headline, 'Seattle Beetle Invasion Causing Power Outages All over Town,' when he was interrupted by someone pounding on his door. Hearing someone banging made him slightly nervous. It wasn't possible to get to his door without first getting past the doorman, Witherspoon. The delivery boy from Arnüd's had already been by with the croissant and the paper. There was really no one that he could think of that it could be. He tried to ignore it. Thinking it was maybe a mistake or something. But the banging persisted. And then he thought that he heard someone shouting his name, saying that they knew that he was in there. But the voice was muffled and he couldn't place it.

He looked through the peephole and thought at first that he was being visited by a large tropical bird. It wasn't a bird though. It was Mabel. He opened the door.

"What are you doing here?"

"What kind of a way is that to greet your grandmother? I've been on a plane all night. Come and give your Mabel a hug."

"How did you get past Witherspoon?"

"I'm your grandmother. Witherspoon remembers me just fine. We had drinks one night after his shift while you were still at the office."

"Please don't tell me about this."

Mabel grabbed Duncan by the neck and pulled him down to her. She looked up his nose and took a peek behind his ears first to make sure that he was taking care of himself.

"Would you stop that?"

"Stop what? What? Can't I look at you? I haven't seen you in over a year."

"I look the same."

"Your hair is different."

"No, it's not."

"It is. There's a little bit of gray on the side."

"Stop it, Mabel. You can look at me but you don't have to examine me. Christ. I didn't even know you were coming. Couldn't you have called?"

"Why? What do I need permission now to come and visit my grandson? Is that why I put all that effort into raising you? So that I could call and ask if it's *okay* when I feel like getting on a plane to come and see you?"

"You're here because you wanted to *see* me?"

"What's wrong with that?"

"Nothing's wrong, Mabel. It's just that the last time you showed up unannounced it was because a UFO had been hovering over your farm in Tennessee. Are the aliens after you again?"

"Are you making fun of me? Those aliens were real, Duncan. I am lucky to have gotten out of there alive. Jesse Oozehazen started dressing like a ballerina after that ship started showing up. And Elizabeth Johnson had an entire flock of white sheep turn black overnight. You think that's the kind of thing that just happens?"

Mabel seemed about the same as ever. She had always been petite and more or less bouncing off the walls. Her hair was pink, with some silver roots showing. She was wearing some hip new fragrance. Duncan didn't know, he only knew that she didn't smell like an old woman. Her skin was fairly smooth for her age thanks to regular mud masks and make-up. She still moved like a younger woman. She walked fast and talked fast. Her clothes were tight fitting and in the kinds of dayglo colors that travelers should probably leave at the airport when they fly out of Florida. He doubted that he would ever get used to the breast augmentation that she had done in her seventies. Mabel has hugged her grandson thousands of times and could instantly tell that she had to stretch a little more than usual in order to get her fingers to clasp behind his neck. She looked down at his feet and beamed.

"You're wearing the boots I sent you!"

"I was just trying the vile things on when you started knocking."

"Vile? You ought to be ashamed of yourself, Duncan. Joubert's got buddies from back home in Cuba that have risked open ocean crossings just to get a pair of those boots."

"You sure it wasn't to escape Cuba?"

"Oh, what do you know?"

"I'll admit that they're a good fit."

"They look wonderful on you."

"I said they're a good fit. It doesn't mean I like them. It just means that your new husband is a talented cobbler even if his taste is poor."

"We're getting a divorce."

"Another one? Why?"

"He's an old man." Duncan gave her a sardonic look. "Oh, I don't mean old in years. His spirit's old. It's used up. He told me that he's lost his desire to travel. He told me it's enough for him to stay in southern Florida, run his airboat business and take care of his mother. And his mother is a serpent, let me tell you. Only speaks in voodoo. Spends all day rocking in a chair, staring with those ghostly eyes of hers. She's over a hundred already but she'll never die. I think that she's fixing to put some kind of awful curse on me. She might even try to kill me with black magic. I can't stay there, Duncan. You know I've never even seen the fjords? I told Joubert I'd never seen the fjords and he said that he'd try to take me up to Portsmouth after the Christmas season. Do you believe that? I ask for fjords and he offers me coastal Maine when the wind chill will be minus fifty."

After her little rant Mabel looked worn out. Duncan invited her in to warm up and have some breakfast.

"I have a croissant that we can share."

"Croissant? Oh, you're as bad as Joubert. I've been flying through the night. I don't want a damn croissant. We're going out to breakfast. Somewhere nice. Your treat. I want to go somewhere that knows how to make a Benedict, where they toast both sides of the damn bun. Somewhere with crispy bacon and stiff Bloody Mary's. And don't you dare think about taking those boots off."

Duncan consented to taking his grandmother out to breakfast. It was early yet. He hadn't heard from Herman, Hal, or Quincy, but he doubted that there was any news. He was hoping that after some heavy food and a drink that Mabel would conk out for a while and that he could get some things done. He was at that point of the day where he permitted himself to think about work and when he thought about it he was pissed. His tolerance for mistakes was very low.

"This is really comfortable," Mabel was referring to the passenger seat in Duncan's Tesla. He pulled the car out of his private garage and up the hill. Duncan knew a place at the south end of Lake Union called Mumu's with a good brunch menu. The brightly-colored California style bistro was a rather incongruous destination on such an overcast day. But he thought that Mabel's clothes would at least fit in there. He knew they had a whole page of Bennies. And most importantly, the drinks were big and strong.

It was a surreal drive through the city that morning. There weren't a lot of cars on the surface streets but the freeway seemed jammed up. A lot of traffic lights were out. Particularly in Belltown. There was a line of people waiting to get into the food bank that seemed to stretch for a mile or more. Mabel had gone quiet in the passenger seat. Most of the fire that she showed up with had died out. Could be that she was just tired and hungry. She was eighty-six-years-old and had been up all night. She deserved to be a little cranky.

"It isn't just the fjords, you know?" she said as she peered out the window.

"Sorry, Mabel?"

"It isn't just that Joubert doesn't want to go to the fjords. It isn't even about his possessed mother."

"What is it then, Mabel?"

"I caught him cheating on me. It was with a younger woman."

"How much younger?"

"Still a grandmother but quite a bit younger. She's part of our country line dancing group. I came home early on Thursday after my water-aerobics class was canceled. Joubert's Airstream trailer was rocking back and forth. I went in and found the two of them with their shorts down around their ankles, fucking on their feet like a pair of washed up porn stars. I didn't even know that Joubert liked it standing up."

Duncan tried to look sympathetic as he whipped around an old Chevy sedan that was struggling to make it up a short incline. The Chevy had a couple of ancient bumper stickers on it. One of them said 'I Heart Viaduct,' which had a double meaning for Seattleites. There was the obvious, and then there was the reference to an elevated waterfront freeway called the viaduct that had been demolished after being replaced with an underground tunnel. The other sticker said 'Fuck Ballard.' That one was tough to come by and you simply had to be a local to comprehend it.

"I lost my temper badly. I grabbed a yardstick from my sewing room and started beating on them with it until it snapped. Then I packed my suitcase and left. Sat in the airport by myself for a full day and night trying to figure out what the hell to do. I decided to come up here because there just wasn't anywhere else for me to go. I'm getting tired, Duncan. Maybe it's finally time for me to get old and die."

Delivery

"**W**hat time is it?" Barbie wanted it to be early, so she could stay in bed much longer—rest up for what was definitely going to be a huge day—but it was obvious that the sun had been up and veiled behind the clouds for several hours. She was contracting but only about every thirty minutes and the sensations weren't painful. She was lying on her side with a pillow over her face. Another pillow was propping up her knees. The belly was laid out to the side. The covers were wrapped tightly around her. She looked like a giant snail. She needed to pee. She always needed to pee. Her belly felt empty and was groaning and she started feeling an intense need to eat. The baby was coming. It was bound to take a lot of energy. She needed to eat while she still could. She started pushing on Kenovan with her heal. She was going to need his help.

"Good morning, mama," he said but his head still wasn't visible. His hand came out from beneath a sheet and groped around until it landed on her thigh.

"I'm not sure it's morning anymore."

The power was still out in their building but outside the clouds suddenly broke, there were rays of golden light and the room was bright and cheerful.

Kenovan sat up and rubbed the sleep out of his eyes. He swung his legs to the side of the bed, landing his size thirteens on the floor with a thud. Before moving into the loft Kenovan did a painting of the Ethiopian flag on the bedroom floor. His

feet were half in the green stripe and half in the yellow. On a
cardboard box that doubled as a nightstand, Kenovan found his
glass bubbler shaped like a sting ray. It was still half-packed
and he lit it up. It blubblubblubbed as he took a long draw.
Kenovan then exhaled a massive cloud of smoke, coughed up
some mucus and headed off to the bathroom to spit it out. He
came back drinking a glass of water, trying to find the alarm
clock. It was still plugged in and he used the cord to fish it out
of where it had fallen between the bed frame and the wall. He
found it but the power was out anyway so the clock was no
help. He rooted through the pockets of his Smash jeans and a
couple of his hoodies and eventually came up with his phone.

"Is midday, mama. And I ain't got but five percent battery
left."

"The baby is coming."

"Today! Did you call Zen neZ?"

Barbie groaned. "Not yet, I think it's still going to be some
time. I need some food, baby," as soon as she said it the belly
tightened up again. Everything turned rock hard and she just
breathed like they had taught her in the class and waited it out.
It didn't last long. Maybe thirty seconds. "Will you go get me
some?"

"I will, mama," Kenovan was a little flustered when it came
to how best to help with the early labor. "Gretta's guy with the
ganja is supposed to be here soon. What you need, mama?
Something close?"

"I want one of those gluten free spinach ricotta pinwheels."

"From the 5B?"

"Yeah."

"Okay, mama. I'll go get that."

"I also want vegan fried chicken."

"From Charte's?"

"The one that they make with the jack fruit."

"Okay, mama," Kenovan nodded with his whole body. He
was stoned. She was sending him to two places in two separate
directions but he didn't seem to mind. So far he was only

wearing white underpants and he gave his cock a good long scratch. Then he pulled on his Smash jeans and fastened them with a big brass belt buckle so that they barely hung from his narrow hips. He put on a wrinkled t-shirt that said 'Uprising.' His dreads barely made it through the neck hole. Even though it was partly sunny it looked cold out so he threw on a hoodie that zipped down the front. His wallet was attached to a chain that he clipped to one of the belt loops on his pants. The wallet went in the back pocket. He picked his classic Seattle Super Sonics cap up off the floor, situated it on his head and twisted the brim to two o'clock. He kneeled beside the bed and massaged Barbie's face. She smiled at him.

"Eye be right back wid your food, mama."

Fresh air was sucked through the apartment when Kenovan opened the door to leave. The stale marijuana smoke followed him out like a loyal dog. He locked the deadbolt behind him with his key.

Barbie was never a fast mover in the mornings but that day was especially bad. She was dead tired. She zonked hard for a few hours after her water broke but she still felt like she had been awake for days. The baby was getting very heavy. And even though she hadn't stood up yet, she could tell that the baby had dropped. The baby didn't karate chop her as much as it just seemed to lay like a heavy bullet in the warm chamber of her loins beside a perpetually full bladder. Then there was something that felt like a bite or a pinch but it was a little high up above her pelvis, not where she expected the head or fingers to be.

"Ow!" she wagged a finger at the unborn kid, "cut it out, will ya?" she rolled to her side and then started lifting herself up so that she could go to the toilet. She felt like she needed a crane.

Either she was starving or the baby was. It was impossible to tell. But she knew that she couldn't wait for Kenovan to get back. In one of the kitchen cupboards she had a candy bar stashed. It was a jumbo version of a grape-toffee bar called the Curve Ball; manufactured by an obscure candy company called

The Peanut King. When she was a kid it was her favorite type of candy bar and it seemed like you could get it everywhere. The only place she knew that had them anymore was the oriental grocer on sixth, and she worried sometimes that they might be really old.

It was delicious either way. As she was chewing the bar, she spread the curtains to let in some more light. She was in the mood to hear some music that wasn't reggae or dub and she decided to see what was on the bike-messenger's iPod. She hooked it up to the auxiliary cord that was connected to the stereo and put it on shuffle. She didn't know the first song by name but she knew that it was Motorhead. An ex-boyfriend of hers who was a tattoo artist was a big fan and played them all the time. While it was playing, she scrolled down and hit play on the first track of something she used to love and hadn't heard in a while—an album that did as much to put Seattle on the map as Boeing or Microsoft ever did—Nirvana's earth-changing debut record, 'Nevermind.'

Her belly contracted again and she had to sit down on the couch to get through it. It didn't exactly hurt but it seemed like they were getting stronger. She knew that she probably should have been timing them but she didn't have a watch and the clock they kept by the bed was digital and it wasn't working. She estimated twelve minutes in between, which she knew was still pretty spread out. Prudent thing to do would have been to call Zen neZ and get her on stand-by. But she wasn't in the mood just yet. She was hoping that she could hold out until Kenovan got back and then he could just be the one to call her. After the second chorus, when the music backed off and found some space inside of it, Barbie heard someone rapping on the door to the loft. It was kind of bad timing, her being home all alone.

She kept the music loud and shuffled over to the door and looked out through the peephole. She knew that it probably didn't seem like the smartest thing in the world for a woman—especially by herself and in early labor—to open the door for a total stranger who was delivering a large illegal shipment of regulated substances, but she could tell looking at Saint that he was no threat. It was partly the way he wore the Hawaiian shirt unbuttoned and the way he had sunglasses dangling from his neck. It was partly the soft expression that he wore and his kind eyes. Mostly it was the dog. People can be deceptive and two-faced but dogs don't lie. Moe sat there, patient, alert, and loyal. Being protective without looking aggressive or threatening. It was Moe that convinced her that Saint was trustworthy and why she wasn't worried when she opened the door. Saint cocked his head and looked kind of puzzled, but still friendly. There was a huge pile of large duffel bags sitting near him on the floor in the hallway.

"You're not Kenovan are you?" he said.

Barbie laughed. "I'm not."

"Do I have the wrong apartment?"

"No, this is it. Come on, bring that stuff inside."

"Sorry about the dog. I just couldn't bear to leave him in the car. He's really shook up. Fucking trucker almost killed him."

"It's fine. I like dogs. He looks shook up."

"I don't know how he survived. Double oil tanker headed straight for him. Moe here hit the pavement and the thing sailed right over top of him like a freight train. Not a scratch on him but there were a few moments there where I was sure that I'd lost him. Sorry to be throwing all this at you. You look like you got your own life and death issues here."

"You can tell?"

"Is Kenovan here?"

"He'll be right back. He went to go and get me some lunch. Can I get you something? Like water or some juice?"

"Why don't you sit down and I'll get you something," said Saint. "I'm not carrying another person around inside me."

"I don't think I'm going to be carrying this one much longer," said Barbie, pointing at the belly.

"Yeah, it's looking pretty ripe. When is your due date?"

"Not sure. To be honest, I think that this baby is going to come today."

"Are you serious?" Saint shuttled the bags inside and they shut the door behind them.

"I've been having contractions since the middle of the night."

"How far apart are they?"

"I'm not sure. The clock is stopped. I'm thinking like ten or twelve minutes."

"Do you have help coming?"

"Kenovan should be back in a few minutes. We'll call the midwife when he gets back. I'm just in the mood to be mellow. Shit, I think another one is starting."

"Let's get you over to the couch." Saint helped her over to the couch and she plopped down. 'In Bloom' was coming on and Saint turned the music down so it was a little easier to talk. "I'm sorry, did you want that louder?"

"It's fine," she said, breathing through her nose with a lot of intention. "What's your name by the way?" Saint was checking the time on his phone so that they could get a sense of how far apart the contractions were.

"Saint Stephen," he said. "You can call me Saint. My dog's name is Moe."

"Barbie." They had an awkward handshake as the skin on her belly loosened up a little bit.

"It's 12:21," said Saint. "Let's see how long it is until the next one."

"You know, there are a couple of apples in the refrigerator. Could you grab them for us?"

"Sure," said Saint and he scampered off toward the kitchen. Moe staked out a corner where he could stay out of the way as well as guard the weed. Saint came back with two apples and started peeling the stickers off. "These are Summerwood apples," he said.

"Summerwood Farms?" asked Barbie.

"Yeah, my mom works in their offices over in Wenatchee."

"Do you know if Summerwood Farms is supposed to be being bought by someone?"

"Why would you ask that?"

"I guess I just overheard something."

"What did you overhear?"

"Just that someone was buying that business from whoever owns it now," said Barbie.

Saint looked confused. "I think that someone *is* buying it. At least that's what my mom has been telling me for the past few months. I just—it's weird. It doesn't seem like the kind of thing that people would be talking about in Seattle. Do you like, know someone who works there or something?"

"Can I tell you something?" she said. But before she could get any further the belly contracted again. This time it was more severe and she was wincing hard and rapid-fire breathing to get through it.

"That was only five minutes," said Saint. "I really think that we need to get someone over here to help you."

"Okay," said Barbie, still breathing hard. "My midwife's number is on the fridge. Can you call her?"

Saint shot over to the refrigerator where he found Zen neZ's number underneath the Southwest Plumbing Bob magnet. He tapped the digits into his cell. It rang five times and then the message kicked on.

"Hi, this is Zen neZ. If I'm not coming, I'm probably going. Leave me a message and I'll call you back in between. Remember that this moment is a gift, that's why it's called the present." And then it beeped.

"Umm, my name is Saint Stephen and I'm with a girl named Barbie who is having a baby. She asked me to call this number. Please give me a ring back as soon as you get this. Her contractions are five minutes apart and they seem to be ramping up in intensity. At the moment it is just me here. Her boyfriend is somewhere getting food or something. Please call right back or come right over. Thanks." He hung up. "I didn't get her," he said to Barbie. The contraction subsided and then suddenly someone else was knocking on the door.

"Kenovan probably forgot his keys. Can you get that?" she asked. And Saint went over to answer the door. Moe was standing right behind him. Saint stood with the door cracked having a conversation with someone that she couldn't hear. She wanted to go and see who it was but she couldn't get up. She was too tired. Saint shut the door and was back in a minute.

"There's a guy out there looking for you. Private detective named Hal Baranoff," said Saint. Barbie didn't understand.

"Why?" she said.

"He doesn't seem to want to tell me. But he described you perfectly and he knows your name. He even knows that you are super pregnant."

"What does he want?"

"Like I said, he won't tell me. He did tell me to tell you that he isn't a cop and that he just wants your help with something. He says that you are not in trouble."

"Would you mind asking him exactly what it is that he wants? He can't come in here right now. Kenovan will kill us if we let him in. Are you sure he didn't follow you here?"

"I don't think so. He's asking for you."

"Help me up," said Barbie. Saint gave her an arm and helped her to her feet and over to the door. They opened it up a crack. Saint was standing right behind Barbie and Moe was right behind Saint. The man in the hall looked like a private detective. He had the long trench coat on and the hat and everything. He took one look at Barbie's belly and it seemed to make him a little nervous. "Who are you?" she asked.

"I'm a private detective," he handed her his card. "I'm not here to do you any harm. I'm just looking for something. And I think that you might have it."

"What is it?"

"Nothing exciting really. A bag that a bike messenger was carrying yesterday afternoon. It had a stack of paperwork in it that a client of mine would like to get back. It shouldn't be of any use to you."

"Well, what kind of papers are they?"

"Do you have them or not, mam?"

"How do I know if you won't tell me anything else about them?"

"I'll give you ten-thousand dollars in cash right now in exchange for the bag. No questions asked."

"Hang on a minute please," Barbie shut the door on Hal and walked Saint over to the living room. "I need to tell you something."

"Okay," said Saint, sort of jacked up on adrenaline. Suddenly the whole marijuana transaction seemed like nothing compared to this girl who was embroiling him in espionage while giving birth to a baby alone.

"Yesterday I kind of stole a bag that someone was carrying."

"Okay."

"The bag had all these papers in it about Summerwood Farms. That's how I know about that sale."

"You think that is what he came here for?"

"It has to be."

"What else was in the bag?"

"iPod that we are listening to. Some clothes. Nothing really."

"And he's offering you ten thousand-dollars for it?"

"What do you think that I should do?"

"Hmm, well, if I were you, I'd fork the bag over and take the money and try to get it done in the next thirty seconds."

"I can't risk Kenovan walking in on this."

"Where's the bag?"

"It's under the bed."

"You want me to get it for you?"

"Can you tell him you'll meet him somewhere in an hour?"

"You want me to meet him?"

"I think I'm going to be busy."

"Why me?"

"Isn't this what you're good at?"

Another contraction hit and Barbie moaned and squeezed Saint's hands until his fingers nearly broke. When she was finally able to let go Saint ran off to set up the rendezvous with the detective who seemed rattled. Hal wasn't a guy that was easily shaken but he did not want to be around to see any babies being born. He heard the moan through the door and he knew that she wasn't faking it. Saint had the detective's card and agreed to phone him in one hour to schedule the handoff of the bag.

The contraction lasted about thirty seconds and then Barbie retuned to relative normal. "Can you get the bag out from under the bed. I can't get it."

"Sure," said Saint. He ran off to the bedroom and laid under the bed. He was skinny and his arms were long so it was pretty easy for him to get a finger on the strap and pull it out. "How am I supposed to get the money back to you?"

"You can keep some."

"I don't need to keep any. Consider it a present or something for the new baby. I just need to know what you want me to do with it. Should I bring it back here?"

Suddenly the door to the loft burst open and Moe barked a couple of times. It was Kenovan.

"Mama," he said. Casting a suspicious glance at Saint. "What's going on here?" The grunge music that was playing on the stereo seemed to be driving him toward a breaking-point. It wasn't all that loud but Kenovan rushed right over to turn it off. "Why is you listening to the devil's music? Baby gone come out angry, with horns on da head."

"The baby is coming, Bub."

"Eye know it's coming soon, mama."

"I mean it's coming now."

"*Now* now?"

"Yeah, Bub. This is Saint by the way. His dog's name is Moe."

"You the guy with the weed?"

"I am," said Saint. "Sorry, I didn't mean to interrupt—"

"Is alright, mon. Is alright. But—"

"I know that you don't have time to weigh it."

"Kenovan, Bubby, I need to eat something before this baby comes. I'm really hungry."

"Eye got your pinwheel, mama. And eye got the jack fruit fried chicken. Which one do you want?"

"Oh, I don't want either of those, Bubby. Can you heat me up a can of alphabet soup?"

"Sure, mama," he said, looking a little overwhelmed. But Saint beat him to the kitchen.

"Why don't you just help her out and I'll heat the soup," said Saint. He wasn't a great chef or anything, which was probably why he happened to be exceptionally good at heating up soup. "Anything to go with it?"

"How about some bread with some melted cheese?"

"Toast and cheese?"

"Not toast, mon. She like the bread soft but the cheese just melted on it."

"I got you," said Saint. Luckily the range and stove were gas and still working even though the power was out. Saint found the soup cans and a pot and got it heating up. He put the oven on broil and covered a couple slices of bread with some slices of Swiss that were in the dark, lukewarm, fridge.

"You can take a look at the pot, Bubby. I'm okay," Barbie knew that Kenovan had to be wanting to get the transaction out of the way. Normally he double-checked the weight of everything on his triple-beam, but for close to fifty pounds, that took a lot of time. Barbie's belly contracted again. It was the first time since Kenovan had gotten back and she clung to his arm hard during the almost full minute that it lasted.

"I think they are getting longer," said Saint from the kitchen. The soup was already hot and he was pouring it into a bowl and setting it out on the table. He put the bread with the melted cheese alongside on a small plate and found a spoon for her to eat with. "And closer together. Four minutes," he said.

"Can eye take a look at the duffel bags, mon?"

"It's all yours."

"Is it all weight?"

"I checked a bunch of them myself. After I subtracted the weight of the bag nearly all of them was coming in at one-hundred-fifteen to one-hundred-twenty. They're way over."

"Eye have to trust you, mon."

"I'll tell you what. Don't weigh the weed, and I won't count the money. We'll trust each other."

"Thank you, mon," said Kenovan, and then he handed Saint the REI duffel with the hundred-thousand that had to make its way back to Gretta.

"Deal, now I really think we need to get her some help. I tried calling your midwife but no one picked up. Should I try again?"

"Please, mon. Eye would be much grateful. Heard many things about Zen neZ but she don't know eye."

"It's cool, I'll call," said Saint as he was hitting the redial on the phone. It rang endlessly and just before the answering message was about to play, someone picked up on other end of the line, and it was definitely not a woman."

"Zen neZ's phone," mumbled whoever picked up the call. He had a low gravelly voice and sounded like he was in some sort drunken stupor at the same time.

"Is Zen neZ available?" asked Saint meekly.

"She's hurt."

"Hurt?"

"Hurt."

"How hurt? I've got a friend of mine here who is in pretty heavy labor," Barbie unleashed a scream in the background as the belly contracted, severely this time and with a lot more pain. "Zen neZ is supposed to deliver the baby, I think. Is she too hurt to come over?"

Whatever scary animal had been on the other end of the line suddenly perked up, as if he were listening to a higher calling. It was the same man, but his voice cleaned up and acquired a surprising amount of professionalism as compared with the moment before. He started asking all the technical questions that one would expect a doctor to ask and eventually realized that he needed to get there right away. He asked for the address and Saint gave it to him, not knowing what else could be done.

"We're not far," said the man on the other end of the line, who had still declined to offer up his name or any kind of credentials. "Keep the mood quiet and calm, treat the mother gently. It's important that she is relaxed. We can make it in twenty minutes."

"Alright," said Saint, ending the call and walking back toward the expecting parents.

"What happen, mon. Did you talk to Zen neZ?"

"I didn't," said Saint. "There is some bad news about the midwife. She was injured somehow and can't deliver the baby. But someone else picked up who seemed to know a thing or two and is on his way."

"Who?"

"I'm not a hundred percent sure, he didn't give a name."

"Is he a doctor?"

"He sounded like a doctor."

"Eye no likes this, mon."

"I don't love it either," said Saint. "I'd be happy to drive you to the hospital but the streets are a mess and the baby would be born in my rental car. I think this guy is the best chance we have."

"Eye need to trust you, mon."

Barbie was going through another whopper and squeezing Kenvan's hand so tight that his fingertips went white. When the contraction ended Barbie lapsed immediately back into her usual self. She seemed barely to have heard the news and was completely unconcerned with the last-minute disappearance of her midwife and the expected arrival of a suspect substitution. Barbie's faith was extraordinary.

"Aren't you guys going to smoke?" She asked. Barbie got up and was making her way over to the table to eat her lunch.

"You don't mind, mama?"

"Well, you've got to try it out. Don't you?" Kenovan and Saint both looked at one another. There were probably a lot of things that they had in common, but one of them was definitely that they both thought that it was always a good time to get high. They shrugged and Kenovan cut open one of the vacuum sealed bags, and it was as though a skunk had suddenly entered the room.

"Smell's good, mon."

"This crop is lights out. I been smoking it for a couple of weeks and it keeps knocking me on my ass." Kenovan took the glass bong out of the gun locker where he kept his gear and loaded the bowl and passed it to Saint. Saint filled up the stem slow, until it was full of dense white smoke, then he pulled the slide and took the whole thing in one lungful and held it. He put the bong down and hustled over to the window, where he tried to blow the hit outside so that the room didn't get so smoky. The wind was sucking in and it didn't really work but at least he made the effort.

"Nice, mon," said Kenovan as he loaded one up for himself.

"This may be your last bong hit before you're a dad, you know," Saint pointed out. Kenovan acknowledged that that could be true and started inhaling slow while he held a flame to the bowl. Barbie had eaten most of her soup between contractions while the boys were inhaling the smoke. Toward the end she was doing what she always did, making anagrams with the last few letters. Yesterday she used her last five letters to make PALM, PLEA, LAMP, LAP, PALE, PEA, APE, MEAL, and MAPLE. Today, with her last five letters, she made the word ONE and RAN. Then she sat back and watched the letters jiggling around in the bowl. Seeing if anything else might come to her. Kenovan exhaled a monstrous plume of smoke and was seized by a coughing fit that lasted a solid half-minute. The E floated off on its own and the four letters that were left came together to form the word NORA. But only for a brief moment. The N kept twisting until it was a Z and the word that she was looking at was ZORA. That was it and she knew it. She was about to have a girl, and she was going to call her Zora.

The moment Barbie made the decision Zora gave another signal that she was about ready to start her big trip through the birth canal. The contraction that she was suddenly hit with didn't feel like the ones before it. It had a whole different level of power and she felt pee dribbling down her leg. Kenovan rushed to help her, stoned out of his mind and still coughing. Saint's phone rang and he picked it up and tucked himself into the bathroom so that he could hear whoever was on the line. Barbie was screaming and in pain. The contractions were getting closer and closer together. They were lasting for longer and they were getting more intense every time. When it subsided and Barbie looked like she was capable of having a quick conversation again, Saint stepped out of the bathroom.

*   *   *

It wasn't twenty minutes, but it wasn't much longer, when Captain Spaulding—looking like a dirty walrus with a stethoscope dangling around his neck—and Baby came knocking on the door. Saint was the one who opened up the door and the sight of the grisly couple that had arrived to deliver the baby was more than he was ready for and catapulted him into a momentary waking nightmare that kept him frozen and unable to move at all. Moe even let out a bark that signaled the potential for danger. Saint might have stayed petrified like that forever if the blood curdling "Let them in!" hadn't rung out from Barbie's little mouth with the kind of conviction that conjured up more terrifying images from 'The Exorcist.' This wasn't the Captain's first rodeo—it was rodeo number 10,000—and he was used to people, especially men, clamming up and becoming useless in the face of birth, it had always seemed paradoxical to him, practically inhuman. In many ways Captain Spaulding was as much of a dude's dude as one could imagine. He had a taste for ribaldry, intoxicants, and farting while watching football on Sundays, but deep down he harbored a far deeper and more genuine respect for women and all the sacrifice to advance the species. He stepped around Saint with a calming gait and lapsed into his bedside manner, adopting a soothing tone of voice and introducing himself to Barbie and Kenovan as Dr. Albert Meade; his assistant Baby he assured them was an experienced phlebotomist at a children's clinic and a very capable assistant. He called her Debbie.

The interval between the contractions wasn't so much shrinking as it was evaporating. They were coming one on top of the other like waves in a stormy sea, there was nowhere to rest in between them, and nowhere to seek shelter. Barbie was sweating like she was laying asphalt in the tropical sun, breathing hard but with intention, soaking up the pain and never once blurting out anything that could be construed as a complaint. Admirable as it was, this caused Dr. Meade some concern. Tough women were the hardest to read. He asked in a polite, almost hypnotic tone, if he could touch her belly and Barbie nodded and squeezed her eyes shut and hunkered down. Dr. Meade laid his hands on her abdomen, pressed lightly in various locations and discovered the reason that Barbie had continued to feel the baby doing its martial arts moves in her pelvis late in the pregnancy: the head was still up and the Dr. was fairly sure the baby was facing anterior. He turned to Kenovan.

"Do you know what Barbie's blood type is?" he asked.

"Other than that, she got the red kind, Eye no sure, mon."

"Okay," said Dr. Meade. "Here's how this is going to go," the Dr. had a way of addressing Barbie while looking at Kenovan that was not only clever but respectful. "The baby is breech. Do you know what that means?"

"Yes!" shouted Barbie.

"Okay, good. We don't have the time for a hospital transfer and considering it looks like World War III outside I don't think we are going to be able to get you a transfusion if you need one. We are going to have to have a little luck here. What I need to do is put my fingers inside of you," he was putting on some sterile gloves as he spoke, "and make sure the feet don't come out first. I'm going to use my fingers to hold them where they are and when it feels like the right time you are going to push and what we need is for the little butt to come out first, okay?" Odd the way the doctor's high from the bath salts injection honed his receptiveness. He relaxed his fingers, like he was reading brail, and trusted to the right side of his brain to intuit how to steer the baby through the birth canal without widening it at all. It wasn't the first time that the doctor had vaginally delivered a breech baby, but the last time the circumstances were somewhat less intense. Still, nothing resembling a worry passed through his mind at all. It was as if all of the knowledge that ever existed in the universe had collapsed into that moment; and that it was guiding the doctor, and guiding Barbie. Or perhaps it was just that the little one knew just how to navigate this complicated terrain on her own. In either case, he found the baby's heels and held them lightly where they were as Barbie was seized by another contraction. "Push," whispered the doctor.

"Okay!" shouted Barbie. She looked possessed by all of the power, pain, pleasure, fury, and ecstasy of every mother who had ever given birth before her; utterly unafraid. And as she pushed and the doctor pressed lightly on the heels, he let his fingers slip out as he could feel the baby's curled up bottom coming through the canal. It was at this point that he adopted what midwives in the industry call the 'hands off' approach. Breech births are all so unique so he knew that it was best to simply surrender to nature and let Barbie and the baby do this on their own. Kenovan was hovering in just the right spot above Barbie's shoulder, massaging her and holding on to her hands when the contractions were at their worst. Debbie was getting blankets cleaned up and ready to receive the baby. In a matter of minutes, the small group had galvanized into a formidable birthing team.

Except for Saint who was not on the team and absolutely consumed with worry. He felt so useless and so unable to think that all he could do was lean against the wall. He may have been sweating nearly as much as Barbie, surviving only because his good buddy Moe was leaning on his knee and making him feel like he had a friend. And he wasn't so daft as to realize that his friend was reminding him that what they were witnessing was far tougher on Barbie than anyone else, so he had better pull it together. Saint knelt down by the dog and wrapped an arm around his neck and noticed the messenger bag. Saint had a mission here. He had a way to help out and it had nothing to do with delivering the baby. He had made the call and gotten help and the help seemed suspiciously competent. Saint had a detective to go meet. He picked up the bag and slung it over his shoulder, along with the duffel with money in it, and opened the door. Just as he and Moe were slipping out, he glanced back over his shoulder and saw two little white cheeks sliding out of Barbie's vagina in a slick of mucus but without much resistance or blood. He didn't want to interrupt with some sort of ridiculous goodbye so he gave a slight bow in the direction of the birth mama, wishing her all the luck in the world without saying it, and then he and Moe shut the door behind them and set out to go make this new mom some money.

Saint's Dilemma

"**X**anadu," said Saint in response to a question that his mother Dolly had just asked him: "Ten down, six letters, starts with X. Synonym for Paradise or Shangri-La?'"

"You're good, Saint Stephen. How did you get that?"

"Come on, it's the title of that Olivia Newton John record you used to play all the time."

"Good memory. Where are you?"

"City. Taking care of some business. I've got some good news."

"Good, because I've got some bad news."

"What's that?"

"You first."

"Why?"

"I'd rather hear the good news than talk about the bad."

"Is Frances okay?"

"Well, she's having a migraine. But that's not it."

"I've got some money for you."

"What are you talking about?"

"I mean that I've got some money for you. You won't have to sell your house."

"How much money?"

"Enough."

"What's enough, Saint Stephen?"

"Like ten-thousand."

"Where did you get it?"

"Mom, don't worry about where I got it. It will be enough to hold you over until the new job gets going, right?"

"I don't think I have a job anymore, Saint Stephen. I think that I'm going to lose it. You figured out my bad news, Sweetie. It sounds like the new owners are going to fire everyone, and cut down all the trees," she was sobbing and it was hard to make her out. "There's a rumor now that they are going to replace the orchard with a golf course, a big hotel, and a water park."

"Weird."

"Weird? It's sad, sweetie. But it isn't weird. People, they just don't know what beauty looks like anymore. When they look up from their phones, they need to see things that are bright, and shiny, and new. They can't recognize anything. It makes me feel nauseous in my stomach. I wish you were here."

"Not that part."

"Huh?"

"When did you hear all this?"

"I just got off the phone with Hartmut and Renata. They're in Seattle now. They signed the papers to close the deal yesterday."

"The deal is done?"

"Actually, it's not quite official. But I think it's just a matter of time."

"I thought you said they signed."

"They did. But the documents that they signed have gone missing. Everyone is looking for them right now."

"Did Hartmut and Renata know that the new owners wanted to destroy the orchard? I thought that they were holding out for a buyer that was going to take the orchard over. Wasn't that the point?"

"Of course not, Saint Stephen. They were duped. Taken advantage of because of their age. They only found out the truth after the deal was supposedly closed. An intern who went with them to the city, Lupita Bevilacqua—who you should remember by the way because she is very sweet and I've tried to set you up with her like a hundred times—actually ran into two men who work for the new ownership group and overheard them talking in the waiting room at the E.R."

"Was she hurt or something?"

"Who?"

"The woman who works for the Frenzels."

"Lupita?"

"Yeah."

"No. Why?"

"You said she was in the waiting room at the E.R."

"Good point. I don't know why she was there."

"Mom."

"What, sweetie? You don't have to give me your money. I'll be okay."

"Mom. I know where those missing documents are."

"What? How could you know that?"

"It's a long story. I'll probably have to tell you when I see you. I am coming back tomorrow."

"Where are they?"

"Umm. Right now, they are in a hip bag in my van. Moe is guarding them."

"Saint Stephen, what are you talking about?"

"It's hard to explain it all. I just met someone who had them. It was a total coincidence."

"Who?"

"She's pregnant."

"Did you get someone pregnant?"

"No, Mom. I just met her. She has a boyfriend but she showed them to me. I think that she just found them."

"Lying on the street?"

"I know it sounds crazy but that's what she said."

"Saint Stephen, everyone is looking for those."

"I'm starting to realize that. About an hour ago a private detective came to her place looking for them. He offered a lot of cash, no questions asked. I'm supposed to deliver them in an hour and collect the money."

"So that's where you're getting the money that you're offering to save my house? From selling these documents? Saint Stephen, you can't do that."

"No, Mom. No. This is something totally different."

"How did you get mixed up in all this?"

"I don't know. I just said I'd do it."

"It sounds dangerous. We need those, or we need them destroyed."

"But I promised her."

"The pregnant woman?"

"Her name is Barbie. She's actually having the baby."

"Now?"

"She was in labor when I left."

"In the hospital I hope."

"Not at the hospital, too hard to get there anyway. She's with an OBGYN who seems to have a good idea what he's doing. He also seems to have been up all night."

"Where on earth did you find this doctor."

"Mutual friend of the midwife who was injured in a yoga accident."

"I'm speechless."

"Mom, I'm really sorry about all this. I really just came over here to help you out."

"Saint Stephen. You need to take those papers to the Frenzels at the Edgewater Hotel right now."

"Do you think they will give me the ten-thousand?"

"You want to extort money from the Frenzels?"

"I don't want to extort anything from anyone, Mom. I'm just trying to help a friend out."

"I thought that you said you just met."

"We're still friends."

"Half an hour and you're such good friends that you'd sacrifice a thousand acres of apples, the Frenzels, all the people who work for them, and your own mother for her. Are you in love with her?"

"No! She has a boyfriend. Mom, what should I do?"

"The right thing, Saint Stephen."

*   *   *

Loven was sawing logs on the couch in Herman's apartment while Herman wrapped up in the shower and slid into a pair of 31x34 Larkee cut Diesel jeans, a quarter-zip fleece from The North Face, and tied the laces of a single bright blue Asics running shoe. The other foot was in a soft cast. Two of the toes were going to need pins but the surgery was going to have to happen after the swelling went down. He already had an appointment with a specialist on Wednesday.

Ever since Loven had appeared, things had gone decidedly better. Their cab reached the E. R. At Harborview without incident. Finding its way through the snarled downtown corridor like it had its own special lane. The driver chose streets that were one-way and knew which intersections were still functional and which ones were all seized up. It was the first thing that had gone without incident for Herman in what seemed to him like an eternity and he took it as a sign that things were looking up. There wasn't a wait. The staff tended quickly to his foot and took a good long look at the embroidery the mini-mart clerk did on Herman's face but they didn't replace any of it. They said it was top notch. There were even a few jokes that having a guy around in the E.R. that could sew a man up like that would be helpful. They prescribed cephalexin as an antibiotic to safeguard against the possibility of infection, Naproxyn for the swelling, and more oxy for the pain—though they were pretty stingy with it, only eight pills. When they left it was brisk, but dry. There was a stiff wind blowing out of the northwest, perfect leather jacket weather. High clouds were chugging toward the east but it didn't feel like rain was imminent. They went to Lola's and ordered half the menu. At breakfast Loven filled Herman in on the status of the deal to buy the orchard. And just when Herman was finally feeling like himself again, ready even to confront work, Loven's cell phone began vibrating on the table. Duncan was calling.

"Duncan," Herman picked it up. "It's Herman."

"Where the fuck you been?"

"Sorry. Things got a little away from me last night," said Herman.

"Apparently. Are you hung over? You sound fine."

"No. I didn't even drink. At least not later on. I was in an accident though. Gonna be on crutches for a few months."

"You'll heal."

"I heard that the documents from the sale are missing."

"Benny Greene's delivered his last package for Cronkey, Mitchell and Wolfe."

"Sounds like it might have been his last package for anybody. Is he dead?"

"I have no idea. Kind of beside the point, don't you think?"

"He wasn't a bad guy."

"'Herman, this is not a girls' softball league, where the real winners are whoever has the most fun. It's business."

"We'll get the docs back."

"Yes, we will."

"I can help look. Any idea where we should start?"

"No need. I already found them."

"They're back?"

"Not yet, but I know where they are."

"Where?"

"Doesn't matter. Hal found them."

"The detective that you went to college with?"

"He's good."

"He must be. That was fast."

"He wants to get together to give them back soon but I'm not sure that I can make it. My grandmother surprised me with a visit. She's lost inside of the Nordstrom's shopping for a new wardrobe or some shit. I've got to wait for her to come out."

"You want me to go?"

"If it isn't asking too much," his tone was lethal and patronizing.

"Whereabouts?"

"I'm not sure yet. I'll have him call you. Hard to tell yet. The power is out in a lot of places. This ridiculous beetle invasion is causing big issues with the grid. I don't think we can even get into the office."

"I think it's actually being caused by a hybrid species of insect called *Agrilus suprema*."

"How the fuck you know that?"

"I met a biologist last night. Told me they are breeding fast and feeding on the power lines and fiberoptic cables. Taking out the electric and the web. You know the bugs are probably the reason that the internet went down at the office yesterday."

"Maybe you don't sound too good."

"I'm fine, Duncan."

"You're blaming this situation on bugs."

"I'm fine."

"Not going to disappear again?"

"I won't."

"Is your phone charged?"

"I'm using Loven's ."

"Tell Loven that belongs to you now. Is it charged?"

"Appears to be."

"I'll make sure Hal has the number."

Sheetrocking Lucky's Apartment

Yellow boxer briefs with a mesh pouch attached to the front so that a man's penis and testicles can hang loose and get a little breeze were draped over the shade of a desk lamp belonging to Lucky Soul. The two-time-academy-award-winning actor was sitting in an office that was part of an entire floor that he owned in a high-rise near the shopping district on 4th Ave. Just barely outside of what the local news anchors were calling The Infested Zone. The yellow glow from the bulb beneath the underpants gave the room a sunny feel the way shooting glasses or tinted ski goggles can make the world appear brighter. Lucky was wearing a short silk robe with seahorses on it and he was naked from the waist down. The robe was wide open and Lucky was on the speaker phone and in the midst of making plans with one of the co-executive producers of his latest film to do some location scouting for a car chase that ends at a gelato cafe, when there was a light knock upon the door. Lucky told his producer he would call him back after finishing up some important business and putting some clothes on.

"What is it?" he called out, gazing across his desk and out the window.

Lucky had been lucky in that the breeding pair of insects that hitchhiked over to Seattle on his bed frame disembarked at the port when the container was opened and flew out on a gust of fresh wind, starving and horny. It is for this reason ground zero for the invasion wound up being the south end of downtown and was taking its time making its way to the building where Lucky occupied the top two floors. By that point those two bugs had offspring in the billions and were taking down the city around him from the inside out. He was either unaware or dismissive of the news of the invasion. It was possible that his assistant had given him some sort of early warning and recommended he take the private jet out in the middle of the night but he was busy and had a foggy recollection of laughing at the idea and waving him off. Once he got up, his head started to fill with obligations surrounding the upcoming shoot, plus he was having the entirety of his accommodations remodeled. It seemed like a good idea at first and a totally appropriate way to commemorate the arrival of the bed frame—which had to be moved into its new home at the top of a skyscraper using a mounted crane that was working on a new high rise nearby but had Lucky's suite in range of its boom. It wasn't legal use of the equipment but Lucky tipped the operator twenty-thousand and he did it just before the sun came up. The foreman either didn't notice or was on the take as well. Lucky wasn't sure. What he was sure of was that now that he was sleeping in Genghis Kahn's bed, he wanted his office to resemble the Mongolian grasslands where the warlord was from, and was having the entire room done up in the newly conceived diaspora. It was hard for Lucky to picture the warlord ever sleeping a wink. But Lucky was sure that thousands of women had helped him make use of the bed.

The ceiling and wall painting was going to be executed over the course of the following two weeks by a crack team of Chinese landscape painters that were being smuggled in to the U.S. illegally in order to avoid the added costs and paperwork of temporary visas and having to give them reasonable wages, much to eat, or anything resembling an actual break.

"Sheet rockers are here," his assistant was shouting on the other side of the closed doors but he could barely hear him because the doors were so thick. Lucky closed his browser windows, fastened his robe, and took the back way out of his office toward the showers. He sent his assistant a text that the drywall team could head in.

There were only two guys sticking around to hang the rock but it took a crew of six to shuttle the 4x10 boards from the freight elevator into the space. They also brought in a couple of buckets of mud—one hot one for the big holes—Dewalt drills with chargers, cartons of screws, and saw horses. The furniture all got moved out and stacked up in a corner of the living room and the walls and floor were protected with thin plastic sheeting. By the time the crew had gotten that far it was pretty hot in the space and the one in charge—Monty—propped open one of the refinished sash windows to let in some air.

Most sheetrock hangers need to rely on lifts, ladders, and stilts to get the job done but not Monty. He was six-foot-eight, with old school phone books for hands. He could pick up a 4x12x1/2" sheet, step onto a short stool, and hold the piece flat against a nine-foot ceiling while his short Italian assistant—Valentino—bounced around on his ladder like a leprechaun, sinking screws into the boards and securing them. As far as hanging ceilings go, it was a very easy job. Since they were overlaying the cedar, they didn't have to look for framing members and every screw bit in nicely. An hour and a half into it they had five sheets hung and Valentino started getting cranky. Even though it was damp and cool out and there was a nice humid breeze coming in, he was drenched in sweat. His black hair was loaded up with pomade and slicked back but it was starting to lose its shape. Monty trimmed the next piece which was a little bit too long and held it in place. Valentino repositioned his ladder.

"Got any idea why we are redoing this place? Seems like it's already pretty nice," asked Valentino, gazing at all of the expensive cedar paneling that was getting covered up. Monty ignored him for a moment while he held the piece steady and Valentino got it anchored, working his way out from the middle so that it wouldn't bow. Once it was done, he admired his work. "I'm hungry. You got any food?"

"Boss told me that it belongs to some kind of art fanatic who wants a smooth surface to paint on," said Monty. "There are some baby carrots in my lunch box. Help yourself."

"How the fuck does a man your size live on baby carrots?" Valentino asked while biting into one of the little orange bullets.

"I don't. I just eat them during the day and then I eat a big dinner when I get home."

"Your mom still cook you dinner every day?"

"As a matter of fact, she does, Valentino. You got a problem with that?"

"No, Monty, I am just asking. I wish I had my mama cooking me dinner every day."

"Sophie can't cook?"

"No, Sophie can't cook for shit. Anyhow, she's busy taking care of the baby all day. I do the cooking when I get home."

"That's scary. Hey, how's little Skylar doing?"

"Who?"

"Who? What the fuck do you mean who? Skylar, your daughter."

"Oh, we changed her name to Christina."

"You changed your baby's name? When?"

"When she was about six months."

"What the fuck for?"

"I just started hearing all these bad news stories about chicks with the name Skylar. I heard like two or three on the news in one week. Then I was driving by a strip club on Lake City and the marquee read pornographic film star Skylar Price was appearing that night. I caught a glimpse of a poster of this other Skylar. She was bound and gagged and—I decided I'd had enough. I told Sophie we were changing her name to Christina."

"And she didn't care?"

"Nah, Skylar was a stupid name anyway."

"You kill me, Valentino," Monty slung another board across his broad chest and braced it up above him. As he did so a kind of peculiar looking bug dropped out of a slot next to the electrical box that contained one of the old can light fixtures that they were drywalling over. New can lights were slated to be installed and this time recessed into the floor so the scene would be uncorrupted.

"Goose it just a little to the left."

"Better?"

"That's perfect."

"Hey, Valentino, isn't your wedding coming up?" After he was able to let go of the piece Monty squashed the bug against his broad chest and let the guts seep into his work shirt. He swore he felt a bite of some sort or a pinch when it died.

"Sure is, my friend. Next weekend. Which reminds me, I got to call Papa John's."

"Congrats, man"

"Thanks, big guy. It's no big deal really, just some family, couple of friends, Justice of the Peace. Afterward my mama's gonna keep Christina for a couple of days, while I take Sophie out to the coast."

"Looks like the weather is starting to turn?"

"When is the Washington coast ever nice? Anyway, I don't give a shit. Wasn't planning on spending a whole lot of time at the beach if you know what I'm saying, Monty."

"No, Valentino, I don't know what you're saying." Monty tried to elbow Valentino in a rib but he actually got him up around the neck.

"Big fucking mama's boy like you probably doesn't what I'm talking about."

"Watch it, Valentino. Hey what's next?"

"Eight foot by thirty-three-and-three-eighths. After that we can hang one more twelve-footer in front of the chimney and then go to lunch."

"Nice," Monty measured the piece and made crow's feet at the appropriate locations with the contractor's pencil that he kept parked behind his right ear. Valentino didn't have room behind his ear for a toothpick, Monty could have carried bazookas behind his. Monty snapped chalk lines over the crow's feet, aligned his drywall square with the mark and dragged his blade along the line. After three passes the drywall snapped nice and easy. He trimmed the width down first and in the absence of anywhere good to put the long scrap, he let it span the distance between the window sill and one of the sawhorses.

"You wearing a tux to the wedding, Valentino?"

"Hell yes, my friend. My mama helped me pick it out. It's light blue, with blue silk lapels. It's fucking sharp. Mama says I look *molto bello* in it."

"You're getting married in a baby blue tux?"

"I said light blue. Why, you got a problem with a blue tux?"

"You probably could have saved a few bucks on the tux rental and just wore your pajamas."

"Pajamas? What the fuck are you saying, Monty? That my blue tux is gonna look like pajamas?"

"That's exactly what I'm saying. You want to look at the pictures in twenty years and see yourself in a baby blue tux? Trust me, Valentino, take it back and get a black one."

"Fuck you, Monty. You live with your mama. What the fuck do you know about weddings or tuxedoes or any of that shit?"

Monty held up the little piece while a slightly pissed off Valentino anchored it. There was only one piece left to hang when Monty's contractor grade Sprint phone busted out its Run DMC ringtone. Monty looked at the caller ID. It was one of the new guys, Mudder Dale. Office had already clued Monty in that the normal guy, Mudder Mitch, never showed up for work that day. Which was ludicrous. Mudder Mitch never looked or smelled very good but he always found a way to get his blind ass to work. Joke was that what he couldn't figure out how to get home.

"Mudder Dale, what's up?"

"You two clowns got the rock hung yet?"

"Almost done, you can start whenever you want."

"Did my mud get dropped off?"

"Yeah, Dunn dropped off some five gallons."

"Fucking five gallons? I told Jess I wanted it in boxes, that I always work out of boxes, it's easier that way."

"I don't know what to tell you, Dale. The driver's long gone. I know you mudders like working out of the boxes, but Connie does the ordering, and she usually gets buckets delivered anyway, cause they're cheaper."

"Makes me wonder who's wearing the Levi's over at headquarters. For fuck's sake. Bucket it is, I guess. I'll be there within an hour."

Monty hung up. Valentino waited for the end of the call before yelling for the final piece. Monty hoisted it up above his head and then walked backward, using his toe to drag his stool into the right position. Another one of those weird bugs fell, landed on his hand, and made him forget having set the last scrap between the sawhorse and the window and when he bumped into it with his big hips, it was with enough force to skid the narrow scrap so that it wound up teetering with its center of mass just on the outside of the building. The part of the board that was outside started to fall while the inside started to lift.

"*Merda!*" cried Valentino when he saw what was happening but he couldn't get there in time. The twelve-foot-long strip of drywall was accelerating towards the streets of the shopping district like a missile.

*　　*　　*

About half an hour before the two sloppy contractors dropped the drywall scrap out of the window of Lucky's office, Mabel was shopping for jeans in the Young Ms. section at the Nordstrom's. She selected a pair made of space age denim, iridescent green, and held them up against her legs to see if the fit and the style suited her. She tried to get the opinion of a pair of young girls who were browsing on the other side of the rack. They just rolled their eyes and left the department altogether. Mabel tried not to take it personal. She took the jeans, and a few other garments she was way too old to pull off into the dressing rooms.

She took her pants off and lamented the worsening of a varicose vein in one of her calves. As she leaned over to examine it her large breasts felt heavy and her lower back ached something terrible. There was also a gurgling in her stomach and she felt like she maybe had to release some liquid stool. She tried using all of her might to close her sphincter but it wasn't a lot of might to begin with and it may not have been working. She couldn't really tell. No time after she was hit with a wave of nausea and she had to curl up on the dressing room floor, feeling alternately cold and hot, like microwaved food. She felt alone. Like millions of miles away from safety, even though her grandson was theoretically nearby. Claustrophobia set in. She thought about shouting for help, and she almost did. Except for someone beat her to it. It was another woman somewhere on the other side of the door and she was shrieking in a pitch so high you'd think that only dogs could have heard it. More joined in and it was as though the world outside of the little room was coming apart at the seams.

Something struck Mabel on the cheek. It wasn't heavy but it stuck to her and she had to summon all of her strength to reach up to her face so that she could pull it off and see what the thing was. It was a terrifying little insect, with two red stripes on its back. Almost too small to be of consequence but its legs were flying through the air like with a disturbing sense of purpose and and its mouth was opening and closing and looking like it wanted to devour anything that came into its path. There were two bent horns on its head, connected by the oddest thing, a little spark. At least that's what Mabel thought that it was. Right afterward the lights in the store flickered and then the screaming in the store approached a deafening crescendo. More bugs started to fall out of the ceiling and land on Mabel. They were pouring out of a small hole they had made next to the light fixture. There was the sound of a muted explosion that seemed to come from below. Then the inside of the store went completely black. In the darkness the foul creatures started to rain down in incredible numbers. In no time there was an inch of them on the floor, and then a foot. Mabel finally mustered the will to scream but when she tried, she only wound up swallowing a mouthful of the bugs. They filled up her throat and suffocated the sound. It didn't matter. No one would have heard her anyway.

* * *

Shoppers who were close to the exits of the Nordstrom's were storming the doors with the same intensity that the bugs had been dropping from the ceilings. Duncan had just gotten off of a phone call and was nearly trampled by a stampede of well-dressed mothers and children. Security guards rallied to the exits, but they seemed as disoriented as everyone else. They were powerless to stop anyone from leaving, even if many of them were carrying—or in some cases wearing— merchandise that they had yet to pay for. Instead, the row of guards focused on making sure that everyone got through the door safely. Duncan overheard someone say something about a terrorist attack inside the store. But Duncan hadn't heard any gunshots. And the panicked crowd somehow didn't seem like they were *that* kind of panicked. A woman in an expensive looking pantsuit with the tags still on it was dragging a friend of hers across the floor toward the row of guards. The friend was unable to walk and clutching a foot that was bent completely backwards. When two of the guards abandoned their posts to help her out, Duncan did what no one else was doing, he slipped into the store.

Duncan was on a mission to find Mabel. But it was no desperate attempt by a doting grandson to save his beloved grandmother—who took him in after being orphaned young—

from the Saturday afternoon apocalypse inside of the department store. This was more like an angry grandson—who had been up all night committing horrific crimes, who had a business to run and an apple orchard to level, who was in the midst of being asked to pay an exorbitant amount of cash to reacquire something that was his in the first place—acting out. In a way, Duncan was still the same little kid who kept swearing that he wasn't tired as the clock struck ten, and then eleven, crossing his heart and hoping to die, and then being the first one up in the morning so that he could make sure that Mabel got her coffee right away. He needed a nap. He'd earned a nap. He needed to sleep off the past twenty-four hours the way people need to sleep off a long vacation or an acid trip. He needed to reset. But there was no way that was happening any time soon. Besides the exhaustion, Duncan had some other things gnawing at him.

While he was waiting outside for Mabel, he found out that Hal had located the sale documents transferring ownership of Summerwood Farms to Cronkey, Mitchell and Wolfe. It was good news, but he didn't have them in his possession yet. He needed another fifty-thousand in cash. Duncan didn't waiver on the price even though it did seem like extortion for a bundle of papers that were essentially worthless to all but a few people. It was a lot to come up with on a moment's notice but he put Quincy on it and Quincy assured him that it wouldn't be a problem to get the cash to Herman. But it wasn't just the request for the cash that was the strange part of the conversation with Hal. The private detective asked Duncan if he had been home at all that morning and Duncan told him that he hadn't. Hal also asked if he had been to the office, which was in an area that was under quarantine. Duncan said no and asked why that mattered. But Hal didn't respond to the question. Instead he asked for the money. After hanging up with Hal, Duncan got a little nervous about Hal having asked him where he'd been. It wasn't like him to pry. He tried to dismiss his thoughts as baseless paranoia but it didn't work.

There was too much at stake. And Duncan wasn't the type to make assumptions anyway. He put a call in to Witherspoon, the doorman at his building. He picked right up.

"Hello," he said.

"Witherspoon. This is Duncan Klevit, from the top floor."

"Ah, Mr. Klevit. How are you today, sir?" It felt very much to Duncan like he was being patronized but he couldn't remember if Witherspoon was always like that.

"Witherspoon, has anyone shown up looking for me today?" There was a long pause while the doorman cleared his throat and searched for an answer.

"Ah, yes," he finally said. "The lovely Ms. Mabel was here looking for you early and I escorted her up. I hope that wasn't too presumptuous of me, sir."

"That's fine, Witherspoon. I meant after that. Has anyone else come looking for me?" There was a similar pause after the question and Duncan could feel Witherspoon wanting to say *no*. But he didn't say *no*.

"Mr. Klevit," his voice was suddenly very quiet and Duncan was having a hard time hearing him because of all of the crowd noise behind him. "Two men in suits came in looking for you about an hour ago, sir. They asked if I'd seen you and I told them I hadn't, sir."

"Did they say who they were?"

"They said that they were friends of yours but I had not seen them before, sir. To be honest, they weren't very friendly. They seemed more like—"

"Like what?"

"To be honest, I thought they were either detectives or well-dressed, you know, like *wise guys*."

"Did they show you a badge or leave a card?"

"No, sir. But I feel as though they meant to come back."

That was the moment in which Duncan hung up the phone and charged into the store looking for Mabel. In a normal state, Duncan would have abandoned her and fled the city. But circumstances being what they were, he wasn't in the mood to head out on the lamb alone. Trying to get into the store was like swimming against a current. Using the flashlight feature of his phone he managed to glimpse a sign pointing toward the Young Ms. department and he assumed that that was where he would find her. But he didn't make it very far before a large black man gripped him by the shoulder and the left wrist. He was a much bigger man than Duncan and the kind of grip that he had on him was designed to subdue. He was obviously trained in the martial arts and could have broken Duncan's arm if he wanted to.

"Just where do you think that you're going?" Duncan knew a few moves himself. He moved into the man's body, rather than away, dropped an elbow into his solar plexus, broke free of the grip and started to run off into the deepening darkness. He hardly got anywhere before being tackled from behind. Besides knowing martial arts, the big man was apparently an ex-linebacker and this time he wasn't going to let Duncan get away. Duncan was still wearing the alligator skin boots that Mabel's latest ex-husband had made and the wood soles weren't getting any purchase on the slippery floor. The man chasing him turned out to be a security guard that worked for the store, and it made perfect sense that in the midst of the evacuation, certain enterprising individuals would be trying to get inside to do some looting. He slapped one side of a set of handcuffs onto Duncan and then yanked him to his feet and attached the other side to a circular rack of Hugo Boss sport jackets. "Man, I ain't got time for this shit. Stay here." As if Duncan could have gone anywhere else. Duncan was furious with himself for bothering to try and find Mabel and when the security guard returned with a lady cop, Duncan was red-faced and snorting. Before the cop could say anything, Duncan started in.

"Look," he said, "I'm just trying to find my grandmother who was shopping in the store when the lights went off. I'm just worried about her." Neither the guard nor the cop seemed inclined to believe him.

"I see. Do you realize that we have an emergency situation here and that you just ran through a security blockade and evaded a security officer?"

"I apologize. Like I said, I'm just worried about my grandmother."

"What's your grandmother's name?" Duncan wasn't prepared to answer the question. So many things were happening that he wasn't sure of. It was a foreign feeling to him, the feeling of being lost in the dark. The cop and guard seemed to interpret Duncan's silence as debunking the whole lost grandma bit. "How about your name, mister?" When he failed to respond to this question as well the lady cop asked for help from the guard, who held onto Duncan's free arm while she searched his pockets for identification. She found his slim wallet tucked into the front pocket of the jeans that he was wearing. "Duncan Klevit?" It was kind of a question and kind of not. She held his license beside his face to be sure that the image matched the man and then she strode a short way off, just out of earshot, and made a phone call. The guard stayed with Duncan. By that point, most of the shoppers had made it out of the store and it was quieter inside. Duncan could see the cop nodding as she spoke on the phone but he couldn't make out any words. She hung up the phone and walked back over. "Mr. Klevit," she said, her tone was icy and mean, "are you aware that there is a warrant out for your arrest?" Duncan, kept his mouth shut. There was a momentary stand-off while they looked into each other's eyes. "Danny," she finally said to the security guard once she was through sizing Duncan up, "would you help me get this other set on him?" She withdrew another set of handcuffs from her belt and the big guard twisted his wrist so that both arms were close together and so that she could get the bracelets on. She cranked them down as tight as she could get them. "I'll be back for you in a minute," she said. And then she disappeared.

Oddly enough, the paranoia that had gripped Duncan just moments before had evaporated. He wasn't even tired anymore. He was trapped, but he wasn't scared. His muscles felt powerful and ready. His vision was perfectly clear and time suddenly seemed to have slowed down for him. He was looking for an opportunity. He could hear perfectly. His breath was slow and through the nose.

When the cop returned, she read Duncan the Miranda Rights and had Danny un-cuff him from the rack of clothing.

"You got him?" said Danny.

"I got him," she said. And then, with a firm grip on both his wrists and his shoulders she pushed him toward the doors, and then outside onto the sidewalk and toward a Ford SUV labeled as a Seattle Police Department vehicle that was waiting for them at the corner. Duncan was actually a little insulted that the lady cop thought that she was going to be able to handle him on her own. She was a tough lady, but not that tough, and arresting someone for suspicion of aggravated assault or murder should require some back-up. For all he knew she had requested some and was denied. Outside on the streets there was a mixture of chaos and gridlock. All of the downtown traffic lights had gone out and the honking that ensued as the drivers tried to navigate the impassable streets sounded more like Bombay than any American city. Seattle was falling apart. Nordstrom's wasn't the only big store having problems. People were running to and fro trying to escape something that couldn't be seen. A group of youngsters threw a cinder block through the window at the Arc Ter'x store and helped themselves to some new winter coats.

Sensing the intensity of the moment, the cop—who had to be nervous as well—released her grip on Duncan's shoulder and drew her gun. With one hand she kept an incredibly strong grip on Duncan's wrists, driving them into his lower back and causing the cuffs to dig into his skin. She shoved the barrel of the gun in next to his spine and then said, "no funny business." For Duncan, everything was still happening in slow motion and he wondered what it was that she meant by *funny business*. Like exactly what was it that qualified. And as he was considering the point, something occurred that likely did qualify as *funny business* but he wasn't the one responsible for it. Something was falling from the sky. Sort of like a meteor but it was much smaller and because of the flat planes that comprised its shape, the object had a decidedly man-made appearance. To Duncan, the high velocity projectile was like something out of a dream. He could trace its path perfectly through time and space. He smiled at its approach but he still had the wherewithal to duck just before it hit him, and the free-falling scrap of drywall pounded right into the face of the arresting officer. The gypsum board was pulverized on impact and nearly decapitated the cop. She wound up laid out on the sidewalk with blood gushing from her neck and pooling around the hat that had fallen off of her. She was also twitching like a zombie and at one point she thrust out her palm, kind of a last-ditch effort to keep control of her suspect. But the look on her face was that of a person left stranded on the platform watching her train pull away from the station, picking up speed, and leaving her behind to face death alone.

Duncan obviously didn't linger to help out. He put his hands below his ass, sat down, and slipped the cuffs around his knees and feet. He took the officer's gun which had fallen onto the sidewalk, engaged the safety, and tucked it into the back of his pants below the shirt. Then he took off running toward the bus tunnel.

*   *   *

North of downtown Seattle sat a complex of buildings that were constructed for the World Fair that Seattle hosted in 1963. The event took place in August, and it rained every day. It is mainly for that reason—that the week Seattle invited the world over to visit it never stopped pouring—that the world assumes that the rain in Seattle continues to fall relentlessly during every season of the year. Of course, that was never exactly true. And the reputation, deserved or not, morphed into the region's greatest defense against being overrun by forward thinking liberal Americans who longed for refuge from the Jesus freaks and the rednecks that populated their hometowns. But as massive tech companies started locating their headquarters in the northwest and driving up property values, and the Seahawks kept making the playoffs every year, people started taking notice of what was going on in the northwest. Once it was identified as being a liberal stronghold, with excellent food, stunning views, and an active healthy population, it began to swell. Rain or not, people were moving there. One of the buildings that was built specifically for the 1963 fair was the iconic Space Needle. And Lupita was parked as close to it as you could get in a car.

She was behind the wheel of Saint's rented Impala, and Moe, the loyal bloodhound, was perched on the passenger's seat beside her. It was just after noon. Dark clouds hung low in the sky—it was not raining outside at the moment—and the wind, while it had acquired a sudden hint of autumn, was mostly humid and warm. Lupita was taking her nascent sleuth skills to a new level. Around her neck she wore a pair of binoculars, and she used them to keep an eye on Saint, as he loitered outside of the remodeled Key Arena, underdressed in his Aloha shirt with the bike messenger's bag around his neck. He was trying to look natural and failing. Lupita and Saint had just met that afternoon in the Frenzels' hotel room. He arrived an unlikely hero. Tall and conspicuous looking. Dressed in loud summer clothes and shivering. He had a big slobbering dog with him and he was definitely stoned out of his mind. He was also sweet. Clearly a good guy but a guy who couldn't resist telling the truth. He wasn't cut out for covert operations. Just too busy being himself to be able to be false. Lupita was instantly drawn to this purity in him. It stood in such stark contrast to the men who worked at the venture capital firm and most of the Latino guys she knew. If the world were run by men like Saint, the world would be absolutely fine.

She checked her watch and it read 12:27. Just three minutes shy of the proposed rendezvous with the private detective. When she looked up from her watch, she could no longer see Saint, at least not from the driver's seat. A box truck in the employ of a plumbing company was suddenly idling in the loading zone between them. Her heart rate sped up and even Moe was getting antsy. He didn't like it when he couldn't keep an eye on Saint either. And Saint was a guy that someone had to be keeping an eye on. The dog was probably the only reason that he had made it as far as he had. Which wasn't really all that far. Thirty-years old with no concrete skills, education to point to, or much experience in the trades. He didn't have a house or any money. He had a van that was paid off, even though it was broke down. The dog was a gem. And Saint's soul came off as intact, a rare thing that made him potentially richer than any white man she had met so far. Damn, she had to get eyes on him. The plumbing truck had this goofy advertising image on the roll-up back door, with a suspiciously enthusiastic plumber, complete with gray beard, thick forearms, and shirt tucked way-in so there is no threat of crack emerging from behind, waving like an idiot in front of a very well-organized arrangement of parts and tools that are supposedly what is behind the actual rolling door once it goes up. The waving plumber was even wearing a name tag that read 'Bob.' Classic. But in the fucking way. Lupita had to get out of the car and walk over to the front of the plumbing truck to get Saint back into her line of sight.

Since she was on foot, she had to hold the binoculars so they didn't swing when she ran. The camera she had stashed in a coat pocket. Once she could see around the front of the plumbing truck it was obvious that the private detective had arrived. He was just as Saint had described: an upright baby elephant in a trench coat and hat with curly gray hair popping out below the brim. From inside the trench coat he withdrew a manila envelope and handed it to Saint, who opened it up and took a glance at what it was inside. Saint then forked over the bag that was draped over his shoulder and handed it to the detective, who also confirmed the contents by quickly flipping through what was inside. There was an awkward moment afterward where Saint wasn't sure if they were supposed to shake hands or not. Apparently not because the detective just turned and walked away casually as though nothing had just transpired. He was walking east toward the McDonald's on Fifth. Lupita jumped back in the car and made a left onto Denny, praying that she was going to be able to catch up with him.

The private detective had parked in the lot next to the fast food restaurant. It was an old brown Tercel with a cute furry dog panting in the passenger's seat. Lupita pulled over and pretended to be fiddling with her phone while the detective got into his car and exited the lot. He looped back to the west on Denny and made a left onto Second, the one-way that would get him back into the heart of downtown. But he didn't get far. Traffic was snarled because so many of the lights weren't functioning and the detective must have gotten annoyed with the inability to get anywhere. He parked his Tercel in a pay lot in Belltown, and then continued making his way south on foot.

Lupita was tempted to follow him into the parking lot but it felt a little too exposed. The detective had never met her before and had no reason to be suspicious of her, but he was a professional and she figured it was wise to extend him the respect that he deserved. It was a risky call because she got stuck at the next light and it seemed like she was going to be there forever. It was flashing red and the drivers were treating it like a four-way stop. Good thing the fat detective was a slow walker. Once she made it through the intersection, she was able to pull into another pay lot. She didn't actually have enough money in the bank to cover the twenty bucks that the parking spot cost. There was nothing she could do but take the chance. She parked at an angle that would make the car harder to tow and locked it up. In her purse she stashed the binoculars that were loaned to her by Omeed Gazipurah, the Frenzels' lawyer, as well as the fourteen-megapixel Nikon with the powerful zoom. Omeed was an amateur ornithologist and was never without his optics. Poor Moe was going to have to wait with the Impala.

When she hit the sidewalk and started hustling south after the detective he was barely still in sight, crossing Virginia with a throng of tourists that was obscuring him from view. She might have lost him if it weren't for the pork pie hat bobbing above the crowd. Lupita ran to catch up. The detective swung right onto Pine. When Lupita rounded the corner, he was no longer visible. She moved west, frantic, trying not to look frantic. She poked her head into a convenience store and didn't see him. As she moved closer to the waterfront and the Pike Place Public Market the crowds thickened and the chances that she was going to find him again shrunk. She crossed First Ave. and descended the steep hill. He wasn't in the lobby of The Inn, nor was he having lunch at Cha:n. Her momentum was carrying her toward the market but she was worried about descending the steep hill. If it was the wrong direction, she would lose him for good. Instead of dropping down she kept her elevation, covered her eyes from the glare and let her gaze relax on the sea of pedestrians below, looking for the familiar brown trench coat. She didn't see the detective, but on the grassy field at the north end of the market where there was always a gang of vagrants smoking pot, she did spy someone that she recognized. It was Herman. He was staring out across the sound toward Alki Point, leaning on a set of crutches, and toting a red backpack. Lupita removed the compact set of birding binoculars that Omeed had loaned her and watched him from the corner of First and Pine. She was almost shy about watching him through the lenses. She was spying on him and it felt unfair, even though he had been an incredible asshole to her. Taking advantage of her to get more information about the orchard. Pretending to be interested in her and then never once calling her afterward. He was a jerk. Yet at that moment he seemed different. He was always so busy, and she had never seen him waiting for anything. But he didn't seem to be in a rush at all. He even seemed like he was enjoying the view. His foot was in a cast but he looked perfectly at ease on the crutches. His face was taped up but it was shaved smooth and his hair was neat. And he was wearing the standard issue casual clothes for a cool day in Seattle. Designer blue jeans. Long sleeve polyester quarter-zip shirt with a North Face vest over it. He was still an asshole, but a handsome asshole. At that moment it was as though he heard her thoughts, because he spun around to face her.

He wasn't really facing Lupita. Lupita was way up the hill. The person that had gotten Herman's attention was the private detective that she had been tailing. He was carrying the messenger's bag. Lupita had to wonder if she was really getting this lucky or if she was just this fucking good of a stalker. She put the binoculars away, picked up the camera, and found the two men again in the view finder. They had to know each other because neither of them looked nervous. But then again, they had chosen a very public place to meet, and that had to mean something. The detective tried to hand the messenger bag over to Herman but Herman stopped him and took off the backpack. Lupita was taking a photo every couple of seconds. It was clear that Herman wasn't going to be able to handle the messenger bag on the crutches so the detective wound up removing a thick folder from the hip bag and handing it to Herman. Herman flipped through it quickly just to make sure that it was what it was supposed to be. The detective opened up the backpack and stuck his hand inside of it. Then he nodded at Herman and withdrew a thick manila envelope and tucked it inside of his trench coat. Lupita must have gotten fifty good shots of the exchange. The two men didn't shake hands before parting ways. The detective kept the envelope and deposited the messenger's bag in a garbage can as he walked off in the direction of his car. Herman tucked the folder of the sale documents into his backpack and slipped his arms back underneath the straps. Lupita scurried up the hill out of sight and put a call in to Saint, who was still waiting for her back at the Seattle Center.

"Lupita," he answered. "How did it go?"

"I got it."

"You're serious?"

"I am."

"Fuckin' A. Nice job. How's Moe?"

"He's in the car."

"Where at?"

"I had to park it and follow the detective on foot. I am on my way back to it now."

"You still picking me up?"

"Give me like twenty minutes to get there."

Lupita hung up with Saint and started jogging back up First. But she only made it a few strides before the phone started ringing again. She figured Saint forgot to tell her something and she stopped quick to pick up the call.

"What's up?" she said.

"Lupita?"

"Yeah?"

"It's Herman."

" ... "

"It's Herman. Herman Glüber. From Cronkey, Mitchell and Wolfe."

"I know who you are."

"I'm sorry, Lupita."

"For what?"

"Are you by any chance still in the city? There's something that I'd like to give to you."

The Philosopher King

"Zealots will always have their greedy little fingers wrapped around the throats of this planet. And the fact that it doesn't pull any punches is the reason why 'Zoolander' is more than just a film, Marcus. Straight out of the heart of Generation X comes a three-hundred-sixty-degree discourse on the human condition that spans, at least the last several-thousand years," Nevil was pontificating while putting up bench presses. His nephew Marcus was spotting for him.

"How do you figure, uncle Nevil? Seemed like just a silly comedy. It definitely didn't feel like they were trying to make an important film."

"That's how you know they nailed it. Incongruity. The absurdity of what manages to become a success on this planet is something that is almost too far-fetched to believe. But it happens every day. It's pretty much all that happens." Nevil got the hundred-ninety-pound bar up for the tenth rep and Marcus helped him land it safely back on the rack. Nevil wouldn't have needed a spotter for that weight if they were on the ground, but it just so happened that the two of them were pumping iron aboard Nevil's customized Boeing 747 and it was sort of an unspoken rule that if you wanted to work with free weights on the plane while in flight, you had to use a spotter, in case there was some sudden turbulence. The bench press was centered on a Persian carpet, just a few paces inside of the skee ball machine. The decor inside of the plane was what one would expect of a young, philanthropic hipster with unlimited means. It was kind of a cross between an old school video arcade—complete with reconditioned Spy vs. Spy machine and Dig-Dug—and the green room at a Pink Floyd concert. The walls were lined with ornate tapestries from Nevil's travels and if he engaged the black lighting it was like flying through the sky in a gyroscope.

"You mean in the last few decades or so?"

"I wish I meant that, Marcus. I mean forever. It's just so easy to see now that it's impossible to ignore. Which leads to some other interesting questions. One of the great paradoxes facing the world today is: how does one make stupid become aware of itself? The lack of self-awareness is implicit in the stupidity. It's Democracy's Achilles heel. It's the most functional system that has ever existed, yet it will always be held back by the lowest common denominator."

"Are you saying that people shouldn't get to vote?"

"No way, Marcus. It's dangerous letting the uneducated make decisions but it is far more dangerous to leave the decision making in the hands of the powerful. Power is naturally defensive. Power is selfish. Power only cares about maintaining itself. It can't relax"

"You're powerful. And you relax."

"I don't relax, Marcus. It's hard to see how that makes sense. Until you acknowledge the real truth. Which is that nothing makes sense."

"What about you?"

"What about me?"

"You could do anything you want. Why is it you always just seem to do the right thing."

"There's nothing special about me, Marcus. I'm a slave to my own ego like everyone else. I just happen to like wild animals a lot. And a lot of people take serious issue with how I conduct myself. There are a lot of legitimate contradictions. I'm a preservationist by name, who is lifting weights with his nephew aboard his own private luxury jet. I'd be full of shit if I

told you I didn't like the attention. We could be flying coach."
Nevil laid back down on the bench to get ready for another set.
"I feel like we should change the subject, Marcus."

"Why?"

"Because I promised your mom that I would talk to you
about girls." Marcus's face went slack at the mention of *girls*.
"Look, Marcus. I know that you really aren't interested."

"In what?"

"In girls. As in, it's pretty clear that you are more taken with
the male form. At least sexually speaking."

"Uncle Nevil, please."

"It's fine, Marcus. It's nothing to be ashamed of. And as far
as this conversation goes, it doesn't really matter anyway."

"What do you mean?"

"Well," Nevil was talking in between reps. He had added
twenty pounds to the bar and the muscles on his upper body
were taut and bulging under his mint green tank top. "You're at
that age where you are going to start playing with your penis.
No matter what is going on in your mind. And I just want to
talk with you about that. You know, so nothing catches you off
guard."

Marcus was eleven-years old. "Nothing is going to catch me
off guard."

"How can you say that?" Nevil could only get eight reps with
the added weight and Marcus's assistance in getting it back
into the cradles was clutch. He was a strong kid. "Has your
pubic hair grown in yet?"

"This is so embarrassing."

"No, it's not. Look, none of us was born with pubic hair. We
all just sort of got it one day. Tell me, has it come in yet?"

"Yeah, I got some."

"What color is it?"

"Dude."

"Let me see."

"No. Why?"

"I just want to see if it's all the way in, or if it's just starting."

"Am I supposed to be braiding it or something?"

"No. You don't have to braid it." They both laughed. Nevil picked up some dumb-bells to do some bicep curls and Marcus picked up one of the spring-loaded grips and started squeezing it to build up his forearms. "Have you started jerking off yet?"

"Uncle Nevil, come on."

"Come on what? When I started jerking off, I had no idea what I was doing. Didn't even know what the stuff coming out of my penis even was. Want to hear how I first learned to do it?"

"No."

"I'll tell you anyway. My dad had this electric shoe polisher. And I used to—"

"Uncle Nevil, I really don't think I need to hear this."

"You feel like you know how to masturbate?"

"Yes. I know."

"How many times a day?"

"None of your business."

"Well, I will just say that, when you are young, you feel like you can just go and go forever. But we're all here waging a losing battle against the law of entropy."

"Against what?"

"Look, Marcus. All I'm really getting at here is that, no matter how you feel now, you've only got so much life force in you. And you need to be careful how you parcel it out. There are some tricks, you know."

"Like what?"

"Have you ever heard of the Tantra."

"Nope."

"What the hell are they teaching you in school?"

"We are adding up fractions and practicing geography."

"What grade are you in?"

"Fifth."

"Maybe they'll get to Tantra in sixth."

"I doubt it."

"You're missing the point of the bigger conversation we are having, Marcus."

"Which is what?"

"Don't doubt anything."

"I'll try to remember that."

"Okay then. Are you ready for your first lesson in the Tantra?"

"What is it?"

"It's easier if I show you." Nevil put the dumb-bells down, dropped his shorts to his ankles, and was standing naked in front of his nephew. "You don't want to go spilling your seed all over the place. It takes time and energy for your body to create it. You can extend your life curve, and enhance the quality of your life, simply by not wasting yourself all the time. Especially if it's just, like, you in the shower, stroking the monkey."

"The monkey?"

"You know what I mean, I learned this from Mantak Chia himself."

"Who? Uncle Nevil, please put your shorts back on." Nevil had a modest-sized but attractive penis.

"I will in a second," Nevil then spun around and bent over. Marcus was left staring at his gaping butt hole.

"Uncle Nevil, stop it," Marcus was shielding his eyes from the graphic view.

"Nonsense. I wish someone had shown me this when I was your age. You see this area in between the anus and the scrotum?" Marcus nodded even though he was looking away. "Your urethra runs through there. So does your vas deferens. You know what that is?" Poor Marcus was really too stunned to speak. "Well, it's like the tube that delivers the seminal fluid to the tip of your penis when you have an orgasm. If you time it right, you can use your index and middle fingers," this description was accompanied by a live enactment, "to pinch it off and keep all of your, you know, your semen, your stuff inside of you. It can be super handy if you need to last a long time, or if you don't want to get a girl pregnant." Marcus looked at him askance. "Maybe that won't matter to you so much but you get my drift, right?" It was a good thing they were on an airplane, or Marcus probably would have taken off running and never come back. Nevil pulled his shorts back on. Then he turned around and looked at his traumatized nephew. "Got any questions for me?"

"No."

"Should we hug?"

"You should wash your hands."

"I need to take a shower before we land."

"Can I play video games now?"

"Sure, but don't tell your mother."

"About what?"

Besides being a billionaire entrepreneur with enough of his youth still in front of him to really enjoy it for all it was worth, Nevil was unwavering in his altruistic pursuits, and even more passionate about wildlife habitat preservation. Since RocketFuel took off, Nevil had been purchasing gigantic swaths of land all over the North American continent and then placing them in the hands of trustees that managed them as refuges for endangered animals and native vegetation. He was only a couple of years into the environmental conservation game, but already his strategically positioned natural areas had come to be known as the Horsetrainer Park System. They were always open for recreation and never for commerce. To the more exploitative private businessmen, Nevil Horsetrainer was considered a cold-hearted foe. Impossible to buy off. He wouldn't permit hunting, fishing, logging, grazing or even agriculture on his land. He didn't build bridges or roads and he certainly didn't allow wind prospecting, solar power generation, or fracking. What he did allow was for the sounds of nature and untainted darkness to reign uncontested. Leave No Trace camping methods were all that was permitted within the interior of his preserved holdings. Only established campsites and fire rings were to be used. Off-trail trekking was permitted but was only for the well-prepared. Nevil considered men to be trespassers in his wild lands and venturing into uncharted terrain and getting injured was practically a death sentence. Search and Rescue teams were not allowed to operate within the system and helicopter evacuations were strictly prohibited. All of these details were laid out in a waiver that entrants to his lands were required to sign. Nevil didn't have any interest in collecting money from people to enjoy natural beauty, but he was realistic enough not to risk liability on what was technically private property. In being that way, he had made a lot of enemies. He had also made a lot of friends.

One of those friends was an outspoken liberal from Wenatchee County, named Caroline Kilpatrick, who sat on the city council board in the small agricultural town of Peshastin, Wa. She was recently made aware of the deception that was happening in the valley; that there was a venture capital firm from Seattle that was intending to lay waste to nearly a thousand acres of mature apple trees in order to make way for a gaudy resort destination. Nevil—whose vast wealth and comfort with technology afforded him almost instant access to the inner workings of whatever interested him—was intrigued, and did a bit of research. When he got out of the shower the plane was clearing Mt. St. Helens and Marcus was looking out the window.

"Thanks for coming," said Nevil to the kid.

"What exactly are we doing here?"

"In Washington?"

"Yeah."

"Two things. First, one of the employees of the advertising department of our Pacific Northwest offices had a little mishap with the car yesterday and we are going to make amends for some of the damage that he caused."

"Was anyone hurt?"

"Yeah, Marcus. In fact, someone died."

"What are we going to do?"

"Unfortunately, we can't land in Seattle because they are on the cusp of an environmental disaster."

"What's going on?"

"Uncle Jodie was just over in Mongolia researching a new mutation of beetle that can conduct electrical current and wiped out the power in a major swath of the country. It appears that the same beetle has made its way over to Seattle and the city is almost entirely blacked out. If we land this plane there, it may never take off again."

"What are we going to do about it?"

"We're going to buy an orchard."

"What's that?"

"It's like a forest of fruit trees."

"How is that going to help with the bugs?"

"To be honest with you, Marcus, I'm not sure. But we need a base of operations that is big, without much electricity running through it, but still good access to high voltage lines. We are also meeting Jodie. He has some ideas about how we can defeat the beetles, but he is trying to talk me into ignoring the situation and flying up to the Yukon Territory. He thinks this is the beginning of the apocalypse."

"What do you think?"

"You know I love your Uncle Jodie, but he tends to be a bit more pessimistic than I am. I'd like to be a part of solving this problem. After that I want to make sure that the mother of the young man that was killed by our driver yesterday is taken care of."

"What kind of fruit grows in the orchard?"

"Mostly apples. Maybe a few pears."

"Are you going to put them in your energy drinks?"

"Like, release a new apple flavor?"

"Something like that."

"I might."

"Who is going to be in charge of growing the apples? It sounds like you are going to be busy trying to deal with the beetles."

"That's a good question. There's an older couple that has had the orchard for many years and they want to retire. I do need to find some new people to run it once we get past the bug problem."

"Do you have anyone in mind?"

"I sort of do."

"Are you promoting someone from your company?"

"I don't think so. I'd rather see someone more local take it over."

"Like who?"

"Well, Marcus, many of the people who work at this orchard are Mexican. Most of them are in the country illegally."

"Are you going to give it to them?"

"I can't exactly give it to them, since many of them aren't citizens. But there is this one woman, her name is Lupita. Both of her parents have worked at the orchard since before she was born. I think I'm going to give it to her."

*   *   *

Herman spent a cathartic half hour on the phone with Lupita. He came clean about all of Cronkey, Mitchell and Wolfe's plans for the orchard. He told her they intended to fire everyone. She told him that she had followed him the night before, and saw a lot of what he went through. Herman cried again, it was turning into his new thing; whenever something heartwarming happened, he recognized it and gushed tears, it was an embarrassing new characteristic but it felt good. He would have given the sales documents back to her, but it didn't even matter anymore. She told him about the photos of Herman accepting the documents from the private investigator, the Frenzels and their legal team had enough ammunition already to challenge the deal and keep it from closing. After signing, the documents needed to stay with an uninterested third party—like escrow, or the messenger service. Once they were back in the hands of an employee of one of the businesses involved, they could be tampered with. Together they decided that the best thing to do was to let Herman hang onto the documents. That way he could at least hang onto his job. Not that he even wanted it anymore. In the past decade, despite having expensive taste, Herman had amassed a savings of over four-million dollars. He didn't have a family to take care of, and he was a decent investor. He was thinking about quitting. Not only that, he was thinking about asking Margot if she and the kid felt like maybe knocking off for a while and taking a trip somewhere, maybe around the world. They could leave heading west and return from the east. Whatever happened to them in between would be, *what?* He wasn't sure. *Life?* Whatever it was, it had to be better than what he had been devoting himself to: being a high-paid lackey at a corporate scrapyard, accelerating the destruction of empires. Laying waste to everything he could get his hands on, like a lightweight imperialist nation. Changing things for the sake of changing them, just to have something to do. People were nothing like crocodiles or ginkgo trees. Two species that seem to be able to glide through geologic time unchanged. Two species that do nothing to help quell the forest fire that the peoples of earth have become. Or maybe this idea of doing nothing is the very thing that they are stubbornly enduring epoch after epoch in a vain desire to teach. They don't quell the fire, but they also don't fan the flames.

By that point of the afternoon, most of the buildings downtown had lost power and there were far more people than usual on the streets. People who had nowhere to go and no idea what to do. Herman was in luck being on crutches. He was given a wide berth, even crossing the street. He rounded the corner onto Second Ave. and slipped into Bedlam Coffee where Loven was waiting for him. The power in the coffee shop was off but they were making cups for a few customers using propane burners to boil water and filtering the coffee into individual mugs. Outside it looked more like Bedlam. Herman took the backpack off of his shoulders and set it on a chair and then sat down across from Loven. The only things in the pack were the folder with the documents, Herman's wallet, and his keys.

"Did you get them?" Loven asked.

"Yeah."

"You don't seem too happy."

"It's fucking Armageddon out there."

"You want a coffee?"

"Nah. I'm supposed to meet Laverne in fifteen minutes. It's going to take me that long to crutch over to The New Luck Toy. I hope the world lasts that long."

"I bet it will. I'll walk you over there."

Herman and Loven crossed over to the east side of Second, where it looked like there were fewer lost souls, and started working their way north toward Herman's rendezvous. They were in the midst of another rainless gap between squalls. Up ahead they could see the marquee outside the Moore Theater. Herman looked up at it and noticed that that evening's scheduled performance by Gillian Welch had been cancelled. When he looked down, he was standing face to face with a woman who was incredibly familiar. She was more than just familiar, she was his secretary, Anita Zottlemoyer. And the fact that he was obviously having difficulty remembering who she was just added to the insult that he had heaped upon her the previous day. She had no trouble remembering who he was.

If Herman was a more attentive boss, he would have known that Anita was supposed to be attending the bachelorette party of her best friend Joanne in Las Vegas that weekend. She had told him at least a dozen times. She'd been planning it for months. They had a suite at the top of the Luxor. She had two new short dresses for the trip and she'd saved up seven-hundred-dollars-worth of spending money. At the last minute she had to cancel when Herman threatened her with her job. Her eyes were red and puffy. She'd obviously been crying.

She was out walking with her husband Luke, whose breath smelled strongly of beer. Luke wasn't in a good mood either.

He was downright pissed off. Partially at Herman for hurting his wife. Partially at himself. A few things about Luke that Herman should know because Anita had told Herman about him before: Luke was a transplant from Liverpool, when he was young, he was a pretty tough rugby player, in America he was just a plumber who was trying to get into ultimate fighting. He was especially mad because on Thursday night he was knocked out by a Filipino kid twenty-two pounds lighter than him. Still sore and licking his wounds, Luke was looking to take his anger out on someone. He had one very black eye. He was also missing a middle tooth and his cheeks were swollen. He stood with a nasty smile on his face, pretending to be honored to be meeting the man who was making his wife's life a living hell. Anita was shaking. She didn't seem like she was going to be able to handle any more drama.

"So, this here's your boss, honey buns?"

"Yeah, Luke," her voice was quaking. She knew the situation was volatile. She knew her husband's temper could easily cost her her job. Or land him in jail. He was drunk. She was drunk. And she was at least a little thrown off by the crutches. "Luke," she meekly said, "this is my boss, Herman Glüber."

"Erman Gloober, eh? It's good to meet you, mate," Luke took Herman's hand in his and crushed it. Herman folded over. "And how's this Herman as a boss, honey buns? Good bloke?"

Anita was frightened and barely audible. "He's good, Luke," she said. "He's a good boss."

"Well that's not what you was telling me over lunch, honey buns. Told me he's an arsehole."

"No, Luke. I didn't say that. I didn't mean that. Please. Just let's go home, baby." Loven tried to step in on Herman's behalf but Luke stiff-armed him and Loven backed down. Luke was clearly full of rage, going directly for him wasn't going to likely cool the man off. Plus, he was a hell of a lot tougher than Herman or Loven. That much was obvious. It was a chilly afternoon but Luke was in nothing but a tight-fitting white t-shirt and blue jeans. His arms were huge and covered in hooligan tattoos. Blue veins, thick with blood, dilated on the edges of his forehead. He was also chewing gum and there was the trace of the scent of cinnamon mixing with the beer.

"What we got in here?" Luke said knocking Herman's crutches out from under him and stealing the backpack from his shoulders. Herman fell onto the ground and tried to protect his tender foot from getting trampled. Loven collected the crutches for Herman. Luke started rooting through the contents of the bag.

Herman was stuck on his ass on the sidewalk.

"What's this here?" said Luke as he pulled out the folder with the sales documents from the backpack. "Something important?"

"It doesn't mean anything," Loven said. "Just please give it back." Luke tucked the folder in his armpit and glared at Loven, daring him to come and get it.

Luke let his face soften. "Aww," he said. "Does this have some sentimental value for you or something?" He extended the documents toward Herman and Herman leaned forward to take it. Then Luke stepped forward and kicked Herman in the nuts with steel toe of his work boots. Herman keeled over backwards, howling in pain, clutching The Herminator with the hand that Luke didn't crush. Luke then took the folder of documents out from under his arm and threw it at the front of a crowded and slow-moving southbound Metro bus. The folder blew up like a bomb, sheets of paperwork flying through the air. Anita was hyperventilating when her husband grabbed her by the forearm and pulled her along behind him as he stormed away. Loven laid Herman's crutches down beside him, and then ran out into the road to try and retrieve what he could of the documents that were scattered all over the place. Herman was in blinding pain, but he fought his way to vertical with the help of an old lady who witnessed the fight.

"You ought to be ashamed of yourself, young man," she hollered at Luke as he and Anita were walking away.

"Fuck you, decrepit old mum," Luke shouted back.

Herman thanked her and levered himself out into the street without even looking and was nearly mowed down by a blonde woman on a Vespa, long scarves trailing behind her pink helmet. He scurried back to the curb to wait for the light to change, but it had gone out. There was a flash of lightning, followed by a thunder crack. It was so loud that people ducked when they heard it. By the time the sound dissipated, the skies had opened up, rain was coming back down in buckets, and water was sluicing down the roadways. The documents that Loven was trying to recover were being reduced to an inky pulp by the puddles and rain.

The sudden resurgence of the storm sent the masses of displaced scrambling to find cover under awnings and in the entrances to businesses that were mostly closed already because of the outages.

Herman hung back on the curb and just watched the reversion to primitive behavior playing out before him; his buddy Loven frantically trying to get his hands on a bunch of inconsequential pieces of paper that were disintegrating before his eyes. It was actually incredible, Herman thought, that in the midst of all that was falling apart around them, Loven still interpreted those silly pages as something of value. Most of what had mattered to Herman twenty-four hours ago had experienced some sort of cosmic shift. Like he was seeing everything through new eyes, or in a different kind of light. It was madness all around him and somehow, he felt more detached and relaxed than he ever had before. About most things. Punctuality still mattered to him, and he had made a silent resolution to be honest from now on. If he didn't get a move-on he was going to miss his meeting with Laverne, and he didn't want to fail to arrive at what he thought would be a defining moment vís-a-vís this bizarre weekend. With some reluctance, he quietly levered away in the direction of The New Luck Toy and didn't say goodbye to Loven, who was still involved in a futile approach to save something that could no longer be saved.

The traffic was totally locked up and Herman ventured out into the street where there was a bit more room to move. Unfortunately for him, things had changed a bit and being on crutches only qualified him as one of the desperate many, and on that afternoon in Seattle, he was exempt from the kind of special treatment he was getting earlier. It was every family or person for itself at that point. Seeing it firsthand made Herman fear that that was all there ever was. He was trying to slide through a small gap between the hood of a Kia Sportage and an old Renault. The Renault was likely a stick shift with a new driver behind the wheel because when the car attempted to move forward, it first rolled backward and pinned Herman between the two vehicles. He screamed, more from fear than because of pain. And before his legs were completely crushed the Renault lurched forward and he was able to continue to lever across the road. But he couldn't ascend the curb on the other side, there simply wasn't any room for him up there. A large crowd was encircling someone who was laid out on the ground and another person was shouting and pleading with the crowd to give her some space. Herman skirted the edge of the crowd. There wasn't enough room even to use the crutches so he hopped on one foot with the crutches in his hand. And then suddenly the crutches were wrested away from him. He didn't even see the person who took them but he did see them being swung at the window of the gelato cafe until the glass broke. A daring youngster pulled his coat up over his head to protect him from the shattering glass and went through the broken window. Once he was inside, he unbolted the door and people started to storm the entrance, trying to get out of the torrential rain.

Herman was soaked through and cold. So cold that he had acquired a shiver that was vibrating every cell in his body. He was without his crutches and some of that panic that had taken him so long to let go of started rearing its vicious head again and threatening to derail the entire plan. But his luck had shifted at least somewhat to the better and it turned out that the individual who stole his crutches to smash the glass of the gelato cafe was really just trying to get his kids out of the rain and he sought out Herman afterward and returned them. He was exactly Herman's height, but with a kinder, rounder, face, and Herman could see that he wasn't a brave man but that he was trying to be strong for his family. His tears betrayed him and he apologized when he gave the crutches back. Herman told him not to worry, wished him luck, and that he was happy that they had served a good cause. Then he turned his back on the man and double-timed it to The New Luck Toy to meet Laverne.

The gastro-pub that had to close in such a hurry the night before was actually open for business. The Chinese ownership wasn't intimidated by bugs and the chef had already come up with an idea to put them on the menu. The New Luck Toy was part of the first wave of the bug invasion and the owner had been quick to hire a cleaning crew and purchase a generator from the Home Depot that could power the kitchen and the dining room. It was rather busy for it being only the middle of the afternoon but with so few places open that was understandable. Herman had a big smile on his face and he was feeling okay despite still looking like a drowned rat and having the bum foot. He looked around for Laverne but he didn't see her anywhere. Jordan was back behind the bar, alternately mixing drinks and doing some heavy-duty cleaning behind the wells. He noticed Herman and came out from behind the bar to talk to him.

"Hey, Herman," he said. "You okay?"

"Tough night but I'm okay. Hey, Jordan, did you happen to notice if that woman that I was talking with last night came by today?"

"Tough night? Were you in a car accident or something?"

"It was more like a series of unfortunate events."

Jordan's gaze perused the stitches in the forehead, the heavy bandage with a small blood stain that was attached to his throat, and eventually the crutches. "Seems like you might be putting it a bit mildly? Did you have any fun at least?"

Herman was a little thrown by this question, bizarre as it sounded, he actually rather did. "It wasn't a boring Friday, let's just leave it at that. Anyway, you know the woman I'm talking about."

"You sure that was a woman, Herman?"

Herman shrugged like it didn't matter.

"I haven't seen her today."

Herman was dejected. He felt sure that she was going to be there.

"But when I opened up, I did find something odd."

"What's that?"

"There was an envelope on the bar, and it had your name on it."

Herman looked down and in Jordan's hands he saw a brown paper envelope with his name 'Herman Glüber,' written out in calligraphy. Jordan let Herman have the envelope.

"Can I get you a drink?"

"Thanks, Jordan. But I'm okay" Herman went back outside where the rain and clouds had given way to another sunburst. He opened the envelope and took a peek inside. There was no note, just one of those ancient cards of hers. He didn't look at it, only glimpsed the back of it before he closed the envelope back up and took his backpack off to slide it inside, when out of some long-gone period of his life he heard a familiar voice using his name.

"Herman? Herm, never-passes-the-puck, Glüber, is that you?"

The mob of people who had to flee their downtown high rises, had collected in several locations like sheep, but the street in front of The New Luck Toy was relatively empty. And the burgundy-leaved maple tree by the entrance appeared to have perked up with wind having dusted off its leaves and having gotten a nice drink from the sky. It was underneath this tree that Herman found himself face to face with his old buddy, who had gone and shocked Herman by recognizing him first.

"Herman? That's you, isn't it? Are you alright?" said the two-time-academy-award-winning-actor Lucky Soul.

"Ork?" said Herman, pretending to be caught off guard. "How are you?"

"I'm good."

"You're beyond good, Ork, you're a movie star."

Lucky laughed. "Any idea how long it's been since someone called me *Ork*?"

Lucky's producer hung close by, along with the muscle that was at the restaurant the night before, and even though these two were clearly old acquaintances, they weren't taking any chances. Lucky was well-disguised, nothing like the night before. Herman wouldn't have recognized him since a make-up artist had changed his complexion somehow by shading his cheeks and his eyes were hidden behind a cheap pair of sunglasses; not the type you would expect a movie start to be in. He wore a tweed jacket that screamed college professor caught out in the rain, and his jeans were the furthest thing from designer, he was wearing Dickie's. Herman had never considered what approach he would take if he were like the movie star that he grew up with, having to hide in plain sight. Herman was impressed that Ork resorted to such humble threads so he could move about more easily. He was also feeling rather touched that Ork had recognized him and reached out.

"It's technically not even your name any more, is it?"

"Like hell it isn't. Being famous doesn't mean that I'm not the same person I was before all that happened. And I certainly haven't forgotten my youth. To be honest, Herman, I might even owe all of my success to you."

"How could that possibly be true?"

"If you weren't such a puck-hog I might have kept playing hockey."

"You may have still become famous."

"And toothless, with a mullet and arthritic ankles that don't work when I'm fifty. No thanks. Shit, Herman. You obviously know what I do, or at least that I'm in the movies. What happened to you? Are you alright, man? You look like you were in a nasty bike wreck or something."

Herman just went with it. "Good guess. I got myself a custom made fully-suspended Fuji mountain bike; overestimated myself and went over the handlebars at Galbraith last week. I'm a little banged up but to be honest, better me than the bike. Fucking thing cost me eight-grand and at least it doesn't have a scratch on it."

Lucky laughed. "Man, you are the same old Herman Glüber. If you aren't competing against the club from The Dalles, or chasing after Cindy Rhoda, you were always pushing yourself at something else. What kind of work are you into?"

"Last week I worked at a venture capital firm that is housed in a building that has been overrun by energy sucking beetles. At the moment I'm not sure how things are going to pan out."

"Alright then," the narcissistic actor appeared to be struggling with what to say to that and instead changed the subject. "Do you remember that time that my parents took us to Ocean Shores together?"

Herman was derailed by the question; mostly because the repressed memory came back to him so suddenly, and with complete clarity. For some reason he had clung to all of his negative experiences with the other kids he grew up with but it wasn't all bad. They had some fun together, and not just on the ice.

"You were so obsessed with the bowling machines, I remember you making a big deal out of turning that twenty your mom gave you into two-hundred dimes, and that you were going to win that big nutcracker that looked like the grim reaper."

"That's right. And you had your focus on some stuffed animal that looked like a wolf and you were rolling for the hundred every time as well."

"I think in the end we won enough tickets for a wooden backscratcher and jar of Superballs that turned out to be a lot of fun."

"Until one ricocheted around in the parking lot and hit that little baby square in the head. You remember that?"

"How could I forget, her mom fucking reamed us."

"And the baby wasn't even hurt."

"Are you sure about that, I remember there being some blood."

"No blood. Kid didn't even cry, thought it was funny, it was just the mom that lost it over basically nothing."

"I'm sure she turned out fine."

"The mom or the kid?"

"The mom was already a lost cause. I was talking about the baby?"

"That was a pretty fun trip. I remember boogie boarding and the waves seemed huge."

"My parents thought we were nuts for swimming in that ocean water all day without wetsuits on."

"I don't remember feeling cold."

"Me neither. Damn, it's good to see you, man. We were just going into the New Luck for a drink. Why don't you join us?"

"I would but I just left that place. And I've got to make a rendezvous with some people, arrange to get out of this town. It looks like it's going to be hell here for a while."

"Because of the beetles, you mean? I know, I wonder where those little fuckers came from."

Herman thought about telling him but there really wasn't any use. The beetles had arrived, how they got there wasn't important anymore.

"You know," said Ork, "some venture capitalists make the leap to becoming great producers of films. There's a lot of verisimilitude. If you ever think you might have an interest you should give me a call. I'd bet you've got a good eye for bullshit, which is exactly what a producer needs." Ork removed a business card from his pocket. It was plain and simply said

'Lucky' on the front. On the back there was a phone number with a local area code. Presumably his private cell. Herman was thankful that it didn't have the extended and unavoidable long version of Ork's new name.

"I'm sorry, Lucky," said Herman. It was the first time he ever referenced him that way.

"About what?"

"Not sharing the puck more. Your wrist shot from the top of the circle was an arced laser beam. No one could stop it."

Ork laughed. "No need to apologize, to be honest, I'm just glad someone remembers. I've been all around the world and I've done damn near everything there is to do. But still, some of those hockey games we won, I think they were some of the best times I ever had."

"Better than winning an academy award?"

"Let's not be ridiculous. Lots of young kids excel at sports. Being a two-time-academy-award-winner is rarefied air."

"You've gotten cockier,"

"Maybe you just rubbed off on me more than you realized."

"I was a cocky prick, wasn't I?"

"We were teenagers, if we had gotten everything right, we wouldn't have learned a fucking thing."

"Congratulations, by the way, on the awards."

"Thanks. I believe I deserved the first one but," Ork leaned in closer and whispered so only Herman cold hear, "the second probably should have gone to Steve Carrell."

*   *   *

New parents Barbie and Kenovan still let their days unfold according to primal instincts that were increasingly latent in the world, especially since the internet showed up. Neither of them cared much or knew anything about what was happening outside their orbit. They tended to ignore news feeds, periodicals, the status of the stock market, and the opinions of basically anyone but themselves. They preferred to hang out on the right side of the brain. Kenovan liked his music, and he liked to know that his jars were full of nice ganja. Barbie liked reading fiction, talking to squirrels, and watching trees shed their leaves. It was already pretty obvious that their daughter Zora was going to be a lot like them.

Doctor Albert Meade delivered the baby, who came out perfectly healthy after a wild, ninety-minute trip through the birth canal. Not ideal but somewhat expected during a breech presentation. Barbie must have been in terrible pain during that part of the birth but it was never visible in her face. The doctor didn't even have a heart rate monitor with him but he could tell from experience that the baby's heart rate was decelerating during the contractions and the cord was likely wrapped around the neck. With a deft hand he managed to turn the baby and unwrap the cord in one smooth motion. After that, her butt and feet popped out and a lot of the pressure was relieved but it was still a while before the head came all the way through. Kenovan was the first to get a really good look at the baby and he was gushing tears when he first kissed her on the head. She looked just like Barbie, but with brown skin and the beginning of a little afro. They weighed her on Kenovan's triple-beam. She was just under six pounds. The perfect size.

They left the umbilical cord attached until the placenta came out on its own and the birth was over. Kenovan and the doctor were in the bedroom with the door shut, smoking a celebratory cone of the El Diablo. They had a wet towel coiled up and placed underneath the door and they were trying to blow the smoke out the window but it was all coming back in. Barbie was on the couch, too tired to move, but it was fine since she had nowhere in the world to be but right there, with Zora staring up into her eyes, working the first bits of colostrum out of her nipples. Baby—who was back to using her given name, Debbie—was working in the kitchen. Normally she was a strict vegetarian, believing that killing animals for food was wrong. But she had a lot less sympathy for people and nothing had to die to eat a placenta. She had a piece of it sizzling in a frying pan with butter and chorizo seasoning. She was also whipping up some of her famous French toast. She hadn't felt the need to scratch herself once since the baby came. In its own unique way, it was a moment of pure peace, not interrupted, but added to, by the sound of someone knocking lightly upon the door. Barbie was mostly asleep. Kenovan and the doctor could be heard coughing up their lungs through the closed bedroom door. Debbie turned down the heat on the burners and opened up the front door for Saint, Lupita, Moe, and a gigantic stuffed teddy bear.

"You're back," she said.

"Did the baby come?" Saint whispered.

"She's beautiful," Debbie couldn't keep from crying as she shared the news and Lupita cried with her even though they hadn't met. The two women hugged and then introduced themselves. "Come in."

"We don't want to bother anyone," said Saint.

"Tell him it's okay," said Barbie from the couch. And Saint walked over to where she was resting on the couch. "Want to see?" she asked. And she lifted up the corner of the blanket that little Zora was swaddled in. The baby looked him right in the eye and smiled and Saint was sure that most babies couldn't be that smart. She didn't cry. And she didn't look away. Saint couldn't come up with anything to say. He just kissed Barbie on the top of her head. Lupita set the huge teddy bear on the floor and Moe sat down right beside the bear and sniffed at the top of Zora's head. The baby reached a hand out toward Moe's face and he gave it a little lick.

"I hope we get to see her again," said Saint. Barbie took his hand and squeezed it.

"You better come and see us again," Barbie said. And then Saint handed her an envelope containing ten-thousand dollars in cash.

Epilogue

New Deadland

Every downtown building, even most of the ones that were equipped with emergency generators, had gone completely dark. As soon as the auxiliary systems kicked on, the bugs relocated to the new food source. It made them even stronger. The National Guard was on its way and the mayor had declared a state of emergency between South Lake Union and SODO. Police were setting up barricades and double-decker buses were being utilized to shuttle all of the displaced dwellers of the swanky apartments—where even the functionality of the plumbing was dependent upon a series of high-powered pumps that needed electricity to run—to tents in quarantined rural areas. It was all a waste of time and resources. Herman knew it, but who was going to listen to him?

The sun was back out which wasn't actually helping. It was turning out to be one of those classic Seattle Saturdays when the weather had decided to be, indecisive. Lots of the loitering masses who were waiting to be transported had thought to grab rain gear. The rains would swoop in and by the time folks got into their slickers the rain backed off and it was way too hot to be trapped inside of your own personal greenhouse and the coats and bibs had to come off. Some people were sweaty and others were cold but no one was comfortable and there was nowhere to sit and nowhere to go. Most of the retail shops had not only closed up but boarded their windows for fear of looting. But the Nike store had somehow retained some light from a backup system and had stayed open to seize the opportunity to sell off its inventory to members of the desperate mob who wouldn't have normally shopped there. Herman himself slipped inside the store and grabbed the attention of one of the store's employees who was dressed in black and white stripes like a basketball referee; she was even wearing a whistle around her neck. She helped Herman to come up with a pair of new running shoes (though he only needed one), socks, a pair of heather gray sweatpants with red piping on the sides, a long sleeve cotton t-shirt that had 'Fly Emirates' on the front and the number 27 on the back, and a thick red hoodie with a zipper down the front and the Nike swoosh on the left chest panel. At the last moment he added a nylon pull-over in case he got caught out in the rain again. Herman paid with cash since the internet was not functioning, although they were trusting people with unexpired cards by taking down the numbers, expiration dates, addresses, and CCV codes. It didn't have quite the same effect as the generous merchants that trusted the wet hippies at Woodstock, but it was more than they had to do. The nice girl who helped him out tallied up the bill and applicable sales tax with a calculator and was happy to dispose of the second outfit that Herman had destroyed in the last twenty-four hours. Before tossing the garments in the bin she checked the pockets and discovered two more hundred bills and the envelope from Laverne. Herman let her keep one of the hundreds, he would have been furious with himself if he had lost that tarot card.

In his new clothes, he crutched toward the east and the fringes of the melee that had absorbed the downtown corridor. The police had a barrier set up along Fifth Ave., and they were technically not letting anyone through it. There was a fear of the displaced residents swamping the adjacent neighborhoods that were still unaffected by the beetles and the city didn't want to risk scattering them around. The goal was to have everyone loaded onto the buses, which were doused with pesticides, before exiting the protected zone and driving to an encampment in Snohomish where temporary shelters were being erected in a large field away from any electrical lines. Either luck was back with Herman or there was an exception made for him because he was on the crutches and obviously quite injured. He showed his license to a police officer at one of the gates with his Capitol Hill address on it and the sympathetic officer actually created a mini-diversion, announcing the arrival of another bus at the north end of the enclosure that wasn't actually there yet. Like Titanic passengers looking for a lifeboat, the desperate mob redirected itself to the north and Herman was allowed to slip through the barricade and make what qualified as a high-speed getaway on crutches. His arms and hands were feeling strong and he was levering himself along at an impressive clip. The area to the east of the protected zone was ominously quiet. The streets were largely free of traffic and the people who lived there had either fled already or they were holed up inside. Herman's destination was too far to crutch to so he posted up outside of a donut shop and did something that he had resisted doing for years, mostly out of a misplaced corny sense of pride and brutal investment envy: he called an Über. Herman had never downloaded the app but it was on Loven's phone and that was what he was carrying since his was still shot. It was his first reluctant ride in an Über. He knew all about the conveniences of it, he just loathed the way the juggernaut transportation company rhymed with his last name. He clung to an irrational fear that he would arrive at his destination to a chorus of people singing here comes Glüber in his Über. And the thought of all the money he would have made if he had gotten in early. It stung. He typed in his destination and within just a few minutes he was expecting a driver that was only a few blocks away. He had barely enough time to grab a lemon merengue and a couple of chocolate frosteds from the donut shop before his ride showed up on the curb. It was a late model Mazda sedan piloted by a very friendly woman who had brown skin and a burka on. On the way to the Bush School she informed Herman that she only drives for Über when she isn't teaching ESL or delivering food for the Bite Squad. Herman found her endearing and inspirational, like an entire corporation organized and sustained by a single individual who projected something desirable as it was unfamiliar: contentment. They shook hands when she dropped him off and Herman tipped her with a hundred-dollar bill, which she tried to give back at first but eventually accepted.

In the school's gymnasium the science fair was already well underway. Most of the exhibits were along the walls of the rectangular room, in the shape of a horseshoe. At the open end of the shoe there was a stage and the students were taking turns at the microphone, explaining their experiments to an assembly of adults, who sat rapt as their kids showed off their respective brains and creativity, making the future look alternately promising and bleak. Herman entered the room during a short lull between presentations, while a nerdy but nice-looking man was helping his daughter drag a kiddie pool up onto the stage and fill it up with water. While the pool was filling up there was some murmuring and some head turning and Herman and Margot's eyes found each other across the crowded room and when she saw him her smile was like the north star. She waved him over even though the seat beside her wasn't empty, but she must have convinced her neighbor—the pimply-faced red-headed sibling of someone—to stand at the back of the room so that Herman could take his chair. The kid most likely relented because of the crutches that Herman was learning to love. People were being nice to him because he was encumbered and his appreciation of it wasn't even fake. He was really grateful. The seat was creepily warm under Herman's butt. He laid the crutches on the floor and interlaced his fingers with Margot's and she kissed him on the neck. Which a young boy in the row behind them was quick to point out as being gross.

"Did he go yet?" Herman asked.

"He's next," she said.

"What's he going to do?"

"He wouldn't tell me. But he was up all night doing research on my hot spot."

"I want to do some research on your hot spot." Just after Herman said that a parent in front of him told him to *shush*, the little girl on stage was ready to present.

"You have to be quiet," said Margot.

"Let's get a puppy, and travel around the world with it," Herman replied. Margot gave him a sideways look that definitely wasn't a *no*. Although she did appear—with good reason—to be speculating on his mental health.

The little girl was dressed in a canvas robe that went all the way past her feet. She was walking funny and seemed unnaturally tall for the size of her head. Her father was laying a configuration of copper pipes into the shallow pool and connecting it to something that looked like a small air compressor, which she explained to the audience was actually a pump and its reservoir was full of liquid nitrogen. When they plugged the little unit in to a heavy gauge extension cord and switched it on, the liquid nitrogen flowed through the pipes and instantly froze the water into a single, solid, glassy chunk. At that point she shed the robe and revealed that underneath she was wearing a pink tutu and figure skates. She then performed a short routine on her tiny rink that included a toe flip and a double-Salchow that she landed perfectly, earning her a thunderous round of applause from the room.

Not only was it a tough act to follow, the pool wasn't going to thaw out nearly as quickly as it froze and the giant blue hockey puck had to be left on stage for the rest of the presenters to work around since it was way too heavy to move. It wasn't a terribly big deal for Ethan, who didn't have too much with him in the way of props. He did have something though. It was a hand-held video camera that he connected to the school's projection system via an HDMI cable and pointed at what was at first a sheet of plain white paper. The crowd sat in what was at first a bored silence. They had just been transported unexpectedly to the Winter Olympics, it was going to take something special to bring them back. And then Ethan dumped the two dead bugs that Herman had given him onto the blank page and they suddenly appeared thousands of times larger than life on the screen behind the stage. The crowd recoiled in horror and it was as though all the air was suddenly sucked out of the room and there was none left to breathe.

"Has anyone heard of the Seattle Beetle Invasion?" Ethan started. It was a rather patronizing intro since everyone in the room obviously had and the hoity toity private school population was chock full of hypochondriacs and germaphobes whose ultimate nightmare was proliferating dangerously close by. No one said yes or actually raised their hand up. At the same time no one seemed to be, in the dark about it. "These are the beetles that have been feasting on the power lines and taking out the internet all over the city. They are increasing in number and spreading out. Last night, I figured out where they came from." That got the room talking in concise whispers and squirming in their seats a bit. The kid's tone was tinged with hope and there wasn't a soul in there that wasn't hanging on his every word. "Not only that, I have figured out how we can live with them." Ethan paused while the room absorbed what he had just told them. "Contrary to what the news reports are saying, this isn't the first time something like this has happened. In fact, there is a region in Chinese controlled Inner Mongolia where they have been living in harmony with these very same insects for many years. The bug is a new species called *Agrilus suprema*." Every single student, parent, grandparent, sibling, teacher, and administrator in that room, whether they were scared senseless by the bugs or not, was invigorated and on the verge of bursting with glorious feelings of triumph and pride. The solution to a localized problem of apocalyptic magnitude was about to be delivered by a tweenage product of their esteemed learning institution, and they were witness to it. Everyone leaned in to be able to better hear the words that would drip from the boy's tongue like nectar, explaining to them how they could run out the legions of tiny villains that were congregating in the dark recesses of the world like cockroaches and buckling the spine of human civilization.

"How did you find out about them?" someone shouted.

"It took some patience, but I eventually discovered a blog post by a man named Gordon Androssus, buried on the fortieth page of the Sino Webo. His credibility has been devastated by the traditional negative publicity crushing machines but his story is true. He has been to where the bugs are from. In fact, he lives there now."

"How do they contain the bugs?" another voice from the back of the room.

"They don't exactly contain them. They control the food source."

"Did they figure out a way to get the power back on?"

"They have. Although after years of living without power, the people who live in the region have decided to leave the power off."

"What on Earth for?"

He never got to explain what the crowd wouldn't have comprehended anyway, because the microphone went dead.

And then the lights shut off.

And then *Agrilus suprema* started to descend.

Margot squeezed Herman's hand and led him toward the end of the row in the semi-dark as he hopped. The building was powerless, but there was a little bit of natural light sneaking through an upper row of windows, enough to locate Herman's crutches. The crowd was starting to panic and it was human gridlock in the gym as half of the people were heading for the emergency exits and the other half were trying to find their kids. Beetles were piling up on the floor in such colossal numbers it was as though the hardwoods had come to life and started to rise and swell like the surface of the ocean. There was a prolonged sizzle up above followed by the smell of smoke and a few ceiling tiles falling to the ground. They were lightweight but the effect was terrifying and whipped the crowd into a frenzy as Margot and Herman burst out one of the fire-exits into the light. Margot was slowing her pace so that Herman could keep up but he was really pretty fast on the crutches.

Ethan was already at the Forerunner. If there was a person anywhere around who wasn't going to shortchange the magnitude of what was happening around him it was him. Margot tapped the button on her remote keychain that unlocked the vehicle and Ethan threw the trunk open so that they could pitch Herman's crutches in and get the hell out of there. Behind them, flames from an air conditioning unit on the top of the gym that had caught fire were tickling the low branches of a Douglas Fir tree and spreading out laterally. There was still no sound of sirens.

It was pretty obvious that Ethan and Margot had spent the night packing for a road trip; or a getaway. The back of the rig had a cooler, a couple of stuffed travel bags, camping gear, and a small cage with Dogwood the cat in it.

Just then there was a shudder that shook the ground beneath their feet and in the sky to the west there rose a monstrous ball of red flame that roared for a moment like the evil, all-seeing eye, and then dissipated into a cloud of black smoke that spread out and marred the whole horizon. Even as it wafted off, plumes of white and gray ash billowed upward from beneath it before losing energy and falling back toward the ground.

Ethan grabbed Herman's crutches from him and laid them neatly across the top of the gear and then helped him to the open passenger side door.

"Get in," the kid shouted.

Herman got a kick out of being bossed around by a twelve-year-old. He loaded up into the car and watched the roof of the building that they were just in implode in the side mirror. The sound that came after was deafening and people were separated from one another, trapped, and screaming like lambs at the slaughter. The implosion then sent up a dust cloud that engulfed the entire structure and it was the last Herman saw of the Bush School as Margot turned the key, went tearing out of the parking lot, and shot north through the Washington Park Arboretum toward one of the bridges that headed east.

Traffic was snarled on the one lane road through the park but Margot was beyond caring. She pulled her off-road beast up over the curb and went tearing down the pedestrian path next to the big London Plane trees, spitting mud from under her tires and swerving but keeping it straight in four high. The solid front axle that Toyota put on these old editions was proving its value. They circumvented the traffic and hit the bridge entrance to 520 heading east, and just in time too. A row of police cruisers was behind them and slowing to a crawl, apparently intending to close the bridge and probably trapping everyone in Seattle with the beetles so the infestation wouldn't spread.

"Where are we headed?" asked Herman, who was buzzing from the adrenaline of their narrow escape.

"Over the pass," said Margot. "After that," she shrugged.

Something occurred to Herman at that moment that seemed tremendously important; he had no idea where Loven was. He reached for his phone to call him and then remembered that the phone he was carrying was Loven's anyway. There was no number he could try. Instead he dialed Dmitri, but all he got was a message that the circuits were busy and to try again later. The last he saw Loven he was running around in the rain, still trying to collect the sales documents that had been run over by the bus. He was endlessly trying to help Herman and Herman barely ever gave him a second thought. Now he was worried about him and had no idea how to help. He looked around the car, and it dawned on him that he had a family now. It made him feel vulnerable, but also happy.

He missed Loven already, and knew that he might not ever see him again. Even if that was true, he was ready to call him a friend. And even if missing him hurt, it helped to break down the useless wall that he had been surrounding himself with. Herman didn't feel invincible anymore as they approached the foothills. He didn't have a superiority complex or a contempt for anyone around him who was just going about the business of trying to survive. He just felt human; and scared of a certain small but highly destructive beetle.

What amazed Herman was that at the same time he was feeling overwhelmed by fear of the beetle, Ethan was having the opposite response. He was sitting in the backseat of the truck, punching numbers into a satellite phone and trying to get a three-way call set up. Eventually the little bugger had the two people that he needed on the line and he laid the phone down on the armrest between the seats so everyone could talk and hear.

"Marcus?" said Ethan.

"I'm here, buddy."

"So am I." Herman recognized this third voice, it belonged to Dr. Jodie Cavendish.

"Everyone, give me their twenty," said Ethan.

"We are in Nevil's plane," said Marcus. "In a few minutes we are going to touch down in Ellensburg."

"I'm at Summerwood Farms, out in Peshastin," said Jodie. "The place is crawling with military personnel but that doesn't mean that there is any concrete plan in place. They want to shut down the grid. I don't blame them. I just know it won't help. Where are you, Ethan?"

"We are just crossing over the floating bridge heading east toward the pass. There are a lot of cars headed this way but it still feels like we are in the first wave of folks trying to escape."

Herman was looking back at the city in the side mirror of the truck. Smoke was still lazily drifting up from where the explosion had occurred and there was an ominous hole in the skyline where the Columbia Tower use to loom above the rest of Seattle's skyscrapers.

"Ethan," it was the doctor addressing the kid, "Marcus and I have been going over this situation with *Agrilus suprema*, I don't even know how much you know. But I'll tell you this, if we shut the grid down, the same thing will happen here that happened in Mongolia where they originated, only here it will happen much quicker since no one has any discipline. The grid will go down, the bugs will go dormant but survive on another food source, and as soon as electricity is re-introduced to the region, the population will either swell back up, or hitchhike out to other cities and towns that feature their favorite food source, which is basically everywhere. These things could be all over the country in a matter of weeks. Days even. I think our best option is to run."

"Do you think that there is an amount of juice that the bugs can't handle?" asked Ethan.

"What do you mean?" asked Marcus.

"We have already determined that we won't get rid of them by killing the power. Instead, what do you think would happen if we overload the grid?"

"You are talking about cooking them."

"I'm talking about crossing the streams?"

"Huh?"

"Ghostbusters analogy, but yes."

"Can the grid can handle it?" Jodie wondered aloud.

"It depends what kind of voltage it would take to kill them. Do we have any live specimens we can experiment with?"

"I have a few in a glass container out here on the farm," said Jodie.

"Do you have any batteries or an inverter with you?"

"I bet I can scare something up."

"We need to figure out what voltage it is that fries these beetles to a crisp, then we need to do some math and see if the lines can handle the flow."

"This will destroy everything electrical that gets the power back-fed into it."

"Which is why we need to get the message out to everyone on the west side of the mountains that we can."

"What's the message?"

"Unplug everything."

"We can't unplug everything."

"That's why the fire trucks will need to be ready. I'm not saying it won't be messy. It's just the only thing I can think of that might work."

"I'll get on top of testing the beetles," said Jodie.

"And stall the cutting off of the power grid as long as you can. We need to convince the military that we need a more aggressive solution."

"Word around here is that the Columbia Tower just fell. No word on casualties. I feel like it was bad though. The military is ready for hardball."

"What should I do?" asked Marcus.

"Organize the juice. If Bonneville's team is out there you have to convince them this is the right thing to do. Once they are on board you need to get every wind farmer that you can between here and Coeur d'Alene to route their power at Western Washington. I'll work on getting Seattle City Light to help up us with the juice they are producing at the dam but they may be a tough sell. This is going to destroy most of their equipment."

"Lot of job security in rebuilding it though."

"Are you saying there's more money in destruction than construction? You sound like my uncle Nevil. He's always saying how there's no money in health, but in sickness there are fortunes to be made."

"Your uncle Nevil is a smart man, and you know that I have always admired his capacity for restraint, considering the truths he is aware of. But this is a crisis, Marcus. I feel like we should reserve the discussion of his philosophies for another time."

"Deal."

"I know this is getting ahead of ourselves, but nuking the beetles is only going to buy time. Any thoughts, Ethan on how we keep them from coming back?"

"It's going to take more experimentation. DC conversion sounds like a last resort. I wonder if the beetles can handle a fractures sine wave. If they need something smooth in order to feed, we might be able to throw them off without destroying every UL Certified object in America."

"You want to monkey with the food source."

"I want to see if we can find a way to make the electricity taste bad."

Herman was listening to the conversation, and when he slipped his hand into the pocket of his new hoodie, he found the envelope from Laverne with the tarot card in it he had neglected to look at yet. It was the Seven of Pentacles. An unremarkable card as it turned out, but somehow welcome in its location. The first time he had looked inside the envelope he had clearly missed something, a small note from Laverne: *The Seven of Pentacles doesn't fail but he doesn't achieve his goals either. His wisdom is in learning to settle for a good thing rather than to sacrifice it for the fantasy of perfection, which is a thing that does not exist. Progress happens, but is always slow. Don't hesitate. Don't be timid. There is no time for that.* Herman could hear Laverne's voice in his head as he read her words and he knew that she, or he, was right; mostly. If he had one objection it was to the impossibility of perfection. This thought occurred to him when he glanced to his left and saw Margot shift from fourth to third to help the old rig get up the guts it needed to get over the hill. Had Laverne met Margot she might have had a different opinion.

Loven's wife's cell phone number was in his phone and it finally dawned on Herman that he could get a message to him through Maggie. While the kids talked with Jodie on the phone, Herman sent her the following text: *Loven and Maggie, this is your friend Herman. You need to go home and unplug everything that you own. In the next twenty-four hours it will be safer to be outside than inside because of the threat of fire. If you two can make it to Summerwood Farms that is where we are going. If you can't make it, we will come and find you as soon as it is safe to come back. Good luck.* He hit 'send' and the message appeared to go through. Although by the time they reached the top of the pass, there was still no reply.

Thanks to my publisher, Michael Thompkins, for having faith in me, and for caring about this project as much as myself. Thank you, Paul, Raven, and Dick for your indispensable contributions. Thanks to the Goddard College MFAW crew, you know who you are. And finally, to The Evergreen State College for fanning the flame.

About the Author

There are some rumors, guesses, and ideas;
but nothing is actually *known* about the author.
Please visit <u>DouglasBrannonAuthor.com</u> to read more of his work.
Photo by Zizi Smith.

CPSIA information can be obtained
at www.ICGtesting.com
Printed in the USA
FFHW012035261019
55768743-61633FF